GOING UNDER

a novel

S. Walden

Penny Press

GOING UNDER

Copyright © 2013, S. Walden

Penny Press Publishing

ISBN-13: 978-1482313123
ISBN-10: 148231312X

CreateSpace paperback printing February 2013

Cover design by Robin Ludwig Design Inc.
www.gobookcoverdesign.com

Editor: Julie Lindy
julielindyeditor@gmail.com

To strong girls everywhere.

ONE

"This dress is bullshit," I said, observing myself in the full-length mirror attached to the closet door.

I was swathed in a boxy knee-length black sheath I bought at T.J. Maxx. It was two sizes too big and hanging in the "Women's Active Wear" section. I knew better. I also knew I'd find nothing appropriate to wear in the "Juniors" section. Not for where I was going.

I walked right by the trendy low-cut tops and designer jeans and headed for a group of 40-something ladies congregated around a circular rack of discounted dresses. *Perfect*, I thought, and began rifling quickly, afraid one of the women would snatch the dress before I could get my hands on it. I received a couple of odd looks that turned hostile when I zeroed in on my target and squealed a triumphant, "Hell yeah!" It couldn't be more perfect. A ghastly dress for a ghastly occasion.

My eyes dropped to the black pumps I borrowed from my mom. They were fashionable for a 35-year-old high power attorney, but I was just an 18-year-old high school senior. They gave the wrong impression, I feared. They screamed, "I'm one amazing person!" and I thought I shouldn't wear them inside a church. Wasn't it appropriate to be humble, or at least give the illusion of being humble, in the house of God? But I owned no closed-toe pumps. I don't know how I made it to eighteen years of age without owning a pair of closed-toe pumps, especially since I considered myself a fashionista. But there it was. I was at the mercy of my mother's shoes.

"These shoes are bullshit," I decided, screwing up my face in frustration.

I turned to the side and looked at my long, straight blond hair pinned in a messy bun at the nape of my neck. Strands were hanging loose, but not in a purposeful way. Not like I pulled them out of the bun to frame my face. No, they were yanked out after a thirty-second walk outside to get the mail. The wind was terrible today, and I considered French braiding my hair, though I knew it would make me look like a 10-year-old.

"My hair is bullshit."

I stared at myself, imagining Beth laughing at me.

"Brooke, where did you get that horrendous dress?" she'd say.

"I know, right? Last minute, and I had no choice," I'd reply.

"And those shoes?" she'd ask. *"All the times I tried to get you to buy pumps, and you refused. Now look what you've gotta wear."*

"I know, Beth. Like I said, I had no choice."

"No, no. You always have a choice. Find something else. I can't be seen in public with you looking like that," Beth would answer.

"Beth, I don't have time. I ran out of time."

"There's still time, Brooke. There's always time to make it right."

"No, Beth. There's no time," I said out loud, choking on the words.

My eyes glazed over. And then I sank to the floor and cried away all of the stupid make-up I had just put on—the stupid mascara on my stupid eyelashes and the stupid blush on my stupid cheeks. I cried for the stupid pins jabbed into my hair that pulled painfully on my scalp.

I cried for the things I should have been doing today. The places I should have been going. I cried for my sad outfit and my sad heart to match. But I especially cried for Beth.

I cried for Beth.

—

I hung around the doors of the church sanctuary. I couldn't bring myself to go in. I couldn't face anyone. My eyes were puffy from constant crying. My body swollen from the heat outside. My hair a whipped-up disaster from the wind. I felt ashamed. I couldn't even look nice for Beth.

"Honey, we need to go in now," I heard my mother say. She wrapped my hand in hers and squeezed lightly. I knew she meant it to be reassuring, but it made me panic instead.

My pulse sped up, and I was certain my heart would explode. I didn't want to face Beth. What if her casket was open? I couldn't stand the thought of her seeing me like this. An absolute mess, like I couldn't even take the time to get my shit together. I would not do that to her—make her think I didn't care.

"I need a minute. I need to go fix my hair."

Mom nodded. "I'll wait."

I teetered on my heels all the way to the bathroom. I pushed open the door and fell into the first sink, clutching the porcelain and hanging my head low, feeling the urge to vomit. My mouth filled with saliva instantly, and then I heaved. I knew nothing would come up; I hadn't eaten in three days. My legs shook violently, and I realized I had no business wearing heels. I was weak and worried I'd fall flat on my face.

I heaved again, this time producing a bit of bile from deep within my stomach that burned my throat on the way up. I turned on the faucet and cupped a hand underneath the running water, bringing it to my lips. The water was adequate in soothing the sting in my throat but not in erasing the vile taste in my mouth.

I stood up and plunged a shaky hand into my clutch searching for the tin of mints. I found it and popped a peppermint into my mouth. Then I began the task of fixing my eye make-up. I was wise enough to pack the essentials in my purse. I retraced the upper and lower lids of my eyes with black liner, rubbing a finger over the lines to smudge them, soften them. I reapplied mascara and swiped my lips with tinted lip gloss.

I exhaled sharply when it came time to fix the damage to my hair. I pulled a wide-tooth comb out of my bag and all the pins out of my head. It was instant relief, and I stood massaging my scalp for a few seconds before running the comb through my tangled locks. It hurt, and it took forever. I gathered my hair in a low ponytail. It was too late to pin it up.

I could see Beth nodding her approval now that I looked presentable again. I took one last look in the mirror, glimpsing the imitation gold chain reflecting the overhead light on my pale neck. I reached down the front of my dress and pulled out a half heart, split in a jagged line down the middle, my portion reading "Be Fri." I imagined Beth's half, the half that read "st ends" and smiled at the memory of my eighth birthday. She gave me my half of the charm, made me swear to always wear it, and I did until the metal started turning green and we grew older. Years later, we discovered one day that we no longer wanted to wear jewelry from each other. We wanted to wear jewelry from boys instead. I felt a pinch in my heart remembering the day I stored away the necklace for good. Until now.

I left the bathroom in a hurry, turning the corner for the foyer and slamming into him. The force of the hit was so great that I stumbled backwards, nearly falling on my bottom if not for his outstretched hand. I grabbed it before going down and wobbled on my too-high heels, clutching him as I worked to regain my balance.

"God, I'm sorry!" he exclaimed.

I looked at his face then, unprepared to see something so beautiful. I think I gasped. And then I averted my eyes out of sheer embarrassment.

"I really should watch where I'm going," he said.

He still held my hand, and I let him. I couldn't remember who I was or where I was going. I couldn't remember where I had just been. I only knew that a very cute boy . . . no, he was more than cute. He was gorgeous. This very gorgeous boy was holding my hand, and I had only one thought. I wanted to make our handholding more intimate. I wanted to lace my fingers with his.

"I think I should," I mumbled.

I chanced another look at him. I made a conscientious effort not to gasp as I took in his light blue eyes. I'd never seen eyes that color. Jared Leto had nothing on this guy's eyes, and Jared's eyes were the color of the Mediterranean. No, the eyes I looked into now were so light blue they looked translucent. I thought if I stared a little longer I could see right inside his head, to his brain, and I don't know why that turned me on so much. I wanted to witness the workings of his mind, the firing synapses, information traveling safely inside neurons to different parts of his body. A few made it to his hand, and they must have told him to keep holding mine because he didn't let go.

I stared shamelessly, licking my lips at one point. He stared back just as boldly. I wanted him to like what he saw. I wanted him to think I was sexy. I wanted him to feel the same instant attraction I did. I'd never felt it before. Not really. Not even with Finn. It was unsettling, and I wondered how people functioned after being smacked upside the head with it. Instant. Physical. Chemical.

Primal.

Just rip my clothes off, I thought. *Just rip my clothes off and do me right here in the hallway!*

He smiled and released my hand. I thought he did it reluctantly, like his brain ordered him to and he finally acquiesced. I smiled back, a flirty grin. I pulled my ponytail forward over my shoulder and played with the strands. I bit my lower lip. And then reality came crashing down like a hailstorm, large lumps of ice banging my head and screaming at me in unison.

"YOU'RE AT A FUNERAL!"

I looked at the gorgeous guy, and my face went white.

"Oh my God," I whispered.

He stared at me for a moment before saying, "Are you okay?"

I shook my head and started towards the sanctuary doors. He followed behind.

"I'm awful, I'm awful, I'm awful," I whispered over and over. I didn't care if he could hear.

What the hell was I doing? Trying to flirt with a guy at my best friend's funeral? How could I even forget for a second that I was at a funeral? I was supposed to be carrying around heavy, black sorrow to match my black dress and black heart, not batting lashes and fantasizing about sex with a stranger. Was I so ridiculous that a hot guy could make me forget to have any kind of decency? Or shame?

I rounded the corner and saw my mother waiting for me. And then I ran to her, threw myself into her arms, and burst into a fit of tears.

"Brooklyn," she whispered, holding me in a tight hug. "It's okay," she cooed as she stroked my hair.

"I'm a terrible friend!" I wailed. I saw the fuzzy

outline of a boy walking past us tentatively through the doors.

"No, you aren't," my mother replied.

"Yes, I am! I don't even know why I'm here! Beth hated my guts! She wouldn't talk to me all summer!"

"Brooke," Mom said. "I want you to calm down. Now, we talked about this. You knew it would be hard, but she was your best friend for all those years. Do you think she wouldn't have wanted you here?"

"No, I don't!" I cried.

"Yes, she would," Mom said. "Now we have to go in."

"I can't!"

"Brooke, Beth was your best friend," Mom said, trying for patience.

"No she wasn't! Not after what I did! I ruined everything! I'm a freaking slut!" I sobbed, shaking my head from side to side.

"Sweetheart, don't say words like 'freaking' and 'slut' in a church," Mom replied.

I only sobbed louder.

"You can do this," Mom encouraged.

I stood my ground, shaking my head violently, refusing to go in.

"Brooklyn Wright!" Mom hissed, pushing me away and grabbing my upper arm. She squeezed too tightly, and I squeaked in discomfort. There was no more tenderness in her voice. "Get yourself together. This isn't about you. So stop making it about you. You're going into that sanctuary and you're going to pay your respects to your friend, and you're going to make it about Beth. Do you understand me?"

I swallowed hard and wiped my face.

"Do you understand me?" Mom repeated.

I nodded grudgingly, and she took my hand, leading me through the doors.

The sanctuary reeked of sorrow and guilt. I imagined everyone thought they were responsible in some way for the death of an 18-year-old. I felt guilty, but my guilt came from an entirely different place. I didn't drive my best friend to commit suicide, but I also wasn't there for her when she needed me. I was too wrapped up in my own selfish desires—desires for her boyfriend, Finn. Sneaking around. Lying to her. Slowly destroying a friendship that was going strong since we were five. I was a deplorable friend, and she discovered it. Then I tried to make it right by telling Finn we were over, explaining that I couldn't betray my friend, and he wanted to know what I thought I was doing to him. Was it not the same thing? Betrayal?

I slunk into a pew in the back of the church scanning the crowd for Finn. I knew he would be here, and I thought he had a lot of nerve. He cheated on Beth. Broke her heart. The worst part was that I was his accomplice. He destroyed my friendship, and I let him. And he felt no guilt over it. *"The heart wants what the heart wants."* That's what he told me once. I think he stole it from some bullshit movie.

I can't believe I fell for him. I can't believe I was sitting here now blaming him for everything. What a pathetic loser. Not him. *Me.* I swiped my fingers under my eyes, no doubt smearing my recently applied mascara. I kept scanning the congregation for Finn, but I couldn't find him. It was desperate disappointment because I needed to find him. I needed to look at his face. Seeing him would compound the anguish I so rightly deserved to feel. I needed him to help me punish myself more for the pain I caused Beth.

I drew in a long, slow breath, exhaling just as slowly, and caught sight of the beautiful guy. There. That's it, and I breathed deeply feeling my heart constrict, feeling it ache for shame at my behavior. I didn't need Finn to make me feel like shit. This guy could. I stared at him, focusing on my guilt, silently apologizing over and over to the girl up front in the wooden box.

I'm sorry, Beth. I'm so sorry. Please don't hate me.

And then my eyes glazed over with fresh tears as the pastor took his place beside the casket.

TWO

"What the hell, Brooke?" Gretchen said. "You met him at Beth's funeral?"

I grunted into the phone.

"A *funeral?*" she emphasized.

"I know, okay!" I said. "I'm a shitty friend."

"You think?"

"I can't help he ran into me," I argued.

"Oh my God," Gretchen said. "This is just like that *Sex and the City* episode."

Here we go again, I thought. Gretchen had an irritating way of likening all of my life experiences to *Sex and the City* episodes. I already knew which one she was going to describe before she started because she made me watch every single episode with her. Multiple times.

"And Charlotte's hat blows over to the guy's wife's gravestone," I heard Gretchen say.

"I know. I remember."

"And it's totally pathetic and you can't date him," Gretchen said.

"I'm not dating him. We barely even talked," I replied. "We kind of just stared at each other for a minute." I screwed up my face in thought.

"You stared at each other?"

"Um, kind of," I admitted.

"Okay. Weird."

"Well, that's what happened," I said defensively. I sat on my bed surrounded by boxes filled with my belongings. In a few hours, they would be packed in the car and driven over to my dad's house. My new residence.

"You really are a bitch," Gretchen said.

"What the hell?"

"You ditch me my senior year and then try to pick up a guy at Beth's funeral."

"Now hold up one second. I didn't have a choice about ditching you. I can't help it if my mom is moving clear across the country. Would you rather me live in California?"

Gretchen pouted on the other end of the line. "Why can't your dad just move into this school district?"

"He's lived in that house for thirteen years. And have you no idea what's going on with the housing market right now? You think he could sell his place?" I cringed at the thought of his yellowed linoleum kitchen floor and floral wallpaper. The house needed a complete interior makeover.

"Oh, shut up, Brooke. Like you have a clue. You're always trying to sound smart about the news."

"Whatever. I am smart about the news. I actually watch it," I shot back, and then added in my best Valley girl impression: "I'm, like, totally fucking smart."

Gretchen giggled. And then I giggled because it was impossible not to giggle when Gretchen did. I relished the sounds until my heart went tight, signaling inappropriate behavior so soon after Beth's death.

"And don't say I was trying to pick up a guy at Beth's funeral, okay? That's just wrong," I said quietly.

Gretchen was silent for a moment.

"I should have gone with you," she said finally. "I just couldn't. I'm a chicken. What can I say? Do you hate me?"

I shook my head but said nothing, feeling the instant lump in my throat. It came out of nowhere, throbbing painfully, especially when I tried to swallow it.

"You there?" Gretchen said.

I nodded, feeling the first hot tears creep over my lower lids to hang on my lashes.

"Brookey," Gretchen said. It came out sounding desperate and soothing and sweet.

The sob caught fast and hard in my chest, louder than I expected, a violent shudder I couldn't suppress. I moaned, knowing I could sound as crazy and wretched as I wanted, and Gretchen wouldn't mind.

"What's wrong with me?" Another sob. Even louder.

"There's nothing wrong with you," my friend whispered.

"Why did I act that way? Why did I try to flirt with that guy?" I cried. "I'm so pathetic." The tears spilled forth, running down the sides of my face and wetting my cell phone.

"You're not pathetic, Brooke," Gretchen said, and then she tried for something light: "You can't cry all the time or else we'd have to admit you into Dorothea Dix."

"They've closed down," I replied, sniffling and wiping my nose with the back of my hand.

"Well, whatever," Gretchen said, undeterred. "The point is that you keep punishing yourself, Brooke, and that's not healthy."

"My best friend hanged herself!" I screamed into the phone.

"And that wasn't your fault!" Gretchen replied. "Why do you think it is?"

"I cheated with her boyfriend, Gretchen. Did you forget?" I spluttered.

"So that makes you a killer?"

The question shocked me. I opened my mouth to

reply but could think of nothing to say. Why *did* I think my betrayal drove Beth to commit suicide? I knew better. I knew the real reason. Still, the guilt hung heavy in my heart, and I couldn't shake it.

"You're a normal person, Brooke. You can't cry forever. You have to be able to function."

"So I flirt with a guy at Beth's funeral?! That's not normal or functioning. That's messed up," I said.

"Well, I don't know much about psychology, but I bet a lot of doctors would say that's normal."

I snorted.

"No, seriously. People do crazy things when they're under a lot of stress," Gretchen explained.

I shrugged.

"Stop punishing yourself, Brooke," Gretchen said. "Finn had nothing to do with it."

"Stop right there," I demanded. "First off, don't mention that name again."

"I'm sorry."

"Second, stop trying to make me feel better for acting like a complete jerk at my best friend's funeral."

"I'm not trying to make you feel better. I'm just calling it how I see it. You've locked yourself up for days already. You've cried more than anyone else I know. You've given Beth every bit of your heartache. You've got to move on," Gretchen said.

"Move on?" I asked, bewildered.

"I don't mean that you forget about her," Gretchen said gently. "I mean that you stop hurting yourself. Hey, maybe this funeral guy can help. Does he go to your new school?"

"Oh my God," I said. "How should I know? And weren't you just saying that I couldn't get involved with him because it'd be totally lame? Not to mention inappropriate?"

Gretchen ignored my question. "He was at Beth's

funeral. How does he know her? Were they friends?"

"I don't know." I grabbed a tissue from the nightstand and blew my nose.

"Gross. Pull the phone away from your face when you do that," Gretchen said.

I laughed in spite of my pain.

And then I heard the familiar whine. It was the same whine Gretchen used on her father whenever she wanted new clothes. It was annoying but sweet.

"Brookey, get better!"

I laughed again. I couldn't help it. Gretchen was the silliest friend I had. And deluded, too. She thought she could will things to happen by just saying them. She discounted effort being a factor in achieving goals.

"I *will* get an A on this history exam today!" she exclaimed last year. But she didn't study and earned a D instead. The most frustrating part of it all was her inability to understand why claiming something out loud didn't make it so.

"Gretchen, you didn't study," I explained to her.

"But I said it," she replied. "I claimed it."

I wanted to tell her real life wasn't a motivational seminar where you're brainwashed into believing that writing down daily affirmations and chanting them over and over made them come true.

"Are you listening to me?" Gretchen asked, and I was yanked back to the present. "I said get better!"

"And how do you propose I do that?" I asked.

"Go fuck that guy from the funeral," Gretchen suggested. "Even if it *is* totally messed up."

"Oh my God. You're sick," I replied.

"I'm not sick. I'm helping you. You need to move on. Move on from Finn and Beth and the whole mess," Gretchen said.

"First off, don't—"

"—say his name again. Yeah yeah. I got it," Gretchen

replied.

"Second, I am not interested in getting involved with anyone this year. Especially not with a guy I met at a funeral. Number One—"

"Wait, I'm confused. First, second, number one?" Gretchen teased. She liked to make fun of the way I listed things out loud in outline form. Headings and subheadings. Sometimes it got a little confusing, especially when I threw in the lowercase letters. It was my thing, though, and it helped me keep my thoughts organized.

"Shut up and just listen."

"Yes ma'am."

"Okay, so Number One, I'm a senior in high school who's planning on attending a very prestigious university when I graduate. I don't have time for boys."

"*Right*. Are we talking about UNC-Asheville?"

"What is your beef with artists?" I asked.

"I'm just saying that it's no Princeton. And I don't really dig scenes with hippies or hipsters or any other groups of people with 'hip' in their names. It's like, girl, go shave your armpits already. Know what I'm saying?"

"Whatever. Number Two. I think it'd be really weird to date a guy that I did, in fact, literally run into at a funeral. I could never admit to people how we actually met."

"True," came Gretchen's reply.

"Furthermore—"

"No, Brooke. There's no 'furthermore'. That's not even a label for an outline anyway, and I don't care," Gretchen said. "This conversation is getting boring."

"Oh my God, and *I'm* the bitch?" I asked.

She laughed. "I want you to tell me all about class registration. Scope out the hotties. I want to know, damnit!"

"Did you not just hear a word I said?"

"Whatever. You may not want to be in a relationship,

but that's not going to keep you from looking. I know you, Brooklyn."

I giggled into the phone, and it felt delicious and wrong. I suppose Gretchen was right that I couldn't be depressed forever. I just wasn't expecting to laugh so soon after Beth's passing, or flirt, however unsuccessfully, with a guy at her funeral. The flirting was definitely wrong, but maybe laughing with my friend wasn't. What was the psychology behind it? What would doctors say about my behavior? Gretchen thought it was normal, and I instantly recalled Scott Peterson shown on camera laughing during his missing wife's candlelight vigil. The wife he was later found guilty of killing. He was a fucking sociopath. Oh my God. Was I a sociopath, too?

"Are you listening to me?" Gretchen huffed.

I shook my head to rid the thought. "Never," I teased. "I never listen to a word you say."

"Total. Bitch," Gretchen said. "Kisses. I gotta run!" And she hung up before I could throw an insult at her.

Gretchen Stevens was the only girl on the planet I allowed to call me a bitch. I knew other girls did, but she was the only one who had permission. She was the only one I loved for it. She was honest with me—brutally honest, especially when I messed up with Beth. She gave me hell over it, but she never rejected me. She remained a friend through all of it, even when I sank into a depression and started therapy sessions again. Gretchen likened the whole cheating incident to the *Sex and the City* episode where Carrie admits her affair with Big to Samantha. Carrie expected Samantha to judge her, but Samantha didn't.

"So it's like I'm Samantha," Gretchen had said.

"Except that you *have* judged me," I replied.

"Yeah, but that's because what you did was totally shitty. I'm still gonna be your friend, though," Gretchen said, and then hugged me until I stopped crying. "I'll always be your friend, Brookey. We're allowed one huge mess-up in our lives."

"Just one?" I blubbered.

"Just one," she said.

I lay on my bed staring at the ceiling thinking of Gretchen's words. We're allowed one huge mess-up. I wish I would have saved mine for later on in life. Eighteen felt like too young an age to already use it. I didn't think it was fair, and then wondered why I kept blaming everyone and everything around me for my bad decisions.

I blamed Finn for the dissolution of my friendship as though I had no hand in it. Like he forced me to sneak around with him and have sex with him and find excuses to avoid hanging out with Beth so I could see him. I actually found myself blaming Beth at one point: if she weren't so mopey all the time, I would have wanted to spend more time with her! I conveniently forgot about her confession to me as the reason for her deep depression. Sometimes I wondered at the size of my heart, if I even had one at all.

I blamed my mother for the fact that I didn't own any closed-toe pumps and had to wear hers to Beth's funeral. It wasn't even important, but somehow I made it out to be a big deal. If I hadn't been wearing those heels, I wouldn't have almost fallen in the hallway at the church forcing me to grab Funeral Guy's hand to keep from going down. I went so far as to convince myself that I wouldn't have even run into him had I not been wearing those shoes. Yes, it was all my mother's fault. She was the reason I flirted.

How could a genuinely intelligent girl be such a fucking idiot?

I felt so tired, but I was reluctant to fall asleep. I was afraid of dreaming about unpleasant things. I knew it was wrong, but I closed my eyes and conjured Funeral Guy's face, imagining the things his blue irises said to me. *I think you're beautiful*, they said. *I think I love you.* And I drifted into a self-absorbed slumber that eventually betrayed me, summoning ghosts from my past in favor of the boy with the translucent eyes.

"Why don't you get that sexy little ass over here?" Finn said playfully. He reached out for my leg, but I was standing too far away.

"Your girlfriend will be here any minute," I replied, giggling.

We decided to meet at Beth's house and ride together to my All-Star cheerleading competition. Beth was running late, leaving Finn and me alone in her bedroom.

"I don't care," Finn said. He jumped up from the desk chair and grabbed me before I could escape to the other side of the room. He wrapped me up in his arms and planted a series of kisses on my neck.

"I care, Finn," I said breathlessly, feeling my body surrender to his mouth.

"No you don't," he mumbled into my neck, walking me over to Beth's bed. He sat down on the edge and pulled me onto his lap, hands resting on my bottom under my cheerleading skirt. "Now, I have a good idea about it, but I want you to tell me anyway," he said. "Why are these little things called spankies?" He squeezed my bottom, and I squealed.

"They're not called spankies anymore," I corrected. "They're called cheerleading briefs."

Finn scrunched up his nose. "Gross. I like spankies much better."

I chuckled and nuzzled my face into his neck.

"You never answered my question," he teased. His forefinger traced the waistband of my spankies then dipped under the fabric. I squirmed.

"I don't know," I said, feeling my face flush.

"Well, I think I know," Finn said softly. "Were you a good girl at school today?" he asked, his lips brushing my ear, hand patting my bottom.

"I'm always good," I managed to get out. I felt myself already growing wet, and I didn't have time to get all hot and bothered.

"That's not what I heard," Finn continued. He lifted me off his lap and laid me on the bed. I tried to get up, but he held me still, wiggling his eyebrows at me before rolling me over onto my stomach.

"Don't you dare," I warned, feeling my skirt flip up.

"Damn, Brooke," he said. "You have one fine ass." He leaned over me and whispered in my ear again. "And I'm about to teach it a lesson." He straddled my back facing my feet and ran his hands all over my backside.

"Finn!" I squealed when his hand came down on me, lightly smacking my bottom. He squeezed me then did it again. And again until I was thrashing about wildly trying to buck him off of me. I didn't realize I was laughing so hard until he mentioned it.

"You're in trouble, young lady," Finn said, trying for a serious tone. "Why are you laughing?"

"Get off!" I yelled between breaths.

"No way," Finn replied. "You haven't learned your lesson yet," and he spanked me again. This time a little harder.

My head flew up and I almost yelled, "No!" but that wouldn't have been right because I wanted him to do it again. I arched my back pushing my ass up and heard the sharp intake of his breath. He spanked me again, but I stayed quiet.

"You're not even gonna cry for me a little?" Finn asked. He spanked me again. Harder. And I let out a tiny whimper.

He climbed off of me and flipped me over, grabbing hold of my spankies before I could protest. He pulled them down my legs along with my panties but was too impatient to work them over my sneakers. Instead, he let them rest around my ankles as he lifted my thighs up and over his shoulders. I was slightly distressed in this position, most of my weight resting on the back of my neck and shoulders.

"Finn!" I screamed completely exposed to him. He had done this to me before—many times—but always in the dark. Right now daylight streamed through the slats of the window blinds giving him a perfect view of everything I liked to keep hidden.

"I'm the luckiest guy in the world," Finn said, and then he ran his tongue over me.

I moaned and twisted my body, but it was useless. He held me still, his muscular forearms pressing into my lower abdomen. He licked me softly, eliciting cries and occasional screams until I thought I wanted to die. It felt too good, and I knew I didn't deserve it. I fisted the sheets on either side of me and begged him to stop.

"I will," he said, his lips still on me. "When I've made you come."

"No no no," I said halfheartedly. "I have a competition. Beth. Beth will be here any minute."

He ignored me and kept up his gentle assault. His tongue all over me. His light kisses. I wanted to come and knew I would harder than he'd ever made me in the past. I don't know why it was so powerful this time. Perhaps because we were being too reckless, too dangerous, and the rush was a powerful, addictive intoxicant.

But I should have paid attention to the unsettling feeling deep inside my heart. It was a warning bell with a big flashing red light. I could hear the smooth, calm female voice over the intercom system—the one in all the sci-fi movies: "Attention. Ten seconds until detonation." And then the ship exploded, and my body along with it. I screamed into space, felt the oxygen ripped out of me, the stars popping one by one behind my eyes, inside my heart, throughout my legs.

"What the fuck is this?"

I lay there sated, frozen. I didn't want to turn my head, but I forced myself to. Beth stood in her doorway. Her face was white, and in my stupefied state, I wanted to tell her that—that there was something wrong with her face. And then somehow I came to, and I realized what I looked like. Lying on her bed with her boyfriend's face between my legs. Finn lifted me off his shoulders, and I scrambled to pull up my spankies.

"What the fuck are you doing?!" Beth screamed.

"Beth, oh my God, I don't know!" I said. I stood on the other side of her bed, trapped like a scared animal.

"You don't know?!" she yelled. "My boyfriend was just eating *you out, Brooke! And you don't know?"*

I opened my mouth to reply, but there were no words.

"Answer me, you fucking bitch!"

"Beth, stop," Finn said.

"Are you kidding me? 'Stop'? What were you doing? How could you do this to me? My boyfriend!"

"Beth, you and I both know it's over. It's been over," Finn said. "You don't even like me."

"You got that right, you fucking prick!" Beth shouted. She turned in my direction. "You were my best friend, Brooke.

The hurt in her eyes broke me to my core. I choked on the sob. I choked on her word. Were. *"You* were *my best friend."*

"Why are you crying?" Beth asked. "Because you got caught? Or you all of a sudden feel guilty? How long has this been going on?!"

I shook my head.

"You're gonna tell me," Beth demanded. She advanced towards me a few paces before changing her mind and standing still.

"A few months, Beth," Finn answered, and I wanted to hit him.

Beth gasped. "A few months?!"

"And we love each other. I'm sorry I hurt you," Finn said. He sounded like a complete jackass. And what the hell was he talking about? Love? We never said anything about loving each other.

Beth laughed derisively. "Wow. Love. Okay." Her face streamed tears. I watched as one clung to her jaw before plopping to the floor.

"Beth, please," I whispered.

"Get out of my house," she said. "Now."

I didn't move.

"Now!"

Finn grabbed my hand and led me out. I thought Beth would lunge at me when I passed by her, but she stood stoic, staring at me as though I were a stranger. And then I heard the door slam, and my entire world shifted in an instant.

THREE

My father stood in the middle of the bedroom looking nervous.

"Well, what do you think?" he asked. He glanced at me for a moment, then turned to the window.

"About what?" I replied.

"The room," he said. "Is it all right?"

"Yeah, it's great," I lied. It looked like a room that belonged to a 10-year-old girl in love with Justin Bieber and the color purple. I would change it immediately.

"That's good," Dad replied, relief evident in his voice.

I grinned. It was impossibly uncomfortable standing together in the bedroom, but neither one of us made a move to leave.

"You feel like pizza tonight?" he asked after a moment. "There's a really good joint up the road. Family owned."

"Sounds good," I said. I plopped down on the bed.

"I usually cook," he went on. "But I didn't know what you like to eat." He scratched the back of his neck.

"I eat anything," I replied. I wasn't going to make it *too* easy for him.

He sighed. "You do, huh?"

I grinned up at him, and he chuckled. And then he relaxed, and I did the same.

"Dad?"

"Hmm?"

"Where did you get these posters of Justin Bieber?"

"Wal-Mart," he answered. "Why? You don't like him? The lady at the store said—"

"It's okay, Dad."

He shuffled over to the curtains framing the one window in the room and tugged on them.

"You probably don't like these either, do you?" he asked.

I smiled again, and he shook his head.

"I'm not listening to those women in the office anymore," he said irritably, but there was humor running underneath the words.

"Well, we can fix anything with receipts," I offered, and he nodded. "Dad?"

"Hmm?"

"I know you didn't really want this, and I'm sorry," I said. I thought it was better to just be honest.

It was a weird situation for all of us. Mom was across the country by now. Dad was still living in the past in the same house that smelled of summers when I was nine years old and hosted the best sleepovers with Beth in the history of sleepovers. Everything looked the same, but it was the smell that made my heart ache. And I was in a new place, too. I knew he didn't understand why I asked to live with him. I didn't really understand it except that I felt compelled to attend Beth's high school my senior year.

"Don't apologize," he said. "I want you here. I really do. I just haven't been a full-time parent in a while, that's all."

"Well, you don't have to worry," I said. "I'm pretty

easy and independent. I just landed a job at that diner you used to take us to. You won't have to worry about giving me money." I shouldn't have said that last part.

"Why would you think I'd have a problem giving you money?" Dad asked. He pulled out his wallet.

"No, I just meant that I don't want you thinking you have to change your whole life now that I'm here. I can take care of myself. I won't be in the way," I said, and I saw the hurt in his eyes.

"What life?" he asked quietly. I didn't know what to say.

He stared out the window while I traced the cheetah print on my comforter. I had no idea Dad wanted me here. Living with him. I looked around the room then. Really looked, and I saw it. The time and detail he put into everything. The bright purple throw pillows on the bed that accented the comforter. The full-length mirror attached to my closet door that boasted a thick frame painted with purple and white flowers. The fuzzy-trimmed bedside table lamps. Purple as well. My old pom-poms attached to the top of the mirror over my dresser. He even found my old My Little Ponies and lined them on top of the dresser. I wanted to cry for how wrong it looked and how right it felt. I wouldn't change a thing, I decided. Well, the posters would go.

"You have any interest in going with me to register for classes?" I asked. I knew I'd be the only senior there with a parent, but I didn't care. I wanted to start over— look sweet and innocent—and I thought that Dad accompanying me would give that impression perfectly. God knows I needed a new identity.

"Well, I don't want to be in the way," Dad replied.

"How would you be in the way?" I asked, hopping up from the bed. "Come on. Afterwards you can take me shopping for school supplies." If he wanted to give me things, who was I to refuse?

"Okay," Dad said, a note of excitement underlining the word.

—

You know when someone is staring at you. You feel it. The hairs on your neck stand up if it's an odd feeling, if you're not quite sure you like it. If the person makes you uneasy, even if you haven't spotted him yet. Or you might feel the wave of heat crash onto you starting at your head and swooshing down your body to your toes. If you like it. If it's a good feeling, even if you haven't spotted him yet.

I felt the hairs on my neck stand up because I knew who it was. And I didn't like it. Or him.

I looked down at my outfit. I don't know why I cared, but I was starting over at a new school, and I wanted the first impression to be the right one. Dark jean shorts with a see-through billowy top. I wore a camisole underneath the top and let it hang off of one shoulder. My feet sported jeweled sandals. I wore just a bit of make-up. Mostly I focused on accentuating my dark blue eyes. Gold tones to make them pop. Thick mascara on my upper lashes. I kept my lower lashes naked. I liked the contrast. I even curled my hair and left my locks loose, cascading down my back in soft blond waves.

This was so important—first impressions. I was trying to start fresh. I was confident that most students at Charity Run didn't know who I was because my old high school wasn't a rival. They wouldn't know my history with Beth, my history as a terrible friend. I had a chance at a real transformation. I would be a good girl my senior year. I would walk the halls every day and feel Beth's ghost—a constant reminder of my betrayal—and welcome the pain. It would be punishment I deserved. And if I was lucky, eventually I would be reformed.

Dad struck up a conversation with the teacher helping me, so I decided it was time to turn my face, to let my surveyor see me fully. I jumped when I saw him. I thought he would be somewhere across the gym, but he was standing right behind me. The heat crashed over me then, but not the good heat. I was nervous, and my skin burned with it.

He smiled at me. I returned my own, shy and uncertain.

"You a senior?" he asked casually.

He towered over me, brown hair buzzed, chocolate eyes dark and foreboding. His arms were thick with years of competitive swimming, and for a split second, I imagined Beth trapped by them, unable to move, to escape as he took whatever he wanted from her. A violation of the most personal nature. Too devastating for Beth to overcome, so she took her life in her bedroom closet instead.

A righteous anger flared in me immediately, and just like that, I discovered a purpose. *My* purpose. It flooded me instantly, a great wave slamming into my mind and my heart, carrying with it the courage and conviction of my newly formed plan. I knew how to apologize. I knew how to make things right with Beth. I was a warrior in that moment, and I was going into battle on behalf of my friend. *I'll fucking bury this guy, Beth. I'll do it. Just watch me do it.* And I transformed into the predator. He just didn't know it yet. He thought I was the prey, and I'd let him.

I swallowed. "Yeah," I said, combing my fingers through my hair. I wanted it to look like a sweet little nervous habit. I cocked my head playfully as I looked up at him.

"That's gotta be hard. Moving to a new school your senior year," he replied.

"Not really," I said. "My old school sucked."

I watched as his eyes roved over my body. He was

covert about it, but I wasn't blind. My skin crawled, and I felt an overwhelming urge to attack him. I'd be no match, I knew, but perhaps I could claw his eyes out before he slammed me to the floor, knocking me unconscious.

"Well, I hope you like this school better," he said after he finished his assessment.

"I guess it doesn't matter either way," I said. "It's our last year."

"True," he replied. "But I plan on making it a good one."

Yeah, I bet you do, you fucking asshole.

"Oh, me too," I said a little too enthusiastically. He seemed to like it.

"I'm Cal, by the way," he said, extending his hand.

I took it tentatively. I didn't want to. Adrenaline was pumping overtime, and I was afraid I'd squeeze his hand so hard I'd rip it off.

"Brooklyn," I replied. "But everyone calls me Brooke."

"It's nice to meet you, Brooklyn," he said, curling his lips into a pleasant smile. He squeezed my hand before releasing it.

Hmm, so he had no plans to call me "Brooke." At least not yet. What was he playing at? Perhaps he didn't want me to think that I had captured his attention. Maybe he didn't want me thinking we would even be friends. He was, after all, one of those popular guys. I, on the other hand, had no social status and had no ambitions to be popular.

"Nice to meet you, too, uh . . . what was your name again?" I worked my hardest to suppress the grin. *You don't wanna give me "Brooke?" Okay then. I won't even give you a name.*

He chuckled. "Cal."

"That's right," I said. "Cal. Is Cal short for anything?"

He smirked and looked over his shoulder before turning back to me. "Yeah. Calvin. But everyone calls me Cal."

"Well, it's nice to meet you, Calvin," I said. I cocked my head to the side and grinned.

"Hmm," he replied, and I imagined he was thinking about the type of panties I wore.

Dad tapped my shoulder at the perfect moment. I had to get away from this guy. I wanted to throttle him, knowing what he did to my friend, and I was heady from the plan still unfolding in my brain. And frankly, I was scared of Cal's physical size.

"Ready?" Dad asked.

I breathed deeply, then thought of the perfect response. "Yes, Daddy," and he looked at me strangely. I watched Cal's reaction to my words, certain of his arousal. "Bye, Calvin." I lifted my hand in a tiny wave.

"Hey wait," he said hurriedly. He reached for my registration card. "Can I see your class schedule?"

"Sure," I said, handing him the card. "Any particular reason why?"

"Uh, well, I can tell you about the teachers," he said.

Bullshit. He wanted to know what classes he could take with me. Gotcha, you son-of-a-bitch, and the image of a big, fat tuna wriggling on a tiny hook came to mind. A slow, tortuous death, and I smiled, imagining the last desperate flop.

"Like Ms. Walker. She'll have you doing all sorts of presentations in class. Good if you like public speaking, but I think most of us freaking hate it," he said.

I nodded.

"And Mr. Hatchet—"

"Yikes, that's a scary name."

"No kidding. He's a jerk. Just so you know. Don't try to win him over with your feminine charms. It doesn't work on him. He won't even take legitimate excuses for missing class. Not even doctors notes."

"Sounds like a jerk," I echoed.

"Um, the rest are okay. I see you're doing Yearbook? I was planning on that, too," Cal said.

Were you, Cal? Were you really planning on doing Yearbook? Give me a break.

"Well, if you do, maybe we can work together. You know, go take pictures together or whatever," I offered. Sickly sweet. Good girl.

"Yeah, maybe," he said, and handed me the card. "I'll see you later."

"Okay. See you next week, Calvin," I said as he walked away.

"Making friends already, huh?" Dad asked as we made our way out of the gym to Dad's old pickup truck.

"Hardly," I replied. "Though he seemed nice enough."

The lie felt heavy in my mouth. He wasn't nice enough. He wasn't nice at all, and I knew it.

—

Make him pay.

That much was settled. I'd make him pay. I just didn't know if I'd do it by taking a baseball bat to his balls, putting a 9 mm to his head and pulling the trigger, or something more subversive. The idea came to me in the gym, and I entertained it now. The idea of letting him have me. Seduce him without him knowing, give him the perfect opportunity to take advantage of me, then make him pay for it afterwards. Could I actually go through with it, though? Could I give up my body as a sacrifice to seek vengeance? Was I strong enough? Crazy enough?

I could never do it if I was a virgin, but I wasn't a virgin. Not that it makes being raped any less painful or traumatic. Still, I thought that having my virginity out of the way made it less life-shattering. And would it really be rape, anyway, if I lured him into doing it?

I'd never been sexually assaulted, had absolutely no idea how that affected a woman, and felt a little ashamed for thinking that I could handle it. Like I had a clue about the reality. My arrogance knew no bounds, and I convinced myself that the emotional impact would be miniscule because I was strong enough to handle it. Honestly, though. Could I really testify in court, go through all of that, without the certainty of getting him behind bars? Could I risk being thrust into the public eye? Not every state protected the identities of rape victims once they came forward. Did North Carolina? I'd have to research it.

My God. My mind was spinning, entertaining grand ideas of revenge. I wanted this for Beth. I wanted this for me. Perhaps it would bury my guilt and grief for good. I considered the type of guy Cal was. What if he'd raped other girls? Was it my duty to seek revenge? I felt in that resolute moment that I had no other choice, that my entire existence was defined by this crazy plan. *There's something really messed up about you, Brooke,* I heard myself saying. Maybe. But it felt right. I hadn't felt right about anything in a long time.

I lay on my bed, my brain flooded with question after question. It was working overtime, and I couldn't keep up with it. Maybe I was just going crazy. Maybe I would wake up tomorrow and scratch the whole plan. But who was I kidding? The anger I felt in the gym when I stood before that predator was too real, too powerful and right to ignore. There's anger, and then there's righteous anger. I felt the righteous anger, and I knew I had to act on it. I would purify my heart by becoming impure.

I fell asleep knowing old events would resurface, creep into the forefront of my mind from my subconscious, make me relive the pain all over again to solidify my decision. I would wake up determined because I had no choice. And if I fought it, the dreams would continue to haunt me until I surrendered to my fate.

"You have to tell me what's wrong," I pleaded.

Beth sobbed into her hands, rocking back and forth like someone on the verge of a nervous breakdown. I didn't want her to have a breakdown. I didn't know what to do if she did.

"Beth, please," I urged, wrapping my arm around her and drawing her into me. She rested her head on my shoulder.

"He raped me," she whispered.

I immediately thought of Finn, and my heart sank. It couldn't be Finn. Finn would never do such a thing. I couldn't believe it, wouldn't believe it, because I was sleeping with him. I was head-over-heels for him.

"Who?" I croaked. My pulse sped up as I clutched my best friend.

"You don't know him," Beth answered. "He goes to my school. His name is Cal."

I pulled away and took Beth's hands. "Beth, you need to tell me what happened."

Beth shook with a fresh wave of sobs as she nodded reluctantly.

"I went to a party. That party I told you about," she began.

I cringed. It was the party I didn't attend. She wanted me to, but I made up some lousy lie about hanging out with my mother when I was, in fact, going to see Finn.

I felt like shit.

"I think he drugged my drink," Beth continued. "I started feeling really out of it. Lightheaded, I guess. He took me upstairs to his room so I could lie down. I didn't want to. I kept telling him I didn't want to!"

She burst into tears, long ragged sobs that sounded painful in her chest.

"It's okay," I said, stroking her back. All I could think was that I wasn't there. If I had been there, this wouldn't have happened. My fault. My fault.

"He took my clothes off," she said. "I told him no. I tried to scream it, but my tongue felt so huge. Like it was swollen. He said I wanted it and that I was just a tease."

"You don't have to tell me anymore," I whispered. I couldn't stand to hear it.

"No! I have to! I have to get it out!" she screamed, and I nodded.

She took a deep breath, trying to settle the hitching in her chest.

"I cried, and he licked my face. I think he was licking my tears. And then he had sex with me while he covered my mouth, and he told me not to tell anyone because no one would believe me. He knew I wasn't a virgin. He knew I had slept with guys on the swim team. Those idiots must brag about it or something."

My head swam with a mixture of guilt: guilt for not going to the party with Beth, guilt for her attack, guilt for sneaking around with her boyfriend, guilt for lying to her.

"He's right, Brooke," Beth said. Her voice quavered uncontrollably. "No one would believe me. He's all-American swim team champ. I'm the girl who's fucked three guys at school. No one would believe me."

"That's not true," I argued. "You have to come forward, Beth. You can't let him get away with it."

"Are you crazy?" she shrieked. It came out harsher than I think she expected. I shrank away from her, confused. "God, Brooke, do you even know what you're asking of me?"

—

I hated the first day of school. This one was made monstrously worse by the fact that I knew no one. Yes, the prospect of starting with a clean slate was attractive, but being as it was my senior year, I didn't know if I wanted or cared to put the energy into making friends. It seemed too hard, and then I had already decided to put all my time and energy into destroying Cal's life. I wasn't sure how a new friend or group of friends would fit into that picture.

I wandered down the main hallway looking for Hallway D. I quickly discovered how complicated the school layout was, mirroring that haunted mansion out west whose owner had workers building onto it every day until she died. Twists and turns that seemed to lead nowhere—a haphazard sort of architecture with no rhyme or reason. A person could get lost in here, and I wondered if it was designed that way on purpose. I imagined teachers snickering in the teachers' lounge watching surveillance video of confused students scurrying about like rats trying to locate their classrooms. Perhaps it was one big psychological experiment.

I don't know how, but I eventually stumbled upon Hallway D. Of course, I had no idea how to get to my first class from here, but I'd worry about that when the bell rang. Right now I scanned the lockers shoved on one side of the hall until I located mine. I stored away the few binders and notebooks I brought with me and slapped a magnetic mirror to the inside of the locker door. That was it. I was ready. I closed the door and looked around.

A few girls glanced my way as they passed by. I decided to smile, but they kept walking, either oblivious to my kind gesture or determined to keep me out of the fold. Whatever. I wasn't looking to make friends. I was looking to annihilate Cal, and I watched as he walked towards me. I tensed, feeling uncertain about the outfit I chose to wear. I was usually only self-conscious around guys I was attracted to. I was certainly not attracted to Cal, but I found myself wanting to impress him. I needed to impress him. That was the whole point. If he found me unattractive or uninteresting, I'd have no chance. My entire plan would spoil like old fruit.

"It's Brooklyn, right?" he asked, breezing right by me.

"Uh huh," I replied, and watched as he disappeared

down the hall flanked by his loser friends.

What the hell was that? And then I realized exactly what it was. He wasn't going to make this easy for me. He was going to make me work for it, work to earn my place in the group of popular seniors. Work to earn the place right beside him.

Fuckhead.

That's fine. I'd do whatever was necessary to achieve my goal. I'd swallow my pride if it meant seeing justice done. I took a deep breath and meandered down the hall, searching the classroom doors for 1A. Eventually I found it, and was pleased with myself that I beat the tardy bell. I walked in to find most seats already occupied and became instantly irritated.

I liked sitting on the outskirts of the classroom. No, that's not quite right. I *needed* to sit on the outskirts of the classroom. But the only available seats were directly in the center of the room. I reluctantly settled in a row four seats from the front and tried hard to push down the instant anxiety.

I struggled with intense claustrophobia for as long as I could remember. I never took elevators, had to be completely sedated on airplanes, and always drove in the slow lane. I had access to the shoulder that way. I had an out. Now I sat with students surrounding me, and for a brief moment, I closed my eyes, imagining I was out in the middle of a great big field, empty space stretching as far as I could see in all directions. I succeeded in slowing my racing heart.

I learned this trick in therapy, discovering its effectiveness in certain situations. But it didn't work in elevators. I learned that the hard way after trying to accelerate my progress, feeling rather cocky after having successfully flown on a plane across five states without a sedative. I thought I could totally handle an elevator, but soon found myself huddled on the floor screaming and breathing into a paper bag.

I looked to my right because I saw something beautiful in my peripheral vision. There he was, Funeral Guy, sitting on the edge of the room against the far window, staring ahead at nothing in particular. I started to shake and closed my eyes again, imagining the field. The problem was that he was in it, walking towards me, and before I could react, he gathered me in his arms and kissed me roughly. My God, he was hurting me, and I wanted him to! I kissed him back just as feverishly, and then felt his hands go to the button of my jeans. He didn't ask for permission but started undressing me, like I didn't have a choice.

My eyes flew open, and I shifted in my seat. This was incredibly inconvenient. Yes, a small part of me suspected that he went to this school. Why else would he be at Beth's funeral? But I wasn't prepared to see him in any of my classes. And I knew I couldn't get involved with him. For one, I had no idea if he was even attracted to me. Two, I couldn't very well pursue him when I was trying to get Cal's attention. Three, I had sworn off boys, Cal notwithstanding.

Stupid Cal. He was already ruining my life, and my plan hadn't even started coming to fruition. I glanced at Funeral Guy again. He was staring straight at me, and my elbow jerked involuntarily, knocking my notebook off my desk. I reached down to retrieve it and slammed my forehead on the side of the desk.

"Motherfucker!" I hissed, and heard a tiny gasp next to me.

"You okay?" a girl asked.

I rubbed my sore head and sat up. "Does it look bad?" I moved my hand so the girl could get a good look.

"It's just a little red," she said, smiling.

I rolled my eyes at the chuckling that ensued behind me.

"I just love being the source of the joke," I said, jabbing a thumb towards the back of the room.

The girl turned around in the direction of the laughter, her smile fading instantly, and I watched as her face filled with something unsettling. I wasn't absolutely sure, but I thought it was fear. She whipped her head back around.

"Don't worry about them," she said quietly, fidgeting with her pen.

"I'm not," I replied, a little offended that she assumed I'd cared so much what those students thought about me.

I turned around to look at them. I've no idea when Cal walked into the room, but I felt my face go instantly hot. He grinned at me and waved. I placed my hand back over my forehead and shrugged, rolling my eyes. He shrugged back, the friendly gesture unnerving me. I didn't want him to be so damn nice, but wasn't that the way of predators? If they came across intimidating or frightening, they'd never have the opportunity to attack.

I turned back around. My forehead still throbbed. "I'm Brooke, by the way," I said, addressing the girl.

"Lucy."

"Nice to meet you."

Lucy smiled but said nothing. She was a pretty, petite blonde with large hazel eyes. She reminded me of a bird— small bones, fragile body. I thought she could stand to eat more, but then maybe she ate like a horse and never packed on weight. I watched her open her notebook when she heard the classroom door open. The teacher entered, and I tried to pay attention, though it was hard with Funeral Guy to my right and Cal to my back. The idea of Cal sitting behind me, watching me when I was powerless to move, really pissed me off. I'm sure he enjoyed it. I'm sure he would enjoy all fifty-one minutes of it, and I closed my eyes again, trying to conjure the field.

—

I had to be at work in an hour, giving me just enough time to do a little investigating.

Lucy.

Something didn't sit right with me about her, not because she seemed like a bad person, but because she seemed genuinely frightened of Cal and his cronies in class this morning. I wanted to know who she was. A tiny part of me suspected the worst, but I didn't want to jump to any conclusions. I wanted my intuition to be wrong as I tore open Beth's freshman yearbook which her mother had given me.

I found Lucy on the third page—Homecoming—and she was the freshmen princess. I studied her. She was posed in a wave, acknowledging the cheers erupting from the stadium bleachers. She looked happy grasping her escort's arm. I flipped through several more pages before I spotted her on the varsity cheerleading spread. There she was, smiling brightly, suspended in the air in a cheerleading move called the Liberty. I knew the move because I used to be tossed in the air to do the same thing. Her form was perfect, and I felt a tiny bit of jealousy. It was stupid, but it was there all the same.

I continued scanning, finding her on a host of other pages: yearbook club, chorus, volleyball. I froze when I landed on the prom page. Lucy was there, dancing with Cal, his arms wrapped tightly around her small waist, holding her protectively. No, possessively. My mind started racing. Was Cal her date? Did he take her home? Did he rape her before he took her home?

I tore open Beth's sophomore yearbook. I scanned all the sports and social activities pages, but found no pictures of Lucy. She was featured only on the sophomore class spread. I stared at her picture, but I didn't see anything in her eyes or the way she smiled that evoked the happy, social freshman. There was something empty about that smile, like she didn't believe it and didn't expect anyone else to.

I flipped through Beth's junior yearbook. No Lucy. Anywhere. Even her picture on the junior class spread was missing, a "No Photo Available" in place of it.

My heart clenched, and I wondered how I could ache for a person I didn't know. I suspected other victims, but I didn't want to discover them. It would complicate my plan. I wanted justice for Beth. I was responsible for her. I was willing to sacrifice myself for her, but I didn't want to be responsible for anyone else. And I didn't want the knowledge of any other rapes to grow Cal into a horrific monster that frightened me. I couldn't do anything to him if I was scared of him.

I tossed the yearbook aside and checked my watch. It was time to go, and I was grateful for the distraction, grabbing my apron that was slung over the desk chair and hurrying out of the house.

—

"What are you doing here?" I asked as I approached Gretchen.

"What do people normally do in restaurants?" she replied.

I smirked and grabbed the pen from behind my ear.

"I told you I would call you when I got home," I said, flipping to a clean sheet on my order pad.

"Yeah, but I couldn't wait that long," Gretchen confessed.

"I'm busy tonight, Gretchen. I can't hang around and chat," I said. I glanced at my other tables. No refills needed. No one looking to get my attention. Good so far.

"I know, Brooke. I'll hang out until the crowd dies down."

"You're gonna hang out at one of my tables all night?" I asked. "You better leave me one hell of a tip. I'm trying to make money here."

"Relax," Gretchen said. "Do your job well, and I'll take care of you." She winked, and I scowled.

"Hilarious. Really," I muttered. "What do you want?"

"This salad thing and a Diet Coke," she answered, pointing to the menu.

"Fine," and I made my way to the order station. I punched in Gretchen's order, then went to pour her a Diet Coke.

I started my waitressing job the day after I moved in with my dad. I got the job because I lied about having experience waiting tables, and the manager was so grateful he wouldn't have to train someone. He repeated that sentiment about ten times during the interview, and I almost confessed my lack of experience out of pure guilt. And fear. No training whatsoever?

I was good at bullshitting, but waiting tables was hard. You had to be quick. You had to remember everything. You had to try your hardest not to piss anyone off, especially your customers. And the hostesses. They wouldn't seat anyone in your section if you pissed them off. The truth was that I hadn't a clue what I was doing, but I learned quickly after a cook, dishwasher, and expediter all yelled at me my first night.

"Put the fucking order in the fucking computer, Wright!" Terry, the main chef, had yelled after I asked him why my order wasn't up for Table 12.

"I wrote it down for you," I said, pointing to my handwritten order form lying on the counter next to his grill.

"Fucking teenagers," he mumbled as he picked up the sheet, crumbled it, and threw it in the flames.

"Hey! What the hell?!" I cried.

He pointed to the computer.

"You burned my order," I seethed.

"You didn't have it memorized?" he asked.

I flipped him off and stormed out of the kitchen, apologizing profusely to Table 12 for needing to retake their order. Thankfully, they were nice about it and asked if it was my first day on the job. I didn't expect a good tip and was surprised when they left me a little extra. It was pity change, but I'd take it all the same.

I was caught off guard when I approached Gretchen once more with her drink. She sat staring transfixed, and I followed her gaze to a family that had just been seated. I nearly dropped the glass but refused to take my eyes off the family. Or rather, *him*. Funeral Guy. Again. Did he know I worked here? How ludicrous, and completely egotistical. I had to keep reminding myself that the world did not, in fact, revolve around me.

"Damnit, Brooke!" Gretchen cried. "You spilled Coke all over me!"

I tore my eyes away from Funeral Guy to look at Gretchen's shirt. There were two tiny dark spots just to the left of her breast. I rolled my eyes.

"All over you, huh?"

"This is Bebe, bitch," she replied.

I grinned. "I don't know what that means."

"Yeah. Sure you don't. You better start setting aside your tip money if this shit doesn't wash out."

"Oh, Gretchy," I said.

"Do *not* call me that," she warned, and then her tone changed in a flash. "Now, check out that hottie over there." She pointed to Funeral Guy. My hottie. I already decided to claim him.

I was itching to see her reaction. "Gretchen, that's Funeral Guy."

"No fucking way!" she squealed, and a couple with three small children seated near her turned in her direction and scowled.

"This is a family restaurant," the mother barked.

"No fucking way," Gretchen replied, mock bewilderment painted all over her face.

"Gretchen," I said quietly.

The mother huffed and turned back to her husband. I could hear them mumbling and wondered how long it would take the manager to hear the complaint and kick Gretchen out. Why couldn't she keep her mouth shut?

"That's the guy you ran into at the funeral?" she asked.

I nodded. "And he's in two of my classes."

"I totally hate you," Gretchen said. "Life is so unfair."

I shrugged.

"Is he sitting in your section?" she asked.

"No, thank God! I'd probably say or do something totally embarrassing," I said. "I smacked my forehead on the side of my desk today. He saw it. It happened because he was looking at me."

Gretchen screwed up her face. "I don't get it. His hotness made you convulse or something?"

I laughed. "No. He made me drop my notebook, and when I bent down to get it, I smacked my head."

"How embarrassing," Gretchen said.

"Yeah, I seem to have a knack for doing embarrassing things around him. I don't know why he makes me so giddy and stupid."

"Because you want to sleep with him. Hello?" Gretchen replied. "And now I totally understand why." She turned back in his direction. "He's fu—"

"Bleh!" I screamed. "Don't say that word in here!"

"Oh my God," Gretchen said. "Whatever. He's *freaking* hot. Happy? Now go over there and talk to him."

"You really are deluded," I replied, and left for the kitchen.

Terry and I had since mended our fragile

relationship. He apologized the same night he yelled at me and burned my order. And for telling the manager to fire me. After work that night, he offered to buy me a drink, and when I said I was only eighteen, he asked, "So what?"

"I don't know," I had replied. "Maybe it's illegal or something like that."

"It's only illegal if you get caught," he explained, and I knew he was bad news. I'd stay away from him and his ten tattoos.

"Wright!" Terry yelled as I walked through the kitchen door. "Get your skinny ass over here and pick up your fucking orders! You're taking up the whole shelf space!"

I saluted him and grabbed a tray, carefully stacking all of my orders for three tables, Gretchen's included.

I made my way through my section, serving food to people who looked genuinely shocked and delighted. I wondered if I acted that way at restaurants without knowing: shocked and delighted to see a plate coming my way, like I didn't know to expect it. I was at a freaking restaurant, after all. People were so stupid.

"His name is Ryan," Gretchen said when I approached her with her salad.

"I know. They take attendance in class. But how do *you* know?"

"I overheard his little sister say his name," she replied, grinning.

"Gretchen, leave it alone," I said.

Gretchen picked up her fork and pushed it tentatively through her salad. I waited. When she finished her assessment, I asked what else she needed.

"Ryan's phone number," she said.

I gave her an even look.

"Hey, if you're not gonna take a shot, then I will."

"I don't think so," I replied and looked over at Ryan. He spotted me, and I watched him do a once over on me with his eyes. It didn't feel sleazy or gross like when Cal did it. Ryan did it blatantly, like he meant for me to see him, and I didn't know what to make of it. I was a progressive woman living in a progressive world. Shouldn't I feel offended? I'm no object, buster!

But I couldn't pretend to be offended. I was flattered, and I smiled at him, though I knew it would be a mistake. He grinned back, and the trouble started. Right there, in that moment. I should have turned and walked away. But I didn't. I smiled, and in that instant, my simple plan to pursue Cal, make him hurt me, then make him pay for it, became anything but simple.

FOUR

The rest of the school week went by in a flash. I made little progress with Cal and even less with Lucy. I thought I could be friends with her, but she remained distant, closed up. She was nice enough in class, always greeting me and asking how work was going, but they were superficial niceties meant to keep me at a distance. By Friday, I figured she harbored horrible secrets. I don't know why I needed or wanted to know them. I told myself not to get involved with anyone else's problems. I had a big enough job for one. I couldn't be the hero for an entire group of victims.

Cal was frustrating. As hard as I worked to come across charming and sweet, he didn't take the bait. He kept me at a distance, too, surprising me every now and again in the hallway in between classes with a "Hello" or "Nice top, Brooklyn." I knew he was doing it on purpose, making me think I had a chance so that I would keep working to get close to him. I was convinced he wanted me close to him. I caught him in class a few times staring at me. It was a predator's stare, and it sought to claim me.

Whenever you try hard to keep from being involved in something, it finds you out, forces you into the situation, and you've no choice but to act out of a sense of moral responsibility because deep down your heart is good, and you want to do good. My desperate desire to do good came more from an overwhelming feeling of guilt for my past than from my moral compass. I knew eventually I would have to say something, do something, that made me uncomfortable because when you're trying to be good, what choice do you have?

It was Friday, and I barely made it to the bathroom at the sound of the lunch bell. I held my pee all morning, unable to find breaks in any of my classes to excuse myself. Actually, that's not true. There was one break between fourth and fifth periods, but Cal happened to approach me at my locker during that time, and I wasn't forfeiting a chance to talk with him. I'd get a bladder infection before I walked away from Cal.

He asked if I wanted to shoot pictures with him of the women's volleyball game this afternoon. Yes, he had decided to take Yearbook after all, and I had been waiting for this opportunity to get to know him better. Discover what made him tick. His likes and dislikes. All the information I would need to store away in my arsenal for future use when the battle really heated up. I agreed to meet him in the gym at four, and he left, giving me just enough time to get to class before the tardy bell.

I flew into a stall and all but ripped off my shorts, sinking down onto the toilet seat because I couldn't squat. I had to use the bathroom too badly. Normally I always squatted over toilet seats, and I probably should have done so now because I'm quite sure I felt tiny droplets on the backs of my thighs.

"Gross," I muttered. "I'm sitting in someone's pee."

But the relief was a little piece of heaven, and I sat in bliss on the toilet, reveling in the feel of an empty bladder, smiling stupidly as I read the obscenities written on the stall door.

Jamie H. is a dirty whore.
I wondered who Jamie H. was.
Carolyn fucked the football team.
Wow, I thought. *That's a lot of fucking.*
Lucy blows guys for money.
Huh?

I leaned in and reread the sentence. They couldn't possibly be talking about my Lucy. Yes, just like Ryan, I decided to claim her for my own. It was instant possession because I thought she was sweet and kind, and I wasn't going to let any bitch talk shit about her. Of course, maybe it was another Lucy, but "Lucy" wasn't a popular name. The Lucy I met didn't seem like the kind of girl described in that sentence. Why would someone write that about her?

I thought back to the few times I saw her outside the classroom. She never walked or talked with anyone. She was always alone, looking morose at worst, empty at best. She didn't have any friends. But why? I thought about the first day of class when I bumped my head. She addressed me then. Why did she do that? And then I realized it was because I was new. I didn't know her. It was safe for her to talk to me. Maybe, just maybe, she was trying to make friends with me. At that moment I was filled with a kind of tenderness usually reserved exclusively for my mother and father. It was familial tenderness, but I felt it for this girl. I wanted to adopt her as my sister, protect her, make her smile.

I froze when I heard the bathroom door swing open. A shuffling of feet, a sniffle, and then a racking sob. I didn't know what to do. Should I make my presence known by coughing or clearing my throat? It was obvious the girl thought she was alone. Who doesn't check under stall doors to be certain of it?

The sobbing continued for a few moments before it stopped abruptly. I was sure she was still in the bathroom.

I didn't hear the door open again. I realized I could be stuck in here forever and thought it was better to just come out. She would be mortified or pissed off, but I had to take that chance.

I flushed the toilet and walked out. The girl whirled around to face me, a horrified look on her face.

"Are you okay?" I asked.

She stared at me for a moment. I didn't recognize her. She looked too young to be a senior, and I never saw her in Hallway D, the senior hall.

She made a move for the door, but I blocked her.

"Can I help in any way?" I asked.

She looked at me, her large green eyes swimming with fresh tears. She was so pretty and frightened. What the hell? This was the second pretty, frightened girl I'd come across in my first week of school. How many were there?

I knew it would shake her to her core, force her to relive a painful event all over again, but I had to ask. "Did something bad happen to you?"

She shoved me out of the way and exited the bathroom, but not before answering me. She nodded. It was barely perceptible, but she nodded.

I left the bathroom after washing my hands, shaken and stunned. Suddenly my eyes were everywhere taking in the scene, scoping out the timid ones hanging in the shadows, wrapped in shameful secrets. I knew they were here.

I skipped lunch and left the senior hall for another. I strolled the junior hall, looking for anything suspicious or odd. I thought I saw her, hanging around a classroom door, mustering the courage to go in. And another, standing by her locker, furtive eyes darting to and fro, looking for a predator. And another, slinking down the hallway quietly to avoid being seen. And another, disappearing into the bathroom to cry away her pain.

Oh my God. I was going crazy! I clutched the wall, taking deep breaths. I looked down the hallway. It was distorted, students stretching and twisting in a circular pattern as they passed by me. Like I had taken a hallucinogen and was having a bad reaction. I didn't know if my feet were still planted on the ground or if I was hanging from the ceiling.

I closed my eyes and tried to focus on the field. But I couldn't summon it. I breathed deeply, feeling pins in my chest that pricked me harder the more I tried to suck down oxygen. I opened my eyes to patches of darkness. *I'm going blind!* I screamed, but no one heard. My mouth never moved. I heard a distant, "Are you okay?" before the blackness swept me up into a silent oblivion.

—

"Do you suffer from panic attacks?" the school nurse asked. She was old—probably in her mid-fifties—and she hovered over me, looking into one eye and then the other.

"I have claustrophobia," I replied. My voice shook. My entire body rattled, and the nurse saw. She grabbed a blanket to wrap around me, but I protested.

"It's clean," she said, and I decided to believe her because I was freezing. And in shock.

I pulled the blanket tightly around my body, huddling into it protectively.

"Do you know what triggers your claustrophobia?" the nurse asked.

And that question told me everything I needed to know about school nurses.

I looked at her with raised eyebrows. Was she an idiot or purposefully ignoring my sarcastic facial expression?

"I don't know," I said flippantly. "Tight places. That's usually what triggers claustrophobia."

"But you weren't in a tight place," she replied. "You were in an open hallway."

It came out smug, like she was ready to trap me. Like she knew I thought she was an idiot for asking me such a stupid question only to prove she wasn't. I wanted to punch her in the face.

"I guess it *felt* closed up," I mumbled. I was angry at the way she made me feel like I had no legitimate excuse for fainting since I was in a large, open hallway. Like it was my fault.

"I see. Have you ever had an attack in any other open spaces?" she asked.

I thought for a moment. And then the memory flooded my mind. It had nothing to do with open spaces. It had to do with an old McDonald's playground, particularly one piece of play equipment: the Officer Big Mac jail. I was seven, and we were on vacation, traveling down to Texas. We stopped for lunch, and I asked to play on the playground because none of the McDonalds back home had a playground like this one. All of ours were plastic and safe. This one was shiny metal—glittering and dangerous in the hot sun—and it beckoned me.

I saw a few children playing in the Officer Big Mac jail, and I wanted to join them. It was a long metal tube that housed a ladder. The top of the jail was a huge flattened sphere in the shape of a hamburger, the top and bottom buns separated by metal poles to resemble a jail cell.

I had my first panic attack from claustrophobia that day as I climbed the ladder to the hamburger. The inside was just large enough to crawl comfortably, but I couldn't stand. And I couldn't lift my head all the way up to see in front of me. I crawled once around the whole thing, and decided I didn't feel right. I wanted out. But the ladder was blocked. More kids were climbing in, so I had no choice but to shrink back, wait for them to get in before making my way down. They kept pouring in, moving to the left and right, trapping me against the metal bars.

I panicked. I tried to move around a skinny boy, but he yelled at me. I felt hot tears roll down my face as I looked out beyond the bars to my parents sitting at a table below. They were immersed in conversation. They didn't see me. They didn't realize I was trapped. I screamed for help, and they finally looked up. They waved at me and smiled, thinking I was playing. *No, no!* I thought, shaking my head so hard I loosened my barrettes. *I'm not playing! Help me!*

I couldn't breathe. I knew I would have to kill someone to get out. Even at seven years old I thought, *Who builds a playground like this?*

I turned to the children smashed inside the jail and screamed at the top of my lungs: "Get me out of here!!"

Their eyes went wide. I must have looked crazy. My hair was sticking out everywhere. My face streaked with tears. The children pushed each other to one side, creating a bit of space for me to crawl around them for the ladder. Once my foot hit the first rung, I felt the panic subside. I looked down the tube at a girl who had just entered and was grasping the sides of the ladder.

"Get out of my way!" I screamed at her.

The girl looked up for a second, bottom lip quivering, then ran off crying.

I slid down the ladder in my haste to be as far away from the Officer Big Mac jail as possible. I sprinted for my parents, flinging myself on my father who pulled me onto his lap and asked me what was wrong. I cried hard into his chest, so hard that I couldn't breathe. A store employee saw me and went for a paper bag. She came back and told me to breathe into it. I obeyed because she was an adult, and I automatically trusted her.

I looked at the adult standing over me now.

"Are you okay?" the nurse asked softly.

I had no idea I was crying. "It's all Officer Big Mac's fault!" I sobbed.

One side of the nurse's mouth quirked up. "I hated that damn jail, too."

—

I hung around outside the gym waiting for Cal. He was late, and I think he did it on purpose. I'm sure he enjoyed making me wait for him. I checked my watch. Quarter after four. I thought about leaving. I wouldn't stay and let someone make me feel foolish. I already felt ridiculous enough after my panic attack earlier.

Thankfully the only witnesses to my attack were juniors and sophomores. The seniors were at lunch. I'm sure the students would gossip about it, but I thought the seniors wouldn't care. I noticed in my first week that the seniors kept themselves separated from the rest of the student body. Snobs, indeed. Every now and then I saw one chatting up a freshman or sophomore girl. Easy target, I supposed.

Another few minutes passed, and I decided to leave. Of course, that's exactly when Cal appeared out of nowhere, sauntering up to me with an easy kind of casualness that made me instantly angry.

"Sorry I'm late," he said. "Something came up."

"You're lucky," I replied. "I was just about to leave."

"You were?" he asked, as though he didn't believe a word of it. Like he expected me to hang out in front of the gym all night for him.

I nodded and turned my face. I didn't want him to see how irritated I was. I remembered that I was trying to woo him, not push him away.

"Those are pretty earrings," he said, observing the diamond stud in my left ear.

I grinned. I couldn't help it. So this was his game. Act

like a jackass and then say something sweet. He could care less about my earrings, and in that moment, my heart constricted, my grin faded. They were my mother's earrings. They were her wedding earrings. She gave them to me when I turned eighteen. They were special, and he complimented them in a cheap, disinterested sort of way. He made *me* feel cheap.

"You ready?" he asked holding up the yearbook camera.

I nodded and followed him into the gym. He opened the door for me like a gentleman, leading me to the bleachers with his hand on the small of my back. I tried to walk faster to get away from his touch, but he kept up with me, never taking his hand away. In fact, he kept it there once we were settled on the first row.

I squirmed.

"Problem?" he asked.

I squirmed again, and he pressed his hand into my lower back before taking it away. I know he wanted me to say something about it, but I wouldn't.

"I'll take the first game. You take the second," he said, readying the camera and taking a few practice shots.

The girls were already on the court, running through warm-ups. I never paid attention to volleyball at my old school, never went to a game. I thought I'd be bored out of my mind, but once the first game started, I found myself cheering and whooping as hard as anyone else in the stands. It was an exciting game, and I felt a deep-seated respect for the girls who spiked the ball hard over the net. I wish I were that strong.

I was barely conscious of Cal moving about the sidelines snapping pictures, but at one point, I noticed he was in the line of fire. Well, that was if the player spiked the ball out of bounds. I hoped she would. I hoped it smacked him right in the face.

But she was too talented, and the spike landed right

in the back corner of the court inside the lines. An "ace," I was later told. And Cal, of course, snapped the perfect picture of the ball heading his way, the player in the background slightly out of focus, still stretched taut in the air with her hand up. He showed me on the camera screen during a timeout. It was a beautiful shot, I had to admit.

"Maybe you should just take all the pictures," I said. "I'm not good with a camera."

"Why'd you join yearbook then?" he asked.

"Well, I'm a decent writer," I replied. "I just figured I'd write all the captions and page summaries and stuff."

He nodded.

I thought it was time to start with the questions. I had to make sure I didn't overwhelm him, though, or make him suspicious. I wanted him thinking I was genuinely interested in his seedy life.

"So what things are you involved in at school?" I asked.

"Well, Yearbook for one," he replied.

I smiled sweetly.

"And I'm on the swim team," he said.

"Oh, so that accounts for your arms," I said.

He liked that comment. I knew he would. His body swelled with flattery.

"Yeah, I swim a lot. I swim when I don't have to."

Whatever that means.

"Is it, like, a therapeutic thing?" I asked.

"I don't know," he said. "I guess I never really thought about it. Speaking of therapy, what happened to you in the hallway today? I heard someone say you fainted."

I flushed a deep crimson and averted my eyes. "Nothing," I mumbled.

"Fainting isn't 'nothing'," he pressed. "You have a medical condition or something?"

I was beyond embarrassed. The question came out

sounding harsh and accusatory. There was zero concern in his tone, but then I looked at his face. It was full of concern, or maybe he was just really good at faking.

I didn't know if I should admit it to him. It would make me come across weak. And then I thought that could work to my advantage. In a sick, twisted sort of way, he might like to hear all about it, feign concern while drawing me into his confidence. I couldn't know now how he would use that information in the future.

"I have panic attacks every now and then," I admitted.

He was silent for a moment, and I shifted uncomfortably in my seat.

"From what?" he asked.

"I have a bad case of claustrophobia," I explained. "And yes, I know I was in a hallway. Not exactly a closet or anything. But I had an attack anyway. I don't really know what triggered it."

That was a lie. I freaked out about all the pretty, frightened girls I saw. Or imagined. I couldn't remember. I just knew that something silent and wicked was happening at this school, and my body went into shutdown mode because of it.

Cal drew in his breath. "So I guess you don't do the whole making-out-in-the-back-seats-of-cars thing."

I stared at him, shocked.

"Oh God, I was only joking," he said quickly. "It was supposed to be a joke."

I didn't know what to say, so I just replied, "I'm gonna get a drink."

He caught my arm as I stood up. "Brooke, I'm sorry. That was a shitty thing to say."

I ignored his apology in favor of focusing on the fact that he called me "Brooke." For the first time. He'd addressed me dozens of times in the hallway. Always "Brooklyn." Now I was "Brooke." He knew he messed up and had to fast-track his plans. For a brief moment, I thought there'd be no more games. No more making me work to get into his little club. He didn't want to miss the opportunity to claim me, especially if he could witness a panic attack as a result.

"It's okay," I said. "But I really *am* thirsty."

Cal jumped up and shoved the camera in my hands.

"I'll go. You stay here," he said. "What would you like?'

"Just a water," I replied, looking down at the camera. I hoped he didn't expect me to take pictures while he was gone. I didn't even know how to use this monstrosity.

"Okay," he said, and hurried to the concession stand.

I stuck my face against the camera tentatively and looked through the lens. I tried the large button on the right side and snapped a picture of the gym floor. I pulled the camera away to study my shot. It was a blur of muted yellow. I tried again, shoving my face against the camera and moving it up and down the bleachers. I couldn't believe the crowd that showed up to watch a volleyball game. Not nearly as big as a basketball game would draw, but it was still a healthy number. The girls' team should be proud, I thought.

I almost put the camera down when I spotted Ryan sitting in the top corner of the bleachers. He watched me looking at him through the lens, his brows furrowed. He didn't look happy. I tried to focus the lens, and succeeded in getting a slightly sharper view of him. His hair was a sexy, tousled mess, like that 1960s throw-back style so popular with the boys right now. I'm glad his bangs didn't obscure his piercing eyes, though. Nothing should ever cover up those eyes.

His jaw was clenched, and I wondered why he was angry. I thought absurdly that he was angry with me, and I couldn't understand what I'd done wrong. I stood paralyzed, unable to take the camera off of him. He refused to avert his eyes. I almost thought he was trying to tell me something, but I was too stupid to understand.

"What are you doing?" It was Cal addressing me from behind.

I whirled around to face him, peeking from behind the camera.

"What do you mean?" I asked.

Cal looked at me, then up at the stands.

"You don't want to have anything to do with that guy," he warned. "He's one of those crazy loners. I think he's on meds or something. A ticking time bomb."

I lowered the camera. "I don't know what you're talking about," I said. "I was just taking pictures of the fans."

Cal snatched the camera and searched the recent shots. "Oh yeah?" he asked, finding no shots at all.

My face flared up again. "Well, I was trying to anyway."

"I'm serious, Brooke," Cal said, handing me a bottled water. "I just want you to be safe."

I took the drink, thinking that "safe" had nothing to do with it. What I really heard underlining Cal's warning was, "You get involved with that guy, and you can forget about me." I was thrust into the middle of another unfair situation. Karma, maybe, for my past mistakes. I was undeniably attracted to Ryan. And I felt an attraction on his end. But I couldn't do a thing about it. I couldn't even talk to the guy, at least not at school. I couldn't risk Cal seeing.

"Did you hear me?" Cal asked. "I want you to be safe, Brooke."

I nodded, looking up at him. He looked at me with the deepest concern, and I forgot that he was a bad guy. He didn't sound like one now. He sounded like he wanted to protect me, take care of me, and I almost believed him.

Almost.

FIVE

The stairs at the end of Hallway D curve down so that it's impossible to stand on the top landing and see someone standing on the bottom landing. Even if you hang your body over the edge and strain your neck. The stairwell is accessible by a door on the top and bottom floors. Secluded, and I imagined couples dipping under the stairs for quick make-out sessions between classes. The stairwell was creepy when you found yourself in it alone, always a little darker than the rest of the school, like the janitors reserved the leftover, low-quality bulbs for this section of the building.

I was on the last stair heading for the first floor hallway when I heard the door to the top floor open and a chorus of hushed voices talking in urgent whispers. My instinct was to move quickly and soundlessly under the stairs, so that's what I did.

I heard a deep male voice. "Is anyone in here?"

I remained silent.

There was a brief pause before the low talking resumed.

"Dude, we can totally trust him. He wants in," the

same deep male voice said.

"How'd he even find out?" another asked. "I didn't tell him. Are you running your mouth?"

"No, man. He found that slip of paper with your name on it."

"What the hell? I told you we shouldn't draw names at school."

I couldn't make out how many boys there were, but it sounded like three. Possibly four.

"Dude, it was convenient. No one could meet outside of school," the first boy said.

A new voice piped up. "When are you sending us the score sheet?"

"Fuck the score sheet. We're not talking about the score sheet right now. I wanna know what Aaron knows," the second boy said.

"I only told him that it's a secret club, and that we'd have to discuss his initiation," the first boy replied.

"Well, if he wants in so bad, he can go fuck that sophomore virgin on the cheerleading squad. Then we'll talk."

A few chuckles.

"Man, her ass is so round and perfect. She's hot."

"How do you know she's a virgin?"

"I've got a spy. Anyway, I'll have to think about it. I don't know about Aaron. There's something about him that rubs me wrong."

"Maybe the fact that his swim times are better than yours?"

"Screw you, man."

"I'm only joking. Look, I know you're all concerned about people finding out, but I'm not stupid. I wouldn't bring his name up if I didn't think we could trust him."

"It's Cameron, right? She's your spy?"

"Dude, shut up."

"Parker, when are you sending the score sheet? I've

got a date this weekend."

"Man, stop deleting shit from your email. I'll send it when I send it."

"*I'll* send it," the first boy said.

"So it's Cameron, right?"

"Shut up! Everyone just shut the hell up! Let me sort this out." It sounded like Parker's voice. "You know, it really pissed me off when Cal put me in charge of all this shit."

I listened as they walked down the stairs and shuffled into the first floor hallway. I took a deep breath. *Secret club. Score sheet. Initiation. Sex with a virgin.* What the hell was going on? And who could I talk to about it?

I crept out from under the stairs and pushed open the door leading to the first floor hallway.

"Parker, grab mine, too!"

I bumped into Parker, who was headed back into the stairwell, and he glared at me, shocked. Then his face changed from shock to agitation and suspicion. Shit. I don't think I put enough time between our exits!

He pushed past me and headed up the stairs, leaving me to wonder if I'd been found out and if my plan had just been thwarted.

—

If I thought I could go the rest of my life without seeing Finn again, I was living in a fantasy world. He attended my old high school, so at least I didn't have to see him on a regular basis. But I worked at a fairly popular diner frequented by people from all over town. He was tactful enough to steer clear of my house, but I knew eventually he'd find out where I worked and show up, all under the guise of simply wanting to eat.

It was a slow Tuesday night, and I was on the verge of asking my manager if I could go home. Amanda, another waitress, wanted my section to try and make a little more money, and I was happy to accommodate her. I was too distracted anyway. All I could think about the entire evening was the conversation I overheard in the stairwell. *Secret club. Score sheet. Initiation. Sex with a virgin.* I kept repeating those words like a mantra because I didn't want to forget them. I also thought that something would magically reveal itself to me if I kept saying them over and over. I was itching to talk to someone about it, but I didn't know who I could trust.

I loved Gretchen with all my heart, but I could not trust her with this. She knew nothing about Beth's rape, and I intended to keep it that way. Beth trusted me with that information, and I swore to tell no one. Not even her parents, though it pained me every time I saw her mother. Plus, I knew Gretchen. She would start a crusade, much like I was doing, except mine was a crusade of one. She'd want the entire world involved, and I wasn't prepared to go there. I wanted to be quiet and wise about it. She'd blow the whole thing with her loud mouth.

"You've got someone at Table 2," Amanda said.

I peered over to my table and instinctively balled my hands into fists. Amanda saw.

"You want me to take him?" she asked.

I shook my head. "You can have the rest, but I've got to take this one. He didn't come here to eat," and she understood completely.

I walked over to Finn and stood silent, waiting. He looked up at me and smiled.

"You look cute in your uniform," he said.

I didn't reply.

"Jesus, Brooke," he said. "What do you want me to say?"

"Why are you here?" I asked.

"I wanted to see you. I didn't get a chance to talk to you at the funeral."

"You think it would have been wise to talk to me at the funeral?" I asked.

Finn shook his head. "No, I don't. But you just disappeared. It took me forever to find out you hadn't moved to California. Why didn't you tell me?"

I shook my head in disbelief. "I don't have to tell you about my life anymore, Finn. We're over."

"Look, us being together had nothing to do with Beth's suicide," he snapped.

"Shut your mouth about it," I hissed.

"You love me, Brooke, but you feel guilty," Finn said.

I hung my head. There was a time I thought I could love Finn. We never said it, and he made me angry when he brought it up to Beth the afternoon she caught us. But I knew I could never love him now. There was too much hurt. Too much guilt, and I couldn't do that to myself anymore.

I looked at him, taking in his soft blond hair and brown eyes. He was cute, would always be cute. He'd just have to go be cute for some other girl.

"I can't take your order, Finn," I said finally.

"I don't want food. I want you," he said softly.

"Please don't say things like that," I pleaded.

"Come home with me, Brooke. We'll just talk. That's all we'll do."

I felt the pull for a fraction of a second, my body leaning into him remembering his mouth, his hands, all the ways he touched me just right. But that's all it ever was, just touching. It was an instant revelation. No love. Just touching, and it was easy to back away.

"No, Finn."

He looked at me with sad eyes. "You break my heart, Brooke."

I shrugged and walked to the kitchen, passing by Amanda.

"He's yours," I said, but Finn had already left the table.

I don't know why I dragged my feet about going home. I hung around the dirty dishes instead, watching Gregory load the machine with glasses and plates. Gregory was a student at Wake Technical Community College with ambitions to be a rock star. He played the drums, and from what I heard, he sucked at it. He was the dishwasher who yelled at me my first night, and unlike Terry, he never apologized. I thought he was a tool, and then I realized a tool was exactly the kind of guy I needed to talk to. I could trust him with the information because he wouldn't care.

"What do you want?" Gregory asked, not looking at me. He continued shoving plates in the washer.

"I gotta question for you," I replied.

"Well, I may or may not have an answer," he said.

I gave him an even look. Okay, I had a few questions for him.

"Why do you dislike me?" I asked.

He chuckled. "Why are girls so self-absorbed? I don't dislike you. I don't think anything about you at all." He looked at me, his facial expression asking, "What else?"

I blinked, then smirked. "Were the popular girls mean to you in high school?" I should have kept that smartass question to myself as I watched Gregory load a handful of knives into the dishwasher.

He paused and cocked his head, considering me. Then his mouth turned up into a smirk that matched my own. "Actually no. I fucked every one of them."

I dismissed him with an eye roll. "Okay, whatever. If you overheard a bunch of guys talking about secret clubs and score sheets and having sex with virgins, what would you make of it?"

He screwed up his face in thought.

"Just a hypothetical question," I added.

"Well, I think you're talking about some kind of sex club," he said.

"That much I figured," I replied. "But score sheets?"

"Maybe they score the girls. How should I know?"

"You mean, like, how good they are in bed?"

"Yeah. Maybe they score the girls on their sex acts."

"Have you ever heard of anything like this?" I asked.

"No, but then again, I don't immerse myself in the kinky sex culture that you apparently do," he sneered.

"Screw you. It was a question."

"Go away, Brooklyn. I have work to do."

"Yeah, whatever. Thanks for your help."

On my way out, I waved goodbye to Terry, who asked why I wasn't going to hang around after work and drink with him. I headed for the parking lot.

It was instant irritation—seeing Finn. I thought he'd gone home, but apparently he was waiting for me. What if I had to work the entire evening? Was he planning to hang around my car for hours?

I walked over to him. "Finn—"

He cut me off with a kiss. My instinct was to draw back and slap him. But I didn't. And I didn't feel any of the things I should have felt: outrage, shock, shame. Instead, I let him kiss me, standing there like a statue, trying to remain emotionally disconnected from it. That didn't last long, and that's when I should have pulled away.

I pressed my lips to him harder, and he took it as a silent invitation to open my mouth with his tongue. It was all so familiar, sensual and frightening. I didn't like how Finn could make my body respond to him so easily, that I could lose all resolve to be a better person with his kiss. I felt his arms snake around my waist, drawing me closer to him, and I slumped against him, letting him hold me while his mouth continued to explore mine. Familiar sparks traveled the nerves up and down my legs. They popped occasionally in various places along my thighs, under my feet, and I was afraid I'd lose the strength to stand.

Get off, get off! I screamed inside. And then Beth's face flashed inside my brain, and my resolve resurfaced, fighting my sexual desire. Thank God the resolve won.

I pushed Finn away. "We can't," I breathed.

"Brooke—"

"We're horrible people!" I cried.

"What are you talking about?" Finn asked.

Was he really so stupid or just completely delusional?

"We treated Beth like shit, Finn! We sneaked around! We lied to her!"

"You're right," Finn replied. "I should have broken up with her before we got together."

"Why didn't you?" I asked. I had never asked him before.

"I don't know," he admitted. "She started getting really depressed. I don't know why, but it seemed wrong to break up with her when she was like that."

I knew precisely what he was talking about, and I knew precisely why Beth was so sad. The heaviest part of my guilt lay in the fact that Beth revealed her rape to me, trusted me with the information, trusted me with her vulnerability, and I continued to sleep with Finn behind her back.

"But it wasn't fair to you to keep dating her," Finn continued.

I looked up sharply. Fair to *me*? He had a lot of nerve. I recognized my guilt, welcomed it, deserved to feel like shit, and he wasn't going to take that away from me.

"What I did was wrong. I hurt my best friend. No guy is worth that," I said.

I watched Finn tense. I didn't mean to be so insulting, but I knew no other way to get through to him.

"So you walk away from me because of Beth?" he asked. "She's dead, Brooke."

"What are you saying? That we might as well get together because Beth's not here to see it? What the hell is wrong with you?"

"Look, I'm not waiting around forever, Brooke," Finn said.

"I don't expect you to."

"Are you trying to tell me that you felt nothing when I just kissed you?"

"Sure, I felt something. I felt horny. That's it," I snapped. "I don't love you, Finn. I cannot be with you. It's wrong on so many levels."

"You'll continue to fight your attraction to me because of some dead girl?!"

It was automatic. I swung my hand with all my might, making contact with the side of Finn's head. It was a sloppy hit, somewhere between a slap and a punch, but it was effective. He grunted and rubbed his temple.

"What the fuck?!"

"You're a heartless piece of shit!" I screamed. "She's not some 'dead girl'! She was my best friend!"

He stood silently for a moment, rubbing his head.

"I feel sorry for you, Brooke," he said. "You'll ruin your life because you can't get past your guilt."

"Ha! And I suppose by ruining my life you mean living without you?" I asked. "Don't worry, Finn. I have no plans to let you ruin my life."

"You'll be sorry, Brooke."

"What the hell does that even mean?"

"We're through. That's what it means," he replied, and started for his car parked a few spaces away.

"Hallelujah," I mumbled, watching him drive away.

——

"I have the perfect guy for you," I said in a singsong voice.
"Oh jeez," Beth replied. "Brooke, it's time you face the truth.

You're not the best matchmaker."

"Okay, Kevin was all wrong, I admit," I said.

"And Jason," Beth said.

I shrugged.

"And Andrew and Ian."

"Oh my God. Okay already!"

Beth giggled.

"I'm telling you that this guy is the one."

Beth sighed. "Describe."

"Okay. So his name is Finn, and he goes to my school, and he's really tall and plays lacrosse."

"What does he look like?" Beth asked.

"I'm getting to that. Chill," I said. "He's got blond hair and brown eyes."

Beth scrunched up her nose. "I don't know if I like that combo."

"What are you talking about? Sandy hair and dark eyes? It's totally hot," I argued.

"Whatever," she said. "Continue."

"And he goes to church," I said.

"So what? That makes him a good guy or something?"

"I don't know. Maybe," I said.

"Hold up. Why would you even bring up the whole church thing?"

"What do you mean?" I asked.

Beth's face lit up with realization. "You think I'm a whore!"

"What?!"

"You want me to date this church guy because you think I'm a whore!"

"Oh my God, Beth. What have you been smoking?" I asked.

She laughed and shook her head. "So what? He's gonna convert me or something? Make me a good girl again? I think I remember you being the one who lost your virginity at fifteen. Not me. At least I waited until last year."

I bristled. First off, I never lost my virginity at fifteen. I lied about it because I was tired of being the only virgin Beth and I knew. Yes, there's just as much pressure for a girl to lose it as there is for a guy. Second, Beth had a lot of nerve comparing my sexual past with hers. Maybe she waited until she was seventeen, but in those ten months since she lost her virginity, she had slept with four guys.

"Go ahead and say it," Beth said. "I can see it written all over your face anyway."

"You're sleeping with too many guys, Beth," I blurted. "It doesn't . . . look good." I averted my eyes.

Beth was quiet for a moment.

"Why can a guy sleep around and it gives him this awesome reputation, but when a girl does it, she's a freaking slut?" she asked finally.

I shrugged. "I don't know. It's the world we live in, I guess. Some things will never be fair." I glanced at Beth, trying to find the courage to ask. She sat on the edge of the bed, staring at her open palms, and I wondered if she was trying to read them. "Why have you slept with four guys, Beth?" I asked, and then added quickly, "And I'm not trying to sound judgmental."

"What if I told you that I just like having sex?" she asked.

I grinned. "That's really the reason?"

"Yeah, that's really the reason," Beth replied. "And so I guess that makes me a whore."

"Stop calling yourself a whore. You're not a whore," I replied.

"You know, it's funny," Beth said. "Guys want a 'good girl' who's pure and sweet and inexperienced, but then he expects her to be this rock star in bed. It's totally messed up. It's a standard no girl can live up to."

"Who cares what guys think?" I said.

"You do," Beth replied. "And I do, too."

I didn't like that answer. I didn't like it because it was true. I did care what guys thought about me. That's why I worked hard to be pretty, to have a fun personality, to come across virginal (because I was anyway) and sweet and kind. Especially kind, and especially kind to other girls. I never wanted to be that bitchy girl who treated other girls like shit. I didn't think most guys liked that anyway.

They wanted someone with a kind heart, and even if I had to fake it, I would to find my perfect boyfriend. I hadn't found him yet, but I knew he was out there.

"Did you give him my number?" Beth asked.

"Who?"

"This Finn guy. Did you give him my number?"

"Would you be pissed if I did?" I asked.

"I guess not," Beth replied. She walked over to her closet and started rifling through her clothes. "I guess I have to wear something conservative on our date, huh? Since he's a church guy and all."

I rolled my eyes. "I said he went to church. I didn't say he was the youth pastor."

"I'm feeling kind of nervous about this," Beth admitted. "What if I come across all prostitute-in-Proverbs-with-the-spiced-sheets girl?"

"That's what you remember from youth group? I asked.

"Whatever."

"Beth, he's just a nice guy. I'm sorry I even brought up the church thing. You're freaking out about it," I said.

We were silent for a moment.

"Is it my fault?" I asked quietly. "Did I make you feel badly for sleeping with four guys? I didn't mean to, Beth."

"No," Beth said. "No, Brooke. It's not you. It's just the world we live in, right?" Her mouth quirked up into a grin.

I grinned back. "Trust me. You're gonna love him."

SIX

"So, what do you think?" Gretchen asked.

"About what?" I replied.

We were sitting in the food court at Crabtree Valley Mall drinking strawberry smoothies from Orange Julius.

"The party tonight! God, you're so spacey sometimes."

"I don't want to go to a party," I said.

"Brooke, you're really starting to get on my nerves," Gretchen said. "Your whole life is becoming school and work. You've got no friends besides me. You've got no boyfriend because you're too chickenshit to talk to that beautiful Ryan guy. And you'd rather go to dinner with your dad tonight than come with me to an awesome party."

I forced a smile. "Gosh, you really have a way of making a girl feel good about herself." I slurped my drink.

"Brookey! I don't want to go alone!"

"Then don't go," I said. "Look, I promised my dad we'd go to dinner tonight. I haven't lived with my dad in years. Hell, I don't even know the man. Is it okay with you that I spend a little time with him? Jeez, you're so selfish, Beth."

Gretchen's head snapped up. "What did you say?"

"I said you're selfish," I replied.

"No no, after that," Gretchen said.

"Huh?"

"You called me 'Beth'."

"No, I didn't."

"Yes, you did, Brooke. You called me 'Beth'," Gretchen said, eyeing me suspiciously.

I didn't remember calling Gretchen "Beth." But I must have. Gretchen's face told me so.

"What's going on?" Gretchen asked. "Is this why your life blows right now? You still feel guilty so you think you're not allowed to have friends or a boyfriend or go out and have fun?"

"No," I replied. I felt suddenly defensive.

"Well, that's what it looks like to me," Gretchen said. And then she lit up like a realization smacked her square in the face. "Are you dreaming about Beth?"

"No," I lied. I wasn't going to tell her that every time I closed my eyes, I dreamed of Beth or Finn. I wasn't going to tell her that I woke up most mornings caked with sweat. I certainly wasn't going to tell her that my nightmare last night was so intense I fell out of the bed.

Gretchen tried for patience. "Beth is gone."

"I know that!" I snapped.

I didn't resist when Gretchen took my hand. "I'm not trying to sound mean when I say that. But she's gone, Brooke. And she wouldn't want you to live like this. Punishing yourself."

"I'm not punishing myself," I argued.

"When you don't allow yourself to have a life, that's punishing yourself," Gretchen said.

"I have a life," I said. "I just can't tell you about it."

Goddamnit. Why did I say that?

"What are you talking about?" Gretchen asked. She looked worried.

"Nothing. I don't know why I said that."

"Bullshit. Don't play games with me, Brooke. What am I not supposed to know?"

I looked at Gretchen's heart-shaped face framed by thick locks of dark brown hair. Her brown eyes bore into me, and I almost caved. The girl in me wanted to confess everything right then and there. Tell her about Beth's rape. Tell her about Cal and my plans to expose him for the monster he was. The girl in me wanted to confess because it was torture keeping secrets, and girls like to talk. I'm no exception. But the tiny little wise woman in me knew it would be a horrible mistake. The wise woman said, "Brooke, Gretchen runs her mouth."

"Okay, maybe I'm having a bit of a hard time," I said. "I still feel guilty about Beth. And Finn came to see me at the diner the other night and we ended up kissing."

Gretchen's eyes went wide. "Are you freaking kidding me?"

"I know!" I said. "But I stopped it. And then I hit him and told him he was a piece of shit and we were over."

Gretchen's body filled to the brim with pride. I could see it bursting out of her eyes and her enormous smile.

"You are *kickass*!" she squealed.

"Thank you," I replied.

"Were you ever planning on telling me this?" Gretchen asked.

"I told you now," I said.

"Yeah, but that's because I caught you."

"I would have told you," I said. "I was just ashamed about the kissing part."

"He's such a jerk. Why the hell would he think you'd want to get together with him?"

"Beats me," I said, finishing my drink.

"Well, I'm glad you're finished with him," Gretchen said. "This is a good step in the recovery process,

Brookey."

I smirked. "I imagine you'll make a fine psychologist someday."

"Get real. I'm totally doing make-up for celebrities," Gretchen replied.

I laughed.

"And I'm sorry about giving you a hard time about hanging out with your dad. That wasn't right."

"No big deal," I replied.

"But if you change your mind about the party, I think some guys from your school are gonna be there. Don't know if you know them, but I think they're on the swim team or something."

My heart clenched immediately. "Who?"

"I don't know their names," Gretchen said. "I just know they have a reputation for being pretty hot."

That meant Gretchen would make a beeline for them, flirt it up and possibly let one of them put his hands on her. She was too generous with her breasts, and the amount of boys who'd seen them and touched them was in the double digits. I couldn't let that number climb any higher, not when I suspected the worst of the swim team members.

"When's the party?" I asked.

Gretchen cocked her head. "So now you want to go? Five minutes ago you were all about spending quality time with your dad, and now you want to go? What? You got a crush on one of them?"

"No, I don't have a crush. I was just curious what time the party was," I said.

"I don't know. I'm not planning on getting there until eleven or so," Gretchen replied.

"Don't go without me," I blurted. It came out sounding like a warning.

"What is up with you?" Gretchen asked.

"I just want to go, okay?" I said. "You're right. I need

to stop moping and being antisocial and all that. Just promise me you'll wait for me. I'll go with you after I have dinner with my dad."

"That's fine," Gretchen said. "But I still think you've got a crush you're not telling me about."

I convinced myself that Cal wasn't the only predator, not after overhearing the conversation in the stairwell. The swim team was up to something. Maybe not all of them, but some of them were participating in a devious game. A sex club, Gregory said. And the slightly paranoid part of me thought they were showing up at this party to find girls. Victims. And there was no way I was letting Gretchen go alone. I made that mistake with Beth and paid the ultimate price.

I sat in the restaurant feeling antsy and irritable.

"So Pam says the customer expects a solution tomorrow, and I'd like to know who she thinks is going into the office on a Saturday morning," Dad said. "If the customer hadn't screwed up the device after we told them specifically not to activate it until clearance from the engineers, there wouldn't be an issue." He shoved the pizza in his mouth.

I nodded, having no idea what he was talking about. My mind was on other things. It raced with thoughts of swim team members snaking their way through the crowded party, brushing past girls and letting their hands graze intimate body parts.

"Am I boring you?" I heard Dad ask.

"No," I lied. "I'm totally listening."

Dad chuckled. "Why?"

I laughed. "Because you're paying for dinner."

"Cute," he replied. "You get that smartass sense of humor from your mother, you know."

I shrugged and watched Dad's face fall. Any time either one of us mentioned my mother, he turned sullen or serious. I didn't want to go there with him tonight. We were at a pizza joint, after all.

"Dad, when was the last time you had a date?" I asked.

He jerked his head up, glaring at me.

"Whoa, it was just a question," I said. I took another bite of my calzone.

I watched his eyes soften and the hint of a smile play on his mouth.

"Five years."

"Holy shit, Dad! Five years?!"

"Brooklyn, must the whole restaurant know?"

"I'm sorry. It's just, wow. Five years. Yikes." I sipped my Coke, eyes wide, eyebrows raised in disbelief.

"Will you wipe that look off your face?" he asked. "There's no one out there. What do you want from me? And anyway, I'm your father. We shouldn't be discussing this."

"What does being my father have to do with it?" I asked. "Now my English teacher is single. And she's cute." I bit into my calzone and continued with my mouth full. "And surprisingly not an idiot."

"Are most of your teachers idiots?"

"Yes."

Dad chuckled. "Glad to know my tax dollars contribute to well-deserved salaries."

"Oh, Dad," I said airily. "Let's not get all political. Let's talk about Ms. Manning."

"Let's not," Dad replied.

I ignored him. "She's in her early forties, I think, but she totally looks like she's in her thirties. Nice skin and hair. She always looks really professional. Dresses to the nines. Her shoes are fabulous."

"Brooke . . ."

"And she's an avid runner. She told me she runs about four miles a day and tries to do a long run of about ten miles every Saturday," I continued.

"Brooke, please."

"And she's competing in her first half-marathon this November."

"Brooke!" Dad interrupted. "I've got a gut, okay? I'm not dating a runner."

I pursed my lips and watched Dad run his hand through his chestnut hair.

"Dad, you barely have a gut. And you're really handsome. It's time you get back out there on the field," I said.

Dad burst out laughing.

"What?" I asked.

"Nothing," Dad snorted. "I just love the way you compliment me, that's all."

I grinned. "Well, it's true. It's barely there," I laughed. "Go date Ms. Manning and start running with her, and it'll be gone in a week. Jeez, it's so unfair. Men can lose weight like that!" I said, snapping my fingers.

"Oh, no they can't," Dad argued.

"Well, whatever. Will you just promise me that you'll keep an open mind and start looking?" I should have left it right there, but I couldn't. "Mom's gone."

"Hmm," Dad replied. He rubbed his forehead and looked at me. "Kind of like how Beth's gone."

I tensed. "What are you saying?"

"Honey, you don't do anything but go to school and work and hang out with Gretchen. I'm not blind."

"As a matter of fact, I'm going to a party tonight."

Dad's eyebrows shot up. "Oh really? Where is it and who's throwing it?"

"I don't know," I said. "Some rich guy whose parents are gone for the weekend." I winked at him.

"Very funny, Brooke," Dad replied. "Where is it and who's throwing it?"

I sighed. "Gretchen's friend, Olivia. It's totally cool. I

mean, I'm sure some people will bring alcohol, but Dad. Come on. You know me."

Actually, Dad didn't know me at all, and I thought he'd say it out loud. But that would have embarrassed the both of us, so he opted for something else.

"And what if the party gets busted by the cops and you're arrested for being there with alcohol?"

"They wouldn't arrest me, Dad. They'd just call you."

"Oh really? You know this from past experience? And anyway, you're eighteen. Legally an adult. They wouldn't call me to pick you up."

I huffed. "Dad."

"Brooke."

We stared at each other for a few seconds.

"I'm not letting Gretchen go to this party by herself," I said.

"Any particular reason why?"

"Um, yeah. Have you met Gretchen? She's ridiculous," I explained.

Dad laughed. "Fine, but she's not drinking either."

"Dad, she doesn't touch the stuff. Empty calories," I said, finishing off my calzone. I eyed Dad's second slice of pizza.

"Don't even think about it," he said, picking up the slice and taking a huge chunk out of it.

I considered him while he ate. "You think we should have done this a few years ago?"

"Done what?" he asked with his mouth full.

"Lived together."

Dad swallowed. It sounded like it hurt on the way down. "You weren't happy with your mom?"

"No, I'm not saying that. It's just, why is it usually the mom who gets the kids?"

Dad stared at me.

"I mean, why didn't I have a choice?"

"Did you want to live with me?" he asked tentatively.

"I don't know. It could have been fun," I said.

Dad stared at his plate. I felt an overwhelming need to hug him, but thought it was the wrong time.

"Well, I guess we've gotta make up for lost time," I said.

Dad looked at me and grinned. "Don't you dare come home drunk, young lady."

"Never."

———

"I'm totally excited!" Gretchen squealed as we walked, arms linked, up the sidewalk to Tanner's house.

Yes, I felt guilty for lying to my dad. It wasn't Olivia's house. There's no Olivia anyway. But I thought it would sound better if the party were being thrown by a girl and not an immature boy. Tanner was just that. An annoying, loud, overbearing football player from my old high school who insisted on being popular whether people wanted him to or not. I think he was only accepted into the club because he had parents who traveled a lot, thus opening his house to the most over-the-top, alcohol-infused, sex-crazed parties in the city. It amazed me that not one of them had ever been busted by the cops.

"What's there to be excited about?" I asked. "These parties are obnoxious."

"Whatever, Brooke. You loved them last year."

"Yeah, that was last year," I said. "God, I don't want to run into anyone I know."

We pushed through the front door and nearly toppled onto Stephanie.

"Oh my God!" she screamed, throwing her arms around my neck and choking me.

"Steph." I know I sounded less than enthusiastic, but I just couldn't pretend anymore.

"I was so hoping you'd come tonight!" she replied,

pulling away and looking me up and down. "You look so pretty!"

I did look pretty. I wore dark blue skinny jeans with a gray sequins top and alligator pumps. My very first pair of closed-toe heels. I bought them immediately after Beth's funeral, and I made sure there was nothing sad about them. Not a hint of black. They were purple instead. I wore my hair in a messy chignon at the nape of my neck to show off my mother's wedding earrings—the diamond studs. I felt confident and sexy.

"Thanks. I love your dress," I replied. "It's really cute."

Stephanie looked down at her outfit. "I know, right?!" She grabbed my hand and pulled me into the living room. "Look who's here, everyone!"

"No no," I said, shaking my head and tearing my hand out of hers. "No one needs to know."

I smiled nervously and looked around. Thankfully no one heard Stephanie or they didn't care. The music was turned up to the max, and half the partiers were already wasted. There was an uneasy energy bouncing about the room, like a huge fight would break out at any moment. I didn't like it, or rather my spirit didn't like it. I could tell because my heart fluttered and thumped, and not to the beat of the song.

I turned around assuming Gretchen had followed me into the living room. I assumed wrong.

Shit. Why didn't I grab her hand when Stephanie pulled me along?

I maneuvered through the dancers, cursing when I felt a foot land squarely on the top of my purple pump, and squeezed into the kitchen. It was the busiest room in the house. Naturally. Liquor bottles and various juices lined the countertops and crowded all the space on the island. The refrigerator door hung open. Guys vied for the imported beers over domestic ones. That's the kind of party this was.

I scanned the group for Gretchen but couldn't locate her. I tried not to panic. We had only just arrived. I doubted anything lascivious could have happened to her in ten minutes.

I pushed through the crammed kitchen to an equally crammed hallway. Cal was walking my way.

"Hey, Brooke!" he called as he approached.

I knew to expect him here, but I still jumped. I hoped he couldn't see.

"Hi," I said.

He backed me against the wall to make room for a few girls rushing by, squealing about how badly they needed to pee. Apparently we were in the way.

"You look really nice tonight," he said raking my body with his eyes. He kept them lowered once he got to my feet. "Sexy shoes!"

What guy says that? What guy compliments a girl's shoes at all?

"Thanks?" I knew it came out as a question. I meant for it to.

He chuckled. "What? I can't have good fashion sense?"

"I don't know," I replied, grinning. I looked down at my shoes. "They *are* sexy, huh?"

"Very," he replied, and leaned in to kiss my cheek. I could smell the alcohol on him. "Is that okay?"

It was most certainly *not* okay. Who the hell did this guy think he was? So what that I was going to let him do me. That wasn't happening tonight, not when I didn't know him. Fucking get to know me first before you act so insolently.

I nodded, cocking my head and twirling my stud.

"So, you know Tanner?" Cal asked.

I debated how much to tell him. I didn't think he knew I went to school with Tanner last year, but then again, why would I be here? Why was *he* here for that matter?

"Do you?" I asked.

He looked at me strangely, then shook his head. "No. But Parker does."

I remained stoic although I screamed inside. Great! Just great! I already had the creeps about that guy, and now he had a connection to my past. I did not want any of them discovering my ties with Beth. It would ruin everything.

"Who's Parker?" I asked. "You say his name like I know who he is."

"Oh, right. I forgot you're new to the school," Cal replied. "Parker's my best friend. He's on the swim team with me. Everyone at school knows him."

"Wow, that's a lot of people," I said.

"No easy job being popular, that's for sure."

I wanted to throw up.

"Anyway, you never answered my question," Cal said. "Do you know Tanner?"

I opened my mouth to tell a big, fat see-through lie, when Stephanie stumbled my way.

"Oh my God! Where did you go?!" she screamed, teetering on her four-inch strappy sandals while holding up a plastic red cup.

"Here, I'll take that," I said, plucking the cup from her hand before she could protest.

She bumped into Cal and mumbled a halfhearted apology.

"Let's go dance!" Stephanie screamed. "Like old times!"

"Old times?" Cal asked. Again, he looked at me oddly.

"She's a friend from a long time ago," I explained. "And she's drunk."

"You bet your ass I'm drunk," Stephanie said. "I'm

soooo drunk!"

"And I'm soooo taking you to the bathroom right now," I replied, handing the half-empty cup to Cal and excusing myself.

"Come find me later!" he called.

Yeah, I'll get right on that. Then I immediately shook my head. *No, Brooke. You need to find him later. You're supposed to be pursuing him, remember? Stop thinking like a bitch and start thinking like an assassin!*

"Brookey, we miss you!" Stephanie said, clinging to me while I helped her through the bathroom door.

"Try to make yourself throw up," I said. "And don't come out of this bathroom until I get back. I'm going to find Gretchen."

"I know where she's is," Stephanie slurred.

"Where?"

"In the basement shatting with some cute guy."

I burst out laughing. "'Shatting'? She's 'shatting' with a cute guy? Do you know how revolting that is?"

Stephanie furrowed her brows. "I don't get it."

"Never mind," I said, and headed out the door. After tonight, no more playing mother to my drunk friends. They were all grounded. I could do that after all. I was the mother.

I forced my way into the basement, half listening to a handful of girls spit insults at me for shoving them aside. When I spotted Gretchen, my heart dropped to my feet. She was standing in the corner with Parker. My instinct was to run and jump on him, sink my claws into him and draw blood. Maybe make him bleed out. Instead, I hurried over to my friend and addressed her cheerfully, trying hard to mask my fear.

"There you are!"

Parker turned around and looked at me. He was clearly annoyed. I interrupted his game.

"Brookey!" Gretchen cried. "Oh my God. I've so

been looking all over for you!"

"Have you?" I asked. I couldn't hide the sarcasm, even at the risk of Parker hearing.

"This is Parker," Gretchen said, ignoring my question. "He's on the swim team at your school."

"Hi," I said.

He nodded. "How do you two know each other?"

"We're best friends!" Gretchen said. "Brookey used to—"

"Hey Gretchen, I think we need to go check on Stephanie," I interrupted. "She's puking her guts out upstairs."

"Gross," Gretchen replied. "Why don't you go deal with her? She drives me crazy."

"She's asking for you," I said, tugging on Gretchen's arm.

"Hey, let Gretchen stay," Parker said. He pushed my hand away. "We're getting to know each other."

I wanted to strangle him. How dare he push my hand away! Another insolent bastard. Was that a personality requirement to get on the swim team?

"Maybe some other time," I said.

"No," Parker replied. "Maybe now."

We stood staring at each other. I learned everything I needed to know about him in the few moments we locked eyes. He always got his way, and he considered himself superior to everyone. The problem was that he underestimated me. And that was a mistake.

"Gretchen's coming with me now," I said, wrapping my hand around Gretchen's wrist. I wasn't about to let go either. He'd have to slice my arm off. "Move."

I shoved him aside perhaps harder than I meant to, but he got the point. He watched as I dragged Gretchen behind me, ignoring her protests to stay in the basement.

"You're not staying in the basement!" I hissed. "So get over it!"

I chanced a backward glance at Parker. He stood with his hands in his pockets, staring at me, deciding how he would deal with me in the future. I'm quite sure he planned to since I stole away his fuck toy for the evening.

Stephanie did what she was told. She was still in the bathroom when Gretchen and I returned upstairs.

"I've got a lot of people pissed at me," she said, as I helped her wash her face and hands. She was successful in making herself throw up—multiple times, I observed—but not so much in cleaning it up. At least she was no longer slurring her words and was slightly more coherent, or as coherent as Stephanie could possibly be.

"There are five hundred bathrooms in this house," I replied. "They'll get over it."

Just then Gretchen decided she needed to get sick, too, and I barely pulled her mass of brown hair away from her face in time before she heaved into the toilet.

"I'm really mad at you, Brookey," she said after the first round. She didn't look at me when she said it. She was wise enough to keep her head in the toilet.

"Don't talk," I ordered. "Just keep going."

I was annoyed, naturally, even though I could recall Gretchen doing the same thing for me, and on many occasions. I can't believe I used to party like this. I can't believe I ever wanted to. What was the point? I wasted all of the following day lying in bed with an herb-infused bean bag stuck to my forehead surrounded by bottles of Gatorade. And if the hangover was especially monstrous, I'd cry, which made it worse. Such a waste of time. A waste of life.

"He was cute," Gretchen continued after the second wave. "I wanted to kiss him."

"I know you did," I replied. "But he's a dick."

"Who's a dick?" Stephanie asked. She was sitting on the sink counter, her already too-short dress hiked up around her hips, long legs slightly spread and dangling off the side.

I turned around and looked at her. "You don't sit like that in public, do you?"

She shrugged. "Who's a dick?"

"Just this swim guy at my school," I replied.

"He's not a dick!" Gretchen said, then heaved again.

"Good grief, Gretchen. How much did you drink?"

I patiently waited for the wave to subside. She wiped her mouth with a bit of toilet paper and addressed me. "How should I know?"

I rolled my eyes. "Was he feeding you drinks all night?"

"He's a gentleman," she replied.

"What the hell does that mean?" I asked.

"He went to get me drinks," she said. No longer able to stand bent over, she fell on the bathroom floor. I could have reached out and grabbed her arm to keep her from going down, but I didn't.

"Yeah, I bet he did," I said. "Stay away from that guy, Gretchen. I mean it."

"You are soooo not fun right now," Gretchen pouted.

True. I wasn't being any fun. The real purpose for coming to this lame party tonight was to do a bit of sleuthing. Well, and to keep Gretchen from being violated. I succeeded in the second, but not in the first. I didn't know what I expected to overhear or see, if anything at all. But I knew in my gut that Parker and Cal were up to something. If they were, in fact, part of a salacious sex club, I was sure they were looking for partners. Unsuspecting partners. I made it my mission to find out, but I realized I'd have to investigate another night. My top priority was keeping an eye on my friends. I would never sacrifice their safety to discover more clues about Parker and Cal.

I walked with my tired, dehydrated friends out of the

bathroom and towards the front door. Stephanie couldn't remember how she got to the party, so I decided to take her home. On our way out, I spotted Cal and Parker talking. They were huddled in a corner of the foyer whispering. I caught Cal's eye, and he waved at me. I waved back, watching Parker scowl. He tried getting Cal's attention again, but Cal was more interested in watching me walk away.

Even when I turned my back on him, I knew he was still watching me. It was the same feeling I had at registration, the hairs standing on the back of my neck. I didn't like it then, and I hadn't met him yet. It was worse now because I had met him. I knew what he wanted from me, and I knew eventually I'd have to give it to him.

SEVEN

The first time I had an actual conversation with Ryan Foster was right after our little spying game. I was vacuuming the living room floor Saturday morning and had pulled back the curtains that usually hung over the large window overlooking the street because I needed sunshine. I realized that part of my dad's problem was that he had gone too many years without sunshine.

He lived in a little box of a house closed up with thick fabric that forbade the outside world to get a peek. I didn't care who wanted a peek so long as I could feel the sunlight on my face when I sat on the couch reading. I lived in my old house a total of nineteen hours before I opened everything, tearing away the dust and heavy seclusion. I could tell it made my dad nervous, but he gave me my sunshine because he'd give me whatever I wanted.

I carefully maneuvered the vacuum underneath the coffee table when I saw him in my peripheral vision. I looked out the window and watched him ride his skateboard down the sidewalk. He didn't look anything like a skater except for his hair. He wasn't dressed in skater clothes. He wore regular straight-legged jeans with a form-fitting blue T-shirt. He had nice arms, but he didn't strike me as the kind of guy who lifted weights. Nobody was just blessed with toned muscles like that, though. He had to do something to work them. I imagined he chopped wood. I liked that image. Even better without a shirt.

He paused in front of my house and looked towards the front door. It startled me, and I knew his eyes would move to the open window next, so I averted mine and continued vacuuming, trying hard to look oblivious and pretty. But how does someone look pretty while vacuuming?

I tried cocking my head to the side and smiling, but felt so stupid doing it that I stopped. I put my free hand on my hip, but that made me feel like one of those models on *The Price is Right*. I gave up altogether and turned off the vacuum. When I braved a glance out my window, he was gone, and the disappointment manifested itself as tightness in my chest. I didn't like the way it felt. I thought I shouldn't feel that way at all about a person I didn't know. I grunted and put the vacuum away.

When I returned to the living room, I spotted him again. He was rolling along in the opposite direction. Again he paused in front of my house, and again I averted my eyes. I looked over at the family portrait still hanging above the couch. I scowled, then thought twice about it. Scowls were ugly. I tried for a smile instead. A sweet smile. But it seemed fake. I lost the smile and tried to look pensive. What the hell?

I looked back out the window and just like that, he had disappeared. I walked over to the window and peered out in the direction I thought he'd gone. He was only a few houses down, one foot poised on his skateboard as though he were about to take off in the direction of my house. I watched him decide, silently begging him to come my way.

What I should have done was close my curtains. I knew it, but he glided past my house a third time, and I decided to check the mail.

He rolled along towards me when I reached the mailbox, and I looked over.

"Hey, Brooke. I was wondering when you'd decide to come out and say 'hello'," he said, stopping short of me and kicking his skateboard up into his hand.

Cocky bastard. I flushed and looked down at the mail. Suddenly it was all so interesting: bills and a craft magazine. Craft magazine?

I felt him staring at me and stopped rifling through the mail.

"You saw me?" I asked, not looking at him.

"I especially liked the hand-on-the-hip look," he replied.

I cringed. "Oh my God. I have to go."

"Please don't," he said, and caught my arm. "I'm only teasing."

I finally mustered the courage to look at him, and he let go of my arm.

"Why didn't you just knock on my door?" I asked. "I saw you pass by, like, three times."

He shrugged and massaged the back of his neck.

"Okay. That's not an answer," I said.

He grinned. "You looked busy. Vacuuming."

I considered him for a moment. "Do you live in this neighborhood?"

"Just down the street."

Well, that was inconvenient. Everything about this guy was inconvenient, from his incredibly sexy face and hair and eyes and body, to the fact that he went to my school, to the fact that he lived in my neighborhood. How had I not noticed him until today?

"But I've never seen you," he said. "Did you just move here?"

"Well, my dad's lived here awhile. I moved in with him when my mom moved to California," I explained.

He looked at me as though he expected further explanation. I don't know why I wanted to give it to him. It was presumptuous on his part, but for some reason it didn't bother me.

"My parents divorced when I was in middle school," I said.

"Jeez, they couldn't pick a better time?" he asked.

"For real. I was already a frizzy, oily, pimple-ridden mess. You'd think they'd have the decency to wait until high school or something when things started leveling out."

He grinned.

"Anyway, I went to Hanover High up until last year," I said. "But I didn't want to move across country my senior year, so here I am."

"But it's still a new school either way," Ryan pointed out.

"True, but at least the area's familiar, and I have a good friend from my old high school I still hang out with," I said.

He nodded.

"So what's your story?" I asked. "I never see you hanging out with anyone at school."

He tensed immediately, clenching his jaw the same way he did when I caught him in the stands with my camera at the volleyball game.

"I don't have a story," he said.

I shuffled uneasily, unsure what to say. It was obvious I hit a nerve, and I thought better about pressing him. A little indignation flared up, though; after all, he clearly expected me to share with him, but he was unwilling to do the same. I never liked one-sided anythings, especially friendships.

"Sooo, where's your house?" I asked, trying for

something neutral.

"It's six down from yours," he replied. "Same side of the street."

"So we're practically neighbors," I replied, and he nodded, dropping his skateboard on the sidewalk.

"I better go," he said.

I felt the disappointment instantly. We had only begun talking, and there was so much I wanted to ask him, to know about him. Why was he at Beth's funeral? Why was he a loner at school? He was hot as hell, so I knew looks had nothing to do with it. Why did he stare at me all the time at school? Why did he look pissed at the volleyball game? Why did Cal tell me to stay away from him? Why did he talk to me just now, seemingly happy until I asked him about his story? God, I couldn't stand not knowing! And watching him glide down the sidewalk farther away from me while my mouth filled with questions put me in a rotten mood for the rest of the day.

—

"Can you believe I used to be a cheerleader?" I asked Lucy as we settled into our seats.

She didn't know how to respond. I'm sure she wondered why I even mentioned it at all. It was random.

"I mean, I so don't come across as the cheerleader type, do I?"

Lucy shrugged and gave me a noncommittal smile.

I kept trying.

"I was a flyer," I continued. "I could do basket tosses all day long, but the Liberty was the hardest for me."

Lucy shifted uncomfortably in her seat. "Do cheerleaders have a type?"

I was surprised and felt slightly encouraged. "Sure they do. They're sweet and bubbly and smiley."

She grinned. "So stereotypical."

I laughed. "Where do you think stereotypes come from?"

She giggled then went quiet. "Not all of them are sweet," she whispered.

"Oh, you're talking about the mean girls," I said.

I felt awful. I knew the conversation was painful for her. I knew it was drudging up old memories she'd rather keep buried, but I had to know what happened to her. After the party, I resolved to be a martyr if I had to, for each and every one of these girls. But I needed more information. It wasn't just about Cal anymore. I could most likely put myself in a compromising situation with him any time I wanted. No, it was more than that. There were others, and I wouldn't be satisfied with just destroying Cal's life. I was taking them all under.

Lucy nodded. She looked like she was making up her mind, debating how much to share with me. She started to speak but promptly closed her mouth when Cal approached my desk.

"Hey, Brooke," he said, shooting Lucy a sidelong glance. I saw her tremble. *Tremble.*

"Hi, Cal," I replied.

"Wish you would have stayed longer at the party," he said. "I wanted to hang out with you more."

"Well, duty called," I replied. "I had to get my friends home."

"Yeah, they looked pretty wasted," Cal said. "One of them was all over Parker."

"I think I remember him being all over her," I corrected.

"Oh, that's right," Cal said, shaking his head. "You really pissed him off." He chuckled. "You interrupted his game."

"Excuse me," Lucy whispered, and vanished from the room.

Cal watched her leave then turned back to me. "Hey

listen, you probably don't want to get involved with her."

"Oh yeah? Why's that?" I asked.

"She's loony, if you know what I mean," he explained. "I think her dad committed suicide or something, and she's just been a nutcase ever since."

I hated Cal. I hated his guts. If I had a shank in my purse, I'd whip it out this instant and plunge it into his heart. Then I'd cut his tongue out for being such a fucking liar. Lucy's dad was alive and well, as I learned last week when she mentioned something to me about his job. The only person who might have turned Lucy into a nutcase, if she even was a nutcase, was Cal himself. He raped her, too. I knew he did.

Suddenly I looked over at Ryan. I remembered Cal's warning to me in the gym, to stay away from Ryan because he was crazy. What happened to Ryan? Obviously it had something to do with Cal. My mind raced in that moment, remembering Ryan's sister at the restaurant. She looked like she could be in high school, but I'd never seen her. Perhaps I just wasn't paying attention. What if something happened to her? What if she was another victim, and Ryan was powerless to do anything about it? Rapes become much harder to prosecute if there's no physical evidence. I doubted any of these girls went to the hospital after their attacks. I doubted Ryan's sister did, being so young and afraid. And ashamed.

My mind was reeling by this point, and it took me a long time to hear Cal's voice in the distance working to get my attention.

"Brooke!" he said. "Damn girl, where'd you go?"

I shook my head. "I have this massive test today in physics. I'm sorry. I just spaced."

I turned my head to see Lucy hanging around just outside the classroom, reluctant to come back in until Cal was safely in his seat at the back of the room.

"Well, think about what I said. Just trying to help you

out. Being new and all," Cal said.

He walked to the back of the room, and only then did Lucy come inside. She slid into her seat soundlessly and didn't acknowledge my presence.

—

"Say 'BFFs!'" Mom exclaimed behind the camera.

"BFFs!" we screamed, holding up our necklaces so that the separate pieces were joined, fixing the crack, making a whole heart that read "Best Friends." It was my favorite birthday present from my favorite person.

Beth hung around after all the party guests left. She was spending the night, and we had big plans that included pizza, movies, make-up, and gossip. I didn't think any of my subsequent birthdays would live up to this one. I decided that eight years old was the perfect age, and I wanted to freeze frame this moment, wearing a pretty piece of jewelry my best friend carefully picked out for me, and never grow older.

"You promise not to take it off?" Beth asked, sitting with me at the kitchen table.

"I won't ever," I said, thinking I couldn't wait to show it off Monday morning to those particular girls at school I didn't like.

Beth grinned from ear to ear watching me finger the heart piece.

"I wanted the 'Be Fri,' but I knew you'd want it," she said.

It's true. I'm glad I had the "Be Fri" over "st ends," but I was willing to exchange. If it made Beth happy, no matter that it was my birthday, I was willing to trade.

"Wanna trade?" I asked.

"No no," she answered. "I like my half now. I'm just saying that when I first saw it, I thought I wanted yours."

I smiled and grabbed another plate with cake. "Wanna share?"

"Mmhmm," Beth replied, reaching for a plastic fork.

"You think we'll be best friends forever?" I asked, shoving a too-big piece of cake in my mouth.

"Why not?" Beth replied.

I laughed somehow, with my mouth full. "Exactly. Why not?"

"As long as you don't turn mean like Courtney," Beth said.

"I would never act like her!" I replied.

"I know, Brooke."

She plopped her left arm over my shoulder in a casual way.

"Happy birthday, Brooke," she said, and leaned over to kiss my cheek. The cake crumbs on her lips stuck to my face.

And I didn't care.

I awoke sobbing. I clutched my stomach and rocked back and forth, back and forth, feeling the threat of a panic attack and powerless to stop it. I heard Beth's voice repeating the question over and over: *"You promise not to take it off?"*

I couldn't breathe when the next wave of sobs washed over me. I clapped my hand over my mouth, but it stifled nothing. I was accustomed to feeling constant guilt, but this was different. This was heavier, scarier. And I feared I would be trapped forever, never able to move on because of the way I treated her.

"I promise!" I screamed before I realized I said it out loud.

Dad flew into the room.

"Brooke, what's wrong?" he asked, sitting beside me and taking me into his arms.

I cried harder, burying my face in his shoulder, liquid pouring out of my eyes and nose all over him.

"I was a bad friend," I cried.

Dad stroked my hair. "That's impossible."

But Dad didn't know what I did. He didn't know the sins I had to repent for, the sickness in my mind that made me hear Beth all the time. Talking to me. Pleading with me. Cursing me. Crying for me.

I pulled away and wiped my nose. "Yes, Dad, I was."

"What do you mean, Brooke?"

"You'll think me so horrible if I tell you," I said. My voice shook uncontrollably.

"I would never think such a thing," Dad replied.

I drew in my breath. "I sneaked around with Beth's boyfriend before she died."

Dad was quiet.

"She found out about it," I said. "I don't think that's why she . . . did it, but I feel so guilty. I never got the chance to make things right." Fresh tears rolled down my cheeks, plopping one by one on my arms and chest.

"Are you still with her boyfriend?" Dad asked.

"No!" I replied. "My God, no!"

"Then you've made things right," Dad said. He put his arm around me, and I rested my head on his shoulder.

"I don't think that's enough," I whispered.

"Did you apologize to her before she died?" Dad asked.

"Yes. I mean, she wouldn't talk to me face to face, so I had to leave messages on her cell phone, but yes. I tried. For months I tried. All summer."

"Then honey? That's all you can do," Dad said. He kissed the top of my head.

But I knew that wasn't all I could do. There was a way I could atone. I had to or else Beth would haunt me forever. I imagined my brain deteriorating, growing black with disease because of guilt. I couldn't stand the thought, and begged my father to stay up with me. I was too afraid to go back to sleep, to see Beth's face, so we went downstairs. He made me tea, and we sat side-by-side chatting into the early morning hours while the television hummed in the background.

———

I stood considering the blank canvas—stark white and full of promise. I had my paints ready and an idea in my head. I was outside on the back patio. I never painted inside, even with acceptable lighting. No. I had to have sunshine if I were to create anything good.

The sun felt warm and delicious on the top of my head, weaker than the summer sun but not altogether ineffectual like the winter one. The seasons were changing, and I observed the first turning of leaves in my back yard. That was my idea: to do a painting of leaves.

I dipped my paintbrush in a glob of oil paints I had mixed. I never painted with acrylic. Mom asked me one time why I couldn't be a "cheap" painter, noting the extreme price difference between acrylic and oil-based paints. What could I say? I couldn't make her understand the difference, how acrylic paint dried almost immediately on the canvas. Impossible to manipulate. Stubborn and unforgiving if you made a mistake. You had no choice but to paint over your mess-up. And then it stayed hidden within the painting, and you always knew it was there.

But oil-based paints were different. They forgave you when you messed up, drying slowly to allow you ample time to fix mistakes, make things right. On many occasions I could leave my painting for days, come back to it, and manipulate the colors as though it were still freshly painted. Oil paints were wiser to the human condition, understanding our imperfections and giving us enough time to rework ourselves until we made things right. I couldn't make my mother understand the richness of oil-based paints.

"Oh, I know all about the richness of them!" Mom said years ago when I took up my hobby. "All I know is that you better not get bored with this."

I had never gotten bored with painting. If anything, I worked each year to become better. Learning new techniques, discovering my strengths. Above all, painting allowed me to escape me. I didn't have to be popular Brooke. Funny Brooke. Sexy Brooke. Witty Brooke. I could be as vulnerable and weird as I wanted, and my friends would forgive me for it because it was art. And they were impressed.

The first contact of brush on canvas is a heady thing. I think it's the promise of something wonderful, beautiful. You can see the finished product in your mind's eye, but it never turns out quite as you expect. It's always better, or at least that's been my experience. And that's where the headiness comes in. You think you know what to expect. You think you have it all planned out. But something in you always surprises you, and it's a buzzing undercurrent that keeps you silently guessing until your picture is complete.

I began, feeling the rush as my brush hit the canvas for its first stroke. I worked all morning creating each leaf, carefully mixing colors I thought would evoke that one last brilliant push for life: jewel tones of rich reds, golden browns, and fiery oranges. But I couldn't get my colors bright enough. They looked bright on my palette, but once I transferred them to the canvas, they turned a muted, uninteresting shade.

I thought my eyes were playing tricks on me. I looked down at my arm where the palette was cradled. The colors screamed to me. I looked at my painting. They moaned before going silent. A flat nothing. But not before they laughed at me a little. I heard them laugh. I heard *her* laugh.

My heartbeat sped up. I felt the rush of rage, an anger far from righteous. It was only anger, and it flowed through me like wicked adrenaline. The kind you shouldn't act on, but if you don't, you know you'll explode. I didn't want to draw attention from neighbors playing next door, so I seethed silently.

I stared at my lifeless painting and mouthed the words: "Beth. You fucking bitch."

EIGHT

Ryan was notably silent after our conversation several weeks ago. He didn't acknowledge me in class, and I never saw him ride his skateboard down the sidewalk. Sometimes I would sit in the living room with the curtains pulled back and watch for him. It was blatant and desperate, and I didn't care. I knew he saw me talking to Cal on several occasions at school, and I wondered if that accounted for his lack of interest. Either way, my feelings were hurt, and my pride along with them. Shouldn't he try to fight for my affections or something? Wasn't that the manly thing to do?

I decided to pay him a visit instead of waiting for him. It was a chilly October Saturday afternoon, so I grabbed a light jacket and headed down the sidewalk, counting six houses from mine. I walked up the stone path to the front door feeling the rapid tapping of my heart. It was that good nervous feeling, an expectation of something wonderful mixed with the fear that it wouldn't turn out as I'd hoped. But the hope made me knock on the door anyway.

A young girl answered. "Yes?"

I recognized her from the restaurant as Ryan's sister.

She had the same color hair as Ryan, the same blue eyes, though hers were a little less transparent.

"I'm Brooke. I live right down the street," I said. "I'm a friend of your brother's."

"My brother doesn't have any friends," the girl replied. "But I'll let you in anyway."

I was startled. What a thing to say, and the way she said it. Matter-of-fact. Not snippy or cruel. Just matter-of-fact.

I blurted what I knew I shouldn't. "How can he not have any friends? He's so cute."

Stupid. Just stupid.

"Gross," the girl said. She cocked her head and studied me. She was so pretty, and I wondered why I'd never noticed her at school. "Do you *like* him?"

I didn't know how to respond. She curled her lips into a grin and moved aside, inviting me in.

"Ryan!" she called up the stairs. "Your girlfriend's here!"

"Nice," I replied, and she giggled. "How come I don't see you at school?"

"I'm not in high school yet," she replied. "I'm in eighth grade."

"Gotcha." I looked up the stairs, heart thumping, when I heard the plodding of heavy feet. Ryan appeared, dressed in plaid pajama bottoms, hair askew, coming down the stairs with his T-shirt halfway on. I got a glimpse of his stomach, rippled with well-defined muscles, before he pulled the shirt down. He was sexier than I'd ever seen him.

"Hey," he said, addressing me. He was confused.

"Hi," I replied, just as confused. Why had I come over?

"Ryan, when did you get a girlfriend?" his sister asked.

"She's not my girlfriend, Kaylen," Ryan replied. "Go

away."

I knew it was stupid, but the thumping in my heart stopped altogether at the sound of those words: *"She's not my girlfriend."* A pinch took its place, and I tried to ignore it.

Kaylen shrugged and left the room. She was no longer interested once she learned her brother's relationship status hadn't changed.

"Your sister's cute," I observed.

"My sister's annoying," he replied, pushing his hand through his tousled hair.

"Did you just wake up?" I asked, noting his clothes.

"No," he answered.

"Sooo, what's with the pajamas? It's like four o'clock."

He stared at me for a second. "Why are you here?"

I hated when people did that: answering a question with a question. It was infuriating.

"I just haven't talked with you in weeks," I said. "I thought I'd come over and say 'hello.'"

"Really?" He sounded genuinely shocked.

"Well, yeah. I thought maybe we could hang out," I offered.

The truth was that I wanted him to pursue me. I think that's inherently female to want to be pursued. And I think Ryan wanted to initially, but I or he or someone else messed it up. So I swallowed my pride and made my interest known, hoping he would pick up where we started several weeks ago outside my house. I knew I had no business doing it. How did I think I could possibly juggle Ryan and Cal? We all went to school together, for Pete's sake. But in this moment, I didn't care. He was standing in front of me with hair I was itching to run my fingers through, and a stomach I wanted to feel pressed against my own.

I admit my vulnerability. I felt it the entire day, trying

hard to keep myself busy to avoid confronting it. Dad had to go into the office, so I was left alone. Beth crept into the forefront of my brain, asking me why I wasn't moving faster, why I wasn't working harder to avenge her, and I couldn't silence her. I tried by wearing the broken heart necklace she had given me. I thought that would appease her, but it only encouraged her incessant interrogation. I had to get out of the house. Ryan would be the perfect distraction.

"You want to hang out." He didn't pose it as a question. He said it with sarcasm, and it irked me.

"Well, if you're busy I can go," I said, turning to leave.

"No," he said, and took my hand. "I'm just confused."

"About what?" I asked, turning to face him. He dropped my hand.

"I don't know why you wanna hang out."

He looked at me with those ocean eyes, his brows furrowed in thought, and I decided in that moment I didn't want to hang out. I wanted to make out. Hard.

"Ryan, you promised you'd take me to Lindsay's house," Kaylen whined from the top landing of the stairs. She had an overnight bag slung over her shoulder.

Ryan never took his eyes off of me. "Any interest in riding over to Lindsay's house to drop off my sister?"

I smiled and nodded.

"All right. Wait here," and he disappeared up the stairs.

While he was changing, Kaylen peppered me with questions, successfully extracting all the important information from me before her brother came back downstairs: my age, grade, family situation, social status at school. I told her I was the most popular girl in my class. She didn't believe me, and told me so, but I think she liked me anyway.

A few minutes later, Ryan came down dressed in jeans and a dark green cardigan. He looked like a poster boy for Banana Republic, and I liked every bit of it.

"Maybe Ryan'll stop being such a mopey loser at school if you start hanging out with him," Kaylen said as Ryan grabbed his car keys from the foyer table.

"Maybe," he replied, and she smirked at him.

The drive over to Lindsay's was filled with Kaylen's chatter. I enjoyed listening to her. She was funny and sweet, quick with the witty remarks, and there was nothing in her manner that suggested something terrible had happened to her. She was bright and talkative. Happy.

I realized I jumped to conclusions in my moment of panic, considering the worst because Cal was so insistent I stay away from Ryan. Naturally I assumed Cal did something horrible to Kaylen and didn't want to be found out. I thought I was becoming paranoid.

Once we dropped off Kaylen, we returned to Ryan's house. He invited me to his room, and I was a little too quick to follow. I kept telling myself not to pounce on him, but it was hard when he made it so inviting by shutting his bedroom door. I felt like a guy. Completely aroused with no thoughts other than sex.

"I didn't have to work today," he said, plopping on his bed. "That's why I was still in my pajamas. I finished my homework then played video games all day."

"You did your homework first?" I asked, and giggled.

"I have a good work ethic," Ryan replied, grinning.

"Indeed." I plopped down on the bed beside him. No point in trying to be coy about it. I promised myself that I would only respond to the kiss, not initiate it. "So where do you work?"

"A game store," he said.

"Like video games?"

"Yep."

"So you play video games a lot?"

"Yep."

"You don't strike me as dorky," I said, then instantly regretted it.

Ryan laughed. "I don't think you have to be a dork to like gaming."

I smiled sheepishly. "Oh."

"I do like the mechanics behind it, though," Ryan said. "So that may be where the dork factor comes in."

I grinned and inched a bit closer.

"So how's your mom doing in California?" Ryan asked. He scooted a little ways away from me. I guess I made him uncomfortable. I should have sat on his desk chair instead, but it would look awkward if I moved now.

"She's fine," I replied. "I talk with her once a week."

"I bet she misses you a lot," Ryan offered.

I nodded. "I'm glad I stayed here, though. I'm getting to know my dad all over again, and it's fun. I probably hang out with him way more than most teenage girls."

Ryan nodded.

"Truth is, I like it. I didn't know we'd get so close so fast. It's almost like there weren't those years in between when we didn't live together."

Ryan nodded again.

We sat in an uncomfortable silence, and since Ryan didn't look like he was itching to say anything, I spoke up.

"So do you plan on telling me anything about yourself other than you like to play video games?"

"What do you want to know?" he asked.

"Well, for starters, how long have you lived here?" I asked. I ran my hand back and forth over his comforter.

"All my life."

"So you've been going to Charity Run since ninth grade?"

"Mmhmm."

"Do you have any other siblings?"

"No."

"And what are your hobbies?"

"I feel like I'm being interviewed," he said.

I smiled. "Well, you don't offer anything. I have to ask."

"Brooke, why don't we talk about you instead? You seem much more interesting."

I started feeling frustrated. "I'm sure that's not true. Why are you so mysterious?" I tried to sound light, but I think it came out as an accusation instead.

Ryan was quiet for a moment.

"Look, you probably don't want to be associated with me at school, okay?"

What the hell did *that* mean?

"I guess I'm a bit of a pariah. And I don't mind. I just don't wanna drag you down."

I looked at him, astonished. "Okay. You just upped the mysterious factor by a trillion."

He laughed. It sounded genuine, dark and rich—that male laughter that's so damn sexy.

I inched a little closer, and this time he didn't move.

"It's your senior year, and you should meet people and make friends and have fun," he said.

"I'm meeting you," I offered. It came out sounding flirty and sensual.

Ryan chuckled. "You're going to be my trouble this year, aren't you?" he asked softly.

Hell yeah I was.

I looked at him and let myself get lost in those translucent eyes. I didn't care if they held a bunch of secrets he was unwilling to share. I just knew that I was hungry to be touched, and to be touched by someone I wanted.

"I don't even know you," he said. He lifted his hand to the back of my neck, brushing me lightly with his fingertips.

"Same goes for you," I replied. I grazed his neck with

my fingertips in much the same way.

It was incredibly intimate, sitting there, rubbing one another's necks, foreheads pressed together so that our lips were mere centimeters apart. I thought it might be more intimate than sex, and I didn't know what I was doing. The rational part of my brain screamed this was much too soon. The sexual part cheered me on. The vengeful part scolded me for seducing the wrong guy.

"I think you're full of secrets," Ryan whispered.

"I know *you* are," I whispered back.

"All right then. We can each share one. But only one," he said.

"Do we get to ask each other?"

Ryan tensed for a moment, hand frozen on the back of my neck. "I guess."

"Why were you at Beth's funeral?" I asked. I didn't even have to think about it.

"I knew her. She went to our high school. I heard what happened and just felt like I needed to go."

I felt the instant, unsettling tears in the back of my eyes threaten to surge over my lids and ruin this intimate moment.

"Why were you at Beth's funeral?" Ryan asked.

I swallowed. "She was my best friend."

Ryan pulled away from me. I knew he would. "Do you . . . do you know why she did it?"

That was a secret I was not willing to share. I shook my head, lowering my eyes. I felt his arms go around me, and I stopped thinking about Beth. I had spent my entire day thinking about Beth. Right now I wanted to think about Ryan and all the things he had planned for me in his bed. I knew it was too soon, but I didn't care. I felt his hand on my chin as he tilted my mouth to his. He hesitated for a second before pressing his lips to mine.

It's always described as melting, and I finally understood why. I thought my body was turning to liquid.

I could feel my bones giving way, threatening to dissolve and leave me one big puddle of goo. His lips were incredible, soft and supple, raining light pecks on my own until I shifted and grunted—yes, actually *grunted*—in frustration.

"What do you want, Brooke?" he asked into my mouth.

I whimpered a reply, and he kissed me harder, finally giving me his tongue. That's what I wanted. I mingled mine with his, feeling a sharp aching deep inside my belly that almost hurt. I thought that this was the guy I was always meant to kiss, that everyone before him didn't count for anything.

Ryan pulled away. "I've wanted to do that since I ran into you at the funeral."

"Why'd you stop?" I asked playfully.

Ryan smiled wearily. "Brooke, I don't think I can be with anyone right now, and I can't tell you why. It doesn't have anything to do with you personally. You're beautiful. It's just—"

"Stop," I said. "Let's worry about your issues later. Will you please just kiss me again?"

Maybe it sounded pathetic. Maybe I was totally pathetic. I had no business getting physical with a guy I barely knew. Oh, who was I kidding? I didn't know him at all! But I was learning his lips, and that's something. Right?

The side of his mouth quirked up, and I took it as an invitation. I lunged for him, pinning him to the bed and kissing him hungrily. Yeah, so I was being aggressive. So what? He didn't seem to mind. He wrapped his arms around my waist and squeezed. It knocked the breath out of me momentarily, and I squealed.

"I'm sorry," he mumbled into my mouth, loosening his hold.

I kissed him harder, and before it registered, I was on

my back being pressed into the comforter by his weight. He moved his lips to my neck, sucking and nibbling, eliciting moans and cries and other sounds. It dawned on me that we were both going at it like we hadn't made out in ages. For me it was five months. I wondered about my mystery man.

I pushed against him, and he released my neck. He looked down at me.

"Did I do something wrong?" he asked.

"No," I replied. "It's just, when was the last time you made out with a girl?"

His face turned pink. "Am I rusty?"

"No no!" I said. "I was just wondering."

Ryan thought for a moment. "I don't know. A year?"

"*What?!*"

He sat up, leaning back on his heels and pushing his hand through his hair.

"I didn't mean it like that," I said. I felt like a jerk.

"No harm done," he replied. He moved off the bed and headed for the bedroom door. "I was planning on going out in a bit."

I stared at him.

"Well, like now," he said.

"Oh. You want me to go?"

"Well, it'd be weird if my parents came home and found some girl in my bedroom," he replied.

I felt humiliated. I *was* just "some" girl, whether he meant it to come across that way or not. I had no business coming over here. No business making out. No business making him feel embarrassed. I was such an asshole. I thought only guys could hold that title, but I realized girls could, too.

I got up and followed him to the front door. We stood in an awkward silence before I walked away. He didn't say goodbye, and neither did I.

—

"Why did you make fun of him?" Gretchen asked.

I agreed to spend the night with her, but only if she didn't make us go to another party.

"I didn't make fun of him," I said. "Or at least I didn't mean to."

"Was he horrible?"

"Far from it. The whole thing was hot until I opened my stupid mouth," I whined.

"Why did you?"

"A year, Gretchen! What the hell? I mean, I could see if he were ugly or something, but the guy is drop-dead gorgeous! I couldn't hide my surprise. What do you want from me?"

Gretchen tossed an emery board in my direction and started in on her nails.

"So, it's like you two have this uncontrollable sexual energy around each other?" Gretchen asked.

"Obviously. We don't even know one another. I lunged at him like a freaking hoochie," I said.

"Oh, Brooke. Stop beating yourself up over it. Make-out sessions can be nice."

"I want more than a make-out session with him," I said, filing my nails.

"So this goes way beyond a sexual attraction thing," Gretchen confirmed.

I nodded sullenly. I felt like a big wet blanket on her fun Saturday night. I don't know why she invited me to stay over. She heard the way I sounded on the phone earlier. Dejected. Slightly bitchy.

"Well, you know what you've gotta do," Gretchen said. "Go back over there and apologize."

"I don't even know what I'm apologizing for!" I argued.

"You're apologizing for making him feel like a loser

for not having kissed a girl in a year. That's what," Gretchen said.

"Fine."

"Brookey, get rid of the 'tude, okay? Tonight is about nails and *Sex and the City* reruns and Bacardi." She plunged her hand into her purse and pulled out several airplane bottles.

"Where'd you get those?" I asked. I was in no mood to take care of Gretchen tonight.

"Why does it matter?" she replied, holding up the miniature bottles of rum.

"I'm not replaying that Friday night with you, Gretchen," I warned.

"Oh, relax. I'm not drinking. You are," she said.

"No way."

"Uh, yeah you are. You need to loosen up and stop worrying about Ryan and have a little fun tonight," Gretchen said. "We're not going anywhere. We're staying right here in my room. This is my 'thank you' for taking care of me after Tanner's party."

"I can't drink straight liquor," I said.

"Hello, Brooke. I'm totally aware. You act like I don't have a clue who you are," Gretchen huffed, and pointed to the Coke bottle sitting on her desk.

Thirty minutes later I was trashed.

"And I'm, like, what? What? *What?* A year? That's, like, completely impossible because he's sooo freaking hot," I said, lying sprawled on Gretchen's bedroom floor wearing only my bra and panties. I've no idea what happened to my clothes.

"Did you want to finish changing into your pajamas?" Gretchen asked, giggling.

Oh. So that's what happened to my clothes.

I shook my head from side to side.

"Hey, don't do that too hard. I don't want you

yakking on my rug," Gretchen said.

"I just wanted to say, 'Ryan, why are you so gorgeous and strange? What are your secrets? Your *secrets*, Ryan. I must know them.'" I rolled over onto my stomach. "God, will you just tell me!" I begged.

Gretchen laughed.

"Gretchy?" I asked.

"Don't call me that," she replied.

"I was ready to do him. I'm totally not joking right now," I said. "I wanted to do things to him."

I crawled towards my friend who sat in front of me leaning against her bed.

"Do you understand what I'm telling you? I wanted to do things. Lots of things," I said, inches from her face.

"Like blow him?" she asked.

"Blow. Him. Up!" I replied, and Gretchen fell on the floor laughing. "What?" I asked, laughing, too, because Gretchen's laugh was infectious.

"I love you," she said between giggles. "Tell me more."

"I want to swim in his eyes," I said dreamily.

"Oh God."

"And marry him and have his babies," I finished.

"And blow him, too, right?"

"To Mars," I sighed, leaning against the bed. Gretchen sat up and joined me. "All the way to Mars."

I looked at my friend. She stared at me, grinning.

"Can I call him?" I asked.

"No."

"I just wanna wish him a good night," I said.

"No."

"But I need to tell him a couple of things."

"No, you don't."

"But I promised him I'd call him tonight."

"No, you didn't."

"But I love him."

"I know, Brookey."

"I love him so much. I've never loved anyone as much as I love him."

Gretchen put her arm around me, and I rested my head on her shoulder. "I know, Brooke."

"Do you think he loves me?"

"I think he's head-over-heels in love with you."

I squealed. "Can I have another drink?"

"You drank it all," Gretchen said.

I grunted and looked at the TV. "Charlotte just wanted to have a freakin' baby, people! Is that too much to ask for?"

"I know," Gretchen said. "They gave her a tough storyline."

"So freaking unfair," I said, and hiccupped.

I promptly fell asleep on Gretchen's shoulder, my head bobbing up and down on tightly packed waves. I heard my friend's voice in the distance before dozing off.

"You're gonna have the worst headache tomorrow."

NINE

Mother. Fucker.

I awoke in Gretchen's bed with a raging headache. She sauntered out of the bathroom, hair wrapped in a towel, smile plastered on her face, looking chipper.

"Hi, sunshine," she said, heading for her dresser.

"I hate you," I mumbled.

"Hey now. I didn't force you to drink all of it, Brooke," she said.

"I still hate you."

Gretchen pouted. "You know you had fun."

My lips turned up in a painful smile. "How stupid did I get?"

"Well, I had to wrestle your cell phone from you," Gretchen said.

"No way! I remember falling asleep on your shoulder," I countered.

"Mmhmm. And then you woke up and you wanted to talk to your dad and then your mom. Finn and then Ryan," Gretchen said. "Especially Ryan."

I placed my hands over my face. "I'm such an idiot."

"You are not," Gretchen said, unwrapping her hair and pulling it up in a wet bun. "It was harmless fun. You got silly, and then I put you to bed. Just promise me you'll never drink by yourself."

"I'm never drinking again, period," I muttered.

Gretchen sighed. "That's what they all say."

I rolled on to my side and nearly screamed in agony. The throbbing in my head pulsed close to an explosion before settling once again into a punishing ache.

"I'm going for breakfast. What do you want?"

The thought of food made me want to hurl. I closed my eyes and swallowed hard.

"You shouldn't go out with wet hair. It's cold," I said.

"It's fine. And I'm making you eat something," Gretchen said. "Stay here. I'll be right back."

I had no plans to leave her bed. Ever.

When I got home around three, I collapsed in my own bed. The day was already wasted, and I wanted nothing more than to sleep away my headache. I convinced myself I wouldn't dream this time because my brain wasn't working right. How could I possibly summon events from my past when I couldn't remember the day of the week?

"Okay, you were right," Beth admitted. "I think I'm in love with him."

"Oh?" I squirmed in the passenger seat.

"Yes. And I've never felt this way about anybody," Beth said. "At the risk of sounding super cheesy, thank you."

She glanced my way for a second before turning back to the road.

"Thank me for what?" I asked.

"For setting me up with him! Hello?" She looked at me again. "What's up with you today?"

"Nothing," I lied.

I couldn't shake the memory of Finn leaning over and kissing me. It happened last night. We went out, the three of us since I had failed at yet another blind date, and we took Beth home first. That left me for last, and he kissed me before I could find the door handle and scramble out of the car.

It didn't exactly come out of nowhere. He had been flirting with me for the past week, always covert and always in Beth's absence. When I mustered the courage to ask him what the hell he was doing, he kissed me. And I kissed him back.

"Brooke?"

"Huh?"

"Wanna tell me what's going on?" Beth asked, pulling into the mall parking lot.

"Nothing," I said. "I swear it."

"You sure?" she pressed.

"Positive."

Beth paused for the briefest second. "Okay then. Can we keep talking about me?"

I smiled. "Sure."

We hurried into the mall. Neither one of us brought an umbrella, and a light April rain threatened to ruin Beth's perfectly styled hair. My hair, however, looked like shit, and I was more than happy to stand in the rain if it melted me to nothing. It was the guilt that made me want to disappear.

"Finn is taking me out tonight," Beth said.

"I know."

"And I think he's gonna tell me something."

My heart clenched. "Oh yeah?"

"Well, he's taking me to that fancy restaurant on Glenwood Avenue. That can mean only one thing."

"He's gonna pop the question?" I asked teasingly.

Beth laughed. "Get real! But now that you said that, it makes saying 'I love you' not nearly as good."

"He loves you," I whispered, somewhere between a question and a statement.

"I think so," Beth replied. "But if I'm totally wrong, forget we had this conversation."

He loves her. That's all I could think of as we roamed from store to store taking notes of the newest fashion trends. Normally I loved doing this. I loved clothes, accessorizing outfits, finding the perfect shoes. But today it seemed so empty and pointless.

I considered telling Beth right there, but I couldn't stand the thought of her reaction. I actually feared it. I feared she would be upset with me, though I never seduced Finn. I never gave him any reason to believe that I wanted to be more than friends with him. He was dating my best friend, for Christ's sake! But I also couldn't deny my physical attraction to him. It started growing about a month ago, but I tried with every ounce of fight in me to bury it. I convinced myself that I was just jealous of Finn and Beth. They had the kind of relationship I wanted. Surely that was the only thing that accounted for my lust.

—

Monday morning was painful. I didn't want to see Ryan and sneaked into first period, tiptoeing to my desk like a burglar. I should have carried my book bag like those cartoon characters carry the sack of money, cinched at the top with my two hands pressed close to my chest. All I needed was a striped outfit and a big dollar sign on my bag.

He was already in his seat, staring out the window, and I hoped he wouldn't turn around. I decided against striking up a conversation with Lucy. I thought if he didn't hear my voice, he would forget I even existed.

"Did you have a nice weekend?" Lucy asked, as I opened my notebook. Ryan turned around and glanced at me. Well, so much for that.

"Yeah. You?"

"It was all right. I went to this crafts antique fair thing up in the mountains with my mom," Lucy said. "I thought it'd be really lame, but it was actually fun."

"Uh huh."

"I think I'm totally digging the shabby chic look. I think when I own my own place, I'll decorate that way," Lucy continued.

Who was this girl? I thought. I'd only been trying to get her to talk to me since the first day of school. Now when she decided to be a chatterbox, I wanted her to shut the hell up.

"We ended up staying in this cute bed and breakfast while we were up there. It wasn't planned or anything. Just spur of the moment. I like that about my mom."

I nodded and looked Ryan's way. He was back at it, staring out the window, and I wished I knew what he was thinking. I was dying to talk to him, but I didn't know what to say. We left things on such a weird note, not even bothering to say goodbye to each other. That was rude and immature on both our parts. Or maybe I didn't realize just how much I had embarrassed him.

"You mentioned cheerleading the other day," Lucy said, and I whipped my head around so fast, my neck popped. She heard it. "Are you okay?"

"Yeah yeah. Fine. What about cheerleading?" I asked, massaging my neck.

"Oh, well you mentioned you used to cheer. So did I," she said.

My eyebrows shot up, and then I lowered them just as quickly. Must I make everything so obvious?

"When?" I asked. "Where?"

"Here in ninth grade. I quit though. Obviously."

"Why?" I pressed.

Lucy fidgeted for a moment with the buttons on her blouse. "It just didn't work out."

I couldn't leave it at that. "Did you have a falling out with one of the girls or something?"

Lucy shook her head. "I just became disinterested, I guess."

Yeah, like everything else in her life. The girl did

nothing at school now, but in ninth grade, she was involved in everything.

"Any particular reason why?" I asked.

"I guess I didn't like being a flyer," she said.

Bullshit. Those pictures I saw told otherwise, unless she was really good at faking it, and Lucy didn't come across as the type of girl who was good at faking anything. That's why I liked her.

"The Liberty was my specialty, though," she said. "I know you said you were good at basket tosses and not so much the Liberty." She thought for a moment then whispered, "I was good at the Liberty."

I saw the pain and anger deep within her eyes, a hurt that's only felt by someone who's suffered a major indignity. And I'm not talking about being called a nasty name or having a rumor spread about you. I'm not talking about getting your feelings hurt because someone or something didn't live up to your expectations. I'm talking about the kind of indignity that changes you as a person, makes you withdraw, hide from the world because suddenly it's turned into something frightening—full of dark corners and monsters.

"Wanna hang out after school?" I asked. "I don't have to work."

Lucy looked at me confused.

"You know. Come to my house. Watch some TV or whatever," I said. I wish I wouldn't have added the "whatever" at the end. It made me sound indecisive, and I was not an indecisive person.

"I guess," she said, uncertain.

"It won't be too bad," I said, and winked at her. She giggled.

"Sounds fun," Lucy said, and the hurt vanished from her eyes instantly.

—

I wanted so much to invade Lucy's privacy. I needed to know about Cal. I needed to know if she wished to do anything about him or bury her pain for good. But Gretchen showed up unannounced, so all of my well-planned questions had to wait.

"I'm totally loving your name," Gretchen said to Lucy. "It's adorable."

Lucy shrugged. "I hate it, actually. Everyone calls me the Narnia girl. It's so stupid."

"Whatever," Gretchen said. "She was adorable, too."

"How do you know Brooke?" Lucy asked.

"Oh, she used to go to my high school," Gretchen said, and I shifted uncomfortably on my bed. I wasn't sure how much I wanted Lucy to know.

"Really?" Lucy asked, directing the question to me.

I nodded.

"So why do you go to Charity Run?" Lucy asked.

"My mom moved to California. It was either go live in San Francisco or move in with my dad," I said.

"Well, you may have made the right choice. You're kind of a hit with some boys at school," Lucy said. "At least that's what I heard."

"Hold up," Gretchen said. "What's this all about?"

Lucy grinned. "There are some boys at school who like Brooke. And they're the nice ones."

"What do you mean?" I jumped on that comment.

"Just that not all the boys at school are nice. But the ones I heard who like you are," Lucy clarified.

"What boys aren't nice?" I asked. I knew I sounded too aggressive, and tried to ease up a bit. "I mean, so I can stay away from them."

Lucy thought for a moment. "Well, Cal for one. You shouldn't be hanging out with him. You shouldn't even talk to him, Brooke."

Alarm bells were going off in my brain. *"Don't blow it! Don't blow it!"* they screamed, and I tried to draw it out of her gently. I wished Gretchen weren't here, but I couldn't pass up the opportunity.

"Cal seems harmless to me," I said. I watched Lucy's face carefully.

"Yeah, he seems like a lot of things. Good student. Good guy," she said. And then she stared off in the direction of my closet.

Gretchen looked at me as if to say, "What's wrong with her?" and I shook my head.

I tried for lightness. "Lucy, anything you wanna tell me about Cal?"

Lucy continued staring at the closet door.

"Lucy?"

No response.

"Lucy!"

She jerked her head and looked at me. "Huh?"

"I said is there anything you want to tell me about Cal."

Her stare penetrated me.

"Yeah. Stay away from him."

———

I stood near the concession stand surveying the home team's bleachers. The wind whipped my hair about and caused my eyes to tear up, making it difficult to spot him. I wasn't even sure he'd be at the game, but I assumed popular students didn't miss Homecoming.

Homecoming. Packed bleachers. Wild fans. Some painted. Black and red and white all over the place. We were the Crusaders. Don't ask how a public high school could get away with that mascot considering the whole separation of church and state thing. But no one seemed to have a problem with it, evidently, because our mascot came tearing down the field before the game, plastic sword in one hand, plastic shield in the other, screaming about righteous retribution with a large red cross slapped on his chest. It happened every game. Every year. I watched him circle the field now, thinking absurdly that I fit right into this school, though I had no plans to take out my righteous retribution on the football players. I was more interested in the swim team and exposing their secret sex club.

I knew it'd be difficult to spot Cal amidst the fans. Football in the South was a pretty big deal. Everyone was here, even people like me who could care less about the game. Something about tradition draws even the most reluctant observers, and I suspected that if they didn't attend the game, they'd watch it on the local TV channel.

My eyes moved up and down the bleachers methodically until I found him. He was sitting with a group of friends, Parker among them, and I almost squealed at my good fortune. Not because Parker was there, but because there was an empty seat a few spaces down from them, and if I moved now, it could be mine.

I climbed the bleachers and started in on their row. My plan was to fake trip into Cal, landing in his lap. It was time to get my hands dirty. It was time to touch him and see how he reacted. I figured I could seal my fate with a little bit of clumsiness and good girl charm.

Things didn't go quite according to plan, however. As I made my way past Parker, I felt a foot shoot out, catching my ankle, and sending me head first into Cal's lap. I grabbed his thighs on instinct, smacking my head against his crotch. My right knee hit the metal bleachers with a smart crunch, and I cried out in pain. Not the way I wanted to trip. I wanted to be cute about it. This was awkward and embarrassing.

"Wow, you okay?" Cal asked, stifling a laugh. He helped me off his lap, holding my hand until I was safely sitting in the space beside him.

I rubbed my forehead. "I didn't realize how rough

jeans fabric was."

"Here, let me look," Cal said, and pushed my hand away from my face. He brushed my hair aside and studied my forehead. "It's a little red, but I think you'll live."

"Great," I mumbled.

"That's the second time I've watched you smack your face, Brooke," Cal said. "Better be careful. Don't wanna mess up all that pretty you got going on."

I chuckled.

"Is your knee okay?" he asked, noticing me rubbing it.

"I think so," I replied, and leaned forward to look down the row at Parker.

He smiled at me, a smug smile that ignited a holy fire. Fitting, I thought, and wished I were the Crusader but with real armor and a real sword. What would I do with the sword? Simple. Run it through Parker. Or if I was feeling especially generous, maybe just give him a few lacerations here and there. I sat back and shook my head. What was it about these boys that made me so violent?

"You here alone?" Cal asked.

"Yeah. I'm new, remember?" I said lightly.

"Yeah, but it's, like, the middle of October. You haven't made any friends yet?" Cal asked.

I hated the way he talked to me. There was always an underlying note of accusation in his words. Just like when he asked me months before if I had a medical condition. My fault I fainted. My fault I had no friends.

Apparently he had forgotten that I *did* have friends, that I drove them home after Tanner's party months ago. I played to his forgetfulness.

"It's hard making friends when you're a senior and you're new," I said.

Cal shrugged. "Didn't come with your dad?"

So he remembered my dad. Interesting. Perhaps I made a bigger impression on him at registration than I originally thought. I had an idea.

"He works a lot, which leaves me alone a lot. I'm not that close to him." I made it sound just the slightest bit pitiful. I thought it couldn't hurt to give the impression that I was a lonely girl with no real connections to anyone. Maybe that would make me a more attractive target. He could violate me thinking I'd have no one to run to afterwards.

He slipped his arm around my waist, and I jumped. His confidence unnerved me. Why did he think he had permission to touch me so casually?

"Well, I'll be your friend, Brooke," he said, pulling me into him. "Everyone should have at least one friend."

"You're very generous," I said, trying to hide the sarcasm, but he heard.

"I'm not trying to be funny," he replied. "I really want to be your friend."

His words, his demeanor—the whole thing felt weird. Suddenly I wanted to be home with my dad, watching bad TV and talking with him about his nonexistent love life.

"Okay" was the only thing I could think to say. "So who are your friends here?"

Cal looked over at the boys sitting in a long line taking up most of the row.

"Well, you know Parker down there. And that's Mike, Tim, Hunter, and this here is Aaron," Cal said, pointing to the boy sitting beside him.

"Hi," I said, addressing Aaron.

"What's up?"

"Are you all on the swim team together?" I asked.

"Yeah," Aaron replied. "How'd you know?"

"Oh, I just took a guess. I know Cal swims. And Parker, too," I said.

"None as good as me, though," Aaron said, and Cal shook his head.

"Whatever, man."

We fell into an easy conversation, Aaron jabbering for most of it. He didn't seem like a predator, but then there was a lot about Cal that suggested he wasn't. I realized I needed to look at evil in an entirely different light. Most bad guys weren't walking around with eyes bugged out. Most bad guys didn't come across freaky and frightening, hiding in shadowed corners with insane grins plastered across their faces. Most bad guys were your normal, everyday guys moving through life like anyone else. Going to school. Going to work. Going to church, even. They were hard to spot, and that's what made them so good at being bad. They were sneaky. They could get away with it, and they knew it.

Cal bought me a hot chocolate and walked me through the game as our team crushed the competition. I tried to ask him questions here and there, but he avoided most. He wasn't interested in talking about himself. He was interested in football. Unfortunately, I learned more about that tonight than Cal. I realized I'd have to secure information in other ways, but I wasn't sure how.

—

I was cleaning my station for the evening when Terry approached me.

"Hey, wanna make out in the back seat of my car when you get finished?" he asked, sliding into a chair.

I grinned. "Every girl's fantasy," I said, filling the last of my ketchup bottles. "How old are you anyway? Fifty?"

"I'm thirty-six," Terry answered.

"Gross."

He chuckled. "Seriously, what are you doing later?"

"It's eleven. I'm going home. To bed." I wiped down the bottles and placed them in the caddy.

"You're so boring, Wright," Terry said. "Why don't

you have a little fun?"

"Oh, I had fun. A few weeks ago when I had to look after my drunk girlfriends," I said. "Will you please move your feet?"

Terry lifted his feet while I swept underneath him.

"I'm not talking about going to a party or anything. And you wouldn't have to take care of anyone," he said.

"Forget it," I replied.

"Well, you're gonna miss out big time," Terry said. "I'm the funnest person to hang with."

"That would be 'most fun.' You're the most fun to hang with," I corrected, putting the broom aside.

He smirked. "I'm not going to school for an English degree, Wright."

"You're going to school?" I asked. I was shocked. I thought Terry made being head chef at Patricia's Diner his career choice. He *was* thirty-six, after all.

"You're such a brat. I'm going to school for computer programming," he replied. "What? You thought I had plans to work at a diner for the rest of my life?"

I shrugged. "I don't know. You make one hell of a pie."

"Whatevs. I don't need this place. Once I'm through with school I'll be rolling in the dough." He laughed at his own pun.

Suddenly I had a thought. "So I guess you're pretty savvy with computers and all."

"Duh."

"And I'm assuming most of your classmates are pretty savvy, too?"

"Most people go to school for what they're good at," Terry replied patiently.

I tried for casualness. "Know any hackers?"

"Huh?"

I thought better. "Um, never mind," and went back to wiping down the table.

"No, not 'never mind'. Why do you need a hacker?" He leaned into the table, eyes glittering with mischief. "So there *is* a little bad girl in you after all."

My face flushed crimson, and he saw.

"Okay, Wright. Spill it. Who do you wanna spy on?"

"Nobody."

"Bullshit. What if I told you I *did* know a hacker?"

"Are you messing with me?" I asked.

"No."

"Okay, who is it?"

Terry leaned back in his chair and placed his hands behind his head. He looked up at the ceiling. "Yours truly."

"Bull. Shit."

"I'm serious. Why don't you believe me? You think I'm stupid or something?"

"I don't think you're stupid, but come on. What are the chances I'd ask you about a hacker and you are one?"

"Well, you got lucky. Now what's this all about?"

I couldn't believe I was about to let Terry in on some of my secrets. I had no choice, though. Not if I wanted to learn more about that conversation I overheard in the stairwell. I needed him.

"Wright?"

"You have to swear on your life you won't tell a soul," I said.

"What? You think I go around blabbing about doing hack jobs for people?"

"Just swear it."

"I swear," he said, rolling his eyes.

I took a deep breath and settled into the seat across from him. "I think there's something fishy going on at my school."

"Oh God. Okay Veronica Mars."

"Shut up. I'm serious," I said, but I couldn't help laughing.

We were sitting alone under one of the few lights still on in the restaurant. It looked like a scene from some cheesy detective movie. All we needed was the smoke from our cigarettes curling its way up to the ceiling, highlighting the jazzy refrain playing in the background.

"All right. What do you think is going on?"

"I overheard a conversation in the stairwell the other day."

Terry clapped his hand over his mouth to stifle a laugh.

"You know what? Forget it," I snapped.

"No no! I'm sorry. Look, I just didn't know you moonlighted as Nancy Drew in your spare time."

"How many more do you have?"

"Well, those are the only two . . . wait! Jessica Fletcher from *Murder She Wrote!*"

"I don't even know who that is."

"Kids these days," Terry lamented, shaking his head.

"Whatever. Are you gonna stop making fun of me and let me continue?"

"Be my guest."

I took a deep breath. "So I overheard this conversation—"

"Can I ask how?"

"I was hiding underneath the stairs," I explained.

Terry burst out laughing. I got up from my seat and grabbed the condiment caddy.

"Hey! Stop right there!" Terry ordered, grabbing my arm. "Stop being pissy. Now I'm allowed to laugh a little because this is fucking funny, okay? Get over yourself and sit back down."

I slammed the caddy on the table.

"That's the thing, you moron! It actually isn't funny. I think some guys at school are raping girls as part of a sick game!"

That got his attention. I sat back down, watching his

face as he processed the information.

"All right. All kidding aside, tell me what you overheard," Terry said.

"I heard these guys talking about a secret club and how this other guy wanted to join. Someone mentioned that the only way he could join was if he slept with a virgin. There was a mention of a score sheet or something."

"This is all you heard?" Terry asked.

"Pretty much."

"And how do you know they're raping girls? It could all be consensual," Terry argued.

"I know one of the guys who's involved in this club. Well, if it is a club. I know he raped someone. I think others are doing it, too. Maybe not all of them, but some."

"How do you know this guy raped someone?"

"I just do," I said.

"You're gonna have to do better than that if you expect me to get involved in this," Terry said.

I looked into Terry's brown eyes. It was the first and only time I'd ever do it. I had to make sure I could trust him. I searched them, but they only told me that he was honest, would always tell me the truth, even if it ended up hurting my feelings.

"He raped my best friend," I said. "She killed herself over it."

Terry was quiet for a few minutes.

"Why didn't she go to the police?" he asked finally.

"She . . . had a bit of a sexual history," I said. "She thought no one would believe her."

"Hmmm."

I rubbed my forehead. "No one knows about that except for you."

"She never told her parents?"

"You think that jackass would still be in school if she had?"

"So why do you need my help?" Terry asked.

"I want you to hack into one of their computers. I want to know about this club. I want to find out if more of these guys are forcing girls to have sex with them," I said. "Who knows? It may only be Cal, but this Parker dude I met really rubs me the wrong way. I think he's a predator, too."

"You think they're gonna keep a list of girls they've raped on their computers? Get real, Wright," Terry said.

"No, but they email each other those score sheets. I know that much. Maybe the score sheet will tell me something."

Terry shook his head. "You out for revenge?"

"You bet I am," I said.

Terry breathed deeply. "Well, I'll need some more information before we break the law."

TEN

Obtaining Parker Duncan's email address was easy. It was right on his Facebook page. Once I sent it off to Terry, the real fun began. Terry explained his plan. He would email Parker and make it look like a message from Cal. Within the email would be an image for Parker to click on. Terry asked me what the image should be, and I offered the idea of some nude chick. "Fun for me," Terry had said, and I gagged. Unbeknownst to Parker would be a "Trojan," a type of computer virus, hidden within the picture. Once Parker clicked on the image, he would enable the Trojan, thus allowing Terry unlimited access to Parker's every move: sites he visited, passwords he typed into his various online accounts, ability to view his files and folders. Terry was confident he'd have news for me the following day.

He pulled me aside at work that evening.

"I've got a bunch of shit for you," he said.

"Yeah?"

"Come to my house after work," Terry said.

"You're out of your mind," I replied.

"Get over yourself, Wright," Terry said. "You wanna

know what I've found or what?"

I grunted. "Fine. But if you try anything on me, I'll mess you up."

"Please. I'm so over you," Terry said, and I laughed.

I was shocked when I entered Terry's apartment. I assumed it would look like a frat house: mismatched furniture with rips and beer stains, old food cartons and pizza boxes littering the surfaces of tables, the smell of something stale and sour. Terry didn't strike me as the kind of guy who had his shit together. I should have known better once he told me he was going to school for computer programming. I should have known to expect a clean, orderly house. Programmers. Total nerds.

His brown leather furniture matched. He had end tables with lamps on them. Nice lamps that matched and balanced the space. The kitchen was spotless. There were freaking tea towels hanging on the oven and dishwasher handles. I burst out laughing at the magazines fanned out on the coffee table, lying next to scented candles.

"Who *are* you?" I asked, walking about the living room.

"I'm many things, Wright," Terry said.

I rolled my eyes. "May I use your bathroom before we get started?"

"Right down the hall."

I sauntered down the hallway in no rush. I was more intrigued with the pictures hanging on the walls. They looked like Terry's family, and I suspected the kid who sported the same nose and mouth as my hacker friend was his brother. I discovered in one picture that Terry surfed, and thought I should try something new: not stereotyping people the second I met them.

I really just asked to use the restroom so that I could investigate. I wanted to see if it was as clean as the rest of Terry's house. He had some scented plug-in going on. It was vanilla mixed with lavender, I think. I gingerly lifted the toilet seat, expecting to see pee stains and God knows what else, but it was clean. Remarkably clean. I couldn't figure this guy out. He was such an asshole at work—gruff and loud and full of curse words. I figured he owned a Harley on the side and hung out at dive bars on the weekends.

"No, I hang out in the labs on the weekends, you brat," he said when I came back into the living room and asked. "You're too young to be so judgmental."

He was lying on his couch flipping through television channels.

"Actually, teenagers are the most close-minded. Don't let all our talk about acceptance fool you," I said.

"Oh, I'm not fooled. I've worked with enough of you people to know how you act. It's pathetic," Terry replied, landing on Comedy Central. "The hostesses are the worst. I keep telling Francis to stop hiring 16-year-olds."

"How many have you made cry?" I asked, grinning.

"Three."

"Did you get in trouble for it?"

"What do you think?"

I giggled. "You're such a jerk."

"I didn't make you cry, did I?" he asked.

I shook my head.

"Good," he said. "That's good. I never wanna see you cry, Wright." His eyes stayed glued to the television. I don't know why he said it, but he looked like he meant it. It sounded protective, but not in a romantic way. In that moment I thought I could have an older brother. I almost asked him if he wanted to be mine.

"All right. You came here for information, and I've got it. You ready to learn?" Terry asked, opening his laptop.

I nodded and plopped down in a club chair.

"Come over here so you can see the screen."

I moved next to Terry on the couch, and he pulled

up a document.

"Observe Exhibit A. Your score sheet," Terry said.

I looked it over, heart racing with adrenaline at the realization that what I was doing was wrong. I didn't care, though. I thought it was a greater good situation, so Parker's individual rights had to be violated. Oh God, I thought. If my conservative father heard me say the words "greater good," he'd disown me.

The score sheet listed various sexual acts and how each act was scored. Kissing earned the least amount of points. Blow jobs were a high scorer. Sex was at the top. But scores were broken down even more than that depending on the type of girls. A blow job from a virgin fetched a hefty number, the largest score out of all of them if she went all the way. Girls who were already considered promiscuous and easy targets earned lesser scores, even if they had sex with the guy. It was confusing at first, but I figured it out fairly quickly.

"I found this score sheet under a file folder labeled 'FSL'," Terry said. "Didn't take me long to figure out what that meant."

"What does it mean?" I asked, tearing my eyes away from the score sheet.

"Lemme show you this first, and you might be able to figure it out," Terry said.

He pulled up Exhibit B, labeled "Game 2." It was an Excel spreadsheet with six boys' names listed. Under their names were the names of four girls. Some girls already had numbers beside their names. Others did not.

"What on earth?"

"They're teams, see?" Terry said. "Each of these guys has a team of girls. Like Fantasy Football."

"Fantasy Football?" I asked.

"Jesus, Wright. Get with the program. Fantasy Football," Terry said.

I shrugged, waiting for an explanation.

"God, you're such a girl," Terry said. "Fantasy Football. You play against people in a league. You draw names to decide who gets to pick first. You pick any professional football player you want for your team, and then you keep score of how they perform in their games. You try to win, see? By having the top score."

I nodded.

"Looks like they play four games a year. Well, according to old documents I found."

"Only four?" I asked.

"Well, think about it, Brooke. If they're working with a team of four girls, they've gotta give themselves enough time to go on dates and woo each of them."

"Okay. That makes sense," I said. "Do they play the school year or the entire year?"

"Looks like they play in the summertime, too," Terry said. "And I'll venture to say these girls don't have a clue what's going on."

"What a bunch of assholes," I said with as much feminine indignation I could portray to hide my complete and utter fascination.

He pulled up another document.

"Here they've rated each girl from the start. You've got four categories to cross-reference with the score sheet. There's 'Virgin' which yields top scores for anything she does. A 'Virgin' is classified as any girl who hasn't done a thing except kissing. A 'Good Girl' yields the second top scores—"

"What defines a 'Good Girl'?" I asked.

"Allow me to show you Exhibit D," Terry said. "This is a document that explains all four categories. Each member of the league signed it. I suppose so that there wouldn't be any disputes. I guess they all decide which category each girl falls into as well. Very democratic."

"Very fucked up," I said.

Terry smirked. "So a 'Good Girl' is one who's done a

little more than kissing. Light petting. No oral anything, though."

"Jeez." I scanned the document looking for explanations of the last two categories.

There was the 'Bad Girl' category for ladies known to have participated in all acts including intercourse. But they couldn't have had sex with more than one person. The 'Whore' category was for all those girls who'd given it up to multiple guys.

I laughed disdainfully, shaking my head. "This is outrageous."

"This is what you wanted to learn," Terry replied.

I ignored him. "Show me that spreadsheet with the teams again."

Terry pulled it up, and I noticed letters next to each girl's name.

"How can they possibly know if these girls are virgins?" I asked.

"Spying, I guess."

"You mean you think other girls are helping them out?"

"I don't know. Maybe."

I was mortified. I read down the sheet. The letters beside each name were V's, GG's, BG's, or W's. There was one W listed for Game 2. Her name was Krista Campbell.

"Why would any of them choose a 'whore' if she doesn't score well?" I asked.

"I don't think they get to choose any girls they want. They have to pick from a list. They change out the girls every game," Terry explained. "No girl plays in games back to back."

"I see. Don't want these girls feeling like sluts," I said.

"No, just labeled as such," Terry replied.

I sat back and looked at the ceiling. "So what's

'FSL'?"

"Well, there's your Fantasy Football League."

"Uh huh."

"Sooo . . ."

I looked at Terry. "Fantasy Sex League?"

"Close," he said. "Fantasy Slut League."

I snorted. "So now they're all sluts? What about the virgin thing?"

"I guess the whole point is to make them sluts," Terry said.

"How do you know it's 'Fantasy *Slut* League'?"

"I saw it in an email. Can't take credit for figuring it out myself," he said. "You're scheduled for Game 3."

I nearly shit my pants. "Excuse me?!"

"I found the list of girls for Game 3. You're one of the picks."

My heartbeat sped up so fast I was afraid I'd have a panic attack. I closed my eyes. Fields, fields, fields. Where were the damn fields?

"My category?" I breathed, eyes still clamped shut. I really didn't want to ask, but I had to. How would these guys know either way? Then I thought of Tanner. Oh God. What if Parker asked Tanner about me? What if Tanner ran his mouth about Finn? He knew about Finn. Don't ask me how, but the boy knew.

"'Good Girl'," Terry replied.

I arched my brow and pursed my lips. "How do they know?"

"Spies, Wright. The question is, are you?"

"That's none of your business, you dirty old man," I spat.

It wasn't accurate, though. A 'Good Girl' meant that I hadn't had sex, and that wasn't accurate one bit.

"When does Game 3 start?" I asked.

"Not for several months, but don't worry. I'll let you know when they've drafted their picks," Terry said.

I stared at him. I must have looked scared because he shook his head.

"Nothing's gonna happen to you," Terry said. "I promise."

I nodded.

"But you have to be smart about this, Wright," he continued. "Don't go putting yourself in some compromising position just to find out more information about this Cal dude. I understand why you want to get him, but you've gotta play it safe."

I nodded.

"I mean, I know she was your best friend and all—"

"I got it, Terry."

"But this could really be some serious shit. And I just think it'd be better to—"

"Terry? I got it."

Terry closed his mouth. I chewed on mine for something to do while I thought.

"Let me see that spreadsheet again," I said. I scanned it. "Where's Cal's name? I see Parker, Mike, Hunter, Tim, and Aaron, but where's Cal?"

Terry looked over the document. "He must be sitting this one out."

"Yeah, but why?"

———

At least I'm not a whore. That's all I could think about while I sat on the couch watching my dad read.

"You're home late. Work go that long?" he asked, not looking up from his *Reader's Digest*.

"This couple would not leave," I said. There was no way I was telling Dad I went to a 36-year-old man's house to discover the details of a fantasy slut league.

He nodded, preoccupied.

Suddenly I wanted to talk to my dad. Not about

anything in particular. I really just wanted him to make me laugh. I needed a distraction from all the information I recently learned.

"What was it like growing up in the Northeast?" I asked.

Dad glanced over his magazine. "Really?"

I nodded.

"Cold."

I cocked my head at him and raised my eyebrows.

"Not friendly," he offered.

"Do better," I said.

Dad drew in his breath. "Why are you interested in this all of a sudden? Isn't there a show on TV you watch at this time?"

"Dad, it's midnight."

"Exactly. Shouldn't you be in bed?"

"Shouldn't *you* be in bed? You're the old person here."

"Cute."

I winked at him. He winked back. It was our thing. I remembered doing it ever since he taught me how to wink when I was four. I didn't realize how much I missed it when we lived apart.

"Just tell me," I said.

"All right. I lived in a row home. You know what that is?"

"Those houses that are joined together like townhomes?"

"Yep. Space up north is hard to come by unless you've got a lot of money. Most of the houses are smashed together."

"So no back yard?" I asked.

"Um, a little one. About the size of this living room," Dad replied.

I looked around. "That's sad."

"It was what it was."

"Why wasn't it friendly?"

"I'm sure it was friendly," Dad said. "Just different compared to Raleigh."

I was about to comment when I heard a light knock on the front door.

"Stay right here," Dad ordered as he jumped up from his chair. He grabbed the loaded Colt .45 tucked in the drawer of an end table. I heard him cock it.

"I'm sure it's just—"

"Quiet, Brooklyn."

I obeyed. Whenever my dad got like this, I listened to him. Not listening proved disastrous. I learned from past experience.

Dad peered out of the peephole and sighed. He turned in my direction.

"You know some boy with a skateboard?"

I jumped up and ran to the door. "Yes!"

"What the hell? It's midnight, Brooke."

"On a Friday," I argued.

Dad grunted and returned to his chair.

"Seriously, Dad? You're gonna sit there when I open the door?"

"You bet I am. With my gun right here in my lap, too."

I rolled my eyes and opened the door.

Ryan stood in the doorway staring at me. I could think of nothing to say, so I just stared back. He finally broke the silence.

"I'm really sorry," he said. "For showing up here late and for the other day . . ."

"Let's talk outside," I said.

"It's midnight, Brooke," my father called from the living room.

Oh my God.

"Maybe I should meet your friend first before you go chat outside?" he said.

I had a feeling I knew what was about to happen, but I had no choice.

"Will you come in for a minute?" I asked, and Ryan nodded.

"This is my dad, Mr. Wright," I said.

I watched my father stand up, the gun nestled in his left hand pointing down while he extended his right. Ryan took it and shook it with what looked like trepidation mixed with a desperate attempt at confidence.

"Nice to meet you, son," Dad said. "Now what the hell are you doing knocking on my door at midnight?" He looked at his wristwatch after releasing Ryan's hand. "Correction. Twelve-thirty."

"I'm really sorry, sir," Ryan said. "Completely inappropriate, I know."

"You got that right. Were you thinking I was out of town or something? Did Brooklyn tell you I travel for work sometimes? Were you hoping to get her alone in my house?"

Oh. My. God.

"No sir!" Ryan said. "No no, I knew you were here! I saw you in the window."

"So you're spying on us now?" Dad tapped the gun on the side of his thigh.

"No, Mr. Wright! I was riding my skateboard down the street—"

"At 12:30 in the morning? Are you some kind of hoodlum? What's your number, son? Who are your parents?"

"DAD!" I cried.

My father turned in my direction. There was a hint of humor playing in his eyes and on his lips. I doubted Ryan could see it, but I could because I knew my dad. And I wanted to strangle him.

Dad turned his attention once again to Ryan. "What are your intentions with my daughter?"

I rolled my eyes.

"To talk with her outside for a few minutes?" Ryan offered.

"On the front porch. You leave that porch and I'll come find you. Do you understand what I mean, Ryan?" Dad sank back down in his club chair and rested the gun on his lap.

"Yes, sir."

I forgot all about feeling uncomfortable near Ryan for our past make-out session. I grabbed his hand like we were old friends and yanked him outside, all but slamming the front door in frustration and total humiliation.

"Oh my God," I said. "I'm mortified. I'm so sorry. My dad is just—"

Ryan's face broke out in a wide grin.

"What?" I asked.

"Your dad is awesome," he said.

I was completely confused. Awesome? My dad was a nutcase and an embarrassment.

I didn't know what to say.

"That's how a father's supposed to take care of his daughter," he said after a moment. "I hope I take care of my daughter that way."

I didn't get it. I didn't get Ryan. But he was just as sexy as I remembered him from school earlier today, and now he was standing on my front porch apparently wanting to make things right between us.

"I'm sorry," I said. "For everything. I didn't mean to make you feel embarrassed for going so long without making out. Like it's a big damn deal making out."

"It is a big damn deal," he said. "With the right person."

I shuffled my feet. "Well, I know. But I didn't mean to act so shocked about it. It's just that you're so cute." I blushed, but it was dark outside, so I knew he wouldn't see. In fact, it was easy for me to be honest with him out here on the porch in the early morning hours because it was dark. Like a confessional. I could say everything on my heart, I thought, and not be ashamed.

"Well, I don't know about cute, but there are reasons I've abstained, if you will."

God, I just loved hearing him talk. What guy says, "If you will"? He sounded so intelligent, and I wanted to pounce on him. And here we go again. Was there no end to my out-of-control sexual desire for this guy? Hello, Brooklyn? Your father is right inside.

"I'm sorry I acted like a jerk," Ryan said. "I shouldn't have done that. I didn't even have any place to go. I was just embarrassed. I thought I kissed you all wrong." He hung his head.

"Are you kidding me?" I asked. "I nearly came."

I am the biggest moron on the planet. Why did I say that?

"I mean, I didn't almost come. I . . . I don't know why I said that. Oh my God. I'm so embarrassed. I'm not like that. I've never come in my life. I mean, I'm a good girl." I had no idea what I was blabbing about. "I just think you're a really special guy." *Brooke, turn around and go back inside.* "I just meant that it was really nice," I ended lamely.

"You've never come before in your life?" Ryan asked softly. "That's a shame."

The heat washed over me in an angry tidal wave. It was embarrassment and lust and giddiness crashing down all at once. I wanted to drown in it.

"Well, I don't know," I said just as softly. I didn't even know what that meant. Of course I'd had orgasms in the past, but I realized none of them counted because they weren't with Ryan. And then I remembered my dad was inside, and we were talking about orgasms.

"I think it's late," I said. "And I think I'm tired from today. School. Work." *Spying on the swim team.*

Ryan nodded. "May I see you tomorrow?"

"You mean later today?" I asked.

Ryan nodded patiently.

"I have to work the lunch shift at the diner," I said.

"May I come in for lunch?"

I grinned. "Yes."

"All right then, Brooklyn," Ryan said, and I liked it. I didn't like when Cal called me "Brooklyn" because he did it to keep a certain distance. And just to be an asshole. But Ryan wasn't trying to keep me at a distance at all. He said my full first name, and it instantly drew me closer to him.

"See ya," I said, watching him walk into the blackness of the morning.

ELEVEN

I had no business getting all dolled up for Ryan. I was supposed to be focused on Cal, but somehow he became just some guy in the background, out of focus and unimportant in my life. I thought I heard Beth screaming from a far off place, asking me what the hell I was doing, but I ignored her. She couldn't control my life. I'd get to Cal when I got to him. She had to understand that.

I studied myself in the full-length mirror. I'd never looked prettier for work. I thought I looked like a Barbie doll, my hair pulled up high on my head in a ponytail, locks curled and tumbling in flirty waves from the elastic band. I pumped up the eye factor with heavy mascara. I wanted to go for an Edie Sedgwick look—all '60s glam. I even ironed my uniform, a typical diner waitress outfit. Blue shirtdress that hit just above my knees. I slipped on my Keds and grabbed my apron.

I planned to knock his socks off.

Ryan showed up at one. I assumed it was to beat the lunch rush, but he came in the midst of it. The hostess tried to seat him at the bar. He was alone, after all, and she didn't want to waste a table on him. Normally we waitresses appreciated this. Bigger party meant larger bill which hopefully meant fat tip. It didn't always work out that way. There were your typical cheap ass patrons always looking to find something wrong with the service or meal, thus justifying a poor tip or no tip at all.

I especially loved the ones who ran me to death and then stiffed me. They usually had me going to the kitchen at least ten times throughout the course of their meals needing a refill when their drinks were three-quarters of the way full. Needing dipping sauces when their meals didn't come with them. Needing a fresh salad because they found one wilted lettuce leaf. And if I didn't hover over them, they'd complain of being forgotten, and so would undoubtedly "forget" to leave a tip.

"I've got an open table," I told Kimberly, watching Ryan hover about the bar area. "Just put him with me."

"But yours is a four top," she argued.

"It doesn't matter," I said.

"It does matter. I've got to seat a family with you. They can't sit at the bar."

"Kimberly," I said patiently. "Seat him with me. Now."

"Whatever. It's your tip," she said, and showed Ryan to my table.

I approached him after counting to twenty. I didn't want to seem too eager.

"Hi," I said. I felt bright and bubbly and on top of the world.

"Hello."

I placed my hand on my hip and popped it out. "Come here often?" I couldn't resist.

"Once. The waitress was cute, but she's got nothing on you," Ryan said.

Damn right she doesn't. I went Edie Sedgwick for you, buddy.

"God, you look gorgeous," he said.

Oh, those heart flutters. I wanted to feel those heart flutters forever.

"I'm in an ugly uniform," I said, looking down at my outfit. I smoothed my apron on my stomach.

"Not ugly at all. Sexy more like."

I blushed, and this time he saw. I couldn't conceal it under the glare of the restaurant lights.

"Hungry?" I asked, and pulled out my order pad.

"What would you recommend?"

"Honestly? I've only eaten the turkey sandwich. It was all right," I confessed.

"Don't you get to eat for free?" Ryan asked.

"Are you kidding? A little bit of a discount, sure, but nothing for free," I said. "And anyway, I'm so tired after work, I don't want to stick around and eat. I want to go home."

"I can understand that," he said. He looked over the menu. "Well, I guess I'll try this steak sandwich."

"A man who eats manly meat," I said. "I like it."

"Manly meat, huh?" he asked, chuckling.

"Sure. Didn't you know steak was the manliest of meats?"

"Making a note of it," Ryan said.

I nodded. "And to drink?"

"A Cherry Coke," he said.

"Now that's a little girly, but I'll let it slide."

"Well, I really ordered it for you," Ryan said. "See, I thought you could bring it over here along with two straws. You could sit across from me, and we could drink it together."

It was decided. I was going to let Ryan Foster do me. I had no idea when it would happen, but it was inevitable. If he kept being this cute, it was inevitable.

"I can't take Cherry Coke breaks in the middle of my shift," I said.

"Too bad," Ryan replied. "Just give me a regular Coke then."

I nodded and walked away, glimpsing four boys filing

in. Cal. Parker. Someone. And another someone.

I sighed deeply. Life was so unfair sometimes. Why couldn't I flirt with Ryan in public without being interrupted? And then I realized that a table in my section just opened up. And it was a four top. No no no. I watched helplessly as Kimberly led the four boys to my section, seating them at a table a few feet away from Ryan.

I could feel the instant sweat break out underneath my arms. It wasn't so much Cal anymore who made me nervous, though he should have. Parker was really the person who made me uneasy. He didn't like me; that was evident. And I didn't know what he planned to do about it. One part of me thought he had no plans at all, but he didn't strike me as that kind of guy. He struck me as the calculating, vengeful guy who always paid back his enemies. I inadvertently became an enemy when I ran into him in the hallway. He knew I overheard his conversation in the stairwell. I was convinced of it. And then I landed right on the top of his hit list when I tore Gretchen away from his greedy claws at Tanner's party.

As I poured Ryan's Coke, I surreptitiously watched the four boys, feeling my anger rise, that righteous anger I had not felt in weeks. I think I heard Beth sigh relief. I took a deep breath, trying to steady my nerves, before bringing Ryan his Coke.

Ryan's demeanor completely changed. He was no longer openly flirty, avoiding my eyes as he said "thank you" when I placed his Coke in front of him. I was fine with that. I didn't want Cal seeing us flirt anyway. It was foolish on my part: pursuing a guy who was off limits. I entertained the idea of being secret friends with Ryan, and then scolded myself for being so shallow and selfish. I didn't want to be secret friends. I wanted to be open friends, but it would ruin everything. Could Beth forgive me if I chose to move on instead of getting revenge?

I reluctantly walked over to the four top.

"Hi, guys," I said.

"Hey, Brooke," Cal said. He looked happy. I think it was because I had to serve him.

The other boys mumbled "hellos."

"Decided?" I asked, readying my pen.

"You have to write down orders?" Parker asked. "You can't just remember them? It's not hard. There are only four of us."

I considered what would be the appropriate response, but there wasn't one. So I just repeated my question.

"Decided?"

Parker snorted and asked for Evian water.

"We don't have Evian water," I said. "We have tap water."

"Pepsi then," he said.

"Nope. Coke here," I replied.

"We're in North Carolina. Pepsi country," he argued.

"There's a Bojangles right down the road."

Parker called me a bitch with his eyes, but I stood stoic, refusing to give him the reaction he wanted. I wondered why Cal wasn't saying anything. It was obvious, the open hostility between Parker and me. I felt like this lunch was one big test. I wasn't sure if I was passing, and more alarmingly, I didn't know why I cared.

"Whatever. Give me a Sprite," Parker said. "And this turkey sandwich."

"You got it." *Asshole.*

"And for you boys?"

"Same as Parker," one of them said. Hanger-on. How pathetic.

"Coke and a burger," the other said.

"How would you like that cooked?" I asked.

"Uh, whatever," he replied.

There was nothing more infuriating and unattractive than a guy with no confidence. Who doesn't know how he likes his burger cooked? Get a freaking backbone.

"Medium okay? Slightly pink center?" I asked.

"Gross."

"Okay. Well done then?" I asked. I made a mental note to tell Terry to cook it until it was rubber.

"Yeah."

"And for you?" I asked, turning to Cal.

"Saved the best for last," he said, pulling on the hem of my dress.

I nearly vomited in my mouth, but I forced a grin instead. *Remember, Brooke. Playful. Sweet. Good girl.*

"Exactly," I said, never taking my eyes off Cal.

"I'll have a burger, medium-rare," he said glancing at his friend with contempt. "And a Coke."

"Sounds good," I said, placing my unused pen behind my ear.

I walked into the kitchen to use the computer. I didn't want to use the one out on the floor. I needed to get away from those boys, separate myself by a door, and one they weren't allowed to walk through.

I stood at the computer punching and banging away, mumbling under my breath.

"Wright! Take it easy on that screen! You wanna break it?" Terry yelled from behind the grill.

"Leave me alone," I snapped.

"Don't get pissy with me or your customers will be waiting a looong time for their food," Terry said.

God, I hated working at a restaurant. Servers were at the mercy of everyone: the hostesses who decided what patrons were seated in their sections. The patrons themselves who blamed everything on the server even if those things were out of the server's control. The kitchen staff who decided how fast and how well the meals were prepared.

I stomped over to Terry. "Make sure you cook the hell out of my well-done burger," I said.

"Problem?" Terry asked.

"He's just a little toadie," I said.

Terry laughed. "Toadie?"

"Yeah. You know. Toadie. Part of the gang. Not the leader. Could never be the leader because he's a little bitch," I explained. "Toadie."

"Gotcha."

"And spit in everyone else's food," I said.

"I'll do my best," Terry replied. "Your steak sandwich is up."

I grabbed Ryan's lunch along with the boys' drinks, and headed out the kitchen door.

I delivered the drinks first. I said nothing as the boys chatted, ignoring me. The memory of Game 3 popped into my head. I was on the list. Who would choose me, if anyone?

Terry and I had found another document of Game 2 picks. There were more girls listed than actually made the cut. I guess the boys liked to keep their options open. I thought how lucky those girls were who didn't get picked. The ones who did? Well, I decided I needed to talk to some of them.

"How's it look?" I asked Ryan, placing his sandwich in front of him.

"Good," he replied. "Thank you." He looked at me then, and he smiled.

Well, this was completely different from a few minutes ago. A few minutes ago he acted like I was a total stranger. Why the change?

I couldn't help it. I had to turn around. I caught sight of Cal glaring at Ryan. Why all the hostility? Why was Cal out to get this guy? Ryan never talked to anyone at school. He was quiet. He stayed out of the way. What was the big deal?

I turned back to Ryan. He was staring at Cal. And then his lips curled into a sly grin like he was passing a secret message to a mortal enemy. It said, "Go ahead and try to keep me away from her, motherfucker. I'm not going anywhere." And here I thought Cal had Ryan under his thumb. Maybe in the past, but it looked like Ryan was deciding to fight back. I felt a warm liquid ooze through my arms and legs at the realization that he was choosing to fight for me.

I bent down and whispered in Ryan's ear. "Would you like ketchup with your fries?"

I heard a rumble deep in his throat. "No."

"Would you like anything else?" I asked, lips all but pressed to his ear.

"Yes," he said, and I understood perfectly.

I stood up, and Ryan caught my arm.

"Brooke?"

"Hmm?"

"Will you do me a favor?"

"Sure."

"Don't hang around him," Ryan said.

I tensed immediately. "Hang around who?"

"Cal. Those guys. Don't hang around them. They're trouble," Ryan explained.

"How do you know?" I felt the rapid increase of my heart rate. What did Ryan know about Cal?

"I've gone to school with him since ninth grade, Brooke," Ryan said. "I know he's an asshole. A bully."

I nodded.

"Please just listen to me when I say that you need to stay away from him. I mean, I know you two work on yearbook stuff together. I know you can't avoid him altogether. But please stay away from him as much as you can," he said.

"Do you know something about him you're not telling me?" I asked.

Ryan paused for the briefest second then shook his head. "I'm jealous for you."

My heart skipped a beat then settled into an uneven rhythm. I begged him silently to say those words again, and he read my mind.

"I'm jealous for you, and he's an asshole."

"Okay," I replied, grinning.

When I brought the boys their lunch, I made sure to serve them in my best I-love-being-a-waitress-and-working-at-a-diner impersonation. Everyone looked satisfied except for Cal, who was seething at Ryan's defiance. I decided to fan the flame. How much did Cal really want me?

"Cal, is everything okay?" I asked. It was super sweet and disgusting all rolled into one.

Cal nodded. "What are you doing tonight?"

That caught me off guard. "Well, I . . . um . . ."

"Wanna go to the movies?" Cal asked.

Okay. Yes, I thought that Cal liked me a little. I think he saw me as one big conquest that would be harder than his others, and he liked the challenge. I didn't fawn all over him like most girls. I think he saw it as part of my charm. It wasn't strategy on my part. Truthfully, I just kept getting distracted. And that was mostly Ryan's fault. I thought I should ask my dad about getting tested for ADD though I knew he didn't believe such disorders existed. This guy was ridiculous, though. The second he feared competition, he was ready to date me.

"I have plans, actually," I said. No, I wasn't forfeiting a golden opportunity. I was taking one instead. I wouldn't pass up the chance to spend an evening with Ryan. And I knew that if Cal suspected Ryan and I had plans, he would blow a gasket. Was I using Ryan? Absolutely not, but I couldn't deny the advantage our date would give me over Cal. I thought in that deluded moment I could have both boys: Ryan, the boy I saw myself truly falling in love with, and Cal, the boy who would use me and then regret it.

"What plans?" Cal asked, glancing at Ryan.

"Just plans," I said. "But maybe next weekend."

Cal grunted.

Parker piped up. "Well, everything seems to be right." His tone held a note of confusion mixed with surprise as thought he expected I'd mess up the orders. I smiled sweetly.

"And I didn't even have to write them down," I said, then turned my back on them and walked away.

—

"I feel shallow," I admitted, not looking at him. I was sitting on Ryan's bed that afternoon after work.

"Why?"

"Because I'm so drawn to you and I really don't know anything about you. Is it just your looks?" I asked.

"Is it?"

I shook my head. "No, I don't think so. I think there's a lot more, but you're not telling me."

Ryan rubbed his jaw. "I'm a Big Brother," he offered after a moment.

"I know that. I've met Kaylen."

"No," he laughed. "For the Boys and Girls Club."

"Ohhh. They take people that young?" I asked.

"Well, not usually, but I was pretty insistent. That, and I had a few strings pulled."

"Why?" I asked.

He shook his head and grinned. "Because I'm trying to be a better person, Brooke."

So was I. I almost said it out loud, but I didn't want him to ask me how or why I was trying to be better.

"What? You've got sins to atone for?" I asked lightly.

"Doesn't everyone?"

"Most people just pray," I said. "Doesn't take as much effort as volunteer work."

Ryan chuckled at my irreverence. "Praying only goes

so far, I think," and I chuckled at his.

"So tell me about your Little Brother," I said and patted the bed, inviting him to join me.

"His name's Chester," Ryan replied, sitting down.

"Okay. That's not a name," I said.

Ryan laughed. "Well, for this kid it is."

I nodded, wanting him to continue.

"He'd be considered your typical white trash kid. Ten years old. So-so home life. I tutor him a lot and take him for pizza. He loves pizza. He wants to join the Marines when he grows up, and I asked him why the Marines and not some other branch of the military."

"And?"

"His father was a Marine," Ryan said. "He died a few years back."

"Oh."

"He's a pretty good kid. I got on to him, though, when I found out he got in a fight at school."

"You sound like you really enjoy doing this," I said.

"I do. I mean, it can get exhausting, and sometimes I don't wanna hang out, but I'm so glad when I do because he seems genuinely happy to see me. His favorite is kicking around the soccer ball. He wants to play in middle school," Ryan said.

"You play soccer?"

"Used to. Tore up my leg pretty badly last year, so I quit. The doctors said I was okay to play, but I didn't want to risk damaging it more."

"Don't trust doctors?"

"Don't trust anyone, really," he said.

"Do you trust me?" I asked.

"I don't know you," he said.

"I know." My face fell, and I thought it was a stupid reaction. Of course he didn't know me. Did I expect him to trust a person he didn't know?

Yes.

"But yes. I do. I don't know why but I do trust you," Ryan said.

My face lit up. I could feel it, and suddenly I didn't want to talk anymore. I didn't think Ryan wanted to either. I wanted to feel his mouth on mine, and I wanted to let him kiss me for as long as he liked.

I wrapped my arms around his shoulders and buried my face in his neck. It was unexpected. I had every intention of going for his lips, but a sudden urge to hug him overpowered my desire for a kiss.

I inhaled his scent, that deep masculine smell of soap mixed with . . . something. His essence, perhaps. I breathed it in like oxygen, a faint sweetness that made me want to lick him. That shocked me. I wanted to lick his neck. I couldn't stop myself. I slipped my tongue out ever so slightly—just the tip—and tasted him.

I drew back and looked at him, embarrassed. "I don't know why I did that."

"Did what?" he asked. "Hug me?"

"No, the other thing."

"What other thing?"

I was confused. "You didn't feel it?"

"Feel what?"

"Nothing," I said quickly.

"Oh, no you don't," Ryan said. "What are you talking about?"

I blushed and looked down at my lap. "I kind of licked your neck."

"You kind of licked my neck?" Ryan asked, grinning.

"Does that make me weird?" I said.

"Not in the least," and he leaned over, burying his face in my neck, and ran his tongue slowly all the way from the base to right behind my earlobe.

I squealed.

"Good squeal or bad squeal?" he asked, mouth pressed against my ear.

"Good squeal." I don't even know how I got out the words. I was out of breath from shock.

Ryan pulled away and looked at me. "I think we need to—"

Anything! I screamed inside. *I'll do anything you want!*

"—play some video games," he said.

Excuse me?

My face must have said it all because Ryan burst out laughing.

"Not a gamer?" he asked.

"I don't even know how to hold the controller," I replied. *Just make out with me!*

"I'll teach you," he offered, and jumped up from the bed to turn on his TV and Playstation.

I didn't know what he was up to. I felt the sexual energy coursing through him when his tongue made contact with my neck. I'm not sure why he was trying to fight it, if that's what he was doing. What was so wrong with kissing, anyway? We'd already done it.

"Come here," Ryan said, and I slunk off the bed half-heartedly to sit next to him on the floor. "No, not there. Here," he said, pointing to the space between his legs.

Oh, so *that's* what he was up to.

I nestled between his legs, leaning against his chest as he leaned against the foot of his bed. He gave me the controller, then placed his hands over mine so I was trapped in what I later told Gretchen was the Gamers Embrace. He walked me through each button and how and when to use them. Then he asked me if I was interested in killing some bad guys.

"I have a feeling I'm gonna be really bad at this," I said, feeling my heartbeat increase. It was ridiculous, but I was nervous, and not because I was sitting in such an intimate position with Ryan. I was scared of the freaking game.

"You'll do just fine," he said, and pressed the X on

the controller. The game started, and I squealed.

"You like to squeal," Ryan observed, watching me die in the first few seconds.

"What is this game?"

"Oh, Brooke. You're such a girl," Ryan said, and I instantly thought of Terry saying those same words when he described Fantasy Football for me. I squirmed. "This is *Call of Duty*. Freaking amazing game."

"It's scary," I said. "I don't think—"

"You're doing just fine," Ryan reassured me.

I didn't think I was doing "just fine" at all. I think I sucked. Big time. How could a painter have no hand-eye coordination? I think at one point I made my guy walk on the ceiling.

I laughed when I died again. But I had to admit that I was starting to get hooked. It didn't even take that long. Yes, I was still afraid of the bad guys. I didn't like rounding corners, but each time I died, I was determined to try again. And I started getting better with the controller. Suddenly it became an extension of my hands, just like my paintbrush.

"That's right, bitch!" I yelled when I killed my first enemy.

Ryan laughed. I hadn't noticed his hands on the tops of my thighs when we started, but I definitely noticed them when they spread my legs apart ever so slightly. Did I mention I was still in my work uniform?

I put down the controller immediately, and died in two seconds.

"What did you do that for?" Ryan asked into my neck. He rained sweet little pecks all over my goose-rippled flesh.

"I can't concentrate," I breathed, closing my eyes.

He took his mouth away, and I wanted to scream at him to kiss me again.

"Pick up the controller, Brooke," he said. "And play

your game." *Meanwhile, I'm going to play mine*, is what I'm sure I heard underneath his words.

I did as I was told, but my heart was no longer in it. I didn't care about killing bad guys when I felt Ryan's hands glide up and down my thighs, pushing my dress around my hips. I knew he could see my panties, but for some reason I didn't think I should say it. I thought I had only one task he'd given me, and that was to continue playing my game.

I drew in my breath sharply when I felt his fingers snake around my right thigh and between my legs. He ran them lightly over my panties, all the while watching the television screen. I knew he was watching it because he gave me some advice and a few warnings of enemies hidden in dark places.

When he slipped his fingers under the fabric of my panties, I died. Shot up in a hailstorm of gun fire. My guy didn't have a chance.

"Try again," Ryan cooed in my ear. He stroked me gently, refraining from slipping his finger inside of me.

"I don't want to," I whined softly.

"Brooklyn, try again," he ordered, and I pressed the X on the controller.

I tried to concentrate. I thought that's what he wanted me to do, to see how long I could go before losing myself completely to his touch. We were playing two games, competing against one another, and I knew I'd lose.

I cried out when he slipped a finger inside me, lasting only five more seconds until I was blown to bits.

"I'm really bad at this," I said. I didn't recognize my voice. It was deep and sultry.

"No you aren't," Ryan whispered, stroking me deeply until I moaned and let my head fall back on his shoulder. "No, Brooklyn. Pick up the controller and try again."

"Ryan!" I was beyond frustrated, and I screamed that

frustration when he took his hand away.

"Play your game, Brooklyn," he insisted, shifting behind me. Only then did I notice his hard-on. I shivered with anticipation.

I reluctantly started another game, and almost immediately, Ryan's hand was in between my legs once more, touching, exploring, probing. I was aching for release, and he knew it. The longer he played with my body, the worse I got at the stupid video game. I felt the pleasure swirl around the insides of my thighs and my stomach. I knew it was coming. But I also knew I would hover on the edge of my orgasm indefinitely if I didn't concentrate on Ryan's touch. My brain couldn't stay split in two between his hand and my game.

The explosion was nearly there, so I focused on what was happening between my legs instead of the TV screen. When he finally released me, I screamed something between pleasure and agony, my finger permanently pressed on the button that made my guy fire incessant shots until his ammo ran out and he surrendered to the enemy.

I lay back against Ryan's chest, my head heavy on his shoulder. I was sweating and shaking from the aftermath. I'd never come like that. I didn't know what to say. I wasn't sure how I sounded when he brought me over the edge, and suddenly I felt self-conscious.

"You are the most beautiful thing I've ever seen," Ryan said. He lifted his fingers to his mouth, and while I couldn't see him, I knew he was tasting me. My self-consciousness multiplied tenfold. Did he like it?

"I'm embarrassed," I admitted.

"Why?"

"Because I think I sounded crazy," I said.

"No. Not crazy. Perfect." He planted a gentle kiss on my cheek. "And you taste delicious, by the way. Scrumptious, really."

And just like that, my self-consciousness disappeared. I sat up and turned around, pulling my legs up under me. "Scrumptious, you say?"

Ryan nodded, his blue eyes soft and glassy. Content.

"I think I like playing video games," I said.

"Oh, you do, huh?" he asked.

I nodded, looking down at his lap then back up at his face.

"I think you should play this next round," I suggested. My hands went to his belt buckle.

He shook his head. I furrowed my brows, confused.

"You're new at video games, Brooke," Ryan said. "Let's just take it little by little."

I thought for a moment.

"Yeah, but doesn't practice make perfect?" I asked.

"In small doses."

TWELVE

"Holy shit!" Gretchen screamed into the phone.

I grinned, lying on my bed in a dreamy state, staring at the ceiling. My popcorn ceiling, and I thought it was the most beautiful ceiling in the world.

"Brooke, why on earth didn't you guys have sex?" she asked.

"He said we weren't ready," I replied, the silly smile still plastered on my face.

"What? Does he think you're a virgin or something?"

"I don't know. I don't care," I replied. I had been in a continuous euphoric state since yesterday afternoon. My dad noticed last night over dinner, and asked me if I was dating Ryan.

"How do you know I like him?" I had asked.

"It's painfully obvious, Brooke," Dad replied. "You think I'm an idiot?"

I grinned. "Are you okay with it if I do date him? I mean, we haven't established anything yet."

"Yes," Dad replied, and that word heightened my ecstasy.

I listened as Gretchen peppered me with questions.

"Are you two dating?" she asked.

"No."

"Will you?"

"I hope."

"When can I meet him?"

"Soon."

"Was he better than Finn?"

Silence.

"Oh God, Brooke. I'm sorry," Gretchen said. "That was a really stupid thing to say."

My euphoria started fizzling, and I was pissed.

"Brookey?" Gretchen asked tentatively.

"He's nothing like Finn," I said.

"I know. I shouldn't have asked that. It just slipped out. You know how I don't think sometimes."

I grunted and sat up in bed.

"Are you totally pissed?" Gretchen asked.

"No."

Gretchen didn't believe me. I could tell by her next statement.

"You wanna just talk later?" she asked. I could tell she was itching to get off the phone.

"Yes," I replied, and hung up before we exchanged goodbyes.

I tossed the phone aside and scratched my head.

I was just fine a minute ago. Actually I was ecstatic at the prospect of someone new. Someone who could make me deliriously happy. I actually convinced myself for a second that I deserved to be happy. I don't know why. I'm not sure I'd done anything to earn it, and Gretchen reminded me with the mention of Finn's name. Now the memories came flooding back. Our secret trysts. Beth's obliviousness. Her rape. I could not escape it. Why didn't I just go to that party with her?

My biggest fear lay in the possibility that I would never be able to let go of my guilt, that it would twist and turn me into something wretched. Mom always taught me to never find my happiness or self-worth in another individual, and I tried hard to adhere to that advice, but I couldn't deny how I felt when I was around Ryan. He was a savior to me. When I was with him, all of the hurt and guilt vanished. I thought he had the ability to put my brokenness back together. Maybe that wasn't progressive. Maybe that wasn't all "liberated woman," but I didn't give a shit. I wanted to spend my every waking moment with him because when I was with him, I felt safe.

But the warrior in me who was resolute in her commitment to Beth kept warring with the girl in me who wanted to hide behind Ryan. I recognized that both girls couldn't win out in the end. Still, while I didn't know how I'd make it work, I was determined to have both. To *be* both. I was greedy and selfish, and in my petulant state I thought that Beth would just have to get the hell over it.

—

"You're out," Terry said after work. I was hanging around while he cleaned the grills because he told me he had news.

"What do you mean?" I asked.

"Out. Off the list. Cut."

I knew there was a huge problem with my psyche that I was actually mad about it. *Mad* about it.

"Why?" I asked.

"I don't know. But I wouldn't take it personally," Terry replied. "I'm sure it's got nothing to do with the way you look."

I scowled at him, and he grimaced.

"Yikes. Keep making faces like that and maybe it *does* have something to do with your looks."

I punched his arm.

"Ow!"

"Is Cal scheduled to play yet?" I asked.

"No."

"Well, maybe that's why," I said, mostly to myself.

"What are you talking about?" Terry asked.

"I think he likes me," I said. "Maybe he didn't want me to be chosen for someone else's team after all. Maybe in the beginning he didn't care. And now? Well, it's obvious he does."

Terry eyed me sternly. "You better be careful."

"I'm being careful," I said, pulling my tip money out of my apron and organizing the bills.

"Figured out what you're gonna do with all this information I'm giving you?" Terry asked.

"Yes. I plan on talking to some of these girls," I said.

"And what makes you think they'll tell you anything?" Terry asked.

"Well, I don't know that they will. But I have to try," I said.

The truth was that I didn't know what the hell I was doing. I thought part of my meddling was clearly due to pure fascination with the whole Fantasy Slut League. How could this be going on and no one know about it? It made no sense. And how did these boys know how to rate the girls? Someone was feeding them information, and that someone had to be a girl. It's not as though girls are going to admit their level of sexual activity to another guy. But they would talk with another girl about it. Who was this girl? And why would she participate in something so licentious?

"You gonna give me some of that tip money as payment?" Terry asked.

I looked at him shocked. And then it turned to embarrassment. I felt it on my cheeks, burning red like Christmas tree lights.

"I'm just kidding, Wright! Jesus, calm down," he said.

"Do you want me to pay you?" I asked. I hadn't

thought about it until now. I didn't know if Terry did jobs for other people, but I'm sure if he did, he got paid for them.

"You're a waitress, Wright," Terry said. "So no."

I rolled my eyes.

"And anyway, it wouldn't feel right taking money from you," he said. "Not over this."

I nodded. "Hey, did you bring the Game 1 printout for me?"

Terry reached into his back pocket and pulled out a folded sheet of paper. "What are you planning to do with this?"

"I'll let you know when I figure it out."

That night I sat on my bed cross-referencing names of girls with their pictures in last year's yearbook. I found two girls I immediately wanted to talk to. They both scored points for going all the way, and they were labeled "Good Girls." I basically wanted to find out if the sex was consensual. It wouldn't eliminate Hunter and Tim completely as possible rape suspects, but I thought it was a start. I'd have to get Terry to dig around and find older games to be sure.

Melissa and Tara. They were both juniors this year. It would be difficult to find a reason to talk to them, and even then, I couldn't come right out and ask if they'd had consensual sex with Hunter and Tim. I had to find a way to extract the information gingerly, and I wasn't the best at being ginger. I thought I failed miserably with Lucy and simply got lucky that she offered information, however vague, about cheerleading and Cal.

God must have been smiling on me the following day at school because I spotted Melissa walking down the hallway towards me. I had no plan. I tried to devise one the previous night but could think of nothing. The closer she came, the more I freaked out until I made a split-second decision and started running, slamming into her in a head-on collision. It didn't help that she was wearing heels, and she toppled backwards, landing on the floor with a loud *thunk* before I could grab her. Her head hit the hard tiles and she moaned. God, I actually hurt her. Badly. I scrambled to help her up.

"Oh my God! I'm so sorry!" And it wasn't a fake apology. I meant it. "Let me help you."

"I'm dizzy," she mumbled, reaching vainly for her book bag a few feet away.

"I'll totally get your stuff. Just let me help you up. I think I need to take you to the nurse," I said.

She nodded dumbly and allowed me to pull her into a sitting position. She rubbed the back of her head and looked at me strangely.

"I'm dizzy," she repeated, as though she were saying it for the first time.

Oh my God. If I gave this girl a concussion, I'd never forgive myself. I pulled her to her feet and let her lean on me as we made our way to the nurse.

The nurse forced me to wait outside for Melissa, which really pissed me off. I actually wanted to sit with her and hold her hand because I felt so horrible.

I had no idea how long I sat in the hallway before Melissa emerged looking better, if noticeably bruised. I couldn't see the actual bruise on her head but it was in her mannerisms. She still wasn't quite right. She seemed sedated, slightly out of focus, and when I apologized to her again, she looked at me as if wondering, *Who are you?*

"Melissa, I owe you big time. Lemme do something for you to make it up to you. I feel horrible for running into you," I said.

"How do you know my name?" she asked, walking with me down the hallway.

"Uh . . . doesn't everyone?" I asked. "I mean, aren't you a cheerleader?"

"No."

Shit. That must have been Tara.

"Well, I heard it somewhere," I said.

She didn't seem to like that.

"Who are you?" she asked.

"I'm Brooke," I said. "Listen, I was just so spaced out. My mind has been going crazy lately, and I wasn't paying attention to where I was going."

"It's okay," Melissa said.

"Well, I feel awful," I went on. "I'm just in this weird place right now, you know? I've got this guy I really like, but he's putting pressure on me to do it, you know? I mean, not like you care or anything, but I've got no girlfriends to talk to about it. I'm new here, by the way, which would account for the no girlfriends thing."

I heard myself talking, like I had stepped outside my body and was watching the scene as an interested third party.

"You don't want any advice from me right now," Melissa said. "I don't think I'm all there yet."

I grunted. "Again, sorry. I don't know why I'm running my mouth to you. You're a complete stranger. I guess I'm just dying for some female advice. I mean, I'm really freaking out."

It was lame, but I was praying it'd work.

"Well, you shouldn't have sex until you're ready. If it doesn't feel right, don't do it," Melissa said, rubbing the back of her head.

I eyed her carefully. "So you've never been pressured or anything?"

"Truthfully? I've only had sex once. And I did it because I wanted to get it over and done with, and the guy seemed more than willing. Maybe not the best way to lose my virginity, but he didn't pressure me or anything. It was my decision." She laughed, then grimaced. "Actually, I think he was shocked when I told him I wanted to."

Yeah, he wasn't expecting such a killer score.

I studied Melissa's face. There was no hint of buried secrets. She didn't appear scared or hurt. I believed her, and once I made that decision, I knew in my bones it was right.

We chatted pleasantly all the way to her car.

"Are you sure you're okay to drive home?" I asked.

"The nurse gave me permission, so if anything happens, it's on her, not you," she said, grinning.

Thank God.

I waved as she pulled away, thinking that Hunter might be cleared.

—

I knew the risk I was taking by talking to Ryan at school. I knew I could lose Cal forever and never see my plan materialize, but it was a risk I was willing to take. I simply couldn't stay away from Ryan. My body couldn't. My mind couldn't. He wanted me, that much was evident, but it was the way he slowed me down, the way he forced me to take a breath that hooked me. He didn't want to rush into anything, a concept foreign to me. I never had that with Finn. We had sex almost immediately when we started sneaking around. That was really the whole point of our sneaking around. I realized I didn't want to jump into sex with Ryan. I thought initially I did because of my over-the-top physical attraction, but I found it was a whole lot sexier to wait. And to burn with it.

I sidled over to Ryan's desk Friday.

"Why haven't you said 'hello' all week?" I asked, pouting.

He grinned. "I thought I'd play hard to get."

"So all those secret smiles and flirty winks were just a game?" I asked.

"I gave you flirty winks?"

"A ton," I replied.

He licked his lips. "It wasn't a game. And I was going to cave today anyway. You beat me to the punch, though."

"Well, lucky for you I didn't lose interest," I teased.

"Hmm. I'm not too worried about that. I have a Playstation and you don't. Sooner or later, you'd be crawling over to my house begging to play."

I burst out laughing. "You are soooo cocky."

He shook his head. "No. I'm not cocky. I just know you, Brooke. And you know me, too. It's inevitable."

"What's inevitable?" I asked, blushing.

He answered with a smile.

"That's all I get?" I asked.

Ryan sighed. "I wish we didn't have assigned seats."

"You're impossible," I huffed, and walked to my desk.

I glanced at Cal, who stared at me. I guess he watched the entire exchange. He looked confused and rejected. It was almost comical, like he simply couldn't understand how a girl would choose another guy over him. I was playing a dangerous game, and I prayed I'd come out the winner.

I smiled at Cal then took my seat. I heard a rustling behind me, and before I knew it, Cal was at my desk.

"You busy tonight?" he asked.

"I'm working," I replied.

"What about tomorrow night?"

"Um . . ."

"I thought I could take you bowling," Cal said.

"Bowling?"

"What? Not fun? We could do something else," he offered.

I glanced at Ryan. He was busy pulling books out of his bag.

"Why are you talking to him?" Cal whispered. "I

thought I told you to stay away from him."

Whoa. Alarm bells. Increased heart rate. Mild panic.

"I didn't mean it like that," Cal said quickly. "It's just, that guy's no good, Brooke. I know you're friendly and everything. You're a sweet girl, but that can also make you naïve."

Fuck you.

"I didn't mean it like that," Cal said, shaking his head. He was frustrated, knowing he was saying all the wrong things. "I meant that I would feel awful if anything happened to you."

Would you?

"I'm not trying to tell you how to live your life. You can be friends with whoever you want, but I'm just saying. Some people will only drag you down."

Lucy sat in the desk beside me, listening to Cal's words, and I wondered what she was thinking. I thought about her words: *"Stay away from him."* What would she think of me if I agreed to go on a date with him? Would that be the last straw? She'd either stop being friendly altogether or confess to me what he'd done to her as a warning. I took a chance.

"I guess we could go bowling," I said.

Cal looked surprised. "Really?"

I nodded. I was afraid Ryan might hear, but the classroom was pretty rowdy, so I doubted it.

"Pick you up tomorrow night at seven?" he asked.

I nodded again. He started towards his desk, and I grabbed his arm.

"I didn't tell you where I live," I said.

"Oh, I know where you live," he replied.

I didn't like that one bit, but I refrained from asking him how.

After Cal walked away, Lucy turned to me, a look of betrayal on her face.

"What are you doing?" she hissed.

"What do you mean?" I asked, playing dumb.

"I said to stay away from him."

"Why?"

Lucy shifted in her seat. She was irate.

"Why, Lucy?"

She ignored me when the teacher walked in.

"Why?" I persisted.

She covered her ears with her hands. *Seriously?*

I was going to make her tell me. If I had to go bowling, and go out to eat, and go to the movies, and make out with the son-of-a-bitch right in front of her, I was going to make her tell me.

—

Tara proved much more difficult to find than Melissa. For a full week I didn't see her anywhere and feared she no longer went to Charity Run. I actually attended another football game, thinking I'd spot her tumbling down the field in a cheerleading uniform. After all, she was a cheerleader last year according to the picture I saw in the yearbook. But no such luck. I didn't see her on the field and promptly left before the end of the first quarter.

I did spot her late Friday afternoon strolling the junior hall dressed in black, sporting black hair, black lips, and black Dr. Martens. Suddenly it was 1994 and I didn't get the memo. What the hell? Last year, this girl had strawberry-blond hair, wore a cheerleading uniform, and sported glossy pink lips. I immediately feared the worst. No one changes personas so drastically unless something awful happened to them. It took me a minute to remember she was on Tim's team.

How on earth would I be able to talk to her? I didn't come across as the type of girl she'd be friends with, let alone speak to. It would have to be another accident like

Melissa's, but I knew I couldn't go running my mouth about a boyfriend who's pressuring me to have sex. It just wouldn't work with her. I'd probably have to spy on her, but how? I was no detective. I wouldn't know where to start, and I wasn't even sure what I was looking for.

I surreptitiously watched her at her locker. She was alone changing out her books, and suddenly I had an idea.

I walked up to her and introduced myself.

"Hi, I'm Brooke," I said, extending my hand.

She looked at my face and then my hand and then my face again.

"I'm on the school paper, and I wanted to know if I could interview you about the cafeteria food." *So incredibly lame.*

"Are you kidding me?" she asked.

"I know. It's totally stupid, but I'm new here, so I get assigned the stupid stories," I said, chuckling.

"Just don't do it," she offered.

"Oh," I replied. "I guess I never thought about that. But then my grade would be affected."

"Who cares?"

Okay. This one wouldn't be easy at all.

"Well, I do," I said. "I want to make good grades."

She looked me up and down. "Yeah, you look like one of those."

"What do you mean?"

"You're a goody-goody." She started walking down the hall, and I followed after.

"I am?" I asked.

For a second I forgot about my mission. I was intrigued. Was I a goody-goody? Tara thought so, and she didn't know me from Adam's housecat. I couldn't help but feel a little proud. After all, I'd been working my ass off for months trying to come across that way. Maybe that's why I was given a "Good Girl" ranking by the Fantasy Slut League. They didn't have to spy on me. It

was blatantly obvious my sexual status. Virginal. Sweet.
Naïve.

I swelled like a damn peacock.

"Yeah," she snorted. "Just don't let the wrong people
know how good you are."

Cryptic. Snarky. This girl was a bitch.

"What do you mean?" I asked, but I already knew.

She stopped cold and whirled around to face me. I
nearly ran into her.

"People take advantage of good people. That's what I
mean. So don't be a sucker."

"Did someone take advantage of you?" I blurted.

"Fuck you," she spat, and headed down the hall once
more.

Well, that was settled. Someone did a number on her.
But I couldn't move Tim into the "Rapists" pile just yet.
I'd have to do more digging.

THIRTEEN

I needed a Ryan fix before my date with Cal. I felt so guilty about going, and I had a lot of nerve thinking Ryan wouldn't find out, but Cal didn't strike me as the type of guy who went around bragging about his dates. At least not in a loud, obnoxious way. Maybe he told his close friends, but I suspected that was only if he got a sexual perk out of the girls. Plus, Ryan and I hadn't established anything yet. We weren't technically dating, so I could always say that I wasn't sure what was going on between us.

Dad was working late Friday night. He called me to let me know, and as soon as I got off the phone with him, I called Ryan to invite him over. He was at my door in fifteen minutes.

"Would have been here sooner, but you caught me in the middle of homework," he said.

I grabbed the front of his jacket and pulled him into the house.

"You and homework," I said, planting my lips on his. "Such a nerd," I said against his mouth.

He wrapped his arms around me and kissed me harder. And then he pushed me against the door we'd just closed, trailing his mouth down my cheek to my neck. I cried out when I felt his teeth on my skin.

"Too much?" he asked.

I shook my head. "Wanna see my bedroom?"

"Yes," Ryan said into my neck, and when he pulled away, I took a long, satisfying gulp of air. I had to remember to breathe around him.

I took his hand and led him up the stairs. I had no intention of having sex. I was sure he'd tell me we weren't ready, and I was surprisingly content with that. I forgot how satisfying kissing could be, though I must admit that when he touched me the other day, it ignited a dangerous desire for sex. Rough sex. I wondered what Gretchen and psychologists would say about that.

I opened the door to my room.

"Oh my God," Ryan said, walking in dazed. He scanned the entire space from floor to ceiling, then turned in my direction.

I smirked. "Like it?"

"Are you eighteen?" he asked. "Please don't tell me you're one of those child geniuses who skipped a bunch of grades, and you only look older than you actually are."

I sauntered over to him and snaked my arms around his waist.

"I'm twelve," I said, then kissed his neck. "Is that okay?"

"Not funny, Brooke. Disturbing more like. What the hell kind of room is this?"

I laughed and walked to the bed. "My dad, okay? He decorated my room for me before I moved in. I didn't have the heart to change it. Plus, it's kind of growing on me now."

Ryan sighed relief then furrowed his brows. "He doesn't know you're eighteen?"

I shook my head and smiled. "He's my dad. He doesn't know what 18-year-old girls like. The last time I lived with him, my room *did* look like this. He's stuck in the past, I guess."

Ryan sat down beside me on the bed.

"This purple cheetah print comforter sure does make a statement," he said, running his hand over the bed.

"My favorites are the matching throw pillows," I replied.

"Oh, yes. Matching throw pillows," he observed.

We looked at each other for a moment.

"Oh, just throw me into the throw pillows already!" I cried, and Ryan laughed, pushing me onto the bed and kissing me roughly.

"I wanna make out so hard," I said into his mouth. As usual, I didn't think before I spoke. I never did around Ryan and thought that was okay. He seemed to enjoy it, and I couldn't help myself anyway. He buried his face into my neck, laughing.

"What?" I asked. "Kiss me again."

"Oh, Brooke," Ryan said. "I plan on kissing you all afternoon."

I liked the sound of that and didn't protest when I felt his hand slip up the front of my shirt to cup my breast. And then my shirt was off altogether along with my bra. There was nothing practiced about it, and I liked it. Ryan stared at my nakedness as though studying me. I thought he was burning the image into his brain.

"I plan on kissing you here," he said, and kissed me lightly on my lips. "And here." He planted a soft kiss on my cheek. "And here." He nibbled my earlobe. "And here." He kissed my neck. "And here." He kissed me in between my breasts. "And here." He kissed the curve of my breast.

"And here."

He fastened on to my nipple, and I moaned. Actually, I had been moaning the whole time, but it came out deeper and fuller when he drew my nipple into his mouth.

I arched my body up to his lips inviting him to kiss me and suck me harder. He wouldn't, though. He kept up his gentle assault until I was begging him to make love to me.

"No, Brooklyn," he said. "We're not ready."

"The hell we aren't!" I cried, and pushed him off of me on to his back. I sat on top of him, straddling his hips. He drew in his breath, eyes glued to my breasts.

"What are you trying to do to me?" he asked.

"I'm trying to get you to have sex with me," I replied. "And it's clear you want to," I said, moving my hips from side to side on him.

He grunted. "You were more than happy to wait before."

"Yeah. That's *before* you took my top off and played with my breasts!"

Ryan laughed.

"I want to . . ." But I couldn't say it out loud. I felt my face blush a deep crimson.

"You want to what?"

"It's just that you've done things to me," I said. "And I thought maybe I should—"

"What? You think everything's supposed to be even?" Ryan asked.

I shook my head. "No, I just mean that I want to do stuff to you. Not because I think I'm supposed to but because I want to."

He studied my pink face, like he was making up his mind about something. Then he shook his head.

"You're not ready, Brooklyn," he said.

"What?"

"I said you're not ready."

I huffed. "I'm not a virgin, you know. I mean, I'm no expert in that area, but I've done it before."

Ryan smiled wearily. "I didn't say it had anything to do with being an expert."

"Okay, so what's the problem?"

"There's no problem. You're just not ready yet."

Before I could argue, he rolled me over again, pinning me to the bed.

"Now, there are some things you're ready for," he said, sliding his hand up my stomach and to my breast. He rolled his thumb over my nipple eliciting breathy cries. "Like this." He watched me squirm, arching my back, pushing my breast into his hand.

He moved his hand down the front of my body, slipping it underneath my yoga pants until his fingers were between my legs. I drew in my breath sharply. "And this."

He rubbed me gently, watching my face as his fingers explored my sensitive flesh. I twisted my body, pumping my hips, asking him silently to slide his finger inside me. He seemed to know it, and refrained, playing a game with me I wasn't sure I liked. I turned my face to the side, determined not to beg him.

"Look at me, Brooklyn," Ryan said. His fingers continued to tease me mercilessly. I ached and wanted to scream for it.

"No."

"Why not?"

I squirmed, fighting for or against his hand. I wasn't sure, but the sexual frustration was starting to turn me bitchy. I needed him to stop toying with me and get on with the program!

"Please?" Ryan asked softly.

"No."

He chuckled at my petulance, slipping his finger inside of me as I moaned relief for finally getting what I wanted. I turned my face to him once more, and he kissed me deeply, muffling my cries, swirling his tongue with mine while his finger did something quite similar down below. I bucked.

"Lie still," he ordered.

He was asking the impossible from me. I shook my

head.

"I can't," I argued.

"I want you to lie still, Brooklyn," he said, staying his hand until I obeyed. "And when I make you come, I want you to keep still."

"I can't!"

"Try," he said, and kissed my lips once more, touching me, rubbing me tenderly until I felt the inevitable build, a pregnant ball of electricity, one in each of my ankles, shooting sporadic sparks up my legs.

"I can't, I can't, I can't," I cried, trying desperately to hold still as the sparks kept coming. More of them and faster.

"You can," Ryan said, watching me intently as he continued his incessant touching.

I was ripped in two. Paralyzed. I couldn't move if I tried. I opened my mouth to make a sound, but even my vocal chords were paralyzed. At least for the first explosion. The second had me screaming until my throat went raw. The third had me begging him to stop. The explosions soon petered out until I was left lying numb in a state of semi-consciousness, dazed and stupid.

"What was that?" I asked. My throat hurt, and the words came out scratchy like sandpaper.

"That was you having an orgasm," Ryan replied. It was so matter-of-fact that it made me laugh.

"How did you do that to me? What? Are you some kind of expert or something?" I asked. I needed water.

"Hardly."

"Hardly" my ass. I think the whole neighborhood heard me.

"I think it's just you," he said, and leaned down to kiss my cheek. "Is that cheesy?"

No. Not cheesy. Too hot for words.

I smiled and shook my head.

"Do you need some water or something?" Ryan asked. "You were screaming like a banshee."

I smacked his arm. And then I nodded.

Ryan moved to stand up, but I caught his arm.

"Ryan, why are you doing all these incredible things to me, but you won't let me do things to you? And don't say I'm not ready yet."

Ryan thought for a moment.

"Do you think the things I do to you are solely for your pleasure?" he asked.

I was dumbfounded.

"I'm not looking for things to be even between us, Brooke," Ryan said after a moment. "I'm looking for them to be right."

I didn't think I understood the definition of selflessness until that moment. It was too heavenly. No one was that good. And for the first time, I wondered about Ryan's secret sins.

—

I didn't want Cal to pick me up at my house. I didn't want my father to see. I didn't want Ryan rolling down the sidewalk on his skateboard to see. I wasn't even sure why I was going on this date. After my last afternoon with Ryan, I thought my entire world shifted. My entire purpose. I no longer cared about revenge and guilt and victims. I cared about being with a boy who was nice to me, who treated me like I was the most important person in his life. A boy who made me laugh, talk my head off, say silly embarrassing things, come like an exploding star.

I even thought I could paint again. I had not picked up my brush since trying to paint the fall leaves. But I thought I could do it now. And I thought it could be good enough to hang in a gallery and fetch thousands of dollars. I decided this weekend to spend time with Ryan, to fill up on his goodness, and to paint.

I wanted to meet Cal at the bowling alley. I told him

about the change of plans at school, and I waited until the end of the day to do it. He wasn't happy about it. He told me that guys were supposed to pick up girls for dates.

"Really?" I asked. "Where'd you hear that?"

"It's common knowledge, Brooke," Cal said, completely missing my sarcasm. "I can't even take this date seriously if you don't let me pick you up."

"I'd just rather make it more casual the first time," I said, feeling myself getting backed into a corner. He was insistent.

"No," Cal replied. "Look, I'm not a text guy or a 'Go Dutch' guy. I'm not an 'I'll just meet you there' kind of guy. I'm old school, Brooke. I pick up a girl. I take her out. I pay for it. And then I call her the next day, not text her. I *call* her to see if she had a nice time."

Suddenly he was Prince Charming.

I fidgeted uncomfortably.

"Stop fidgeting, Brooke," Cal said. "You're a grown-ass woman. Start acting like one and let me pick you up."

"I *am* acting like one!" I cried.

"Good. Then I'll be at your door at seven."

I stood in the living room peering out the window every three seconds. As soon as I saw Cal pull up, I'd sprint out the door before he could make it up the walkway. I should have just explained to Dad that I was going on a few dates with different boys to see which one "fit." That way he wouldn't wonder about Ryan. But it sounded like something a college girl would do. High schoolers didn't date around. We were in committed relationships, even if they only lasted two weeks at a time.

"Brooke! Get in here!" Dad called from the kitchen.

"I'm waiting for my ride, Dad," I called back.

"Get in here now!"

I hadn't heard my dad talk to me like that since I let our dog go outside to potty without a leash. I was ten years old. I thought Poppy could handle it. She was always so good. Well-behaved. Plus, I was in the middle of painting my fingernails. I couldn't run the risk of messing up my nails by putting on her leash. Well, she ran away and never came back. Dad lit into me and told me I could forget about ever having another dog because I was too self-absorbed. I cried for a week.

I was reluctant to leave the window, but I knew better than to keep Dad waiting. I sprinted to the kitchen.

"Yes, Daddy?" I asked.

"Don't 'Daddy' me," he snapped. "What the hell is this?" he asked holding up a bill.

"I don't know," I replied.

"It's our cell phone bill," he said. "Now, do you want to tell me what all these charges are about?"

"What charges?"

"God, Brooklyn! This is a five hundred dollar bill! Who the hell have you been talking to? How much data can you possibly use in a month? You got your GPS permanently on? Are you texting while you drive? Surfing the web in class?"

"Dad, take it easy," I said. "I barely use my phone." It was the dumbest lie I'd ever told, and the bill proved it.

Dad looked at me like I'd lost my mind. "Give it to me."

"Huh?"

"Your phone, Brooke. Give it to me."

"Dad!"

"I'm serious. You're done. No phone for . . . a month!"

"What the fu—"

"Go ahead and say it," Dad warned. "I'll make it a year."

"Dad!! You're being unreasonable! And anyway, I have a date tonight. I need it to get in touch with you!"

"A date? With Ryan? I don't think so. You talk to him enough on the phone," he said, waving the bill in my face.

"It's not with Ryan," I said. "It's with some other dude."

"What happened to Ryan? I thought you were in love with Ryan," Dad said.

"I am so not discussing this with you!"

"Well guess what, missy? I'm the parent here. I get to know what you're doing, where you're going, and who you're going with. So I guess you *so* will be discussing this with me. Now hand it over."

"No!"

"Brooklyn, hand over that damn phone."

"Dad, I cannot survive without my cell phone. Please. You don't understand. I need it."

"What the hell is happening to kids these days?" Dad lamented.

"Dad, please. I'll pay the cell phone bill. I've got enough to pay it. More than enough," I pleaded.

Dad looked at me and sighed. "I don't want you to use all your money to pay this bill, Brooke. I want you to be responsible. Ever heard of it? Responsibility?"

I nodded my head vigorously.

"I want you to save your money," Dad continued. "And stop texting so damn much."

"Do I really text that much?" I asked, grabbing the bill and scanning the charges.

"Yes!"

"I'm really sorry, Dad. I am. Maybe I need to change my plan."

"Maybe you need to stop using that thing like a lifeline. Go do your painting or something. Read a book, Brooke. Go to the park. Disconnect for Christ's sake."

"You're right, Dad. Absolutely. I hear you one hundred percent."

"Oh, stop humoring me. That's more infuriating than this bill." Dad rubbed his forehead. "Now tell me who this guy is."

"Gross. You really want to know?" I asked.

"If you're spending the evening with him and he's driving you, you bet I do," Dad replied.

I took a deep breath. "Okay, but I have to tell you really fast because he'll be here any minute."

Dad nodded.

"He's some dude at school who knows Ryan likes me and is trying to get me to like him, so he asked me out on a date, and I agreed just to get it over with. I figured after tonight he won't be too interested in me anymore."

"What, you plan on throwing the date?" Dad asked.

"Sort of," I replied. That was another lie. I had no plans to throw this date. I was going to be my charming, sweet, good girl self. I was going to make Cal burn with jealousy after tonight.

"Does Ryan know you're going on a date with this guy?" Dad asked.

"No, and I don't want him to ever find out. I'm just doing it so this guy will get off my back. Do you understand?"

"You think this is a good idea? I can just tell whoever this is that you're not interested. I can say it while I'm holding my gun," Dad offered.

"No! No, Dad. I can handle it. Just please don't tell Ryan about any of this."

"I think this kind of deception got you in trouble in the past, Brooke."

Bullet to the heart, and Dad wasn't even holding his gun.

"I'm not judging. I'm just saying that you seem to carry around a lot of guilt. I mean, is this the only way to show this guy you're not interested in him? Does he not understand that 'no' means 'no'?"

How could I possibly explain to my dad that I was actually doing this for Beth? That I was doing it to repent for my sins, to clear the guilt? I realized the date seemed convoluted to Dad, but I could never in a million years tell him the real reason. If I did, Cal would be dead in a puddle of blood on our front porch.

"Trust me, Dad. You know how people learn differently? Some are visual learners? Some are auditory learners? Some are hands-on?"

Dad nodded, the side of his mouth turning up in a grin.

"Well, this Cal dude is definitely not an auditory learner. That's why 'no' doesn't work. He's a hands-on kind of guy. So I'm going to let him take me bowling, and then he'll see why I'm the last person in the world he wants to date."

Dad's face sported a full smile now. I think I made him proud in that moment.

"You're not going to let him put his hands on you, are you?"

"Gross, Dad."

"Well, you're telling me he's a hands-on kind of guy. He puts them on you and he's dead."

"Dad, relax. I didn't mean 'hands-on' that way," I said.

He grunted and tossed the cell phone bill on the kitchen table. Just then the doorbell rang, and I kissed him goodbye.

"Can't I meet him?" Dad asked.

"No," I said. "I'm taking my cell phone. And I'll call you before I come home."

"You have a curfew, you know," Dad said.

"I do? This is new."

The doorbell rang again.

"Yeah, you do. Now what's the standard curfew for a girl your age?" Dad asked.

"Are you for real? You know, I didn't think for a second you'd actually make me hand over my phone," I said, walking to the front door.

"Give me an hour, Brooke!" Dad called, still standing in the kitchen.

"One!" I called back.

"Nope! Try again!"

"Oh, for Pete's sake," I mumbled, reaching for the door handle. "I didn't come home from that party with Gretchen until one!"

"Yeah, and that's the last time for that!"

I rolled my eyes. "Midnight!"

"Still not happy!"

"Dad, oh my God!" I yelled, opening the door. "Eleven!"

"Better! I love you! Be safe!"

"I love you, too!" I called, pushing Cal out of the way.

"Shouldn't I meet your dad or whatever," he asked, following me down the walkway.

"Another time," I said.

Oh. My. God.

I wasn't told about the double date, and neither was Gretchen evidently. We stared at one another shocked, and then excused ourselves to the bathroom.

"What are you doing here with Parker?" I hissed.

"What are you doing here with that guy?" she shot back. "What happened to Ryan?"

I hated lying to Gretchen. She could always see through the lies, but she never called me out on them. She just waited until I finally caved and told the truth. I think it was satisfying for her, watching me squirm for minutes or days or however long it took before I finally came clean.

"I can't tell you, Gretchen, but I don't like Cal, and I think I'm completely falling in love with Ryan and if you mess this up for me I'll—"

"Relax," Gretchen said. "But you've gotta do better than that. We're not leaving this bathroom until you tell me why you're on a date with him."

"Me? What about you? Why are you on a date with Parker? I told you he's a dick."

"Yeah? Well I wanted to find out for myself. He was really nice at the party, and I want to get to know him better."

How on earth could I tell Gretchen that I thought Parker was a rapist? How could I tell her that I knew Cal was? I was trapped. It was as simple as that. I had to come clean. I had to tell her what I was doing.

"Okay, Gretchen? I will tell you everything that's going on. I swear to God I will. But we've got to get through this date first."

Gretchen nodded.

"Which means we have to walk out of this bathroom acting normal," I explained.

"Totally."

"Now, you're gonna see me flirting with Cal and acting like a little good girl, okay?" I said. "Just go with it. Don't mention anything about me going to Hanover High last year. Don't mention anything about anyone from my past. And especially don't mention Beth."

"Huh?" Gretchen immediately looked concerned.

"Please, Gretchen. I'm begging you. Just go along with my flirting and sweet girl persona and don't mention anything about my past."

"What if they ask?"

"Just say we know each other from ballet. We used to take ballet together and stayed friends."

Gretchen nodded. "I feel super weird right now."

"No you don't," I said. I couldn't hide the panic in my voice. "You don't feel weird at all. We're gonna bowl. It's gonna be great. And we know each other from ballet."

"Got it. Ballet."

We emerged from the bathroom giggling because I said we needed to and approached the waiting boys.

"We've got shoes and balls," Cal said, and Gretchen burst out laughing. I couldn't help but grin.

"That's what we hope," Gretchen said, and Parker's face broke out in a grin as well.

Cal smirked and handed me my size 6 shoes and the ten-pound ball I asked for.

"Now how should we do this?" he asked the group as we made our way to Lane 7.

"You mean teams?" I asked. "I thought I'd be with you." I sat beside Gretchen as we pulled on our bowling shoes.

Cal shrugged. "I don't know. I thought it'd be fun to switch partners."

Oh no. No no no. There was no way in hell I was partnering with the guy who purposefully tripped me on the bleachers. Why would Cal do this?

I was furious. This was not the date I had intended. I wanted Cal all to myself. I wanted to flirt and be cute and have him eating out of my hand by eleven tonight. And I thought he wanted something more one-on-one as well. After all, what was all that bullshit about picking me up and this being a "real" date? He insisted on driving when I wanted to meet him here. I wanted it casual, friendly, and he didn't like that one bit. And now he was giving me the "friendly" treatment?

"Did you two arrange this?" I asked. I wanted to know.

"Sort of," Cal replied. "It was last minute. Parker told me he was taking Gretchen out, so I just figured we could all do something together. Since you wanted our first date to be more casual." He winked at me. I wanted to poke his eye out.

I looked at Parker, who hadn't directed two words to me since we arrived. This was the guy who thought I was too stupid to remember food orders. I couldn't imagine what he'd think after we bowled. I was lousy at it, and I'm sure he was stellar, which meant he'd bitch the entire time about having a bad partner. But he'd do it in a snarky, subtle way because that's just the kind of guy he was.

"Ladies first," Cal said, and gently pushed me towards the lane.

"I turned around and addressed Parker. "I'm not very good." It was apologetic, and I instantly regretted saying anything at all.

He shrugged. "I figured."

I turned back around and closed my eyes. *Find a happy place, Brooke, and just breathe. Breathe, Brooke. Don't say it. Don't say what you really want to say. Just breathe. Brooke? Don't do it. Please don't do it . . . Oh, just go on and say it!*

"Fuckhead." I didn't whisper it either. I just said it. Right out loud.

"Excuse me?" I heard Parker ask from behind.

I turned around. "I called you a fuckhead. Because you are one."

Gretchen's eyes went wide. I could see the struggle on her face: laugh or stay mute? She opted for mute, which was wise.

"You've had a problem with me since I accidentally ran into you in the hallway at school. I'm soooo sorry I ran into you. It was a freaking accident. But you know what wasn't an accident? You tripping me on the bleachers." I looked at Cal. "That's right. Your little buddy here tripped me. That's why I fell into you."

"Get a grip," Parker said. "Nobody tripped you. And I don't have a problem with you."

I snorted. "Okay. Whatever."

Cal looked at Gretchen, who shrugged her shoulders. A waitress walked by, and Cal asked for a pitcher of beer.

"I'll need to see your ID and all of theirs," she said.

"Oh, they're not drinking. It's for me," he said, and

handed the woman a fake ID. She studied it and then studied Cal. She looked unsure about whether she believed him, but then made up her mind to not care.

"Bud Light?" she asked. "It's on special tonight."

"Sounds perfect."

I turned back to face the pins. What a jerk. Did he think about the fact that he needed to drive me home later? This night was shaping up to be the worst date in history. Thank God I brought cab fare.

I rolled the ball down a fraction of the lane before it settled into the gutter. I cursed profusely in my head, wondering if I wouldn't just abscond the pitcher of beer and make a run for it. I could drink it while I walked home.

My second try was slightly better. I managed to knock over one pin. It teetered for awhile and was painful to watch.

I heard Gretchen behind me saying, "You can do it, pin! I know you can!" and Cal telling her that she wasn't supposed to be cheering for the opponent.

I walked back to the group and plopped down beside my teammate.

"Well, let's see if you can beat *that*," I said. Parker actually chuckled.

Gretchen bowled next, and Cal cheered for her as loudly as possible. I admit my feelings were kind of hurt. My partner didn't cheer for me. Cal was supposed to be my partner. This was our date. Why was he partners with Gretchen? I felt like he was punishing me, and it made me unreasonably sensitive.

Parker's first bowl was a strike. Big deal. His second bowl was a strike, too. Slightly bigger deal. He sauntered back over to me and lifted his hand in the air. Did he expect me to high-five him? Get real.

"Come on, grouch," Parker said. "I promise to stop being mean to you if you'll high-five me."

I stared at him perplexed. "Just like that? Yeah right. You know, I don't know what your problem was with me in the first place."

"Look, I was having a bad day, okay?" he said.

"Are you serious? So you were having a bad day when I ran into you at school? And another one when I took Gretchen away from you at the party? And another when you freaking tripped me on the bleachers? You know, I could have broken a tooth or something!"

"Take it easy," Parker said.

"*You* take it easy," I snapped. "Oh yeah. I almost forgot the diner! Were you having a bad day then when you insulted me?"

Parker rubbed his forehead.

"Yeah, rub your forehead. It's sooo exasperating being called out for acting like a complete asshole."

"Anyone care to watch me bowl?" Cal asked, grabbing his ball from the ball return.

"Sure!" Gretchen said. She smiled at me. It was a smile that said, "I don't have a clue what's going on right now, and so help me God, you're gonna tell me everything when this horrible group date is over."

I returned my own smile. It said, "How many years would I get for bashing Parker's head in with my bowling ball?"

Cal bowled, and Gretchen and I acted impressed because we figured that's what he wanted. I knew in my heart I annihilated any chance of setting him up for rape charges. It was the most ludicrous feeling: disappointment for ruining my chances of getting pseudo-sexually assaulted. I thought up until now I was simply teetering on the edge of insanity. Now I knew I had toppled over, and I wasn't sure where to go from there. I didn't know what Beth would have me do, and as I sat beside one nemesis while watching the other bowl a spare, I wanted to cry for my failure.

FOURTEEN

It was time to get to work. I woke up Monday morning with a new resolution. Well, several resolutions. Number One: Make Beth a priority. Remember my purpose. Number Two: Discover the rest of the boys in the Fantasy Slut League responsible for raping girls. Number Three: Warn the girls scheduled to play in the next game about the boys' intentions. (I wasn't sure how to go about this yet, but it was one of my resolutions.) Number Four: Make Ryan fall in love with me.

I resigned myself to my fate with Cal. After our horrid date, I assumed he'd lost interest. I showed him exactly who I was: not the sweet, shy, timid girl I tried to portray at registration so many months back. Nope. I had a smart mouth and a hot temper, neither of which made me a good candidate for molestation. Surely Cal would cut all ties with me, especially since I verbally trashed his friend. My only chance at justice lay in exposing the league and encouraging victims to come forward. I thought this was the only way I could make peace with Beth.

I cried all of Sunday night as I tried to explain this to Beth. I lay in bed talking things over with her, telling her I never intended to fail her, but that I made a lousy undercover detective. A lousy date. A lousy crusader.

I cried to Gretchen, too. After the date, I called Dad to let him know I was spending the night with her. We took a cab to her house since neither of us had any intentions of being driven by Cal, who was drunk, or Parker, who was an asshole.

"Put Gretchen on the phone," Dad ordered.

I was confused, but I did what he asked, pressing the speaker phone button to listen in.

"Hi, Mr. Wright," Gretchen said.

"Gretchen, is Brooke spending the night with you?"

"Yes, sir."

"Are there any boys spending the night with you?"

"Mr. Wright! I have parents, you know!"

"How can I trust that you girls aren't going somewhere with this Cal person? You know who I'm talking about? Brooke's date for the evening?" Dad asked.

"Mr. Wright, I went on that date as well, and let me tell you. There's no Cal. Ever."

"You went on the date?"

"Long story, but it was a surprise double date that ended kind of badly. My date was a jerk. Brooke's date was a doofus."

"Hmmm."

"I swear, Mr. Wright. Brooke is spending the night, and it's just us two, and my parents are home," Gretchen said.

There was a brief pause.

"I trust you, Gretchen," Dad said.

Gretchen looked at me. "You should. And you should trust your daughter, too."

"I do."

Gretchen and I were both confused now, but she said goodbye to my father and handed the phone to me.

"I know I was on speaker phone. I'm not an idiot,"

Dad said.

"What was that all about then?" I asked.

"It's called being your father, Brooke," Dad replied. "Now, was your date really so bad?"

I sighed. "The worst. But can I just tell you about it later?"

"Yes, Brooke. I love you."

"I love you, too," I said, and hung up.

Gretchen and I sat on her bed while I explained Beth's suicide, Cal, and my plans to expose the Fantasy Slut League.

"She was raped?" Gretchen breathed. She looked stunned.

I nodded. "I know that's why she did it. She was so depressed the last few months before she died. Of course, I didn't help at all. I wasn't even there for her, and then she discovered Finn and me. Can you understand why I feel so guilty now? I knew what had happened to her because she told me. She trusted me, and I betrayed her in so many ways."

I was crying, unable to hide my total anguish.

Gretchen took my hand and squeezed it.

"I'm trying to make things right for her. I . . . I think I can. I know about this league. I know Cal is a rapist. I'm not sure about the others. I'm trying to figure that out."

"How?"

"God, Gretchen. If I tell you these things, you have to swear on your life you won't tell a soul. A friend of mine could get in big trouble," I said. I took the tissue Gretchen passed to me and blew my nose.

"Brooke, I know I can be spacey sometimes and say stupid things, but I swear to you that I'll keep your secrets. You can trust me," Gretchen said. It was the first time she was that serious. I saw a different side of the friend I'd known since ninth grade. I believed her, and so I talked.

I told her everything, but I left out the part about setting up Cal.

—

I studied every game. Parker kept records for years, all of which I received in a black binder from Terry after work Wednesday night. He told me to be smart about it. That's what he always said whenever we discussed anything to do with the Fantasy Slut League. Be smart about it. I thought I was, but when I confessed to him that I told Gretchen about the league, he blew up on me. We were standing beside my car.

"What the fuck, Wright?!" he yelled.

"I had no choice!" I replied. "She caught me, Terry! I had no choice!"

"Jesus, did you mention my name?"

"No! God, no! I'm not stupid. I knew what things to say and what I shouldn't," I said.

"Yeah? Like what?" he asked.

"Well, I certainly didn't tell her your name. And I didn't tell her I planned on getting raped."

Terry looked shocked. "What the hell did you just say?"

"I said I didn't tell her your name. Everything's cool."

"No, after that," Terry clarified.

"I said I didn't tell her I planned . . ." My voice trailed off. *Oh my God. Stupid stupid stupid. What have I done?*

Terry advanced on me and grabbed my upper arm. "What are you doing, Wright?" he hissed, inches from my face.

I tried to pull away. "Nothing. I'm not doing anything."

"Then what was that comment all about?"

"I don't know why I said that."

"Bullshit. Now I'm giving you one minute to explain yourself," Terry said. He kept his fingers wrapped tightly around my arm.

"I can't," I whispered. "Please, Terry. You just don't understand."

"You're right. I don't. And you're gonna tell me," he replied.

I ripped my arm out of his grasp and searched my purse for my car keys.

"You're not going anywhere, Wright." Terry moved in front of the car door, barring my escape.

"He'll keep doing it," I said, mostly to myself. My body felt strange.

"Who? Cal?"

I screamed, "He'll keep doing it! He'll keep getting away with it! He's a monster!" I looked at Terry, eyes wild and unfocused. I thought he didn't hear me or didn't register what I was saying, so I screamed again. "He'll keep doing it! He'll keep getting away with it! He's a monster!"

I felt the panic explode in the base of my chest. Usually there's a build-up. Usually I know it's coming. I have a bit of a warning. But not this time. I couldn't breathe. I kept hearing myself yelling, repeating the lines over and over but never taking a breath between them. I was running out of oxygen. I was running out of time. I had to keep saying it. Someone needed to understand, to believe me.

"He's a monster!" I gasped, feeling my knees buckle, my eyes roll up into my head. White nothingness as I dropped to the pavement like a stone.

I awoke on an unfamiliar couch. It smelled of rich leather, and in my peripheral vision, I saw the flickering of candlelight, warm and comforting. Wherever I was, I liked it.

Someone walked up to me and removed a cloth from my head. I squinted and recognized the face, but I couldn't yet put a name to him.

"You scared the shit out of me," he said.

"Huh?"

"You fainted, Wright."

Wright. Someone calls me that. Who calls me by my last name? It was on the tip of my tongue.

"I did?"

He sighed deeply, and then I felt the couch sink next to my stomach. He must have sat down.

"Does that ever happen to you?" he asked.

"Sometimes," I replied.

Terry! That's who it was!

"Terry, why did I faint?" I asked.

There was a brief pause.

"Well, I think because I discovered something you didn't want me to," he said. He looked down at me and furrowed his eyebrows. "You said something you didn't mean to."

And then I remembered. My slip-up. How could I be so careless?

"Brooke, please tell me I misheard. Please tell me I'm crazy or something. Anything, because I'm freakin' out over here," Terry said.

I breathed deeply and thought about creating an elaborate lie. And then I remembered I was lousy at lying.

"I thought it was the only way," I said. "He's done it to other girls, Terry. I know he has. I know one of them. I mean, she wouldn't come right out and say it, but the signs are all over her. He'll keep doing it. I know he will, and no one will stop him. None of these girls will come forward. They're all scared or unsure or something. She's scared of him, Terry. This girl I know."

"Are you hearing yourself?" Terry asked.

"I'm not crazy," I snapped.

"I didn't mean to imply that. But Brooke, what more can you do but expose these guys? You can't make the girls come forward. You can't make them press charges."

"Exactly!" I said. "I can't make *them* press charges. But I can. Or at least I thought I could."

"Jesus Christ, Brooke. Are you hearing what you're saying? You'll let this guy screw you to what? Get justice for a bunch of girls you don't even know?"

"I do know them!" I shot back. "They're Beth! All of them!"

Terry said nothing. He placed his hand on my forearm, and I didn't pull away.

"I blew my chances anyway, so you don't need to worry."

I sat up slowly, the pounding in my head increasing then subsiding once I sat still, fully upright.

"What are you talking about?" Terry asked.

"I've been trying to get Cal to like me. I figured I could get him to want me and then use me. But I messed everything up. I'm sure he won't ever talk to me again. Whatever. At least I can try to keep these girls safe during the next game."

"How did you mess things up?"

"I don't want to talk about it," I replied.

"Why are you doing all of this?" Terry asked.

I huffed. "I told you. For my friend, Beth."

Terry stared at me, and I shifted uncomfortably.

"You think you're responsible," he said.

"I don't think it. I know it. She told me about her rape. I should have done something. I should have made her tell her parents. I should have been a better friend. I should have gone to that party with her."

I cried unabashedly. I didn't care that I looked unattractive, or scared, or tired; I cried until there was nothing left, until I was dried up. Terry sat beside me and put his arm around my shoulder. He held me like a big brother, saying nothing, just letting me cry out my anger and guilt until I settled down and the hitching in my chest eased.

"I'll help you get them, Brooke," Terry said. "But you have to promise me you'll kill this crazy idea about setting yourself up as a rape victim."

"I told you I had," I argued.

"No, you never said that. You said you think you messed up the chance," Terry countered. "You have to promise me, Brooke. We'll get him and all the others, but you have to promise me you'll stay safe."

I nodded.

"Say it."

"Come on, Terry."

"Say it, Wright."

I sniffed and wiped my face. "I promise."

Terry met my dad for the first time that night. He drove me home, introduced himself as the head chef, and told my dad he was escorting me to my car when I fainted. Dad was sick with worry, and he crushed me a little too hard against his chest, but I was glad to be home and in his arms. I realized in that moment that, despite all the bad I was learning about Cal and Parker and their friends, there were still good men in the world. Terry and my dad were two of them.

—

"This is daunting," Ryan said, staring at the blank canvas, holding my brush.

"No," I replied. "This is the fun part. When it all starts."

We were standing on my back patio Sunday afternoon. I thought it would be fun to paint a picture together. Ryan was unsure when I explained my plans over the phone, but he agreed to try. I stood mixing the colors on my palette while he stared, obviously frightened, at the awaiting canvas.

"Now don't be nervous," I said. "There's no right or wrong to it. That's what makes it art."

"Hmm." Ryan sounded dubious.

"I'm serious. Create whatever you want."

"Yeah. I'm more concrete than that," Ryan said. "We've got to have some sort of idea in mind."

"Okay. How about a winter scene?" I suggested.

It was surprisingly mild outside for mid-November. But the striking fall leaves had long since vanished from the trees. Everything outside looked like winter, even if it didn't feel that way. Bare trees. Muted sky. Gray.

"You gotta narrow it down, Brooke," Ryan said.

"All right," I said, and came up behind him. I stood on my tiptoes and spoke into his neck. "Snow."

I handed him the palette, showed him how to hold it, then placed my right hand over his to help him guide the brush.

"A sloping hill," I suggested, and steered the brush to the paint, swirling the tip in a light green and bringing it to the canvas.

"I thought it was snowing," Ryan said, giving up control of the brush as I grazed it over the canvas fibers.

"Soon," I said. "Now feel what's happening with the paint. Notice how it glides effortlessly over the canvas? How the brush doesn't pull or tug?"

Ryan nodded.

"That's because this is primed canvas. If it weren't, you'd see the paint soak deep into the fibers immediately on contact. But this canvas forces the paint to hover on the top, waiting for you to let it dry, rework it, whatever you want."

I dipped the brush once more and continued the curve of my line, creating the rolling hill that would be the backdrop of our snowy scene.

"You wanna try by yourself?" I asked, releasing his hand and backing away.

"I don't know, Brooke," Ryan said. He shifted on his feet.

I grabbed another paintbrush and stood beside him.

"You can't mess it up," I said.

"I'm sure I can," Ryan countered, and I giggled.

"No you can't," I said, and showed him by dipping my brush in gray paint and swirling it all over the top half of the canvas.

"Wait! Shouldn't that be blue?" Ryan asked. "You know, for the sky?"

"Sure," I replied, and waited for him.

He cleaned his brush and dipped it in blue, hesitating before bringing it to my gray swirl.

"Don't be afraid," I encouraged.

He took a deep breath and ran the blue on top of my gray, mixing the colors to slate, and I thought our snowy scene had just taken on a blustery effect.

"A winter storm," I said, and continued with my gray, dotting and gliding, twirling and smashing until the sky was filled with the promise of snowflakes. Ryan mingled his blues, discovering by accident the effects of flicking his brush to create a 3-D impression with the paint.

"That's so cool," he said, staring at his work.

We painted all afternoon, creating the winter sky, stopping only to kiss once. Neither one of us was interested in making out. We wanted to create a different kind of art together, one Ryan could hang in his bedroom.

"And why do you get it?" I asked.

"I figured we'd share it," he suggested. "I'll take it for a few months, and then you can. We'll switch off."

I liked that idea. It meant that Ryan planned to keep me around for awhile, and suddenly I thought of many more paint projects we could undertake together to make me a permanent fixture in his life.

———

Parker was stupid. Why would he keep a record of all the league's previous games? Certainly not to remind himself of all his past wins. He didn't have many, after all. Cal did, though. I assumed most of his wins came by force. I already knew he was bad news, and I thought Tim was as well. My brief encounter with Tara in the hallway a few weeks back suggested his violent behavior, but I had to be sure.

I cleared Hunter. Melissa seemed fine, and for a week, I tracked another girl at school who had supposedly given it up to Hunter two years ago. She appeared happy. She was heavily involved in sports at school and had a group of close friends she hung out with. She smiled a lot, and I just knew in my heart she was okay. I crossed Hunter off the list.

Parker was an asshole to me, but I had a hard time finding out if he was a monster like Cal. There was only one girl he'd slept with in all four years' worth of records, according to the scores. And she no longer attended Charity Run. I did a Google search for Jessica Canterly, but came up empty-handed. I realized Parker would probably be my hardest target.

Mike was a non-issue at the moment. He started the league a year ago and never scored above a blow job. I tracked a few of the girls who bestowed that lovely gift on him and decided they were fine. None of them seemed depressed or broken. A few were complete bitches, however, and it was hard for me to feel sorry for them for their ignorance. Aaron was new, and Game 1 of this year was his first. I had no idea if he was simply in it for innocent fun—if there was even such a thing—or if he had other motivations. All I could do was wait to find out.

I was doing more research using Beth's old
yearbooks when I came across the picture. I gasped. It
was the girl from the bathroom—the one sobbing
uncontrollably. She was the one I was sure nodded when I
asked her if something bad had happened to her. She had
been a player in Game 4 of last year. The game right
before the current one. She was on Tim's team and was
classified as a virgin, scoring the ultimate points for having
sex with him.

I wasn't really searching for her, but by divine
providence, we ran into each other again. And again in a
bathroom, though this one wasn't on the senior hall. I
slipped into a bathroom on the junior hall before leaving
school Tuesday, and there she was, hovering over the
sink, reapplying her lip gloss. She froze when she saw me.

"Oh, hey," I said.

"Hi," she replied, unsure.

"How's it going?"

"Fine, I guess." She turned on the water to wash her
hands.

I assumed she'd try to escape as quickly as possible,
but she hung around. It almost seemed as though she was
silently inviting me to ask her questions. I took a shot.

"It's just that after that day a few months ago . . ."

She wiped her hands and threw away her paper
towel.

"Are you okay?" I asked.

"Yeah."

I nodded and smiled.

"I was just having a bad day," she said.

"I totally understand that. It's bad enough being in
high school, right? Then on top of that you've gotta worry
about fitting in, getting good grades." I paused for the
briefest second before adding, "Boys."

She tensed. I saw it.

"Boys," she snickered.

"For real," I said, trying to encourage her. "Why are they so lame?"

"Don't ask me. I don't understand them at all," she replied. She swung her book bag over her shoulder. "They're awful."

"The worst is when they're mean," I said. "I slammed my head on my desk at the beginning of the year—the first day of school, actually—and they laughed at me. Like we're back in second grade. What the hell?"

She shrugged. "Well, at least when they were mean in elementary school, it usually meant they liked you."

"True."

"Now it just means they're assholes."

I laughed. She laughed, too.

"I'm Brooke, by the way," I said.

"Oh, I know," she replied. "I'm Amelia."

"Wait, how do you know my name?"

"You're the girl who fainted in the hallway."

Super. People knew me as the fainter.

"And you kind of have a reputation for not being very friendly," Amelia admitted.

"What?"

"Well, I just heard that you don't have any friends here. Girlfriends, that is. That you don't really like girls."

I was pissed. I worked my ass off every day to appear friendly to the bitches who strolled the senior hallway like they owned the place. They were the ones who gave me major attitude. What the fuck?

"I shouldn't have said that," Amelia said. Apparently my anger was written all over my face.

"No, it's fine. It's true I like to keep to myself," I said. I was getting unfocused. I wanted the conversation back on Amelia and why she thought boys were assholes.

"Maybe they're just jealous," Amelia offered. "Maybe they think you're going to steal their men since you're really pretty." She smiled shyly.

I laughed. "Hardly. But thanks for the compliment. I have no intentions of dating any of the losers at this school, though I have to admit that this Tim guy in my class is kind of cute."

I silently cheered for myself. That last line came out of nowhere, and it was perfect.

Amelia's demeanor changed in a flash. She didn't look scared. She looked pissed off.

"Did I say something wrong?" I asked.

She shook her head. "Are you talking about Tim Shelton?"

"Yeah."

"Word of advice. Stay away."

She moved to the bathroom door.

"Wait! Why?" I asked.

"He's one of the assholes," she said, and opened the door.

I ran up behind her and slapped my hand to the door, slamming it closed again.

"Tell me why," I said.

"Huh?" Amelia fidgeted with her book bag, moving it from shoulder to shoulder, unable to find a comfortable way to hold it. "I've gotta go," she said.

"Amelia, I . . . I really need you to tell me why Tim's an asshole," I said gently.

"I've gotta go," she repeated.

"Please," I begged. "I won't tell a soul."

"Get out of my way."

"Did he make you do something you didn't want to?"

Amelia backed away from the door like a scared rabbit.

"What have you heard?" she whispered. "Are they starting up that rumor again?"

"What rumor?"

"Don't play dumb!" she screamed. "That rumor

about me. It's not true! I didn't want to do it! I told him 'no'!"

She dropped her book bag and wrapped her arms around her stomach.

"I don't know about any rumor, Amelia," I said.

"Yeah right! Everyone was talking about it at the end of the summer, right before school started."

"I'm new here. I didn't hear any rumor," I said. I walked towards her, and she flinched. "It's okay. I'm one of the good people."

I saw tears forming in her eyes, and then they spilled over, plopping on her white, eyelet blouse. It was instinct. I wrapped her in my arms before thinking. It didn't feel strange at all, holding someone I barely knew because in a way, I did know her. She was Beth. Like I told Terry. They were all Beth.

"I think he drugged me or something," she cried into my shoulder. "People were saying I got topless at this party. In front of everyone, and that he was egging me on. I don't really remember. I mean, I think I do, but I'm not sure. I remember a bed. I remember bleeding the next day, but I wasn't supposed to start my period. It didn't feel like my period, and it only lasted a day."

I felt sick. I swallowed hard, forcing down the urge to vomit.

"Did you . . . did you tell your parents?" I asked.

Amelia pulled away. She wiped her face and shook her head.

"I wasn't sure what happened. I should have told them, but I wasn't sure," she said, and then added more quietly, "I was ashamed."

"You didn't do anything wrong," I said.

She nodded like she wanted to believe me but didn't have the heart to.

"I mean it, Amelia. You did nothing wrong. He took advantage of you. Like you said, he's the asshole."

She looked up suddenly, her face full of concern.

"You can't tell anyone," she said. "Promise me."

I sighed. "It's not my business to tell."

"Good."

"But I wish you'd tell your parents, Amelia."

"What can be done about it now, Brooke? It's been months. It's not like I went to the hospital afterwards. There's nothing to prove he did anything," she said.

"There's your word," I offered.

"Yeah," she snickered. "That's good for just about nothing."

FIFTEEN

"Beth? I thought we could go to the mall today," I said, lingering in her bedroom doorway. She lay on her bed facing the window.

"What for?" she asked, disinterested.

"Well, there's a sale going on at The Limited," I replied. I walked over to the bed and tentatively sat down.

"No thanks," Beth said.

"It's Friday afternoon," I said. "What do you feel like doing?"

"Lying here."

"Oh."

We were silent for several minutes.

"You don't have to stay, Brooke. Go hang out with Gretchen or something."

I took off my shoes and lay down beside her.

"I don't want to hang out with Gretchen. I want to stay here with you."

Beth rolled over and looked at me.

"I think Finn is getting frustrated with me," she said. "I don't want him to be physical with me, and he's getting all restless about it."

I tensed, unsure what to say. It was weird hearing Beth talk *about Finn and their physical relationship. I knew they had sex. I knew they were probably still having sex even though he and I were. Did I have no self-respect?*

"I feel lost, Brooke. I don't know what to do," Beth said.

I took her hand.

"You don't have to do anything, Beth. You can just lie here. That's okay."

"You'll stay here with me?"

"Of course."

"But don't you want to do something fun tonight? Go to a party or something?" Beth asked.

"Nope. I want to hang out with you."

"I'm not very much fun right now," she admitted.

"That's okay," I replied.

We lay in silence for a time. I started counting the dots on her ceiling.

"How do I get better, Brooke?"

I wanted to tell her to talk to her parents, to talk to a doctor. I wanted to tell her to press charges. I wanted to tell her to be brave. But I didn't.

"It'll just take time."

"How much time?"

"I don't know, Beth."

There was another moment of silence. I stared at Beth's ceiling wondering how to make my friend come back to me, wondering where to find the strength to stop sleeping with Finn.

"Look what I'm wearing," Beth said, pulling the tarnished half heart out of the front of her shirt.

I rolled over to face her.

"I thought it went with my outfit today," she said.

I giggled.

"We should start wearing them again, don't you think?" Beth asked.

I nodded. "We definitely should."

Beth grinned. "Do you think we'll be best friends forever?"

I grinned, remembering Beth's answer to this question when we were eight years old. "Sure. Why not?"

She laughed, remembering it, too. "Exactly. Why not?"

"You're going to kill me, Beth," I breathed into the blackness of my bedroom.

I paced the length of the room wearing fresh pajamas because I soaked my other ones with sweat. I was so sick and tired of waking up every other night drenched with sweat. My face felt tight from the dried tracks left by tears. I rubbed my cheeks roughly trying to erase the tightness, but all I managed to do was make my face hurt more.

"I'm doing the best that I can," I said.

Do better.

I whirled around and stared into the opposite corner of my room.

"Who's there?" I whispered, feeling the jolt in my chest, the aching in my fingers.

Nothing.

"Beth?"

He raped me.

I wanted to run for the bedroom door, but I was certain she'd block my escape. Should I call for my dad? I was scared out of my mind.

He raped me, Brooke. What are you doing about it?

"I . . . I'm working on it. I know about this league, Beth. I know about some others."

I don't care about the others. Why haven't you gotten Cal?

"Are you hearing yourself?" I cried. "Do you hear what you're asking me to do?!"

It was your plan, Brooke. I didn't come up with it. But now that I've had time to think about it, I rather like it.

I stood dumbfounded, staring at the ghost.

I mean, don't you deserve it? You slept with my boyfriend. You lied to me. You're a despicable human being. Don't you deserve to be treated like shit?!

"No! I don't deserve it! I don't!" I yelled into the

corner of the room.

Yes you do. Yes you do. Yes you do. Yes you do . . .

"Shut up!"

Yes you do. Yes you do. Yes you do . . .

"DADDY!" I screamed. "DADDY!"

I heard my bedroom door ripped open and felt my father's arms go around me. I opened my eyes, dazed and confused.

"It was just a dream," Dad said. "You're okay, honey." And he rocked me side to side while I cried into his chest.

"I'm scared!" I wailed.

"Don't be scared. I'm right here," Dad reassured me. He continued to rock me, stroking my hair and shushing me as my sobs became fewer and more infrequent.

"Please don't leave me," I begged, clutching him.

"I'm not going anywhere, Brooke," Dad replied.

I eased my desperate hold on him, and he looked down at my face.

"Did you dream about Beth again?" he asked.

I nodded reluctantly.

Dad didn't say anything. He just held me until I asked to leave the room and sleep somewhere else in the house. He walked me out, and I could feel an angry, unsatisfied Beth hovering in the corner of my bedroom.

—

Dad eyed me cautiously over breakfast the next morning. I was pale; I could feel it. I think my dream within a dream drained half the life out of me. I was so terrified. I tried to steady my hand as I brought the cereal spoon to my mouth, but it was no use. I shook violently, and Dad, unable to bear the sight of me struggling to eat, plucked the utensil from my feeble grasp.

"Dad, I'm not a baby," I said. But I felt like one in that moment, and I wanted to cry all over again.

"Who said anything about anyone being a baby?" he asked.

He dipped the spoon in my Corn Flakes and brought it to my mouth. I acquiesced to being fed because I was hungry, and Dad was doing a much better job than I did.

After I woke up screaming last night, Dad brought me downstairs. He made me tea and turned on a Christmas movie. It was the middle of November, but I think he chose *Miracle on 34th Street* because it was innocent and pleasant. And full of hope. And I think he thought it might lull me into a peaceful sleep, listening to the sweet voice of a young Natalie Wood scrutinizing Kris Kringle's whiskers. I nuzzled my father and fell asleep against his chest, hearing the famous line at the end of the movie repeated over and over in my sub-consciousness: "You've still got to believe!"

"Brooke?" Dad asked after I took my last bite of cereal.

"Hmm?"

"I think you should talk to someone," he said. "I thought about your old psychologist. I could set up an appointment. What do you think?"

I leaned back in my chair and crossed my arms over my chest.

"It's so self-indulgent, Dad," I said after a moment. "And I still have panic attacks. What did all that talking really do for me?"

"Well, while you were going, you were better," Dad said. "Remember? The attacks subsided."

I sighed.

"Will you think about it?" he asked.

I nodded.

"And it's never self-indulgent to do something that makes you happy and healthy," he said.

I smiled just to placate him. I wasn't convinced.

—

By Wednesday I felt like my old self. Still guilt-ridden but no longer shaking. No longer terrified to sleep in my bedroom. No longer convinced that Beth was an angry ghost who hated my guts. Something else was going on in my brain, and next week I planned to discover it with the help of my former psychologist, Dr. Merryweather. God, I hated her name. It made me feel like I couldn't talk to her about any of my problems—like I had to be all sunshine and smiles in her office because she was happy. Or at least her name suggested it.

"I want you to do something for me," Dad said over dinner.

"Oh yeah? What's that?" I replied.

"Thursday is Family Night at the Y," Dad said. "I want us to go."

I laughed. "Are you freaking kidding me?"

"No. I think it would help you to run around and lift some weights and work out some of this stuff going on with you," Dad said.

"Dad, you cannot be serious. Family Night? Can we say, 'Lame'?"

"Totally lame. And we're going," Dad said.

I narrowed my eyes at him. Only then did I realize that Dad had been to the gym three times this past week. He bought a membership at the beginning of the school year for us, but he rarely went. I went on occasion, but I'm not really a gym girl. I prefer to take solitary walks or do a workout video in the comfort and privacy of my living room. Curtains drawn, of course.

"Who is she?" I asked.

"Huh?" Dad gathered the dinner plates and took them to the sink.

"Who is the woman you've been working out for? And will she be there Thursday night? Is that why you're so insistent on going?"

"Brooke, I have no idea what you're talking about," Dad replied, but he wouldn't turn around and look at my face when he said it.

I jumped up from the table. "Oh my God, Dad! I want to know!" I squealed, and just like that, Beth, my nightmare, my guilt, all dissolved to nothing.

Dad finally turned around, a silly grin lighting up his face.

"Did you completely forget about fall conferences, Brooke?" Dad asked.

"What?"

"With your teachers," he clarified.

"No, I didn't. You met with Mrs. Hayes," I said. "She's older than dirt. And married."

Dad chuckled. "Yeah, I met with Mrs. Hayes. But then I popped into English class."

My mouth dropped open.

"Just spur of the moment kind of thing." He looked proud about it.

"Where have I been? Why didn't Ms. Manning say anything to me?"

"Because it's not your business," Dad said lightly. "At least not yet."

"Oh my God! Did you ask her out?!"

"No. I introduced myself, and she seemed to know more about me than I did. I assume you had something to do with that." Dad smirked.

I grinned.

"I didn't know she lives around here. She goes to the Y, too," he said.

"So now *you* go to the Y," I said.

"I've had a membership for months, Brooke."

"Ha! One you've never used!" I held up my hands,

fingertips touching in a steeple-like gesture. I felt like Mr. Burns, devising my plan.

"Stop right there," Dad said.

I dropped my hands. "Oh Dad. This is the cutest and most disgusting thing ever!"

Dad laughed. "So will you go Thursday night? She's gonna be there. We're gonna work out together."

"Oh, I'm not missing this for anything," I replied.

—

I have to admit that Family Night at the Y was pretty fun. I ran a mile with Dad around the indoor track before we moved on to the weight machines. Ms. Manning showed up during Dad's set on the biceps machine, and he asked me to increase his weights.

"No, Dad, I'm not doing that," I said.

"Brooke, come on," he begged, but I shook my head. I would not be responsible for his injury.

"Hi, Brooke," Ms. Manning said, approaching us.

"Hi," I replied, and giggled.

She ignored it, and Dad shot me a look. I shrugged. "You've got another set."

Dad completed his curls as he talked to "Johanna." She was "Johanna" now, and I wondered what she'd say or do if I called her by her first name. It was obvious Dad was trying to impress her, lifting his weights and contracting his biceps for all it was worth. I snickered.

Clearly, they were attracted to each other, and while their whole show of outward affection was embarrassing, I couldn't help feeling a little proud. I talked up my dad incessantly to Ms. Manning, but I didn't think she heard a word of it. Still, it wasn't all me. Somehow, be it curiosity or craziness, Dad found the courage to go to her classroom and talk to her.

I spotted Kaylen hanging around the outskirts of the

weight room and excused myself, making a beeline for her. I didn't know Ryan's family were members at the Y.

"Hey," I said, and she grinned at me.

"I cannot believe you're dating my brother!" she squealed. No "hello" back; just right into it.

"Why's that?" I asked.

"Because he's my brother! Totally gross." Kaylen scrunched her nose at the idea.

I rolled my eyes. "Are you guys members here?"

"Yeah."

"You came for Family Night?"

"Duh."

I exhaled. "So your brother's here?"

"Gross. And yes he is. He's in the pool."

"The pool?" I had to catch my breath.

"Yes, Brooke. The pool."

"Thank you, Kaylen," I said sweetly, and made my way to the opposite end of the building.

Ryan was in the far lane, and oh my God, he didn't have a shirt on. Obviously. In all our make-out sessions, I had not once seen him shirtless. Yes, I ran my hands over his arms and chest from time to time, but there's a big different between feeling and seeing.

He was in the middle of a swim stroke. I don't know the name. He was bobbing in and out of the water, arms circling overhead. He stopped at the end of the lane on the far side of the pool and pulled himself up onto the ledge.

Dear God in heaven.

He was beautiful. I thought it was unfair how beautiful he was. Why does God do that? Make some people so beautiful that it almost hurts to look at them? Meanwhile the rest of us look like a bunch of frumps in comparison. I studied my workout clothes. I actually wore a cute outfit, and I thought I looked okay, but when I gazed at Ryan, watching the water stream, curving this way and that over his taut muscles, I instantly felt ugly. I wanted to leave, but I couldn't take my eyes off his chest. I wanted to be crushed underneath of it. And I didn't want him to dry off first before he crushed me.

My feet moved instinctively, and before I knew it, I was standing over him.

"Well, if I would have known you were coming, I'd have brought my bikini," I said.

He looked up sharply, staring at me as though he'd been caught. And then his face relaxed.

"Hey, Brooke," he said.

"Wow. Goggles and a cap and everything," I said. "You're hardcore."

"I guess," he replied, holding the swim accessories in his hand.

"So what was that last stroke you were doing?"

He stood up and walked over to a bench to grab his towel.

"The butterfly stroke," he said.

"It looks hard," I replied, watching him dry off his arms. Now I understood the arms. No wood chopping. Swimming instead.

"Not my favorite." He wrapped the towel around his waist.

"Do you swim a lot?"

He nodded.

"How come you don't swim for the school?" I asked. Not that I particularly wanted him to be a part of our swim team.

He smirked. "You're full of questions, aren't you?"

"Just curious, is all."

"Well, you know what happened to the cat," he teased.

"Lame," I replied, rolling my eyes, and he laughed.

"I swim for fun. I don't swim to compete. I just do it for me," Ryan said.

"But you look so good at it," I said. "I mean, not that I know the first thing about swimming, but you looked really good. Good enough to eat. I mean compete! Good enough to *compete!*" I stared at his chest.

"Oh, Brooklyn," Ryan said, grinning and shaking his head. He knew what I wanted and decided to be generous. He wrapped me in his arms and held me close against his naked chest. It wasn't Y appropriate, and I didn't care. I refrained from kissing his pecs, however. I had *some* class.

I let myself get lost in his muscles. If I concentrated hard enough, I could feel each one, pressing into my shoulders, pressing into my face, my back. I was engulfed in them, and the slightest movement made them contract, made me heady with sexual want. His skin was smooth, smelling of his essence mixed with a hint of chlorine from the pool. Chlorine? No salt system? This gym was old school.

Ryan released me when his sister approached.

"I'm so grossed out right now," she said. Such a drama queen. But sweet, so I didn't mind.

"What do you want, Kaylen?" Ryan asked.

It was funny the way he said it, like he was already exasperated with her and she'd only just arrived. But it wasn't mean-spirited. Instead, he seemed to secretly enjoy his sister's interruption, and I thought in that moment that he loved her very much and wouldn't mind if she kept interrupting him for the rest of his life.

"You promised you'd show me how to use the weight machines," Kaylen said.

"I know." Ryan didn't move. He was teasing her.

"Well?" She put her hands on her hips.

"Well, what?" Ryan asked.

"Are you coming?"

"Coming where?"

"Ryan!" She stamped her foot in consternation.

He smirked. "Ohhh, you wanted me to show you

now?"

Kaylen looked at him flatly. "Funny, Ryan."

He chuckled. "I've gotta change first. Why don't you two go in there and I'll meet you in a minute?"

I wanted to follow Ryan into the changing room, but I think that would have gotten me in major trouble. I followed his instructions instead and walked with Kaylen to the weight room.

"Ryan really likes you," Kaylen said as we hung around the door waiting for her brother.

"Does he?" I felt my heart flutter.

"Mmhmm. Did you guys paint a picture together?" she asked.

"Yes. Why?"

"Just curious. Ryan told me but I didn't believe him because he can't draw or paint or do any of those kinds of things," Kaylen said. "And the picture's pretty, so I didn't think he helped you."

I laughed. "Well, he did. Maybe he'll take up painting with me," I suggested.

"If he can find time in his video game schedule," Kaylen replied.

I grinned and waved as Ryan approached thinking I didn't mind if his gaming schedule left little room for painting as long as he included me when he played.

SIXTEEN

"Good afternoon, Ms. Manning," I said, sliding into my usual seat. I was fifteen minutes early for class. I didn't feel much like eating in the cafeteria. I knew this was Ms. Manning's planning period and thought I'd like to chat with her instead.

"May I help you, Brooke?" she asked.

"Yes, you can, as a matter of fact," I replied.

She drew in her breath and stared at me.

"I would like to know what you've done to my father," I said. "Because all of a sudden he's running and stocking the fridge with disgusting healthy food and singing in the shower. Yes, I heard him the other day singing in the shower. And it was terrible."

Ms. Manning giggled. A grown woman giggled. I raised my eyebrows in disbelief.

"Brooke, I'm not discussing this with you," she said.

"Ms. Manning, come on! Did he ask you out on a date?"

"None of your business."

"Do you like him?"

"Brooke, please."

"Am I gonna get A's on all my papers in your class from now on?"

"Brooke!" She looked outraged, if a person can look outraged when she's smiling.

I thought I'd keep goading her.

"I just figured that if you're gonna marry my dad someday, I should get A's in your class. Seems fair to me. I set you up."

"Who said anything about marriage?!" she cried.

"Ms. Manning, these are progressive times, but I'm old school. I cannot allow you to live with my father in sin. You have to be married first before you live together."

"Brooklyn Wright! This is completely inappropriate!"

I smirked but kept quiet.

"Now, if you choose to stay in here until class starts, then you have to be quiet. I'm grading papers. I don't have time to talk about your father who happens to be taking me out this Friday night." She didn't look up from her work, but I saw the tiniest smile playing on her lips.

"Got it," I replied, and thought about all the advice I needed to give my father before his big date.

—

I weighed my options. I really didn't have options, but I pretended to. It was completely unfair, but I had to stop being so freaking selfish for at least one night out of my life. I would have had the house to myself—Ryan to myself—and the thought left me feeling desperate and empty. And then I remembered Melanie and Taylor, two girls I was positive would be at the party, and I couldn't throw them to the wolves. I had information, and I had to act on it. The worst timing possible, but then I thought maybe this was character building. I would not sacrifice those girls to sex they didn't want just so that I could have the sex I wanted.

"Cal's having a party, and we're going," I said to Gretchen over the phone Friday afternoon.

"We are?" she asked. "Why?"

"Because I know some girls who will be there, and they happen to be players for the current game," I replied. "I want to keep an eye on them."

"Ohhh," Gretchen said. There was a pause before she continued. "You know, Brooke, you can't keep them all safe all the time."

"I know, Gretchen. But I can in this instance. I know who will be there, and I have a pretty good idea what will happen if I'm not there to stop it."

"So what happens after that? You'll keep attending parties? Thwarting these guys' plans? Eventually they'll get what they want. You can't be everywhere at once. You can't go on their dates with them. You need to take this shit to the media."

I sighed with frustration. "Gretchen, I'm working on it. But I'm not ready to expose anyone yet. I don't have enough information. Will you please be patient?"

Gretchen huffed. "How do you know Cal even wants us there? I mean, after that date and all?"

"He invited me," I replied.

"He did?"

"Yep. Today after school," I said. "He seems to think the date went rather well."

Gretchen burst out laughing.

"Is he deluded?" she asked.

"What do you think?" I replied.

Gretchen grunted. "He makes my skin crawl. I don't know how I'll face him after what you told me."

"I know, but you've got to play it cool. Don't mess this up for me, Gretchen," I warned.

"I won't! Calm down. It's just frustrating knowing something so horrible about a person and feeling powerless to do anything about it," Gretchen said.

I thought for a moment. "Yeah. How do you think those girls feel?"

"You think the others are drugging girls as well?" Gretchen asked.

"I do."

"How many do you think there are?"

"Well, I can't find any concrete evidence on Parker yet. He's a sneaky son-of-a-bitch. But I think he's one. And I think this Tim guy is another. Actually, I know he is."

"How?" Gretchen asked.

"A girl at school told me," I said.

"She did?!" Gretchen sounded shocked.

"I was disgusted by what she told me. It made my heart sick." I recounted the conversation with Amelia, leaving out her name. Gretchen and I sat in silence for a time.

"That poor girl," she whispered. "She won't come forward?"

"I think maybe she would if others would. Strength in numbers kind of thing," I replied.

Gretchen sighed. "I've never gone to a party with any other purpose than to get drunk and have fun. This feels weird."

"What feels weird?"

"Going to a party with a mission," she said. "I want to help these girls, Brooke. I want to protect them."

I smiled. "I'm glad. But Gretchen? Please don't punch out one of the guys. It would kind of mess up the whole covert thing I've got going on."

"Gotcha. No punching," she said.

After we hung up, I went to pester my dad about his night out. I listed off all the appropriate behaviors for a first date, and the inappropriate ones.

"Brooke, I've dated in the past, you know," he said

patiently.

This was news to me. I thought he knew Mom since birth, started dating her in middle school, and married her right out of high school.

"You have?"

"Funny," Dad replied. "I dated quite a few ladies in college."

"Gross. Don't tell me anymore," I said.

Dad chuckled.

"What time are you picking her up?" I asked.

"Seven."

"And are you wearing what we discussed?" I raised my eyebrows at him, daring him to object.

"Brooke, you spent three hundred dollars of my hard-earned money on that outfit," he replied. "Yes, I will wear it."

I used Dad's credit card after school on Wednesday to buy him a pair of dark wash straight-legged jeans, fitted collar shirt, and a casual tweed blazer for his date. I was proud of myself for getting everything on sale. Dad, on the other hand, was pissed and wanted to take it all back.

"Just try it on first!" I demanded. "You're not going on the first date you've had in a trillion years looking like a typical nerdy dad!"

Dad relented and put on the outfit.

"Five years, Brooke. It's been five years," he said, walking out of his room and standing in the hallway looking lost.

I think for the first time in years he felt stylish, and it made him uncomfortable. Then the more he moved around in his new clothes, the more confident he became. It was interesting watching the transformation unfold before my eyes. From dork to dashing in ten minutes.

"I'm ashamed this cost so much," he mumbled, fingering the fabric of his coat.

"Dad, these are classic pieces. They never go out of

style. You can wear them forever," I explained.

"Oh, I can, huh?"

"Absolutely."

I stood in front of the full-length mirror assessing my outfit: skinny jeans tucked into knee-high brown boots accessorized with large buckles around my ankles and upper calves. My favorite boots. The heel was the perfect height. They were the only shoes I owned with a perfect heel, adding two inches to my 5-foot-4 frame. I wore a floral button top with a fitted cranberry color corduroy jacket. I looked cute and casual, long straight blond hair pulled back with a thin, clear headband. I wore gold hoop earrings and gold bangles on my wrist. It was my version of a police uniform. I was ready to serve and protect.

I informed Dad that Gretchen and I were hanging out. I failed to tell him we would be attending Cal's party. I figured he didn't need to know. It would only confuse him. I felt mildly guilty lying to Ryan, though. He asked if I was free tonight, and I told him I already made plans with Gretchen. He seemed oblivious to my lie that we were having a girls night at her house, and it only made me feel worse.

I picked up Gretchen around ten, and we made our way to the party. I had no idea what to expect when we pulled up to Cal's house. I'd never seen it. We parked down the street and walked to his house. It was one of those ridiculous $900,000 homes with the brick and stone and every other design element you could think of decorating the façade. Overly manicured lawn. I thought I was standing in an office park.

It was already dressed up for Christmas. White lights all over the trees, outlining the house. Wreaths on the windows; candles inside them. I liked the decorations, but I was tempted to come back another evening and put up one strand of colored lights on a bush. The house needed a rebel strand.

We knocked on the door, but no one answered. I heard music from inside, and thought it was loud enough to keep the guests inside from hearing anyone on the outside. I pushed open the door.

This party was much more subdued than Tanner's. Cal's house was expensive. The furniture looked expensive. The floor we were standing on looked expensive. Hell, the paint color on the walls looked expensive, and everyone seemed to understand. No one would be getting rowdy in this house. There was still dancing, but Cal made sure to push the furniture to the side, covering it with sheets. I suspected he put away all the expensive glassware and accessories. The tables and bookcases were bare. He was careful, and that made sense. He was careful about everything he did.

"Hey, Brooke," Cal said, approaching us.

"Hi," I replied. I flashed a sweet smile, and that seemed to encourage him.

"So, um, I'm sorry about ordering beer on our date. I should have apologized days ago, but you looked busy," he said. It was cryptic, but I knew exactly what he was talking about. He spotted me several times chatting with Ryan in between classes. He knew there was something going on between us.

"No worries," I replied.

"No no. I was a total dick. I shouldn't have drank all that," Cal said.

Shouldn't have drunk.

I didn't know what to say. "It happens."

"No, Brooke." Cal was insistent. "It doesn't happen. I have manners. I know better, and I feel like a complete jerk. I just freaked out about the whole Parker situation. I had no idea he was being mean to you. Did you girls get home okay?"

Cal was difficult to understand. There were instances

of complete idiocy followed by knight-in-shining-armor acts. It's like he had split personalities.

"Yeah. But you owe us cab fare," Gretchen said.

I tensed.

Cal furrowed his brows for a half second before relaxing his face once more into a pleasant smile. "You're right."

"No, she's not," I objected. "It's fine. Don't worry about it."

"No, I want to give you cab fare," Cal said. "It's the least I can do."

"Please, Cal," I said. "I cannot take your money. I won't take your money."

I watched him pull out his wallet and placed my hand over his.

"I won't take it," I whispered. "It's okay. The apology was all I needed."

Cal hesitated. He wanted to argue, but instead, he tucked his wallet back in his pocket.

"You girls thirsty?" he asked, looking towards the kitchen.

"Um, just a water for me," I said. "I'm DD tonight."

"Gotcha. And for you, Gretchen?" he asked.

"I'll have a water as well," she said.

Cal looked at her strangely. "You're the DD, too?"

"I can party without drinking," she said, staring him down like prey she was ready to maul.

Cal chuckled. "I didn't know that was possible."

Gretchen opened her mouth to reply, but I cut her off.

"We're gonna be hanging out on the dance floor," I said. "Thanks for getting us those waters," and I dragged Gretchen away before she had the opportunity to make another flippant remark.

"What is wrong with you?!" I hissed, trying to find the rhythm to the song while running the conversation over in my head. I wasn't good at multi-tasking.

"You look like a retard, Brooke," Gretchen replied, shaking her hips like a belly dancer.

"Gretchen, keep your mouth shut for the rest of the evening," I demanded. "Got it?" I stopped altogether and closed my eyes, concentrating on the beat of the song until I thought I discovered it. I started dancing again, and Gretchen burst out laughing.

"Can you move away from me, please? Cute boy over there is eyeing me up, and you're totally killing my mojo."

I rolled my eyes and gave up. Usually I was a good dancer. No, not good. Great. And usually I had someone tiptoeing around me within the first ten minutes on the dance floor trying to get my attention. Tonight I looked stupid. Just plain stupid, like someone who doesn't get out much. I knew the problem. I was wound up like a top, terrified of spinning out of control because I was trying to be braver than I actually was. I put the sole responsibility of taking care of strangers on my shoulders, and the party was so packed I feared I wouldn't even find them until it was too late.

"I'm going to do some rounds," I said. "See if I can spot Melanie and Taylor."

Gretchen became serious like she suddenly remembered why we were here.

"You worry about Melanie," she said. "I've got Taylor."

We made a plan before we arrived. I showed Gretchen Taylor's picture from last year, made her study it, commit every detail to memory so she could track her at the party. I did the same with Melanie. The goal was to intervene in any activity we thought looked sketchy. Taylor was a player on Aaron's team, and I wasn't sure about him yet. Melanie was one of Tim's drafts, and I knew he was trouble. If he had the opportunity to take advantage of her tonight, he would.

Cal arrived with our bottled waters before we started. He wanted to talk to me some more, and suddenly I realized he planned to stay close to me all evening. Gretchen slunk away to start investigating, and I felt helpless, trapped.

"So, are you liking Charity Run?" he asked.

"Sure," I replied.

"I noticed you're not involved in any sports," Cal said. "Amazing considering you have a nice figure."

And we're back to idiocy.

"Thanks, I guess," I replied.

"Any reason why you don't do sports?"

What was up with the weird questions?

"Just not really sporty, I guess. I mean, I try to work out some," I said, scanning the crowd for Melanie.

"Well, you should definitely do active things," Cal said. "If you want to keep that body."

I ignored him as I continued searching the room.

"Looking for someone?" Cal asked.

"No, just people-watching."

He took another swig of his Heineken.

"So, I thought I'd invite you to a swim meet," Cal said.

"Why?"

He looked at me funny.

"I mean, when?" I laughed. "Did I just say why? I meant when. Good grief, my brain is mush. When is your swim meet? I'd love to go."

Bad recovery, but hopefully it would work.

"Well, not 'til the spring actually," Cal replied.

"Thought you'd seal the deal early?" I asked lightly.

He grinned. "Yeah, I guess. We've gotta practice in the off-season, you know."

"Uh huh."

"And we're practicing Friday afternoon. Care to swing by and take a couple of shots for the yearbook?"

This was interesting. Ryan and I weren't officially dating, but we talked at school all the time. Sure, we didn't touch each other—we weren't into the whole PDA thing—but it was obvious we were interested in each other. And Cal didn't care. He caught me in the hallway on more than one occasion chatting it up with Ryan, and he simply didn't care. I would venture to say he was *more* interested in me because of it. And a week or two ago, I would have reveled in that realization, welcomed the opportunity to trap the son-of-a-bitch. But I was changing. I wasn't sure I liked that plan anymore.

Once I accidentally told Terry, everything shifted. He was a reflection staring back at me, mouth agape in disbelief and disgust, and I saw for the first time how messed up I was. How the guilt had twisted me into a monster and a victim. I wanted something better for myself now. I still wanted justice for Beth, but I didn't think I could make myself a sexual sacrifice anymore. The fact that Cal was still interested in me, though, made me doubt my decision.

"Uh . . . sure, I guess."

Cal looked pleased. I imagined he had plans to show me just how ripped and awesome he was. "Okay. Practice starts at 3:45. So—"

"Dude, Collin's got the game set up." It was Hunter who interrupted us, and thank God. I had things to do.

"Interested in beer pong?" Cal asked.

I held up my water and shook it.

"Oh that's right. DD. Mind if I split for awhile? I'll come see you later," he said.

"Go. Have fun," I replied, and started meandering through the crowd.

Gretchen grabbed my arm in the upstairs hallway.

"Taylor's not here," she said.

"How do you know?"

"I asked."

"Oh." Asking never occurred to me. "Who told you?"

"Her friend, Carrie. She got sick last night. Food poisoning. So bad she actually had to go to the hospital."

"Well, I'm sure Aaron's disappointed," I said.

"Yeah, poor Aaron," Gretchen replied. "Dickhead."

"I just got away from Cal," I said.

"Okay. Not good." Gretchen grew worried. "This party's been going on since nine."

I pulled out my cell phone. Eleven-thirty. How was it already eleven-thirty?

"It's time to open some doors," I said, and Gretchen nodded.

We made our way down the hallway—the longest hallway in the world, with about a hundred doors.

I heard muffled talk through the sixth door I came upon and pushed it open.

"Get the hell out!" Tim yelled, lying on top of a girl I suspected was Melanie.

"Oh my God! I'm so sorry! I thought this was the bathroom," I lied, trying to get a better look. She was awake but not altogether lucid. "Melanie?"

She turned her face in my direction, eyes out of focus, and grinned.

"That's *my* name!" she squealed.

"Melanie, I've been looking all over God's green earth for you!" I said, walking towards the pair. Gretchen followed me in. Tim looked irate.

"I thought I told you to leave," he snapped.

"Will you get off of her, please?" I asked pleasantly. "Her father is pissed off ready to come over here with a loaded shotgun. She wasn't supposed to come here tonight. Now either get off of her and let me take her home, or get your balls blown off a little later when Mel's dad gets here. Your choice."

Tim slunk off his obviously drugged date and sat on

the edge of the bed.

"What's wrong with her?" I asked, trying to pull Melanie up in a sitting position.

"Nothing," Tim mumbled.

"Melanie? How much did you have to drink?" I asked.

She smiled stupidly. "My name's Melanie."

"I know," I replied. "Now put your arm around my neck. We're gonna help you out of here."

"Where am I?" she asked, flopping her arm over my shoulder.

"A very bad place," I said, and shot Tim a nasty look.

"What the fuck?" he asked.

I wasn't planning on saying anything to him, but I couldn't hold my tongue.

"She's obviously drunk or whatever. Why were you on top of her?"

"Fuck you. Like you've never made out drunk?" he asked. He was defensive, jaw clenched, ready to do damage. I knew it was time to leave.

"Come on, Melanie," I said, and Gretchen helped me walk her out of the bedroom.

We made it all the way to my car before the shaking started. Gretchen saw and took the car keys.

"I'll drive," she said.

I sat in the back with Melanie trying to comfort her, but I was a mess myself. Total fear. I'd never felt it before. I realized I was functioning on pure adrenaline the entire time I helped Melanie out of the house, and now it was gone, leaving panic and dread in its wake.

"You're okay, Brooke," Gretchen said in the rearview mirror. "Keep it together, and tell me where Melanie lives. Do *not* faint on me."

I had come prepared. I recorded Melanie's and Taylor's addresses on my cell phone in case I needed to take them home and they were too drunk or drugged out to tell me where they lived. I didn't actually think it would come to this. What if I had gone to the wrong room? What if I had burst in too late? What if the door was locked?

My body shuddered violently.

"Brooke! You are fine," Gretchen said. "Breathe in and tell me the address."

Right. The address. I was clumsy pulling out my cell phone, and I punched about ten wrong buttons before pulling up my notes.

"Twenty-six fifty West Moreland Avenue," I said.

"Of course I have no idea where the hell that is," Gretchen mumbled, and pulled over. She punched the address in her GPS then pulled back out onto the road.

Melanie's house wasn't far away, but it gave me enough time to compose myself and get the shaking under control. Both Gretchen and I walked her to the front door and rang the bell.

Melanie's mother answered, gasping when she took stock of her daughter.

"Mommy!" Melanie said. "I love you so much, Mommy!"

"What is this?" Melanie's mom whispered.

"Mrs. uh . . ."

"Graham," she said, moving aside to let us in.

"Mrs. G, we were at the same party as your daughter," Gretchen said. "We don't know Melanie, but we saw that she was pretty wasted and thought we better take her home."

"Oh my God," Mrs. Graham said. "Oh my *God*." And then Mrs. Graham lost it completely, bursting into a fit of tears while Gretchen and I stared at one another.

"Okay," I said. "First thing is getting Melanie some water and food. Go see what's in the kitchen."

Gretchen nodded. We sat Melanie on the couch, and Gretchen disappeared.

"Mrs. Graham, is your husband here?" I asked. Mrs. Graham was slumped in an armchair bawling uncontrollably.

"Things like this don't happen in our family!" she wailed.

"Mrs. Graham, where's your husband?"

"We attend Mass every Sunday. Melanie is an honors student!"

"Mrs. Graham! Where is Mr. Graham?" I demanded.

"He's on a business trip," she cried.

"Of course he is," I muttered. I now felt responsible for taking care of a drugged-out daughter and her emotionally distraught mother.

Gretchen—thank God for Gretchen!—made a sandwich for Melanie and a cup of tea for her mother. I wondered what the hell took her so long, but I was so happy for the tea as it appeared to settle Mrs. Graham's nerves.

"Girls, I'm sorry," she said, hand shaking, rattling the teacup. I told her not to apologize but that we couldn't stay all night. I was close to missing curfew, and Dad had already extended it tonight until 12:30 because he was delirious about his date. I couldn't push it.

Gretchen tried to feed Melanie, who was more interested in kissing the sandwich than eating it.

"I love you, sandwich," she said. "You're my favorite sandwich."

"Melanie, do you know what you drank? What you took?" I asked.

"I drank a cup of looooove," she said. "Can I have more?"

What? I was no drug expert, never caring to do anything myself. I smoked weed once but hated the stench of it. I didn't really get high either. I just sat like a fat toad on a log gobbling up any food that flew by me. I decided weed would do nothing but make me overweight and stupid, so I never touched it again. But Gretchen knew about drugs. She went through a stint of moderate drug use in tenth grade before she finally found better friends. Weed, acid, cocaine. You name it. She stayed away from meth, though. She understood all about the picking and didn't want to ruin her pretty little face.

"What's she on?" I asked Gretchen. I didn't care if her mother heard.

"Ecstasy," Gretchen replied. "She's in love with everything. Total ecstasy, and a large amount, I think."

"Like, take-her-to-the-hospital amount?"

Melanie promptly threw up all over the couch, and Mrs. Graham jumped from her chair.

"Yes," Mrs. Graham said. "Like, take-her-to-the-hospital amount."

All of a sudden she was in control. Mother mode. What the hell was in that tea? She took a deep breath and wiped her face.

"Girls, I want you to follow behind me until we get there," she said. "Then you can go home. I know it's late. I just want to be sure I have some help just in case. If you need me to explain to your parents why you were late getting home, I will."

"No!" we said in unison.

"It'll be fine," I said.

I helped Mrs. Graham lift Melanie off the couch. She threw up all over the floor, and I panicked.

"Does this happen with ecstasy?" I asked Gretchen.

"I think that's from the alcohol," Gretchen said, opening the front door for us.

Neither Gretchen nor I said a word as we followed Mrs. Graham to the ER. I was terrified. I never saw someone so drugged and drunk out of her mind. I felt naïve in that moment, and I was ashamed of it. I can't explain why. There's nothing wrong with being naïve. There's nothing wrong with having abstained from drug use. Still, I felt helpless, having to rely on Gretchen for information. *I* wanted the information. *I* wanted control. I was lost without it.

I followed the tail lights around the bend to the hospital entrance thinking I would kill Tim—murder him in cold blood—if anything happened to Melanie.

SEVENTEEN

Terry caught me as I made my way through the back door at work.

"News?" he asked.

"About?" I said, tying my apron around my waist.

"Don't make me spell it out for you, Wright," Terry replied.

"Ohhh, *that* news. Well,"—I smacked my gum a little louder and leaned in close—"we plan on doing it tonight. He's totally dreamy, and I think I'm in love." I winked at him, and he huffed.

"Please keep your too-young-to-be-having-sex life to yourself," Terry said, "and tell me what's going on."

"Why do you care?" I asked, walking over to the order station to sign in.

"Do I have to state the obvious?" Terry replied, following me.

I lowered my voice. "I've already got one dad. I don't need another. And everything's fine. I haven't tried to get myself molested, if that's what you're concerned about."

Terry breathed a sigh of relief.

"I have, however, discovered another rapist," I continued. "And I know he's taking a girl to the movies tonight."

"What's he gonna do in the movies?"

"It's not what he'll do inside the theatre that I'm worried about," I said. "I plan on stopping it before it starts. I was already successful once. At a party last week."

"Wright . . ."

"Hey, if I didn't burst through that door, she would have been raped," I said.

Terry's eyes bugged out of his head.

"Yeah, that's right. She was high on ecstasy, we think."

"Who's 'we'?"

"Gretchen and me."

"So now she's playing crusader, too?"

"Strength in numbers."

"Is the girl all right?" Terry asked.

"Yes, thank God. I waved to her at school today, and she looked at me like she had no idea who I was. Apparently she remembers nothing from that night. Just as well. She'd probably be more messed up if she did."

Terry sighed. "I told you to be careful. You think these guys won't catch on to what you're doing? Have you thought about consequences?"

"Nope. But they should. Once I collect all my data, they and their little slut club are history."

"Taking it to the streets, huh?" Terry asked.

"You better believe it," and I left the kitchen to greet my first customer.

—

Every girl goes to the bathroom right before a movie. We're conditioned or something. I knew to expect Ashley between nine and 9:20. The movie she was seeing with

Tim started at 9:30. I wasn't worried at all about the time they spent in the theatre. I didn't think he was that bold. But I was very worried about his plans for her after the show, and I thought I could scare her into ditching him and getting a cab home. I even brought cab fare for her in case she had no money.

I hovered over the sink pretending to fix my make-up. The mirror gave me a perfect view of girls coming and going without me having to turn around and check. And just like that, as I had expected, Ashley strolled through the door at 9:18. I let her use the bathroom before I said anything. She was washing her hands two sinks down from me when I spoke.

"You don't know me from Adam," I said to her. She reached for a paper towel. "But that guy you're with is bad news."

"Huh?"

"That guy you're with is—"

"No no," she interrupted. "What you said before. What does that mean?"

"What are you talking about?"

"That thing you said about Adam. Does Adam like me?" she asked, her face flushing a rosy pink.

Dear God.

"I mean. He's never said it, but I've been giving him all the signs. You think he likes me?"

Who was she talking about?

"It's an expression," I said. "It's just an expression meaning you don't know me at all."

"Oh." Her face fell.

"But Adam might like you," I said. "And he'd be a lot better than the jackass you're on a date with right now."

"How do you know I'm on a date with Tim?" she asked.

"I saw you, and I'm telling you, Ashley, the guy is

bad bad news," I said.

"Wait. How do you know my name?"

Shit. I was always doing that. Think quickly, Brooke.

"Didn't you know you were popular? Like, everyone knows your name," I said.

"They do?" Her eyes went wide in a dreamy kind of disbelief.

I felt awful.

"Sure. Now listen to me. I want you to get in a cab and go home," I said.

"What?"

"Ditch him, Ashley."

"Why?"

"Because . . . because Tim is seeing a whole lot of other girls. Not just you. He wouldn't be faithful to you for two seconds," I said.

"Oh, I don't care about that," she replied. "I plan on dropping him the second Adam looks my way."

I stared at her.

"Okay, Ashley? It's not just about Tim being unfaithful. He's a bad guy. He does bad things to girls," I said.

She looked intrigued. "Like bondage kind of stuff?" she asked. She leaned in close and whispered, "That's okay with me. I'm kind of into it."

What the *fuck*?

"No, Ashley," I whispered back. "Like rape kind of stuff."

She jumped back, eyes going wide again, but this time not in a dreamy state of disbelief. This time she was scared. I shouldn't have said it. I mean, technically it wasn't slanderous because it was true, but I didn't want this airhead spreading it all over school.

"I think," I said quickly. "Listen, I think he's done it."

"How do you know?" she asked.

"Not important. What's important is that I don't want anything to happen to you. So go home. Don't talk to him over the phone or at school. Don't mention me. Don't say anything. Okay?" I knew it was wishful thinking, but I had to try.

She nodded.

"Ashley? I'm serious. When he calls you, do not answer. When you see him Monday—because it's inevitable, you will see him Monday—tell him you can't talk to him anymore. Don't say why. Just do it. And then walk away. Understand?"

She nodded again.

"I'm gonna call you a cab," I said. "Here's money."

She took it without speaking.

"Are you okay?" I asked, dialing the number for City Star Cabs.

"He was going to rape me?" she whispered.

"I don't know. Maybe. Maybe not. But you're safe now, okay?" I said, wrapping my arm around her shoulder as I spoke to the dispatcher.

I watched Ashley climb into the cab before going back inside. I had to pee, the irony being that I had hung out in the bathroom all evening. I rounded the corner and smacked into Tim. He laced his fingers with mine in one deft movement and pulled me down the hallway. I looked like his reluctant date, digging in my heels. I should have screamed then, but I was too surprised at the turn of events. I had planned on sneaking out of the theatre without him ever spotting me.

"What the fuck are you doing?" he demanded, dropping my hand and backing me into the corner of the hallway.

"I'll scream to high heaven if you do anything," I warned.

"Is there a reason you keep fucking up my dates? I mean, who are you anyway?"

"I don't know what you're talking about," I said.

Tim snorted. "You think I'm stupid or something? I saw you send Ashley off in a fucking cab! Did I do something to you that I can't remember? You got some vendetta with me? What the hell did I do to you?"

I wanted to tell him it's not what he did to me; it's what I knew he'd do to Ashley. It's what I knew he did to Amelia.

And then the righteous anger bubbled up, and it spilled over at the wrong time with the wrong words.

"I *know*," I said so softly I thought he wouldn't hear.

Tim reared back as though I slapped his face. He stumbled into a couple on their way to Theatre 5. He mumbled an apology while rearranging his stunned face. And then he leaned into me once more, hands on either side of my head.

"Oh, you know?" he asked. It came out as a sensual whisper. "What is it you think you know?"

He was taunting me, raking his eyes up and down my body. Suddenly I wasn't brave anymore.

"I . . . I know y-you're trouble," I stuttered.

"You're right," he cooed. "I am trouble. So you better watch out."

"Don't threaten me," I said. I was so happy I got the words out without faltering.

"Oh, I'm not threatening you. I don't have to threaten little girls like you because you'll do what I say," Tim said.

I trembled now from outrage and humiliation. I wasn't some "little girl".

"Fuck you," I spat, and pushed against his chest with all my might. He could have kept me pinned in the corner easily, but he moved aside, allowing me the illusion that I'd pushed him away with my strength.

"Stay away from me, bitch," I heard Tim say as I booked it down the hallway.

—

"So, what trouble have you gotten yourself into lately, Brooke?" Dr. Merryweather asked.

I tensed.

"Hey, take it easy. Everything in here is confidential. Remember?" she said good-naturedly.

"No trouble," I lied.

"Brooke. You know the drill. If you don't open up to me, then my hands are tied. I can't help you the way you need, so you've gotta trust me. Remember all this?"

I nodded.

"Okay. So tell me about these nightmares."

"Wait. How do you know about my nightmares?" I asked, shifting uncomfortably in my seat.

"Are you serious? Your dad called. He set up this appointment. You think he didn't tell me what was going on?" she asked. She wrote something down on her pad of paper, and I thought she was taking notes about me. I imagined they read, "Dip shit."

"I'm not a dip shit," I muttered.

"That's not what I wrote, Brooke," Dr. Merryweather said patiently.

"Whatever."

She smiled pleasantly and showed me her pad. She was right. She didn't write "dip shit." She wrote my name and birth date.

"Oh," I said. I tried for an apologetic smile. "My bad."

"So what's got you all upset that you're having nightmares?" Dr. Merryweather continued.

"Oh, I don't know," I said airily. "I sneaked around with my best friend's boyfriend. We had sex behind her back. Then she killed herself because she got raped. Now she's haunting me in my dreams and telling me I deserve to have bad shit happen to me. Oh yeah. I've discovered a group of boys at school who fuck girls and score themselves on it."

I leaned back in my chair feeling smug. Take that, Doc! And here you thought I was just sad about my mommy moving away.

"Maybe all that combined has something to do with it," I concluded for good measure.

Dr. Merryweather drew in her breath. "Well, it looks like we've got some work to do."

"Evidently."

"Brooke?"

"Hmm?"

"Perhaps you've considered that it's not your friend who's haunting you? Rather, it's you who's haunting you?"

Score one for the doctor.

"Of course I have," I said. I felt defensive and stupid. Of course I thought that it was probably me, my psyche, telling me I was a bad person and deserved horrible things to happen to me. Wasn't it simply my brain conjuring my own guilt in the form of an angry ghost? What? This doctor thought I was a moron? A dip shit?

"Lemme see that paper again," I said.

Dr. Merryweather smiled and showed me her writing. Still my name. And birth date.

"Let's talk about the betrayal," the doctor said.

"I'd rather not," I replied.

"Brooke, talking it out helps."

"What is there to say? I was a horrible friend."

"So how do you make amends?" Dr. Merryweather asked.

"Really? I thought you were supposed to tell me," I said, feeling my irritation grow. I crossed my arms over my chest.

"That's a defensive move, Brooke," Dr. Merryweather said. "You're better than that."

I dropped my arms and huffed.

"Now, I can't tell you how to make amends. You have to discover your own peace. But I can tell you that it's no angry ghost haunting your dreams. You're punishing yourself for the past. Unable to move on. Is there something you think you have to do in order to move on?"

Yes. I needed to do something. I had a purpose once, but I thought now I couldn't do it.

"Brooke? You've got to open up to me. Do these boys have anything to do with your deceased friend?"

I swallowed. "Huh?"

"Well, you mentioned them in the same breath. You told me about your cheating, your friend's rape, and these boys. Are they connected?"

"Um . . ."

Dr. Merryweather thought for a moment. "Did one of those boys rape her?"

My eyes went wide. Was she a psychologist or an investigator, or were they one in the same?

"I see," the doctor whispered. She wrote something else down on her pad.

"What are you writing?" I asked quickly.

She ignored me. "Brooke, it's clear you think you owe your friend. What is it you plan to do?"

What I plan to do? I have no plan. I have nothing.

"Brooke?"

"I'm not planning anything. It's just that I go to school with this jackass every day, and it's hard to move on from my friend's death when I have to see his face."

"I can understand that," Dr. Merryweather said.

"No one knows he's a rapist. Well, no one who counts, anyway," I said.

"What do you mean?"

"The police. People who could put him away. No one knows because girls aren't saying anything," I said.

"There are more victims?" she asked. "How do you

know?"

I sighed. "I've been digging around."

"Is it dangerous what you're doing?"

I shook my head. "Just illegal."

"Well, I'm not your moral compass, but anything illegal may not be the healthiest thing for you right now. How can it possibly help you move on from your grief?" the doctor asked.

I considered her for a half moment. I knew I could trust her. She took an oath or something like that. She couldn't repeat anything I said unless I threatened to kill somebody. I think, anyway. I don't know all the details of the doctor-patient confidentiality thing. But I knew I could trust her. Mom and Dad had no clue about the things I confessed to Dr. Merryweather years ago when I started therapy because of my claustrophobia. I knew this to be true because they looked at me every day like I was the sweetest, most innocent child in the world.

I drew in my breath and let it out slowly. Deliberately slowly. Dr. Merryweather knew what that meant. She resituated herself in her large club chair to get comfortable.

"Okay, so, it was like the best of times and the worst of times," I began.

"Would have been better if you didn't include the word 'like'," Dr. Merryweather said.

I sighed. "I slept with Beth's boyfriend behind her back."

"I fail to see the 'best of times' in that."

"Well, the sex was incredible, but the cheating and lying were unforgiveable," I replied.

I laid out the entire story for Dr. Merryweather, right up to my discovery of the Fantasy Slut League and the boys I suspected were rapists. I even confessed to the doctor my old plan to self-sacrifice but didn't receive the shocked reaction I expected. I did, however, receive a slew of questions about my emotional state and my struggle with guilt and forgiveness.

I listened politely to the psychobabble wondering what 18-year-old girl with half a conscience *wouldn't* be guilt-ridden and have a hard time forgiving herself. I didn't want my own fucking forgiveness anyway. I wanted Beth's, and she was no longer here to give it to me.

The session concluded with a hug. I never thought that was professional, even when I started therapy at eleven years old, but I had come to view Dr. Merryweather as more of a wise, if a bit self-important, old grandmother than a psychologist. If nothing else, I got to dump my problems on someone for a whole hour without being interrupted or made to feel guilty over it.

I scheduled another session for the following week.

—

Ryan and I were officially dating by Christmas, but not before I came clean about going on a date with Cal and attending his party.

"I swear I don't like him!" I had cried.

"I knew about the party, Brooke," Ryan said. "Even a reject like me hears about the parties." He eyed me curiously. "I'm not mad, but why did you go?"

"My friends were insistent, and I didn't want them going alone. Drunk girls are easy targets," I said. It wasn't exactly true. Melanie and Taylor weren't my friends, but I went to the party regardless to protect them. And that part was true.

Ryan nodded. "And the date?"

"He wouldn't leave me alone about it. And I know what you said about him being bad news. I just thought I could go and show him how lame I was and then he'd stop harassing me about a date," I said.

"You're far from lame, Brooke," Ryan replied.

I shrugged. "Well, I was pretty lame on the date."

Ryan thought for a moment. "You could have just told me. I could have beaten the shit out of him for you."

I smirked. "I didn't want you getting blood on your hands."

"Oh, I'd love to get blood on my hands," Ryan said. He sounded dead serious.

I shivered involuntarily. "Why does he hate you, Ryan?" I asked softly.

Ryan rubbed his jaw. "Because I don't want to be like him."

We were quiet for a time before I spoke. "Are you upset with me about the date?"

Ryan shook his head. "No, Brooke. But I do wish you would have listened to me in the restaurant. I wasn't kidding when I said that Cal was a bad guy."

I nodded. I wanted so much to know why Ryan thought Cal was bad. A tiny part of me suspected that he had some knowledge of Cal's devious sexual behavior, but I was unwilling or too scared to ask him. I don't know why, but I didn't want Ryan involved in my investigation. I liked him on the outside, and I liked escaping to the outside every time we were together.

"I should have asked you a long time ago to be my girlfriend. Officially speaking. Will you?" he said.

Were we just talking about Cal? Because I couldn't remember. All I knew in this moment was that Ryan wanted me as his official girlfriend, and it felt like a huge box of fireworks had been set off all at once inside my heart and mind. An ecstatic explosion.

I nodded enthusiastically and crushed my lips to his.

I'm sure people at school knew we were together even though we kept our relationship low key. We talked with one another when we got the chance between classes and sat together at lunch. We were never physical, though. He preferred to keep that behind closed doors, and I was never one for open displays of affection anyway. I think Cal understood that Ryan and I were together, and he stopped bothering me with his "That guy is bad news" rhetoric.

Perhaps making our relationship official right before a major holiday like Christmas wasn't the wisest idea considering neither one of us felt comfortable giving each other presents. We didn't want to deal with the pressure of it and thought time spent together was the most appropriate gift we could give. He took me to dinner one evening and then to the North Carolina Museum of Art to see a Picasso exhibit. He listened intently while I jabbered about lighting and colors and meanings that were even over my head. It was a perfect night, made all the more perfect by what he asked me on the way back to our neighborhood.

"I've been doing a lot of thinking, Brooke," Ryan began.

"Mmhmm."

"And I sort of had this planned out in the hopes that you'd say 'yes'."

My heartbeat sped up. "Okay."

"My sister is at a friend's house for the night, and my parents went out of town for the weekend on their annual Christmas trip for two," he said.

"Where did they go?" I was curious.

"They went to some bed and breakfast in the mountains," Ryan replied.

I smirked. "And they trust you at home alone?"

"Oh, I'm very responsible, Brooklyn. You haven't figured that out by now?"

I shrugged as he pulled into his driveway.

"So would you like to come in?" he said.

I was nervous. I'd waited an eternity to have sex with Ryan. I thought I even acted too brazen or too impatient from time to time, coming across as a common street hussy. Now, he was asking me, and I felt clammy and awkward, like a virgin. I tried for humor.

"Come in for what?"

Ryan grinned. "Coffee."

"Oh, I don't drink coffee," I teased.

Ryan leaned over and whispered in my ear. "Then perhaps you'd like to come in so that I can kiss all over your body and then make love to you."

Yes. I would definitely like to come in for that.

He placed his hand over my heart, feeling the rapid, uneven beating. "I'll take that as a 'yes'."

The last time Ryan saw me topless, I wasn't timid about it. I remember straddling his hips and giving him a good view of my breasts, knowing he liked them, knowing I was in control. But now I was suddenly shy, and I crawled into his sheets, pulling up the comforter to hide my half-naked body from him. He had stripped me down to my bra and panties during an intense kissing session. Afterwards he asked me what I wanted him to do to me. I blushed fiercely and made for the covers.

"Oh, Brooklyn," Ryan said, crawling in beside me. "Why so shy?"

I shook my head and grinned. "I don't know."

"Well, I like you this way," he said, kissing my cheek.

I feared it would come out sounding corny, but I took the chance. "I just feel like this is really special, you know? What we're about to do. I just want to do it right."

"What do you mean by 'do it right'?" he asked.

I turned my face away. "I just want to be good for you." My cheeks were burning, and then the burning moved down my arms and legs. Suddenly I didn't need the warmth of the sheets anymore.

Ryan turned my face to his. "Brooke, you will be good for me. Better than I deserve. Do you understand? I'm not expecting us to make love like experts. We're eighteen. How about you just relax and let me do all the work."

"But that's not fair," I argued.

"Who said anything about fair?" he asked, and kissed me before I could object.

Ryan didn't do all the work, however. He did for awhile, cradling me gently underneath him while he stroked me softly, then more urgently when he told me he needed to feel all of me. I wasn't sure I understood what that meant until he reached under me, lifted my hips, and drove deeper, eliciting screams that he promptly stifled with his mouth.

He rolled us over and forced me to straddle him, holding my hips and helping me move to a slow, almost tortuous rhythm. I felt utterly exposed, and he stared at me unabashedly, making my nipples harden without him touching them.

"I love your body," he breathed, increasing my speed.

I couldn't sit up any longer, and leaned into him, but he shook his head and smiled.

"Sit up, Brooklyn," he said.

"I can't." It was exquisite torture now, my legs shaking from the work.

"Yes you can," Ryan said, and gathered my wrists behind my back, holding them there with one hand while his other rested, fingers splayed, on my stomach.

He tickled my skin, and I squirmed, but he kept his hold on my wrists. The hand on my stomach inched lower, lower until his thumb found my trigger, and I cried out for him to stop.

"Do you really want me to stop?" he asked, rubbing me slowly and gently.

I answered with a moan.

"Do you want me to stop, Brooklyn?" he asked again, and I shook my head violently. He smiled, satisfied.

"I want you to ride me, Brooklyn. Nice and slow."

I think if he told me to jump off a bridge or rock climb with no safety ropes, I would. I moved my hips, feeling him swell inside me while he stroked me with his thumb. How did he do that so perfectly? Usually I was the only one who could touch that intimate spot exactly right to send myself over the edge. But he understood my body, bringing me to the heights of ecstasy every time he touched me there. It was skill. That was certain. But I thought that perhaps he and I had a deeper kind of connection, like he always knew my body before we even met.

My legs were beginning to scream in protest, and it was a delicious mixture of pleasure and pain. I couldn't hide my face from him when I came. He kept my wrists trapped, and I struggled vainly, wanting so much to cover my face with my hands. I'm sure I looked ridiculous, and he was kind enough to let go of my wrists towards the end so that I could collapse on him and bury my face in his shoulder. He wrapped his arms around me, murmured things in my ear I couldn't comprehend, and then moved his hips.

I tensed immediately, then tried to break free of his hold.

"No Brooklyn," he whispered, and held me tighter. There was no use trying to struggle. He was too strong, and I had to accept what was about to happen. I was spent in every way, but he made me work a little longer.

"I'll die," I cried in his shoulder.

"Look at me," he demanded gently, and I lifted my face to his. "You won't die. I promise," and he kissed me while he moved his hips against me, finding a rhythm that I knew would send him over the edge and me to my grave.

I cried in his mouth, struggled some more as his rhythm came faster, but he held me still, forcing me to feel every bit of it, something new and frightening and beautiful. A mixture of heaven and hell.

I buried my face in his shoulder once more as his thrusts became more urgent. Then jerky. He grunted from the force of it, coming hard in me, his body drenched with sweat.

My hips and thighs were sore from my legs being spread for so long. I rolled off of Ryan and pulled my knees to my chest, sighing deeply as my muscles relaxed. He went to the bathroom to dispose of the condom before climbing into bed again.

"Did I hurt you?" he asked.

"Not at all," I replied. I stretched my legs, burying them once more under the sheets, and turned to face my boyfriend.

"Did you like it?" he asked.

"What kind of question is that?" I asked, chuckling. "Did I look like I liked it? Did I sound like I liked it?"

Ryan laughed.

I eyed him curiously. "It's not my business, really, but how many girls have you slept with? I only ask because you've got mad skills."

Ryan pushed the sheet down over my hips. "I like you like this. Full frontal."

I tried to pull the sheet up once more, but he pushed my hands away.

"You want to know the truth?" he asked.

"No, I want you to lie to me."

"Funny." He scratched his head and screwed up his face in thought. "I've slept with six girls."

"Holy shit." The words escaped my lips before I could stop them.

"And I suppose now we fight about it?" he asked.

That irked me. I had no plans to fight with him about anything. "No. Why would we fight about it?"

"Well, it's happened in the past, is all."

"Well, I'm not your past. I'm your present. And I'm fine with it," I said. I didn't know if I was completely fine with it, but I didn't think I had a reason not to be.

"What are you thinking?" Ryan asked.

"You said you hadn't made out in a year," I said, just now remembering our first make-out session.

Ryan shifted uncomfortably. "Yeah, well, I slept with those girls in tenth grade and part of eleventh grade."

"That's kind of young," I said.

"I know it's young. And I know it's a lot of girls in a short period of time. That's what you're thinking, right?"

"Well, no and yes. I mean, did you love those girls?"

"When I was making love to them, yes."

What the hell did that mean?

"Were they all your girlfriends at one point or another?" I asked.

"No."

"Are you a player?"

"No."

"Then I don't get it."

Ryan looked like he was debating how much to share with me. I didn't like that either. I was his girlfriend. I thought he should feel comfortable telling me anything.

"Some of the girls were my friends. I lost my virginity to one of them. We both wanted to experience it with someone we could trust. We dated briefly after that, but we weren't right for each other."

"Uh huh." I was utterly fascinated.

"Sometimes I did it as an escape, but I always made sure she understood that."

He rolled on to his back and placed his hands under his head.

"Sometimes I did it because I wanted . . . I needed to make someone feel good. It made me feel good to make someone else feel good."

He glanced at me briefly. "I suppose you think I've

got issues."

"No. I don't think you have issues." But I did think he was hiding something from me. Some sort of terrible pain that made him seek solace in sex. No wonder he was so damn good at it. What was that talk about not being "experts"? That we're just eighteen? He certainly was no amateur, and I suddenly felt foolish and unstudied.

"And, really, if I'm being perfectly honest, I just love a woman's body. I love to touch it. I love to kiss it. I love to make her feel important and special," he said. "And I really love to make her come."

"Are you a sex addict?" Again, I did not mean for those words to slip out of my mouth.

He chuckled. "No Brooke, but I can understand why you would ask that."

What I wouldn't give to open his brain up right now and peek inside. Get an idea about this stranger I'd just given it up to.

"I hope this doesn't make you look at me differently. I mean, I understand if it does. I understand if you can't be with me."

Whoa! Back it up, buddy!

"Who said anything about that?" I asked. I curled into him, resting my head on his bicep and wrapping my arm around his waist. "Please don't ever say something like that again."

He kissed my forehead. "I won't. I'm sorry. It's just I know what I must sound like. A sex-crazed teenager who's got an unhealthy obsession with the female body."

I giggled. "I don't know that I mind all that much." I thought back to my orgasm. No, I didn't think I minded at all.

But one little unsettling feeling poked and jabbed at my heart. I was no psychologist, and I thought therapy was a load of bullshit, but Ryan was sleeping with women because he felt guilty. That was my assessment. I'm sure

Dr. Merryweather would concur. Guilty of what, I didn't know. But he felt guilty.

EIGHTEEN

I missed the swim practice three weeks in a row. I kept forgetting about it, and only showed up today because Cal reminded me right after school. I still didn't know how to use the yearbook camera, and I wasn't sure I felt comfortable being in the same room with three predators.

The pool atmosphere was exactly as I expected: sticky and humid. I had to work harder to breathe, taking long, moist gulps of air in my mouth and holding it deep in my chest before expelling it. I breathed through my mouth the entire time. Boys were diving in here and there, swimming laps, yelling and calling each other names the way men do to show camaraderie. I felt out of place and turned to leave.

"There you are," Cal said. "Glad you could make it."

He had on his swim gear which amounted to basically nothing. Speedos, goggles, and swim cap. I could see why girls thought he was hot. He had cut muscles, a ripped chest, and strong, thick legs. *"All the better to pin you down, my dear,"* I could hear him say.

"It only took close to a month," I replied. I got right to the point. "Listen, I don't really feel all that comfortable taking pictures. I still don't know how to use this thing."

"That's not true. You used it during that chorus production," Cal said.

"Yeah, but did you see those pictures?" I asked, chuckling. "They sucked."

"Well, nothing like taking pictures of a practice to give you some practice, huh?"

Cute.

I smiled begrudgingly.

"Here. Lemme give you a quick tutorial," Cal said, and ran through the buttons for me once more, watching to make sure I understood how to zoom the lens correctly. "You're a pro," he said afterwards, and dove into the pool.

I got splashed a little, and it annoyed me to no end.

I walked up and down the side of the pool methodically taking horrible pictures. In the beginning, I pulled the camera from my face after each shot to look at it. And every picture was the same: fuzzy splashes, and if I got lucky, maybe a hand or part of a head poking out of the water.

I quit looking at my work halfway through and decided it was time to leave. It wasn't so much my irritation at being the world's worst photographer. I didn't care. It was really that I grew increasingly nervous the longer I stayed. Where was the swim coach? There was no adult, I realized, and only a handful of swimmers. Where was the rest of the team? I counted them. Just six. The swim team had at least twenty members.

I caught Parker and Tim glaring at me from time to time. I tried to ignore them. They were trying to intimidate me, and I knew why. Tim probably told his buddies about his thwarted dates and how I was responsible for them. He climbed out of the pool along with Cal.

I turned towards my book bag sitting in the far corner of the room.

"Hey, Brooke!" Cal called. "Hold up!"

I should have kept walking.

I should have.

"Let's see what you've got," Cal said, extending his hand for the camera. I walked over to the edge of the pool and turned it over with a huff.

"They're really bad, Cal," I said. "I told you I was no good."

Cal sported a furrowed brow as he flipped through the pictures.

"You're right, Brooke. You can't take a picture to save your life."

I shrugged, then screamed as I was pushed into the pool. I broke the surface breathing heavily, wiping my eyes to discover my attacker. I let loose a string of filthy words as I watched Tim dive in beside me. He hid beneath the water, and I feared he was circling me like a shark. I couldn't touch the bottom and started panicking, kicking my legs hard to tread water.

I moved closer to the edge of the pool and was nearly there when Tim popped up blocking my way.

"You're a jackass," I hissed.

"Just having a little fun, Brooklyn," Tim replied. He pushed off from the edge, wrapping his left arm around my waist and pulling me along in the water.

"Let go!" I screamed, struggling against him. My head felt heavy from the water pulling on the ends of my hair, raking wet furrows in a trail behind me.

I turned to look at the others in the water. Oh my God. How could I be so stupid? There was Hunter hanging on the edge of the pool watching. Aaron oblivious to the scene as he continued his laps. Mike, slipping through the changing room doors, ignoring my plight. Parker staring at me from a bench on the far side of the pool. All the boys in the Fantasy Slut League, and no one was coming to my rescue.

I twisted harder, pushing against Tim's arm with all my might. But he was too strong, and in that second I cursed God for making women so fucking weak. "Get off!"

"Okay," he said, releasing me and pushing me under the water.

I fought ferociously, certain he would drown me. I hadn't the opportunity to take a breath before being plunged beneath the surface, and already felt my chest burning for air: just one small breath of life.

Tim eased up, and I shot out of the water breathing in hungry gulps of wetted oxygen.

"What are you doing?!" I screeched, pulling away the matted hair from my face.

"Playing around," Tim replied. "Jeez, we're just having a little fun. Take it easy," and he plunged me beneath the surface once more.

I dug my fingernails in his wrists, but it did nothing to loosen his grip. He was holding me down longer, I could tell, as my chest began burning urgently, demanding the oxygen I couldn't provide. I wriggled this way and that to no avail, feeling the urgent burning move down into my belly, through my legs to the tips of my toes. My body was screaming silently, and I couldn't save it.

Tim hauled me out of the water, and I clung to him on instinct, breathing deeply between coughs and splutters. He took advantage of my vulnerability by wrapping my legs around him, settling me on his hips so that I could feel his arousal. I tried to break free, but he held me tightly in his arms, shaking his head at my silent plea.

We were at the shallow end of the lane, a place where he could firmly plant his feet and move us round and round in small circles. I thought he was trying to lull me

into a false sense of safety, and I had no choice but to
cling to him harder, praying he wouldn't dunk me under
the water again.

"Did you have fun?" he asked.

I felt the tears spill over to those words as I shook
my head. I imagined I looked a mess with wet, matted hair
and black mascara running down my cheeks. Not only
was he successful in making me feel weak and helpless,
but also in making me feel ugly.

"Brooklyn," Tim said. "It was only a little bit of fun.
Why are you upset?"

He slid his hands over my bottom, and I squirmed.

"Keep doing that," he said, and I stopped.

"I hate you," I sobbed quietly.

"Brooklyn, you don't hate me. But I should hate you.
Why are you spreading rumors about me at school?"

"I'm not spreading rumors about you," I choked.

"You're not? Then why did Ashley think I was a
rapist?" Tim asked.

"You are a rapist," I said, trying once more to free
myself from his grasp.

"Stop struggling," Tim ordered. "Now, lucky for you
she believed me when I told her you were a crazy psycho
bitch ex-girlfriend. And lucky for you, she got her friends
to believe me, too. So you get a free pass this time, huh?"

He slipped his hand between my legs. "But just this
once. Now give me a kiss, and I'll let you go," Tim said.

I shook my head.

"Just one little kiss," Tim cooed.

"Hey, man, what's the deal?" Cal asked, hovering
above us. "Give her to me."

I can't believe I wanted to be passed from one
predator to the next, but in that moment I thought Cal
was the good guy. He was my rescuer.

"Chill out, man," Tim said, releasing me. I reached
for Cal who pulled me easily out of the water. He

wrapped a towel around me and held me close.

"Not cool, dude. She was scared to death," Cal snapped, running his hands roughly over my arms to warm me up. "You can't rough house with girls like you can with guys, you douchebag."

He walked me over to my book bag then out of the pool area to my car. If I were in my right mind, I would have noticed two things: first, Cal never jumped into the water to come after me. He was no rescuer. And two, he had a towel in his arms ready for me. I pictured him, watching the entire scene then strolling lazily to the towel rack before intervening.

Later that night as I lay in my bed shaking with fear and anger, I realized they planned it. There was no real swim practice. They lured me to the pool under false pretenses, then to the edge of the water for Cal to look at the pictures I took. And Cal stood there and watched as Tim pushed me underwater, forcing me to endure minutes of torture that felt like hours. He let Tim grope me before feigning outrage. Throughout the entire ordeal he was silently telling me one thing: "Don't fuck with me. Don't fuck with my friends."

I pulled the covers over my head and burst into tears. I wouldn't mess with him anymore tonight. The truth was that I was genuinely afraid of him for the first time. So I chose to entertain the fear, let it grip me and manifest itself in the sounds of quiet, desperate sobs. But I would only let him do this to me tonight. Tomorrow the fear would be gone.

———

"Jessica Canterly," Terry said on our way to the parking lot.

I whirled around to face him, stopping cold. "Yeah?"

"In and out of psych wards since tenth grade. Family

moved out of state after her freshmen year. Serious shit. She did everything. Cut herself. Developed every eating disorder in the book. Pulled her hair out," Terry said. "I'm talking serious shit."

"I knew it," I whispered.

"Now, hold up," Terry replied. "Just because she has all these psychological problems does not mean she was raped."

"It doesn't?" I asked. I wasn't trying to be a smartass.

"No," Terry said. "I found stuff on her dating back to seventh grade."

"So maybe Parker saw her as an easy target," I replied. "If she's already crazy, who's going to believe she was raped?"

Terry shrugged. "It's not right, Brooke."

"Too hard to say, 'It's not right, Wright'?" I asked.

"You're a dork and completely unfocused. I was saying it's not right to assume something without hard proof. You know that."

I scowled. "That asshole is a rapist. I know he is!"

"Okay then. Have you figured out how you're going to prove any of this?"

"I have, actually," I replied. I smiled a smug little smile, and Terry rolled his eyes. "Can we have this conversation somewhere else? It's freezing out here."

"Get in your car," Terry said.

"No way. We'll get in *your* car and waste *your* gas on the heat," I replied.

"Whatever."

We slipped into Terry's unassuming Acura and blasted the heat.

"Okay, Wright. What's your plan?"

"I'm going to ask them to come forward," I replied.

"You're what?"

"The girls who've been raped. I'm going to ask them to come forward."

"Why would they agree? It's been years for some. No rape test. No DNA evidence. Their word against the guys'. Are you serious?" Terry asked.

"If I can get them together—"

"So you're a group therapist all of a sudden?"

"Shut up. If I can get them together and encourage them to come forward together, I think there's a real chance these boys will get some well-deserved justice," I said. "Strength in numbers."

"That's the stupidest plan I've ever heard."

"Hey! It's not stupid. It's the only thing I've got!"

"You might have to come to the realization that these boys may never see justice. Okay? You may have to be satisfied with exposing their league and embarrassing them, because that may be all you get."

"No!" I slapped my hand on the dashboard.

"Wright, do not do that to my car," Terry warned.

"I'll never be satisfied with a little bit of embarrassment. I want them in jail. They're criminals who belong in jail."

"So your plan is to trick these girls into what? Coming over to your house for a sleepover? Then you expose each of their painful secrets to the group and tell them they need to take those painful secrets public? With no evidence? No proof? Do you hear how fucking stupid that is?"

"Fuck you."

"Typical teenager response," Terry scoffed.

"I hate you."

"And there's another."

"Shut up and help me then!" I screamed.

"I don't have an answer, Brooke. I don't have a plan. The only thing I can tell you is to go public with your knowledge of their club."

I hung my head. "You said you'd help me get them. That's what you said."

"I know, Brooke. But I can't make them confess to rape. And I can't make those girls come forward. They have every right to stay silent. That's their right, and I think you forget that. You think they have a duty to your friend, but they don't. Their justice isn't her justice, don't you see? They're individuals with individual experiences. I'm not saying it's healthy for them to hold on to their secrets, but it's their right. You can only do so much. And you've done everything you can, and I'm proud of you for wanting to protect them. I really am. Expose the league and you've settled your debt with Beth."

I was crying. I realized it when Terry fished a napkin out of the glove box and handed it to me.

"Can't I just shoot them all in the head?!" I cried, blowing my nose into the musty paper.

"Oh my God. First you want to be a rape victim, and now you want to be a murderer?"

"It's murderess, dumbass. I'm a girl."

"Wright, you need to visit a therapist," Terry said.

"I already do," I blubbered.

"Well, thank God for that."

I shot him a nasty look.

"And quit crying, for Christ's sake. You cry all the time. Aren't you supposed to be big and tough?"

I looked at him stunned. "For real?"

"Yeah, Wright. 'For real'. Straighten up and stop acting like a total wimp. You wanna be some badass fem crusader? Then start acting like one."

"You are the biggest jerk on the planet!"

"Yeah, and one hell of a good friend to you," Terry replied.

Well, I couldn't argue that.

I drove home with "Big Girls Don't Cry" playing over and over in my head. Don't ask me how I knew the song. It wasn't Frankie Valli singing, though. It was Terry instead, and I laughed my ass off imagining him leading the Four Seasons to the tune. No tears. Exactly how he'd want it.

—

"Are you never going to talk to me again?" I hissed, watching Lucy stack her books and binder in a neat little rectangle on her desk. I leaned over and pushed the top book on to the floor.

"Hey!" she yelled.

"Freaking talk to me," I said.

"I've got nothing to say to you, Brooke," she snapped, and leaned over to retrieve her book.

"Why are you so pissed at me?" I asked.

"You're a smart girl, Brooke," Lucy said. "You figure it out."

"Does this have anything to do with Cal?" I asked, lowering my voice to a barely audible whisper.

Lucy looked flustered. "Don't say his name out loud," she replied.

"What the hell? He's not Lord Voldemort."

"And don't say his name either!" she cried.

I sat there confused. And then I burst out laughing. Lucy glared at me. But apparently my laughter had some kind of effect because her face broke into a grin. And then she giggled. And then she laughed, too. Hard.

"Okay okay," I said, wiping my eyes. "Does your not talking to me have anything to do with He-Who-Must-Not-Be-Named? And I'm referring to Cal."

"Yes," she said, her laughter dying away.

"All right. What's the problem?"

She turned around, but Cal hadn't come into class yet.

"I told you to stay away from him," she said.

"You never told me why," I replied.

"Because he's a bad guy," she said.

"What makes him bad?"

"Stuff."

"Like what?"

"For goodness sake, Brooke! Why can't you just leave well enough alone?!"

"Because I think he did something to you that you're not telling me. And I know he's done it to other girls because guess what? I knew Beth. Beth Cunningham? She was my best friend."

Lucy's eyes filled with instant tears.

"No. Do *not* cry. Haven't you given him enough of your tears already?" I remembered Terry's words to me. To stop crying. To be strong.

She stared at me, and then she looked up at the ceiling trying to get the water to recede. She was determined, and focused on the ceiling for a long time before she thought it was safe to face me again. When she did, her eyes were dry.

"Good. Now there's a start."

She smiled wearily. "I want to tell you a story."

"Okay."

"After school."

We sat in a coffee shop ten minutes from school. I initially suggested the one across the street, but Lucy didn't want to be so close to school when she made her confession. There'd be too many students coming and going. It was a popular hangout spot for Charity Run seniors.

We ordered café mochas then tucked ourselves into a dimly lit corner table.

"I can't believe I'm gonna tell you all this," she said, sipping her drink carefully.

"I kind of already know," I said, trying to ease her anxiety.

"No, you don't, Brooke," Lucy replied. "You don't

know anything."

I wanted to feel offended, but I couldn't. She was right. I didn't know anything about her horrific experience. In all honesty, I didn't really know anything about Beth's experience either. She never told me the details. She just described how Cal licked her tears and covered her mouth. And that was too much to know. I wish she had kept those things to herself.

"I was so excited to start high school," Lucy began. "And I was a really happy girl back then. I had friends. I was involved in everything."

"I know."

"Huh?" Lucy furrowed her brows.

"Well, I kind of did some research in old yearbooks," I confessed.

Lucy thought for a moment. "When?"

"When I first met you. That first day in class when I smacked my head."

"Ohhh." Lucy nodded.

I waited patiently for her to continue.

"I don't think I'm the ugliest thing on the planet," she said, "but I could never figure out what attracted Cal to me. I mean, yes, I was a cheerleader, but I don't think I ever fit into that mold. I wasn't popular. I just kind of did my own thing and had fun."

"You must have been kind of popular to win a place on the homecoming court," I said.

Lucy shrugged. "I guess I meant that I didn't really hang out with popular people. I was nice to everyone."

"Ahh. That's why you won," I said.

"Well, whatever it was, Cal liked it, and he started pursuing me from the moment school started."

I shifted nervously in my seat, knowing the conversation was about to get intimate.

"We dated all year, and all year he was a gentleman. I thought I was the luckiest girl in the world, really." Lucy stared off in the direction of a couple huddled at another corner table on the opposite wall. They were telling each other jokes apparently, because they were laughing hysterically.

"You okay?" I asked.

She nodded and continued. "I was so excited about prom. And we had such a fun night until he took me to that motel room."

"He what?"

"Champagne. He fed me champagne all night. He didn't drink a thing. He had a bottle in his car, and I drank some on our way to the prom."

"Hold up," I said. "He was driving? How old was he?"

"He'd just turned sixteen," Lucy said.

"Sixteen in ninth grade?" I asked. "That's kind of old. Did he start school late? Was he held back a grade or two?"

Lucy sighed, then smiled. "Brooke, do you have ADD?"

"Huh?"

"Who cares that he was driving? The point was that he was driving."

I nodded and refocused.

"Anyway, we'd sneak out of the prom occasionally so that I could have a couple of sips. By the end of the night I was hammered. But I mean really hammered, like something-doesn't-feel-quite-right hammered."

I looked at her dubiously.

"Okay, I know that being hammered never feels 'right.' What I meant was I think he drugged the champagne. I mean, yes, I drank a lot of it, but I've had champagne before, and it's never made me feel like that. Really sluggish. Out of it. Like my arms were heavy weights or something."

"I see."

"I remember very little about that evening. I remember making out and getting naked. I was okay with that because we'd gone there before, but then he started getting forceful."

I tensed.

"And there were others."

"*What?*" I was in the middle of sipping my coffee, choking down most of the liquid while some dribbled down my chin. Lucy handed me a napkin.

"I remember that there were others. I don't know how many, but they were talking and laughing." She thought for a moment. "And then they argued for awhile."

I stared at her wide-eyed, one term repeating over and over in my head: gang-raped.

"The last thing I remember was a bunch of hands all over me before I passed out."

We sat in silence. I didn't know what to do, so I finished off my coffee. Lucy was no longer interested in hers. She preferred to watch the young couple holding hands and giving each other occasional pecks.

"Lucy, I'm so sorry," I whispered.

She turned in my direction. It was a reluctant turn, like she didn't want to take her eyes off of the cute couple. Like she wanted to linger in their fantasy a little longer.

"You didn't do anything, Brooke," she replied. "Why are you apologizing?"

I had no response to that. Why was I apologizing? I didn't rape her. But that's what you said when you heard bad news. It was standard. You say you're sorry, like you're apologizing for the wrong or apologizing on behalf of the people who inflicted the wrong.

I shrugged.

"I woke up the next morning wearing my prom dress. It was speckled with blood. I was a virgin, you see, so I figured I must have been raped. But it's kind of hard to make the claim when you can't remember shit."

"What about your parents?"

Lucy snickered. "Well, according to them, Cal brought me home drunk. They got in a huge argument and said he wasn't allowed to date me anymore. Then they got mad at me for being irresponsible about alcohol. Somehow it became all my fault."

I shook my head in disbelief.

"The best part is what happened at school," Lucy went on. "Monday morning I confronted Cal about that night. I wanted to know what happened. Of course, he told me I was crazy. And then he told me he wanted nothing more to do with me, that I was a crazy psycho lush. He spread all kinds of nasty rumors about me. I lost my friends. I quit cheerleading. Somehow, I turned into the psycho bitch at school. People were actually *afraid* of me. Of me!"

Lucy burst out laughing, her fragile frame shaking uncontrollably. "Are you looking at me, Brooke? Are you seeing this?" she asked between giggles. "How could anyone be afraid of this?"

"Lucy . . ."

"I weigh a hundred pounds, Brooke! A hundred pounds! I can't even walk my Saint Bernard because I'm not strong enough! I don't have a mean bone in my body! I don't even know how to be mean to other people. How do they do it, Brooke? How are people mean, 'cause I'd really like to know? I mean, if people are gonna be afraid of me and all, then I'd like to know how to be a fucking bitch!"

Several patrons turned in our direction, and I instinctively jumped from my seat. I put my arm around Lucy and led her out of the coffee shop to my car.

"I mean, if I'm a fucking psychopath lush bitch then I need to know how to act the part!" she screamed in the parking lot. There was no more laughter, only angry tears coursing down her cheeks.

I helped her into the passenger seat of the car and fastened her seat belt.

"He ruined my life!" Lucy dug her hands into the sides of the seat. "And I can't do anything about it! Not a thing!" And then she let out a long, mournful wail. I thought I'd heard it before: complete and utter wretchedness, but I realized I hadn't. Even I, in all my misery and guilt over Beth, had never made a sound like that.

I shook because of it. I was scared of it. I didn't know how to comfort her. I never understood the complete desolation one feels when her will, her rights, are stripped from her. And she doesn't want to hear "I'm sorry" from someone who doesn't have a clue. It's offensive.

I crouched on the ground beside Lucy, letting her cry. Not shushing her. Not feeling embarrassed as people walked in and out of the coffee shop staring at us. Not even offering words of sympathy. I wasn't concerned with anything but my dawning epiphany. It's as though I heard Beth's voice whispering from heaven's gates, and she was forgiving me. Or maybe it was me, for the first time in months, able to let go of my past sins. Able to forgive myself. All because of Lucy, and her revelation to me. I didn't want to be a victim. I didn't want my world ripped apart. I wanted justice, but I realized it had to be sought by different means. I wanted to protect my body, my mind, because I was witnessing what happened to someone when her right to do that was stolen from her.

I drove Lucy to my house. We huddled inside my bedroom all afternoon, and I shared everything with her just like I did with Dr. Merryweather. She breathed a sigh of relief when I promised her I had abandoned my plan to set up Cal, and encouraged me to take my information about the Fantasy Slut League public. I suggested she go forward, but she argued the absence of hard evidence.

"Will you at least tell your parents?" I asked.

Lucy shrugged. "What could they do about it?"

"I don't know, but they're your parents, and they love you."

The side of Lucy's mouth turned up. "I suppose."

"Will you think about it?" I pressed.

She nodded then took my hand. "Yes, Brooke. But I'm only considering what you're saying because you're so nice."

I smirked. "I'm not a nice person, Lucy."

"Yes you are. I know Cal was feeding you all kinds of bullshit about me, but you were always nice, even when I stopped talking to you for awhile."

"I should have told you what I was doing with him a long time ago," I said. "I just didn't know who I could trust."

"It's understandable," Lucy said. "I'm just glad you didn't actually like him."

"Gross. No way," I said, and she grinned.

"I don't think Beth handled what happened to her the right way, but I see why she did it," Lucy said after a time.

I listened, not wanting to interrupt. I wanted to hear the perspective of another victim.

"It's easy to sink into a bad depression. I did. It's easy to withdraw. It's easy to see no purpose in anything: your daily routine, your relationships with others. Everything becomes pointless or scary. For me it was pointless. I think for your friend, it was scary. And when you're scared of the world, you want to escape it."

I hung my head.

"I wish she were stronger. I wish she were still here. It'd be nice to have a friend who understands what I went through. Someone who experienced it, too."

Suddenly I had an idea. I pulled the tarnished half-heart from underneath my shirt. I had started wearing the necklace again about a week ago, hidden under my shirts, resting against my heart. I learned from her mother that Beth was buried with a few of her most special personal belongings, and the half-heart necklace was one of them.

I unfastened the chain and gave it to Lucy.

"What's this?" she asked, fingering the charm.

"Beth gave that half to me on my eighth birthday. She was buried with the other," I explained. "I want you to have it."

"Brooke, I can't take this!" Lucy said, thrusting the necklace into my hands. I pushed back shaking my head.

"I want you to have it, Lucy. I really do. I know you didn't have any connection to her in life, but now you can." I searched for the right words, but I knew my sentiment would come out sounding sappy. "Maybe it can bring you some comfort or something." I averted my eyes. I felt kind of silly and overly dramatic in that moment.

Lucy hesitated for a split second before fastening the chain around her neck.

"Thank you, Brooke," she said softly.

"You're welcome."

NINETEEN

Word spread around school about the boys. None of the girls besides Lucy and me knew about the actual league, but they knew to stay away from Cal and his cohort. No loud talk, just urgent whispers creeping through the hallways like smoke, sending signals and warnings. The impact was immediate. I checked the current scores for Game 3, and no one had earned a single point.

"Sexual frustration is a bitch," Gretchen said, leaning over the back of Terry's arm chair to get a better look at the computer screen. I heard the sharp intake of Terry's breath.

"Stop looking at her ass," I scolded. "She's practically a child."

"I'm about to turn nineteen, thank you very much," Gretchen replied, standing up and turning to face her gawker. "Is sexual frustration a bitch for you, Terry?" she asked in a playful, sultry tone.

Terry ignored her. "Wright, is there a reason you felt the need to bring Gretchen over here?" He pushed past my flirty friend and plopped on the couch.

"She's spending the night with me," I replied,

distracted. I was searching for the picks for Game 4.

"There's no Game 4 set up yet," Terry clarified when I asked.

"Yeah, but shouldn't they have the list of girls by now. They had those pretty early for the other games," I replied.

Terry shook his head. "Maybe they're spooked. I mean, look at those scores. Well, lack of scores. Maybe they know something's up, and they're laying low."

Gretchen sidled over to the couch and sat next to Terry. "I like your tats."

I rolled my eyes.

"I like them, too," Terry replied, then moved farther down the couch.

Terry wouldn't talk to me for weeks after I brought Gretchen to his house for the first time. Yes, I shouldn't have exposed him, but I trusted Gretchen, and we were on our way to the mall. It would have been really freaking inconvenient to make her wait in the car or drop her off somewhere to wait for me while I picked up new information Terry had for me. He eventually forgave me once he learned he enjoyed flirting with my friend.

"Now's probably a good time, then, huh?" I asked.

"What, to blow the whole lid?" Terry replied.

I nodded, and he shrugged.

"I'm sorry you couldn't get all the evidence you wanted, Brooke," Terry said. He sounded genuinely apologetic.

"It's all right. I can be content with this."

"Any of those girls willing to come forward?" he asked.

"I only talked to two of them, and you're right. It's unfair to ask them to expose themselves with little to no evidence. I don't know what I was thinking."

"You were thinking that those boys are assholes who deserve to be punished. There's nothing wrong with that,"

Gretchen said. "I'm proud of you, Brookey."

I smiled. "Well, I guess I'll get all the documents together and then figure out who I want to send them to."

"Do you realize how huge this'll be?" Gretchen asked. Excitement underlined her words.

"I don't know how huge," I admitted. "But I hope it encourages some girls to speak up."

Terry nodded. "I just want you to be safe about it."

"Yeah yeah," I said, dismissing him with a wave of my hand. "You always say that, and I'm always safe." I never did tell Terry about my terrifying pool experience with Tim.

Gretchen leaned into Terry. "So when are you asking me out on a date? It's obvious you like me. That's why you're mean to me and ignore me all the time."

"All the time?" Terry asked, amused. "I've hung out with you a total of four times. And you're too young for me."

"So you *do* like me!" Gretchen said, trapping Terry at the end of the couch and resting her head on his shoulder.

"I'm thirty-six," Terry said, and I watched as he struggled with the desire to put his arm around my very pretty friend.

"I like them older," she cooed, nuzzling his neck.

"Oh my God. I'm still in the room," I said.

Gretchen sat up laughing. "I'm just playing around, Brooke! Jeez, I'm nineteen. Can you imagine? It'd be like that *Sex and the City* episode when Samantha dates that old fart. Remember? She tried to have sex with him but then she caught sight of his flabby ass in the light?"

Terry looked outraged, and I couldn't hide my grin.

"I don't have a flabby ass," he snapped.

Gretchen cocked her head and smiled demurely. "You wanna do me, don't you?"

"Stop!" I screamed. "I can't listen to anymore of this!"

"What does Ryan think about the Fantasy Slut League?" Gretchen asked, changing the subject. It was completely unexpected and made my heart jump.

"What do you mean?" I asked.

Gretchen's eyes went wide with disbelief. "You haven't told him any of this stuff?!"

"I didn't know I was supposed to," I replied.

"Brookey, he's your boyfriend, for Christ's sake! You're sleeping with him."

"Oh God," Terry groaned.

"And you don't tell him about this sex league?" Gretchen looked offended.

"Why should I? I didn't want him worrying, and I didn't want to involve him. It's not his thing, okay?" I said.

The truth was that I didn't want to involve Ryan in the things I knew about Cal and his friends because I liked having him separated from it. I liked that I could escape it all when I was with him, and there was no way in hell I was giving that up.

"But he could have been helping you this whole time!" Gretchen argued. "He could have spied on them or something."

"I don't think so," I countered. "Cal hates his guts. Ryan wouldn't be able to get anywhere near him."

"Still," Gretchen pressed. "He could have been encouraging and supportive or something. Isn't that what boyfriends do?"

"Gretchen, I like that he doesn't know anything. I like that I don't have to talk about this slut league with him. I like that I get to escape it all when I hang out with him, okay? Can you understand that and leave it alone?" I closed Terry's laptop and slid it onto the coffee table.

"Yes, ma'am," Gretchen mumbled, and I rolled my eyes.

"Would it be totally bitchy to say I'm glad you two

haven't met yet?" I asked.

"Yes, you bitch," Gretchen replied. "What? Are you gonna cancel the dinner plans we all have together?"

"No." I felt my face flush.

"Good, because it's high time I met this Ryan person. You shouldn't have kept him away for so long. Don't I get a say in who you date?" Gretchen asked.

"Um, no. Are you crazy?"

"No, I'm not crazy," Gretchen said. "Just feeling a little left out, I guess."

I sighed. "Gretchen . . ."

"Brooke, you're too young to be having sex," Terry said.

I looked at Gretchen, and we both burst out laughing. Perhaps Terry just said it to ease some of the tension. It worked.

"What?" Terry asked. "I'm some sort of ancient or something? Just because I'm a little bit conservative, that's funny?"

"Conservative?" Gretchen said. "You've got tats all over you."

Terry shook his head. "Gretchen, get a clue."

"Terry, I'm not talking to you about sex, okay? Can we change the subject?" I asked.

"Fine, but I don't understand kids these days," Terry replied.

"Oh, who are you kidding? I know all about the '90s, buddy, and I can only imagine the stuff you were into," I said.

Terry blushed and grinned.

"It's not like I'm putting out for every guy on the block," I said.

"Exactly," Gretchen said. "You're in a committed relationship."

I nodded and watched Terry carefully.

"Gross. Whatevs. Just don't let anything get traced

back to me when you take all this crap public. Got it?" Terry said.

"I'm careful. I keep telling you that," I said. "When are you going to trust me?"

"I trust you, Wright," Terry said.

—

"I've never seen you look so sexy," Ryan said, grinning.

It was the springtime, and we were standing in the street, my foot poised on his skateboard. I was wrapped from head to toe in protective gear: helmet, elbow pads, knee pads, even hockey gloves.

"Hockey gloves?" Ryan had asked earlier as he scrounged around in his closet.

"It's inevitable. I'll fall on my hands, and I don't want them scraped up," I replied. "Just give them to me."

Ryan handed the gloves over and kissed my lips.

"You're adorable, and I love you," he said.

My mouth dropped open in shock.

"Don't say anything," he said. He kissed my lips again. "I don't need or want you to say it back. But I wanted to tell you because it's what I feel. And what I know. So when you're ready, you tell me. But for right now, just don't say anything."

I nodded, mouth still hanging open.

"And just because you're so cute standing there in disbelief, let me say it again: I love you, Brooklyn."

I flung my arms around him and smacked the side of his head with my bulky helmet.

"Ouch!"

"Sorry," I said, and crushed my lips to his. I could have stood there in his bedroom all afternoon kissing him, but he wanted to teach me how to skateboard.

I hovered near his mailbox staring at the asphalt.

Suddenly it looked really frightening, especially if I fell face forward into it.

"I'm digging this picture," Ryan said. "I like your foot on my board."

I burst out laughing.

"What?" Ryan asked.

"Why does that sound dirty to me? Like sexual?"

Ryan smirked. "Brooke, keep that little sweet foot right on my board. My board, Brooke. Mmmm."

And I laughed all over again.

"Seriously, though, there's nothing to riding a skateboard. The tricks are a different story, but all riding requires is pushing off with your foot and then positioning your feet on the board that's most comfortable for you."

"I'm afraid of falling over," I said.

"Well, you will. But that's what all your pads are for," Ryan said.

I waved to a car passing through the neighborhood that honked at us. It wasn't a hey-I-know-you honk. It was a girl-you-look-hot kind of honk. I looked down at my knee pads. Maybe they *were* a bit sexy.

Ryan walked me through the basics: pushing off, positioning my feet, stopping by pushing down on the back of the board. I was more than nervous. I was never good at roller skating. I definitely couldn't roller blade. In fact, I hated any wheels besides car wheels underneath me. I was out on the street with him now only because I liked him enough to get scraped up for him.

"I'll hold your hand at first just until you get used to the feel of it," Ryan said.

"You better," I replied.

I kicked off with Ryan holding my hand and jogging beside me. I gripped him hard, wobbling on uncertain feet as we rolled along down the street.

"Okay, Brooke. Stop," he said.

I shook my head. "You stop." And I squeezed hard on his hand.

Ryan stopped short, and I fell, the skateboard slipping out from underneath my feet. It rolled along lazily down the street while Ryan tended to me.

"I'm so sorry, Brooke," he said, chuckling. He helped me off the ground and checked for damage. I think he just enjoyed running his hands up and down my recently shaved legs. "I swear I didn't do that on purpose."

"Yeah right," I said, swatting his hands away.

He trapped my wrists with both hands and held them by my sides while he rained light kisses all over the front of my legs.

"Better?" he asked, looking up at me. The sun was bright, forcing him to squint, and I wasn't sure he could see my nod.

"Let's try again," I said, and he went to retrieve the skateboard.

After thirty minutes I was pushing off and rolling slowly on my own. Always with my arms out, legs slightly bent, body tensed to the max. I knew I'd be sore tomorrow. Learning to turn was a disaster, and I fell forward every time I leaned into the board. I gave up and asked if we could play a video game.

"Now when you say play a video game, what are we talking about?" Ryan asked, helping me up off the street for the last time.

"I mean actually play a video game. You said you had a Wii. Can't we play *Super Mario Brothers* or something?" I replied, walking with him to his house.

"Not into the hardcore blood and guts games?"

"Honestly? I'd much rather jump on mushrooms and flying turtles."

"They have names, you know," Ryan said. "You've got a lot to learn, Brooklyn."

"Goombas and Koopas, thank you very much!" I

said, satisfied.

"Wow, I think I just got a hard-on," Ryan replied, and I smacked his arm. "I thought you didn't play video games. How do you know about Goombas and Koopas?"

"I used to play with Beth when we were younger. It's the only game I did play before you came along," I replied, following Ryan to his bedroom. He stopped at the threshold and turned to face me.

"Well, I don't know how I'll keep my hands off of you, Brooke. Goombas. Koopas. Skateboarding. Not to mention killer mind and body. You're my dream girl," Ryan said.

I grinned. "Don't even think about distracting me."

Ryan threw his hands up. "Never. We're playing together."

"I'm Mario!" I shouted, going for Controller 1, and grabbing it just in time.

"You don't have to have Controller 1 to be Mario," Ryan said, picking up the second controller and settling beside me on the floor. "This isn't the original Nintendo system."

"Oh."

"But I'll still let you be Mario. Only because I love you, Brooke."

And I warmed all over.

—

I read the note again, shaking and sweating.

Some little bitch has been running her mouth. Happen to know who she is?

That's all it said, but it was accompanied by horizontal scratches etched into the sides of my car by a key, no doubt. I was pissed. Pissed and scared out of my mind. I turned around and scanned the student parking lot. No one in sight.

I knew I couldn't wait any longer. I had to take the information about the Fantasy Slut League public immediately. I was afraid of what these boys would do next. They were pissed because they weren't getting any and pissed at me because I was the reason. They told me to back off, but I wouldn't listen. It started with a trip on the bleachers. It quickly escalated to a near-drowning experience in the school pool. Finally it erupted with a keyed car. What was next? I didn't want to find out. I didn't want to imagine. I wanted the story out, the boys disciplined, and someone to pay for the fucking damage done to my car.

"Hey, Brooklyn," I heard from behind. I whirled around to face Parker. Where did he come from? I had just looked over the entire parking lot a second before.

"Did you do this?" I asked, pointing to the scratches in my car door.

Parker whistled low. "Damn, that's bad news."

"Fuck you, and stay the hell away from me," I spat, searching my book bag for my car keys. I felt unsafe. Why could I never remember to pull my keys and have them in my hand before exiting a building?

"Calm down, Brooklyn. I didn't key your car," Parker said.

I didn't believe him for a second. "Yeah? Well, who else could it be?"

"Maybe it's someone pissed at you for meddling in business that's not yours," Parker said. He backed me against the car. "Have you been meddling in business that's not yours?" he asked softly.

"I don't know what the hell you're talking about," I said. I groped blindly for my keys, finally locating them and pulling them from my bag. "Move."

"Well, it appears you are," Parker replied, not

moving. "I can't even get a date."

"Maybe that's because you're a dickhead."

The side of Parker's mouth turned up. "Someone needs to wash out that mouth of yours, Brooklyn. Absolutely filthy."

"Leave me alone or I'll scream at the top of my lungs," I warned.

"Sure you will," Parker taunted. "Now you listen to me."

I looked into his eyes. I swear they were the color of coal.

"Quit being nosy. Let me and my friends do our thing, and we'll be more than happy to let you do yours. A truce sort of thing, huh? I mean, I'd hate for someone to find you face down in the school pool, know what I'm saying?"

I shook violently, rattling my keys.

"Tim was generous. I don't know that I'd be," Parker said.

"Are you threatening me?" I whispered.

Parker burst out laughing. "God, Brooke! I didn't think you were one of the dumb bitches!"

I filled my lungs with the maximum amount of air possible and opened my mouth to scream. Parker slammed me against the car and clapped his hand over my mouth.

"Don't you fucking dare," he hissed in my ear. "Get your ass in your goddamn car and drive away."

He squeezed my face before backing away enough for me to open the car door. I remained composed as I slid inside, turned the key in the ignition and drove off. Once I turned onto the street, however, I burst into tears, crying so hard that I made it just a mile down the road before pulling off on the shoulder to have a satisfactory breakdown.

Fuck them! my mind screamed at me. *Don't let them*

intimidate you. They've been intimidating girls for far too long.

"I know!" I screamed back. "I'll do something! I will!"

But first I cried until I was completely spent. I cried until a police officer pulled up behind me and asked if everything was all right. I told him I was upset that my boyfriend broke up with me, and he told me I shouldn't be driving while I was so emotional.

"Well, excuse me for living," I sniffed.

"Really?" he replied.

"Well then, excuse me for being a woman."

The officer was patient. "Just trying to keep the roads safe, ma'am."

"The roads are the least of your problems," I mumbled.

I watched his mouth turn up in a smile. "How's that?"

I wiped the last of my tears away. "Well, you've got burglars, drug dealers, murderers, all kinds of low-lifes roaming around, and you're worried about a car parked on the side of the road."

"Just doing my job, ma'am. Making sure you're safe."

"Then go arrest some rapists or something."

"I'll do my best. Now make sure that seat belt is buckled tight, and you be careful."

I told him to go fuck himself once he was out of earshot. The exchange was exactly what I needed. It gave me perspective. I wasn't scared Brooke. I was warrior Brooke, and I was about to take some assholes down.

You wanna threaten me? I don't think so, bitch.

TWENTY

Everything was ready. I had all the documents sealed in an envelope addressed to "Patrick Langston," a rookie reporter for the *Raleigh News and Observer*. I decided to go with him after some research into the staff because he was new and I figured this story could be his big break.

I mailed the packed manila envelope Monday morning before school, excitement mixed with dread sneaking out of my fingertips and dampening the package with sweat. I couldn't say that I regretted abandoning my original plan with Cal. I realized it was unhealthy, and who was I to think I could endure what these other girls experienced simply because I was filled to the brim with vengeance? No, I simply couldn't, and I knew I made the right decision in mailing the information about the Fantasy Slut League. I never discovered the "smoking gun" evidence to get Cal, Parker, and Tim charged with rape, but I could hope that after the story broke of their salacious club, some girls might have the courage to come forward.

I could only hope.

I committed to staying after school to take pictures of the boys' baseball game. I promised Ryan I would be over as soon as the game ended. We planned an innocent night of playing video games; his parents and sister would be home, and we were all going to hang out together. It would be the first time I spent any significant amount of time with his family, and I was nervous. I had met Ryan's parents when we first started seriously dating, but this would be the first night I actually talked to them. I wanted them to like me.

"Hey, Brooke," Cal said, sliding into the bleacher.

"I didn't know you'd be here," I said, putting my sunglasses back on as the sun peeked out from another cloud.

It was becoming extremely difficult just to be anywhere near Cal. He made me nervous, and he knew he did. We both knew we were playing at some fake friendly game, but neither one of us would voice it aloud.

"Last minute. Ms. Kerrigan asked me to help you out," he explained. "She, uh, viewed those last pictures you took and thought you might need some help."

I shifted uncomfortably. The last pictures I took were of the swim team "practice" where Tim almost drowned me. I wanted so much to say something to Cal about it, but I knew he would accuse me of being crazy, say that Tim was just goofing off even if it was a bit rough, and that I needed to stop being such a drama queen.

"So, is it okay that I'm here?" he asked.

"Sure," I replied. "In fact, you could just take over if you want."

That worked for me. It meant I could get to Ryan's house a whole lot sooner.

"No no," Cal said, laughing. "You're not getting out of it that easily. You've gotta take notes for your page summary and little picture captions, huh?"

I shrugged and nodded. "I guess you're right." I handed the camera to Cal and pulled a pen out of my book bag. There was something inherently wrong with taking notes on a Friday afternoon after school. I sighed and put pen to paper.

"So how are things going with Ryan?" Cal asked.

I jumped in my seat, and Cal noticed.

"What? I can't ask you about him?" he said.

I thought for a moment. "You said he was crazy. I just assumed you wouldn't think it was a good idea, me dating him and all."

"Well, I don't think it's a good idea. But I've learned that you're gonna do what you want," Cal replied.

I bristled. "He's nice to me, and I like him."

"That's good," Cal said. He snapped a shot of one of our players sliding into first base.

I'm not quite sure I understood Cal's statement that I was going to do what I wanted. I didn't think I really ever gave him the opportunity to see who I truly was, apart from the bowling date. And that really wasn't completely me. I'm not normally an angry person. Parker brought out those colors, but it wasn't the full picture. The full picture was one of a girl who was trying to make up for past mistakes, be loyal to her deceased friend, be a good person.

I said very little to Cal as the game continued. I mostly took notes or doodled when nothing was going on or I didn't understand what was going on. I did ask him baseball terminology from time to time, and he answered happily enough.

Well into the fifth inning, he asked if I wanted something from the concession stand.

"A Sprite," I replied, half distracted on my cell phone with Dad. "Thanks."

Cal returned with two Sprites, uncapping both bottles for us while I took a few hasty notes about a recent homerun. It was the middle of May, but it felt like summer decided to visit early. The sun was blazing, and I was thirsty. After downing half the bottle in one gulp, I thought it would have been better to get water instead. Beads of sweat broke out around my hairline, and the back of my neck felt oddly stiff.

I tried to concentrate on my note-taking, but the words on the page kept going in and out of focus. I looked out on to the field, and asked Cal why there were three players on first base.

"There's only one player, Brooke," Cal replied.

I shook my head and chalked the whole thing up to being dehydrated. I finished my Sprite and thought about purchasing a water.

"You okay?" Cal asked, looking at me with furrowed brows. Actually, there were five Cals, and they were rotating counter clockwise. "Brooke?"

"I feel funny," I said. I slurred it, I think, and tried to push my pen behind my ear. I missed my ear completely, and the pen fell back behind me somewhere. I turned around to look for it, clutching someone's knees behind me to steady myself. "Sorry," I mumbled when she jerked her legs aside, and forgot why I had turned around.

"Brooke? You don't look so good," Cal said. "You're all white and stuff."

"Well, I'm a white girl, Cal," I replied, then giggled. It wasn't even funny, but for some reason I thought it was the funniest thing I'd ever said. I laughed hard, watching as my spiral notebook slid off my lap and on to the ground. Cal picked it up and put it in my book bag.

"Come on, Brooke," he said, lifting me up by my upper arm. "Let's get you some water. You must be sun dazed or something."

I laughed again. I thought "sun dazed" sounded funny. I kept repeating the words over and over until they sounded strange in my mouth.

I stumbled behind Cal who walked me to the student parking lot. I watched him rummage around in my book bag for my keys, open my car door, and throw my bag in.

He tucked my keys in his pants pocket.

"Let's get you feeling better," he said, tightening his grip on my arm.

"I'm fine," I said, but I knew I wasn't. I was looking at him through half-mast lids, unable to open my eyes completely. My body hummed with electric liquid, and I wanted to love everything around me in that moment, the moment I discovered what love truly felt like. Warm and sultry, like an old black and white movie.

Cal helped me into a car, but it wasn't mine. I guess it was his. I was fascinated with all the buttons on his dashboard, and decided I'd like to press them.

"Don't do that," he ordered, when he climbed into the driver's seat.

"But I like them," I argued.

Cal laughed and pulled out of the parking lot.

"Where are we going?" I asked, not caring in the least. I thought I needed a bed to lie down on, and I didn't care whose bed or where it was located.

"Nowhere, Brooke," I heard Cal say as I dozed off to the low sounds of the radio.

I woke up to darkness. Cramped darkness. I didn't know where I was, but the panic set in immediately, my heart racing as I tugged on my arms. My wrists were bound behind my back with something thin and tight, digging painfully into my flesh. I tried to focus, letting my eyes get accustomed to the darkness, and realized I was in someone's closet. And it was packed with boxes and heaps of clothes and other junk that surrounded me. I had only a small space to call my own right in front of the door.

I kicked my foot out by reflex creating a loud *thunk* against the hollow door.

"Is someone awake?" I heard from the other side.

I kicked the door again. It wasn't as loud. I realized I

was tired. My limbs felt heavy and strange, and I pushed my foot out like I didn't really care. Like I didn't truly have a purpose for doing it.

"Brooklyn? Are you up?"

It sounded like Cal's voice, and I nodded.

"Let me out," I said. The words felt like weights on my tongue. It was the hardest sentence I think I'd ever said.

"Brooklyn, I'm trying to help you," Cal said. "Help you get over your fear of tight places."

I thought I would die. My chest hurt from the rapid pounding of my heart, and I was waiting for the inevitable explosion. I was terrified, but my body was trapped in a sluggish state. I couldn't feel any adrenaline pumping throughout my limbs, signaling a fight to live, to escape. Only the focus of pounding at the center of my chest threatening a panic attack of monumental proportions.

Don't panic. Don't panic. Just search for a way out.

"Brooklyn? How are you doing in there? I know it's a bit tight."

I breathed in as deeply as possible, putting pressure on my stressed heart, then let out the loudest scream I could muster.

A sharp banging on the door silenced me instantly.

"Don't do that, Brooklyn," Cal demanded. "Or you'll be sorry."

"Please let me go," I begged, and felt the first of many tears roll slowly down my cheeks.

"Brooklyn, can't you see that I'm trying to help you?"

"You want to hurt me," I sobbed, twisting my body in an attempt to free my hands. The ties felt like they were growing tighter, and my hands started going numb.

"No, Brooklyn," Cal said. "You only think I want to hurt you. But I'm going to make you feel good."

There was something sinister in the words, but my drugged brain couldn't pinpoint it.

"Just breathe," Cal instructed, and I did what I was told.

I breathed in and out, closing my eyes and trying to conjure the field. It was no use, however, as my hands went completely numb save for the occasional tingling pricks.

"I hurt, Cal!" I cried in panic. "Please let me out! My hands hurt!"

"I know, baby. But you're not ready yet," he replied.

I kicked the door in frustration, trying to focus all my energy into my foot. I managed a respectable thud, and Cal raised his voice.

"Brooklyn, stop kicking my fucking door! I'll keep you in there longer if you don't behave!"

I moaned softly.

"That's right, Brooklyn. I want you to moan for me. I want to hear you freak out," Cal said. "Go on. You know you want to. Go on and have the biggest panic attack of your life. I wanna hear every bit of it."

"Why are you doing this?" I cried. My heart thumped painfully, and I knew in a few minutes he'd get exactly what he wanted. I couldn't fight it off much longer.

"Because afterwards, I'm gonna make it all better. I'm gonna fuck that sweet little cunt of yours until you pass out all over again."

"I hate you!" It came from deep within my chest, one last burst of energy. I screamed at the top of my lungs, loud and long, burning my throat until it went hoarse. I screamed for the girls who endured this torture in the past. I screamed for Beth who couldn't survive it. I screamed for my uncertain future, my rights that were being violated, and dropped to my side, passing out at the height of my terror, heartbeat pulsing fast and hard into starry blackness.

I awoke again but didn't open my eyes. Actually, I

couldn't open my eyes. My lids were too heavy, so I had to rely on my ears to help me discover where I was. My arms were lifted over my head, wrists secured together with something thin and tight, and I vaguely remember feeling it once before. Somewhere, a long time ago. I tugged on my arms but couldn't pull them down to my sides. Only then did I realize my shirt and bra were missing, leaving me half naked on an unfamiliar bed.

"You sure she's drugged enough?"

"Dude, she's out of it. I slipped a pill in her drink earlier and gave her another half just a few minutes ago," Cal said.

"I thought we said two pills." I recognized the voice. I just couldn't match it to a name.

"I didn't want to take the chance. People die from that shit all the time, you know," Cal said.

"So?"

The question sent a shiver down my spine.

"Look, I was all over her tits and she didn't feel a thing. Relax. If she wakes up, she'll still be too out of it to really know what's going on," Cal said.

"She seemed to know what the fuck was happening to her in your closet."

"Man, you know how this shit goes. They go in and out. When it's all over, they'll be so fucked up they won't know if it was a dream or reality," Cal said. "You need to chill out."

"What was that shit anyway? Putting her in the closet? You're one sick fuck." I realized it was Tim speaking.

"I really just wanted to see if she'd pee her pants," Cal replied.

Tim chuckled. "Man. You're messed up."

The panic started instantly. My head swam too much for my body to be completely consumed with fear, but I felt my heartbeat from far away increase a little, signaling danger, and I was incapable of fleeing for safety. Out of pure reflex or instinct, I pulled hard on my binds.

"Brooklyn?" Cal asked.

I froze.

"Brooklyn," Cal taunted. "Are you waking up to join us?"

He ran his hands over my breasts, squeezing them hard until I yelped. He pinched my nipples, and then I felt his mouth on me, sucking long and hard. He drew away abruptly, and I felt his hot breath in my ear.

"I love you, Brooklyn," he said, and I wanted to vomit from fear and disgust.

I felt his hand snake down my belly and in between my legs. I fought hard to keep them closed, rolling my hips from one side to the other, but all I managed to do was assist Cal in sliding my shorts off more easily. My panties followed shortly after, and I screamed as loudly as I could. It felt weak and heavy on my tongue, but I screamed anyway until someone's hand clapped down firmly on my mouth, stifling my cries for help.

"Who wants to be first to love Brooklyn?" Cal asked.

I shook my head violently, twisting my body and pulling frantically on the ties around my wrists.

"Now, Brooklyn," Cal said. "There's no use doing that. Why don't you just enjoy it? You wanted this, remember? You were the one snooping around, trying to find out stuff about our league. We figured you wanted in pretty badly, so here's your chance."

I felt two sets of hands pry my thighs apart and another touch me between my legs.

"Let's make her come."

A new voice, and familiar, too.

"That's generous," Tim said.

"Well, it's not rape if they come," the voice replied, and the boys laughed.

Parker! It was Parker's voice!

Three of them, I realized, and I had no chance. I was becoming more lucid, thinking back to the beginning of the year, my ludicrous plan for revenge, and then the forgiveness that came when I realized I didn't have to sacrifice myself, that Beth wouldn't want that. I learned to forgive myself, to move on, and found a new peace in protecting the girls at my school. But now I was trapped, about to experience violence I was certain I could never recover from, and the terror turned me primal. I bit down as hard as I could on the hand covering my mouth, breaking skin.

"Fucking bitch!" Parker yelled.

"Stop!" Cal said, and I heard a slapping sound.

For the first time, I opened my eyes fully though it was painful. Cal was holding Parker's wrist, poised in the air above my face.

"You wanna leave a mark?" Cal hissed.

"She fucking drew blood, man!" Parker cried.

"Then go wrap it," Cal replied. He looked down at me. "Does someone need another dose?" he asked, resuming the probing between my legs.

I shook my head, feeling the tears well up and run down the sides of my face. They pooled in my ears, distorting my hearing.

"I think so," Cal said, moving his finger in and out of me. He looked over to Tim who let go of my left leg and disappeared from the room.

I immediately closed my legs, trying to squeeze Cal's hand.

Cal sighed patiently. "Brooklyn, spread your legs."

"Fuck you," I spat.

Cal jumped on me, knocking the wind out of me, and held my face between his hands. He squeezed tightly, and I was afraid he'd crush my skull.

"No, see, that's what I'm about to do to you. For hours. And then Tim's gonna do it. And then Parker. For hours, until you've been used up like a little bitch ragdoll. And you wanna know the funny part? You won't remember a thing."

I inhaled deeply for another long scream until I felt fingers go around my neck.

"You scream, and I'll fucking squeeze your head off," Cal warned.

I swallowed, or tried to, and Cal took it as a sign that I'd obey.

Tim came back and hovered over my face.

"I don't trust that ecstasy bullshit, Cal. I told you that from the beginning."

"What is that?" Cal asked.

"It's called a Roach or something. That's what the guy said, anyway," Tim replied. "It's supposed to be a memory wiper."

"Where'd you get it?"

"Never mind where I got it. The point is that I don't wanna take any chances with her. She takes it or I'm out."

Cal shrugged and lifted my head, and I fought with all my might, kicking my legs and twisting from side to side. But he was too strong and eventually trapped my face between his large hands, holding me perfectly still while Tim shoved the pill into my mouth. They forced me to drink down the water, and I coughed and spluttered most of it all over my cheeks and neck. But they succeeded in getting me to swallow the pill, and I cried out of fear and frustration for what I knew it'd do to me and what they'd do to me. I would be passed out in minutes, completely vulnerable to their sexual attacks.

"Don't cry, Brooklyn," Cal said. "We all love you. And we're about to show you. We're even gonna let you come first. That's how much we love you."

The boys snickered as I pleaded with them to let me go.

"Parker, you're the best at it," Cal said. He looked

down at me. "See, I never really cared to figure out how to make a girl feel good. I usually just make it about me. Tim? Well, he always makes it about him. But Parker, here, he's a pro. He'll have you screaming in a matter of minutes. The good kind of screaming."

"I don't think I want to make her come," Parker said. "She doesn't know how to behave herself. My fucking hand hurts."

"Now, Parker," Cal said. It was a stupid, placating sort of tone. "Let Brooklyn have a little bit of fun. She's gonna earn it, after all."

Parker shrugged, and Tim and Cal grasped my thighs, spreading them wide until my hamstrings screamed in protest.

"Wow, that's nice," Cal said. "Don't you think Brooklyn has a nice pussy, Tim?"

"I do," Tim said. "I can't wait to shove my dick in it."

"What do you think, Brooklyn?" Cal asked. "You want Tim to shove his dick in you?"

"Stop!!" I screamed, but Parker touched me anyway, one hand pressed firmly on my lower abdomen to keep me still while the other probed me between my legs. It wasn't a predator's touch; it was a lover's touch, gentle yet firm. Experienced.

"Wow, you must really be enjoying this," Parker said, stroking me softly.

"How do you know?" Cal asked, watching me intently as I struggled against Parker's hand.

"Well, she's wet," Parker replied. "Really wet. I think she likes being used this way." He leaned over and whispered in my ear. "You're right. I hated you from the moment I met you. But look how nice I am, making you feel so good. Making you get all wet for me. Because you're my fucking whore, aren't you?"

I don't know why I was moaning. Whatever drug

they gave me turned me to liquid all over again, eventually lulling me into a false sense of security, even tricking me into imagining that the hand touching me belonged to a different boy—a boy I thought I loved. And I should have told him that the day he confessed his love to me.

I fought it. I tried to focus on my humiliation—my nakedness and their hungry eyes. Parker's ugly words. I tried to remember I was being touched against my will, but I was quickly giving up the fight, letting Parker use my body against me. I replayed his earlier statement over and over in my mind while I begged him to stop: "It's not rape if they come."

I wanted to pass out *now*. Then I wouldn't come. I would be safe from that shame, dreaming somewhere far away in a place where evil doesn't mask itself behind boyish charms and all-American façades. I closed my eyes and waited for the darkness to consume me, and it finally did, but not before my body responded to Parker's hand, climaxing painfully while I was held down, stripped of integrity and hurled into some kind of limbo where I knew I was a victim but my body disagreed.

—

I woke up, forehead pressed into the steering wheel. I sat up slowly, head pounding from what felt like a hangover. It was dusk, and the colors beyond my windshield were disorienting. It took me several minutes to recognize the student parking lot at school. Mine was the only vehicle, and I realized I was alone. Instinctively, I locked the doors and looked around for my car keys. They were dangling from the ignition, but I didn't remember putting them there. I didn't remember getting into my car. I had no recollection of the day.

I noticed my wrists hurt badly, and I brought them close to my eyes to get a good look. There were marks on them, and I had a small cut on the inside of my right wrist. The blood was dried and caked in a smear over my skin. What happened to me? My muscles were stiff. My shoulders screamed. My hamstrings felt tight. The back of my neck ached. I felt like someone had beaten me up.

I wasn't sure I could drive home. My head continued to pound relentlessly, and I knew I shouldn't chance it on the road. I looked around for my book bag, locating it in the back seat, and thought that was strange. I never put my book bag in the back seat. I always set it beside me in the passenger seat. I pulled out my cell phone and called Dad.

"Honey? I thought you'd be home by now. Isn't the game over?" Dad asked.

"What game?"

"Funny, Brooke," Dad replied.

I panicked. "Dad, I don't feel so good." I choked back the tears. I wasn't ready to cry yet because I wouldn't know why I'd be crying.

"What's wrong?" I could picture Dad sitting up in his chair, straight as an arrow, ready to go for the gun at my signal.

"I don't know. But I woke up in my car. I must have passed out or something. I don't think I can drive home," I said. "Will you come get me?"

"Lock your doors. I'll be there in ten minutes," Dad said.

I hung up and rested my head against the seat. What game? I thought hard trying to remember the game I was supposed to be attending. I was supposed to go somewhere after school. I was supposed to do something. And then I remembered. The baseball game! I went to the baseball game, but I don't remember leaving it. Think, Brooke, think! But I could recall nothing. Not the slightest memory of events that took place after the game.

Dad pulled up, and I unlocked my door for him. At

that very instant I felt like a little girl, six years old again and bruised and broken from a nasty fall off my bike. I didn't say a word but stretched my hands to him, palms facing up so that he could see the marks on my wrists, the deep wound just shy of a major blood vessel.

I cried then. I cried because I knew why I was crying. Someone had hurt me. That's all I had at the moment, but it warranted tears.

Dad gently pulled me from my seat, and only then did I notice the dull aching between my legs. And then I noticed another ache, a stinging soreness in my anus.

"Daddy," I whispered, clinging to him while I cried into his shoulder.

"It's okay, honey," Dad replied, stroking my back.

I sobbed hard as my father rocked me gently side to side, like we were slow dancing to a terrible tune, one that sang the disjointed melody of a brutal assault.

"I-I need to g-go to the hospital," I stuttered.

And then I heard my father's sob, felt the shaking and shuddering of his chest, because he knew what I meant, and he didn't want it to be true.

—

It was humiliating: legs spread, swabs taken, blood drawn, questions asked. I screamed when my father left the room before the exam started, and they erected a hasty paper screen, separating us so that I could hold his hand while they prodded me.

Most of my answers to the questions were "I don't know." I recalled the faces of each of my attackers, but I couldn't remember what they said to me. It was mostly blackness with a few sharp rays of recollection: the stifling closet, something shoved down my throat, several hands in places they didn't belong.

The exam concluded with "three days."

"We'll get the DNA test results in three days, Ms. Wright."

"Call me Brooke. I'm a fucking kid," I snapped.

The nurse bristled, then remembered I was a rape victim. A brutally raped victim. They had sodomized me, made me bleed, and there was damage done to my cervix. It would heal, and I could have all the babies I wanted, I was told. It was little comfort, but I understood they were just giving me the facts.

"Honey, is there anything else you want to tell me before I bring an officer in here to talk to you?" she asked.

I thought no, then remembered the terrible shame of one event. Right before I blacked out for good. I was embarrassed and asked Dad if he could leave us alone for a minute.

"Girl stuff," I said, and he nodded and left.

I glanced at the nurse before averting my eyes. "I think I had an orgasm."

She said nothing. I waited.

"Did you hear what I just said?" My head snapped up to meet her gaze.

"Yes, Brooke. And it's okay. It doesn't mean anything if you had an orgasm," the nurse said.

"It doesn't?" I wasn't convinced. I thought there was something wrong with me, that my body was telling me I actually enjoyed it.

"Orgasms are physical responses. They don't speak to whether your heart wanted them," the nurse said. "They certainly do not demonstrate consent on your part."

I was quiet for a moment, staring at my lap, thinking through what she said.

"But shouldn't I have been so scared and angry that my body wouldn't respond that way?" I asked after a time. "Shouldn't my body have shut down or something?"

"You *were* angry. And I'm sure you were terrified. That doesn't mean you aren't still going to have a physical response to stimulation."

I cringed at the word "stimulation." The nurse saw and sat down beside me.

"The adrenaline you felt from your anger and fear could have actually aided your orgasm," the nurse continued.

I looked up sharply.

"I'm just trying to help you understand how your body and mind work together to achieve orgasm," the nurse explained. "And it has nothing to do with desire or being in the mood. You did not desire your orgasm. Do you understand?"

"I'm so ashamed," I whispered, and she hugged me.

"Sweetheart, you have nothing to be ashamed about. You did nothing wrong. What you felt was something taken from you against your will. It doesn't diminish or bring into question the validity of your attack. You were raped, whether you had an orgasm or not."

I nodded, trying desperately to believe her.

"There's research out there about this. Not enough, but it's there, and some suggests that as many as one in five rape victims experience orgasm. Women are ashamed to admit it because they think it means they weren't really raped or that they enjoyed it."

I buried my face in my hands.

"Brooke? Please understand that you did nothing wrong," the nurse said. "Your orgasm was not voluntary."

"I hate that they took that from me!" I screamed.

"I hate it, too," the nurse replied. "But if you're brave and strong, you can make them answer for it."

I didn't want to make them answer for it. I wanted to go hide in a cocoon somewhere. I wanted to run from my attack or, at the least, pretend it didn't happen. I must have been shaking my head because the nurse kept encouraging me.

"Brooke, you're brave enough to do it. I know you are. I can feel it. You don't have to settle for what they did to you. You don't have to live with it or try to make do with the situation. You can heal from this. You can get justice."

Just then the officer entered, and I looked at her through tear-stained eyes.

"Officer Patterson is very friendly, Brooke. She's here to take your statement and ask you a few questions."

I nodded, settling into a light shiver. I stared at the chipped polish on my toes, wondering how the paint got messed up so quickly when my pedicure was brand new.

TWENTY-ONE

My mom arrived on the first flight out of San Francisco. It was a little weird, her staying in the house with us. Dad was officially dating Ms. Manning, and Mom was married. She was going to surprise me with the news the following week. I learned that Mom was shopping for a dinner party at the time of my rape. Dad was finishing up his end-of-week reports at work. Ryan was sitting at home with his sister, waiting for my arrival. Everyday, mundane living, and I wish I could have been any one of them during those hours instead of the person I was.

Ryan came over the night of my attack, concerned because I hadn't called him. Dad was reluctant to let him in, but I told him I wanted to see my boyfriend. I wasn't sure if I should tell Ryan what happened, but it was hard to keep it a secret. He knew instantly that something was wrong. He noticed my wrists when he sat down beside me, so I told him the truth. He stayed up with my dad and me the entire night. I was too scared to sleep. Dad wouldn't let me out of his sight, and Ryan wanted to make sure I didn't hurt myself. He didn't say it, but I got the impression.

I didn't go back to school. Neither did Cal, Tim, or

Parker. News broke early Monday morning about my attack, though my identity was kept private. The boys were at least eighteen, so their faces showed up on television screens all over the city. By the following week the story had gone national once the boys were connected with the Fantasy Slut League. It was the most sensational news story to hit the greater Raleigh area since the Duke lacrosse players scandal. I didn't want to see or hear any comparisons between the two stories: the Duke players were innocent. Cal, Tim, and Parker were not.

Tim would prove the hardest to prosecute, I learned. DNA evidence found no traces of semen. That didn't surprise me. I was certain every one of them wore a condom. I was surprised when DNA tests matched a pubic hair found inside me to Cal. Teeth marks on Parker's hand corroborated my story of biting him. The marks on my wrists were consistent with being bound. With zip ties, I later learned. But nothing on my person pointed to Tim.

Hunter, Mike, and Aaron were humiliated for their participation in the league, but they weren't charged with any crime because they had no knowledge of the rapes. The school could take no action against them because their sexual activities occurred off campus. Patrick Langston was able to dig up additional information I could never find: the girl responsible for feeding sexual statuses to the boys about their "drafts."

Annabel Kingsley was the most popular senior at our school. I could never make sense of why she did it, unless she simply loved the power and control it gave her over all those girls. All four graduated quietly and disappeared from the harsh media glare. Their story couldn't stack up to the rape cases, and I'm sure they were relieved to be forgotten.

Ryan visited me faithfully every day after school to check up on me and bring me my class assignments. My mother couldn't be happier. She liked him immediately, told me over and over how good he was for me, and I knew she was right. I showed my appreciation as best I could, but I was still reeling from my attack. Sometimes I couldn't remember the conversations I had with him when he popped by. Sometimes I cried on him for hours. Other times I tried to kiss him because I thought I should do that as his girlfriend, but it felt strange and scary. I was afraid of intimacy. It scared the hell out of me thinking I was too emotionally damaged to ever have sex again.

I visited Dr. Merryweather three times a week after the attack. Suddenly I didn't think therapy was self-indulgent bullshit. I needed her. I needed her to help me sort out my issues. I would not stay wounded forever. I was determined to heal.

Amelia was the first to break her silence. She called me herself to tell me she was coming forward. Tara was the second. I was shocked when I learned she decided to press charges. She actually visited me one morning, and I didn't recognize her.

"Yeah, I decided black hair was too much upkeep," she said, sitting across from me at the kitchen table sporting her old strawberry-blond locks.

I grinned.

"And I guess the goth look really wasn't me. Just something I hid behind, but I suppose you already knew that," she continued.

I nodded, eyeing her surprisingly ordinary khaki shorts and white T-shirt.

"I'm not supposed to be telling you anything, but I think Tim is gonna cave and go for the plea deal. I admit that I'd be relieved to not have to testify in court."

"Understandable," I said. "I'm hoping the same goes for me, but the deal isn't good. We're talking years in prison. Those boys may try to take their chances. Well, Tim, anyway. He's the only one who escaped DNA evidence."

Tara scoffed. "Brooke, you think Parker and Cal aren't gonna try to take Tim down if they know they're going down? There's no such thing as loyalty in those situations."

I nodded, glancing at my cell phone. Ryan should have been here by now.

"Well, I better get going," Tara said. "Again, sorry for being such a raging bitch to you before. You only wanted to interview me about cafeteria food, right?" She winked at me, and I giggled.

"Lame, I know. I'm not the smoothest investigator, okay? What do you want from me?"

Tara hugged me and disappeared out the front door, leaving me alone to wait for Ryan. Dad was still at work. Mom went to the grocery store for milk.

I went into the living room and turned on the TV. The four o'clock news was on, and I thought to switch the channel to MTV or Bravo. There'd be something mindless to watch on those channels, and that's definitely what I needed right now. I froze, though, when an update flashed on the screen about the rape cases. Another girl had come forward claiming to have been raped by all three of my attackers and a fourth. There they were, same pictures as before, lined up in the center of the screen: Cal, Tim, Parker . . . *Ryan?*

Oh my God.

I stared, blinking several times because I knew I was mistaken. My Ryan, displayed at the end of the line, and I thought my eyes were playing tricks on me.

It was instantaneous. I couldn't get to the hallway bathroom in time. I threw up all over the living room rug. And then I collapsed on the floor staring at my mess. I didn't have time to clean it up. I had to get to my phone. Where was my phone? I looked wildly about, locating it on the couch, and hastily dialed Ryan's number. Surely this was a mistake. Ryan was no predator. No rapist. Someone got the wrong guy.

His voice mail picked up immediately. I didn't leave a message. I threw up again instead, then sat thinking about the third girl. I knew someone who was gang-raped like me. Lucy! And I dialed her number.

"Brooke, I don't know what's going on," Lucy said on the other end. She sounded panicked.

"What do you mean you don't know? Did he rape you?!"

"I don't know why they showed his picture, Brooke," Lucy said. "Listen to me. He—"

"What the fuck is going on?!" I screamed into the phone. But I couldn't stand sitting around waiting for Lucy's explanation. My heart pumped madly, threatening to explode, and I wanted answers from *him* before I died.

"He didn't—"

I hung up abruptly in the middle of Lucy's sentence and left my vomit to soak in the carpet as I made my way to Ryan's house. I banged on the door. Kaylen answered, her red-rimmed eyes large and scared.

"Move," I demanded, pushing past her into the house. I immediately saw Ryan sitting on the couch. His parents were with him. "Glad to see you made bail," I snapped.

"Brooke, you really can't be here right now," Mr. Foster said.

I ignored him. "What the fuck is going on, Ryan? Why did I see your face on the four o'clock news? Why are you being charged with rape?"

I shook violently, taking deep breaths when I remembered to in an attempt to settle my nerves and keep from passing out from panic.

"Brooke, we cannot discuss the case with you. Our attorney advised—"

"What the fuck?! Your attorney?! What's going on?!"

Ryan looked me square in the face. "I didn't rape anyone," he said firmly.

Mrs. Foster spoke up. "Ryan, honey, you're not supposed to be—"

"Then why are you on the news? What happened? For Christ's sake, tell me something!" I screamed.

"I was there, Brooke, but I didn't rape her," Ryan replied. He pushed his hand through his hair. "Jesus, I was fourteen."

"Ryan, that's enough," Mr. Foster said. "Brooke, please go home."

"No!"

"Brooke, I'm calling your father to come get you."

"Did you do anything?" I asked Ryan, advancing on him.

He stared at me, eyes full of anguish. He opened his mouth to reply, then closed it.

"I asked you if you did anything, you fucking son-of-a-bitch."

"Don't call my brother that!" Kaylen cried.

I ignored her. "Answer me!" I screamed in Ryan's face.

He understood my question and reluctantly shook his head.

"Then you're as bad as the others," I spat. I turned on my heel and walked out the door. It would be the last time I ever stepped foot in that house.

I returned home and went straight for the wooden knife block beside the kitchen stove. I yanked out the cleaver and headed upstairs to my bedroom.

"What the fuck is happening? What the fuck is happening?" I whispered over and over.

I dropped the knife on my bed and grabbed the winter picture hanging on the wall opposite my headboard: the winter picture I painted with Ryan back in November. It was my turn to keep the painting, and I hung it where I could wake up to it every morning.

I tossed the picture on the floor and picked up the cleaver, considering the colors of our scene and deciding how best to mutilate them. I cried hysterically, tearing and slashing through the canvas until my mother came home, dashed upstairs, and wrestled the knife out of my hands.

—

More girls. They were coming out of the woodwork. I stayed glued to the television, and my parents became worried. I was watching too much news. I was consumed with it, and it wasn't healthy, they said. I ignored them. I ignored everything. My school work. Gretchen, who visited me on a near daily basis and controlled the TV whenever she could. Eating, sleeping, painting. All of it. I ignored my life in favor of sitting, day after day, watching the stories unfold of victim after victim.

Ryan wasn't charged in any other case but Lucy's. I learned about his involvement a few weeks after I graduated. Somehow, I managed to graduate with decent marks, despite studying very little for my final exams. I took them during after-school hours so I didn't have to see the other students.

Ryan tried multiple times to reach me. He called me incessantly, leaving messages I never returned. He came to my house twice only to be turned away by my dad at my request. I couldn't face him. The pain was too much to bear. I thought it was even worse than the hurt and humiliation I felt over my assault.

Lucy visited me one Saturday afternoon during the summer because I refused to speak to her over the phone. I wasn't mad at her; I was just mad in general. I didn't want any of the situation with Ryan to be true, so if I didn't speak to her, I didn't have to know about it.

"It feels weird and amazing, doesn't it? Those boys

being in jail," Lucy said, sitting across from me in my dad's armchair.

I nodded.

Cal, Tim, and Parker pled guilty to a slew of rapes. They took a plea deal for every one to avoid a trial by jury and risk the possibility of receiving the maximum sentences for each. I never had to testify in court. I didn't even attend the preliminary hearing. I was not subpoenaed, the judge requesting I submit a written statement of my attack. At first I thought I wanted to face my attackers at the hearing—that I was supposed to want to go to relish in their misery and fear—but I learned that wasn't strength. Strength for me was giving them no more of my time. I didn't need to see them cry. I didn't even need to hear about it from my attorney, though she told me anyway, thinking the news would give me some satisfaction.

The boys accepted the terms of the plea deal my attorneys and the defense counsel drew up. Their sentence for my attack was the stiffest since they were charged as adults, but it could have been much worse had they opted for a trial by jury. They knew the evidence was stacked against them, so they took the deal: guilty of kidnapping and rape in the first degree, each would serve out a sentence of fifteen years without the possibility of parole. That sentence didn't include the years they racked up for their other offenses. They would be in prison for decades.

"Ryan told me what happened," Lucy began. She watched me carefully. "He was there that night. Fourteen years old, and he was on the swim team with the others."

I immediately feared the worst, and Lucy seemed to know what I was thinking.

"He wasn't part of that league, Brooke. He didn't even know about it until the news story broke."

"How could he not know about it?" I asked.

"Brooke, did anyone at school know about the

league? The other swim team members didn't even
know."

I was so confused. "Why wasn't his picture in the
yearbook? I never saw him in the ninth grade swim team
photo."

"I don't know," Lucy replied. "Maybe he was absent
that day or they took the picture after he quit. Who
cares?"

"Why was he at the motel room that night if he
didn't know about the league?" I asked.

"Well, he thinks now that the boys were going to ask
him to join, and that's why they brought him to the motel
room. He thought he was going to some stupid underage
drinking party."

I scowled.

"Anyway, no one got the chance to tell him their
intentions because he freaked out as soon as he saw me
lying there on the bed."

"He should have fought for you," I said bitterly.

"He did," Lucy replied. "He argued with them: Cal,
Parker, and Tim. He tried to stop what they were doing to
me, and Parker and Tim beat the shit out of him. They
threatened him if he talked. He wouldn't tell his parents
what happened when he got home. They took him to
urgent care, but he wouldn't give up the names of his
attackers. It drove a wedge between him and his parents
for a long time. He just . . . withdrew."

I was furious, unable to contain myself any longer.

"Oh, poor Ryan! He got beat up! So what? Where
were his balls, Lucy?! He should have gone to the police!
He should have told someone what happened to you!"

"Did you tell anyone about Tim almost drowning
you in the school pool?!" Lucy shouted.

I stared at her, stunned.

"No, Brooke. You didn't. Because you were scared.
And what about after your rape? Were you ready to testify

against those boys? I remember you telling me you wanted to run away and forget it all happened. Why? Because you were scared."

I opened my mouth to reply, but Lucy cut me off.

"I'm not saying it's right that Ryan never talked, but they threatened his *life*, Brooke. Maybe they would have followed through with that threat; maybe not. But when you're fourteen and you're scared shitless, you believe it."

I turned my face away, ashamed and disgusted with myself, with Ryan, with the victims. Everyone.

"He came to my house one afternoon and confessed everything. I've never seen a guy cry, and it really freaked me out."

"Too little too late," I mumbled.

Lucy ignored my statement. "He went to the police. He told them everything. I came forward afterwards. If not for Ryan's testimony, those boys would have never pled guilty for what they did to me."

"A pillar of honor," I said sarcastically.

Lucy was patient. "I've forgiven him, Brooke."

My head shot up. "Why?"

"Because he apologized."

My mouth hung open in disbelief. Just like that? Because he apologized?

"All those other rapes," I said.

"Yeah," Lucy replied. "All those other rapes that he didn't know about."

"But he knew Cal was a bad guy. He warned me about him."

"He warned you about the Cal he knew in ninth grade, Brooke. He warned you because of what happened to me. Stop trying to hold him responsible for every subsequent rape!"

I said nothing. I was seething with anger that Lucy was defending Ryan.

"Maybe you don't care, but he got slapped with a

misdemeanor. Community service. Probation. I didn't
want him to get anything, but I wasn't allowed to dictate
the terms."

"A *misdemeanor*? He watched you get raped!"

"Actually, no he didn't. They beat him unconscious.
He only saw what happened in the beginning and at the
end. The boys could have very well succeeded in
challenging his story, but they were already in hot water
with you and those other girls. They knew to concede and
tell the truth."

I shook my head.

"Why are you shaking your head, Brooke? You don't
believe me?" Lucy asked.

"I don't know."

"He shouldn't have been charged with anything,"
Lucy went on.

I was quick to jump on that. "He didn't report it. So
yes, he should have been charged with something."

Lucy bristled. "He made a mistake, Brooke. He was
young and scared."

"Yes, Lucy. You've already said that." I felt impatient
and agitated. And then I had a thought. "If he was so
innocent, why did his picture appear on the news?
Wouldn't the police have protected his identity or
something?"

"He was still charged with failure to report a crime.
They couldn't let him off altogether. And Brooke, you
know how the media is. Someone got word that he came
forward, and that was that. It didn't matter what his story
was. They just jumped on the opportunity to reveal
another rapist, even though he wasn't one," Lucy replied.
"Journalists get it wrong all the time. I could run down a
list of screw-ups for you if you'd like to hear them."

I shook my head thinking back to Ryan's picture on
the news. It was the only one that wasn't a mug shot.
Someone had gotten a picture of him from somewhere,

but it wasn't from the police.

"Well, then I guess his life'll be ruined because of bad journalism," I said. I didn't know if I was pleased with that or heartbroken.

"Don't be flippant, Brooke," Lucy said quietly.

I looked at her oddly. "Why are you so forgiving?"

Lucy smiled. "Because I am. And I wish you'd forgive him, too. He loves you, Brooke."

"Do *not* go there," I warned.

Lucy nodded.

That evening I watched a large moving truck pass my house but thought nothing of it.

———

"I was a terrible friend, Ms. Janie." I hugged Beth's pillow close to my chest. Beth's mother and I were sitting in Beth's old bedroom looking through boxes of pictures and other keepsakes.

Ms. Janie sighed. "Baby, you made a mistake. You think there's any one person in this world who hasn't made a big mistake in their lives?"

"I just wish my mistake would have only hurt me and not someone I loved," I said.

"Well, it seldom happens that way for anyone, Brooke."

We sat in silence for a moment.

"Beth would have been very proud of how brave you were," Ms. Janie said.

I snorted. "The police arrested those boys right after my hospital visit. I was so angry because I wasn't sure I wanted to go through with testifying. That's not brave. That's weak."

"That's not weak. That's human," Ms. Janie said. "And you did, anyway. You did it, Brooke. And look at what you did for those other girls. You made them brave, too."

I shook my head. "I should have told you. The minute Beth told me about her rape, I should have made her tell you." A tear plopped on a vacation family picture I was holding, and I apologized.

"Brooke, I don't blame you in any way. I hope you know that." She wrapped her arm around me and held me close.

"I miss her," I whispered.

"I know. I do too. So much"

A thought occurred to me. "Ms. Janie?"

"Hmm?"

"Why did you bury Beth with that half-heart necklace? You knew all about Finn and me. Weren't you angry with me?"

Ms. Janie kissed the top of my head. "Brooke, you were my daughter's best friend."

I swallowed hard. "But she hated me."

"You think there's no forgiveness in death?" Ms. Janie said. "I choose to believe that Beth would be very upset had she not gone to heaven with that necklace."

I smiled wearily. "I gave my half to a friend. Another victim. She wished she could have known Beth."

Ms. Janie squeezed me. "I think you did a good thing."

I spent the afternoon helping Ms. Janie sort through Beth's belongings. The room had remained untouched until now because it was too hard for Beth's parents to enter it. Now Ms. Janie was ready to let go of the past, and we started by making piles of clothes and accessories we planned to donate to Goodwill. I made a pile for myself of a few clothing pieces. I never planned to wear them though Beth and I were the same size. I just wanted to keep them in my closet to remember her by.

"This feels good," Ms. Janie said a few hours into our

work. "This feels right."

And I thought I was beginning to feel what Ms. Janie felt, not because I was saying goodbye to Beth, but because I felt the guilt start melting away. A promise of healing.

—

I sat on the front porch Saturday morning drinking coffee. Mom had since gone back to California and asked if I wanted to join her. It was a tempting thought, running away from everything here, but my partial scholarship to NC State and a very pushy Gretchen who would join me as my roommate there, kept me from getting on the plane.

The rape stories eventually faded from the spotlight, and I discovered that I was starting to heal. My body—that resilient, God-breathed creation—felt healthy and strong again. My nightmares about the attack became less frequent. I actually woke up happy this morning. I felt a tiny glowing inside my chest. I thought it was hope sitting like a little ball of energy or a fully charged battery pushing me forward. I even thought I was ready to forgive the past, to start over entirely, but one bit of lingering pain kept me from forgiving everyone.

I took another sip of my coffee and watched two moving trucks rumble down the street towards the neighborhood entrance. I glimpsed a familiar car being towed behind one truck. It was Ryan's, and my heartbeat sped up. I jumped from my seat, dropping the paper cup, and sprinted to the mailbox, straining hard to see anyone in the vehicles. I couldn't, and I panicked.

Instinctively I ran to his house and banged on the door. No answer. I peered inside through a front window and saw the bare rooms that were once nicely furnished with couches and chairs, pictures and tables. My heart sank, and I walked back to my house.

I reached for my cell phone sitting on the porch railing and pulled up Ryan's number. My finger hovered over the green receiver icon, and I kept it there until my screen went black. I turned the screen on and hovered over the call icon again. And again I hesitated until the screen when black. I tried once more, my finger millimeters from touching that icon, millimeters from making the connection that could change everything. But I opted to close out the screen instead and wiped the tears from my phone, lying to myself that I'd made the right decision when it was only the fear holding me back.

TWENTY-TWO

Three years later . . .

"And I'm really proud of your progress, Brooke," Dr. Merryweather said over the phone.

"Thanks, Doc," I replied, swiveling in my computer chair. I was alone in my shared apartment with Leslie, my new roommate since transferring to UNC and moving to Chapel Hill.

"Oh, Brooke. I hate when you call me that. It's so flippant, like you're not taking any of this seriously," Dr. Merryweather said.

I giggled and flipped open my laptop.

The doctor ignored me and continued. "Are you dating anyone?"

I tensed a little, and I swear she could feel it through the phone.

"I don't have time for boys," I said lightly.

"Yes you do."

I thought for a moment. "Well, there are none here I like."

"On the entire UNC campus, there are no boys you like?" Dr. Merryweather asked.

I didn't answer her but spun myself slowly in my chair.

"Is there someone at another school you like instead?" the doctor prodded.

I didn't even know if he was in school, so I couldn't answer that question anyway. Plus, even if I did, I'm sure Dr. Merryweather would drill me about unhealthy attachments or emotional damage or something like that.

"Brooke? There's nothing wrong with being in love with Ryan."

I could feel my face draining of all its color.

"There isn't?"

"No, there isn't. And I think that you think you're not allowed to have feelings for him because his picture showed up on TV with those other boys," the doctor said.

This wasn't the first time she explained it to me. She'd been doing it for three years. But I guess I still wasn't convinced, or I was scared. Perhaps both.

"He's not those other boys, Brooke. And deep down you know it. That's why you're still in love with him and want to be with him. You just think it'll discredit you as a true victim to date a boy who knew about a rape and didn't report it."

"Won't it?"

"No."

I expelled the breath I didn't know I was holding at the sound of that simple word.

"You must forgive him, Brooke. If not for him, then for you," Dr. Merryweather said. "But I suspect that you want to forgive him for the both of you because you love him."

I didn't even think about it. I just said it. "I do love him."

"I know. I've known it for three years," the doctor replied.

"I'm sure he's moved on, though," I said.

The truth was that I hoped Ryan *was* able to move forward in some way, to find a kind of peace that allowed him to forgive himself. I wanted that for him despite my lingering anger. I think it was mostly anger for not wanting any of it to be true, not wanting to see him as a flawed individual, because for so much of my time at Charity Run, he was my savior. He was perfect in my very immature eyes, and now I had to confront Ryan as another ordinary human: good and bad and the fuzzy mixture of those things in between.

I hung up with Dr. Merryweather and continued proofing my final paper for Dr. Hoskins' Writing for Teachers course. I wasn't getting a degree in education; rather my bachelor's in criminal justice, but I took Dr. Hoskins' course because I liked him. I had him for freshmen composition, loved his style, and took any class I could with him that fit into my schedule. I couldn't concentrate, though, with Dr. Merryweather's words repeating over and over in my head: *"You must forgive him."*

It was a split second decision on my part, and I'm glad I dialed his number before I lost my nerve.

"I need a favor," I said into the phone.

"What is it, Wright? Don't tell me you've discovered information about another sex club at school," Terry replied.

"Cute. And no. It's not about a sex club," I said.

"Well, can you blame me for thinking it? I mean, here you are going to school for criminal justice. Can we say, 'Clichéd' by the way?" Terry asked.

"Shut up!" I laughed.

"What's next, Erin Brockovich?"

"First off, her big case had nothing to do with sexual violence. It was an environmental case. Second, I happen to be going on to law school."

Terry whistled long and low. "Jeez, Wright. You need to take it easy and go on a date or something."

I shrugged. "You think there's something wrong with me that I haven't dated in three years?"

"Yes."

I rolled my eyes. "Well, that's kind of why I called."

"Wright, you're cute and all, but the age difference would just be too—"

"Gross! I wouldn't date you in a million years!" I exclaimed. "It's Ryan. I'm calling about Ryan."

"Ryan? As in Ryan Foster?" Terry asked.

"Yes."

There was a brief pause.

"Why do you want to know anything about Ryan?" He sounded defensive.

"I just do. I have some things I need to tell him. Will you find out where he is? What he's doing? I tried to search for him and came up empty-handed."

"You sure you wanna go there?" Terry asked. "I mean, after everything?"

I took a deep breath. "Terry? I wanna go there. Will you just find him for me?"

Another pause.

"Yeah, I'll do it."

—

It took me two and a half hours to make the drive from Chapel Hill to Wilmington. I had no idea Ryan was so close. The last I heard, his family moved up north to be near relatives in Pennsylvania. I figured he'd stay there for good, but he did always tell me he wanted to live by the ocean.

I felt slightly guilty for ditching Gretchen. We had planned a girls' weekend in Raleigh since I hadn't seen her in a month, but she was insistent I go once I told her my plans to reconnect with Ryan.

"Well, it's about damn time!" she squealed over the

phone.

"You're not mad?" I asked.

"God, Brookey! Are you kidding me? Go. I command you to go. Go forth and fuck his brains out all weekend. And that's an order," Gretchen replied.

I giggled. "I can't promise you that. I don't even know if he remembers me."

Gretchen burst out laughing.

"What?" I asked.

"Trust me, Brooke. He remembers you."

I understood what Gretchen meant, but I think she misunderstood my statement. I knew Ryan would remember me, but I was unsure if he would remember the love he once had for me.

"Thanks for being so sweet about it," I said.

"Of course," Gretchen replied. "But you better tell me everything. And I mean *everything*, Brooklyn Wright, or I will be so pissed at you."

I grinned. "Okay."

My heartbeat sped up as I crossed the bridge to Wrightsville Beach. Ryan wasn't joking when he said he wanted to live by the ocean. This wasn't a ten-minute drive *to* the water. He lived *on* the water in a tiny oceanside apartment. It took me a few minutes to find. His apartment was actually one of several that made up a massive beach house. I imagined his rent was astronomical no matter the size of his home.

The front door faced the ocean, I realized, and despite a stone pathway leading to the entrance, I decided to take off my flip flops and walk in the sand. It was soft and silky, worming its way between my toes. When I got to his front door, I froze. I wasn't sure what I wanted to say. I hadn't seen Ryan in three years, refused to talk to him before his family moved up north. I regretted that decision ever since, but my heart still warred with my mind, refusing to forgive, believing he was a monster, ignoring Lucy's pleas that he was anything but.

I knocked on the door before I lost my nerve. It didn't occur to me that he may not be home. It was five in the evening; perhaps he was still at work or in class. I had no idea if he was even attending college. I made Lucy promise to stop giving me updates about him after the first year. She talked to him weekly and tried to slip in information here and there during our conversations. It just became too painful for me, and I told her I didn't want to know anymore.

I jumped when the door opened. It was a woman. And she was the most beautiful woman I'd ever seen. Shiny black hair, dark eyes. Her blue shirt hung off of one shoulder to reveal a thin pink strap. She wore jean cut-offs—very short cut-offs that highlighted thin, tanned legs.

"May I help you?" she asked.

"Oh, I'm sorry. I thought someone else lived here," I said.

"Someone else does live here," she replied with a smirk. "I'm just a visitor."

"Oh."

I felt strange—a little lightheaded and ridiculous. I show up after three years, and what? Expect him to be single? To be pining for me? I had a lot of fucking nerve.

I turned to leave.

"Hey, wait!" the woman called. "You looking for Ryan?"

I stopped cold. I didn't want to tell her "yes." I didn't want her telling me that she was his girlfriend now and that I could piss off. But I turned around to face her anyway, head bobbing up and down in a desperate nod. I must have looked on the verge of tears because she closed the door softly and darted my way.

"It's okay," she said, wrapping me in a hug.

I had no idea who this chick was, and I'm pretty sure

S. Walden 325

I was supposed to hate her if she was Ryan's girlfriend, but I was so emotionally exhausted and drained of adrenaline that I didn't care. I let her hug me as I cried into her shoulder.

"I'm a total lesbian," she said into my ear. "It's okay."

I drew back and wiped awkwardly at my face. "Huh?"

"I'm not Ryan's girlfriend. I'm Alyssa. One hundred percent gay," she clarified.

"Okay," I said. "Why are you telling me this?"

She laughed and grabbed my hand, pulling me down to the beach.

"Oh my God. Are you serious? It's obvious you're in love with him and you thought I was his girlfriend," she said, walking me along the water's edge.

"Why are we down here?" I asked.

"Because you need to get your shit together," Alyssa said. "Now breathe deeply and stop crying."

I didn't realize I was still crying. But I think my tears transformed from shock and pain to elation. I had never cried tears of joy before. It felt weird, and I didn't like it.

"Seriously, girl. Straighten the fuck up! You come all the way to see Ryan after how many years? And you're gonna give him—" She paused, looking me up and down. "—*this*?"

"How do you—"

"Oh my God, Brooke. Get a clue! You're all he ever talks about. It's getting so fucking old, too. You know, the second I opened that door, I knew it was you. He described everything about you, right down to your fucking nose."

"My nose?" I asked, instinctively touching it.

Alyssa nodded. "Now calm down and wipe your face. Get yourself together before you go back to that door."

I swiped my fingers underneath my eyes and asked Alyssa if I wiped the runny eyeliner clean. She nodded.

"He still talks about me?" I asked, my voice quavering slightly.

"For three loooong years," Alyssa replied.

"But he never called," I said.

"You changed your number."

"But he never came to see me at school."

"You transferred schools. Remember?"

How did she know all of this?

"If he really missed me, why didn't he try to find me?" I asked.

Alyssa sighed patiently. "He did, Brooke. He did find you. And he wanted to make things right. But then he thought he shouldn't bother you. If you never tried to find him or talk to him, he wanted to respect your space."

"I was scared," I said quietly. I felt defensive, like I needed to justify my behavior to this stranger. "Do you know what he did?"

"He told me everything," Alyssa said.

"How can I still love a person who did that? What does that say about me?" I felt the fresh tears pooling fast inside my eyes.

"It's not what he did, Brooke. It's what he didn't do. And he was young and scared. He made a terrible mistake. And he paid for it. He lost you."

I wiped awkwardly at my face.

"Brooke, why did you come here?" Alyssa asked.

I shrugged. "I don't know."

"Try again," Alyssa said.

"I miss him. I want to see him, but I'm afraid," I replied.

"Of what?"

"Of loving someone who kept such a horrible secret!"

"Brooke? Get over yourself. Everyone makes

mistakes. And yes, some are worse than others, but if you're waiting for the whole world to be okay with you loving Ryan, then you'll be waiting for the rest of your life. Fuck the world. Do what you feel is right, and you have every right to love whomever you want."

I felt the wind knocked out of me.

"Are you sure you even want to be here?" Alyssa asked.

"Yes!" I cried before it even registered that I uttered the word.

Alyssa smiled kindly. "You better? You think you're ready?"

I took one last long breath for good measure, wiped away the remaining tears, and nodded.

"Okay then," she replied. "Let's do this." She grabbed my hand and walked me back up the bank to Ryan's apartment.

"Wait," I said, digging in my heels. "Are you staying around to watch this?"

Her mouth quirked up in a grin. "You want me to?"

I shook my head.

"Didn't think so. I'm going for a swim. Maybe I'll see you around later," she said, then walked back down the beach, tearing off her shirt and shorts to reveal a tiny pink bikini. I watched her meander in the surf before walking out into the waves. I turned back to Ryan's door and knocked again.

This time he answered.

We stared at each other for what seemed like ages. He finally moved aside to allow me in. I walked in tentatively, looking around his apartment to see if anything felt familiar, like his old bedroom back home. It didn't. He was a new person, it seemed. His furnishings reflected a man in limbo: not quite an adult but older than a teenager. He had a dining room table. I wasn't sure any guy his age had a dining room table. The apartment oozed a laidback surfer style: wicker chairs and beach-themed paintings. They weren't kitschy or cheesy, though. They were abstract pieces of art, but they evoked the ocean.

I finally mustered the courage to look at Ryan's face. He had been watching me the whole time. I grew nervous. He had changed. Still the dark, messy hair. Still the mesmerizing blue eyes. But something had changed. He looked tired. Not old and haggard. Just tired, like he needed to take a nap and hadn't found the time for one in the past three years.

"Hi," I managed.

"Hello."

I shuffled my feet.

"You're probably wondering what I'm doing here," I said.

"A little bit."

I swallowed. I didn't know what I needed to say. Nothing was coming to me, so I asked about Alyssa.

"My best friend," he replied. "I met her in a philosophy class at school."

"She's really . . . perceptive," I said. I was going to say "nice," but "perceptive" was way more accurate.

"Yes, she is," Ryan replied.

"So, you're in school?" I asked.

Ryan nodded. "Took a year off before applying to UNCW. I work full time and go to school full time."

I nodded. Ryan didn't elaborate. He just stared at me, and I grew increasingly uncomfortable trying to think of another general topic of conversation.

"I made a huge mistake!" I blurted instead. It came out of nowhere, and I actually slapped my hand over my mouth once I said it.

"Coming here?" he asked.

I shook my head, hand still covering my mouth.

"Can you explain?" he said.

I dropped my hand. "I'm sorry, Ryan. I was unfair to

you."

Ryan averted his eyes. "No you weren't."

"Yes, I was! Jesus Christ, Lucy's forgiven you! *Lucy*! I should have been able to."

"I did a terrible thing, Brooke. I kept it from you because I knew you'd hate me for it. I lied to you. That's not easy to forgive. Lucy's forgiveness is something else entirely. She forgave me for being a coward. That's not the same thing as being a liar. I understand why you couldn't let it go. I do."

I didn't know what to say. I stood, mouth hanging open, dumbfounded.

"But you're here now," Ryan went on. "Will you tell me why?"

"I told you," I said. "I made a mistake. I made a mistake not forgiving you. Lucy kept telling me I was making a huge mistake. I knew it all along. I knew it all those years, but I let my heart harden because I was afraid that if I picked up the phone to talk to you, you wouldn't want to. Or maybe I'd learn that you were with someone else and I couldn't stand the thought. Or maybe—"

Ryan walked towards me, stopping within inches of my face. I closed my mouth. "I want to kiss you, but I'll only do it if you'll let me."

I didn't think twice about it. I flung my arms around his neck and pressed my lips to his. Everything about it was familiar, and I wasn't afraid anymore. I never said the words to him in the past because I was fearful of them. But not anymore. I murmured them against his lips over and over.

"I love you. I love you," I said, until his tongue invaded my mouth, garbling my declaration.

I clung to him with a fierceness foreign to me. I felt I was making up for lost time. Three years of being without him, and so much to learn. I pulled away and held his face between my hands.

"I need you to tell me everything," I said. "Will you? I want to know everything about your life. I've missed so much, Ryan, and I don't want to miss out on anything else."

"I'll tell you," he said. "But first, let me say how much I love you, Brooke. I told you a long time ago in a bad place when I was a bad person. I'm not there anymore, and I'm not that boy, but my love for you has never changed. I love you. I'll always love you. There simply isn't anyone else."

EPILOGUE

I lay naked in our unmade bed, hands grasping the bars of our iron headboard like he instructed. Our bedroom walls were covered with paintings we'd done together, mostly at the ocean where the sun and water created the ideal atmosphere. I stared at them until Ryan redirected my attention.

"I think I'll need to make it up to you for the rest of my life," he said, hovering over me.

"What do you mean?" I asked.

"The secrets I kept from you. Lucy's rape," he whispered.

I couldn't believe I was just now piecing it together. The reason he slept with all those girls. He was trying to atone for his guilt by giving pleasure to other women. I felt sorry for him, but not in a pitiful, condescending kind of way. I felt sorry for him because he was still trapped in the guilt, and it had been a year since we were back together. A year since I had forgiven him.

We were living together in Chapel Hill. I was about to start law school at UNC, and Ryan was finishing a business degree. We led a quiet life, surrounded by a few close friends. We spent most of our weekends in Wilmington when the weather was nice. During the cold months, we hunkered down in our tiny rented house, fire glowing warm and inviting, wrapped in blankets and each other's love.

I looked at my boyfriend and sighed. I could say the words of forgiveness again like I had done a hundred times before, but they seemed to make no difference.

"You don't have to make it up to me, Ryan," I said finally. "I just want you to love me and let me love you."

He dipped his head and kissed me long and slow. Then he pulled away and grinned. It lit up my heart. Nothing explosive. Just lightning bug flickering, and it warmed me through and through.

"Well, then ladies first," he said, and kissed my neck.

I loosened my grasp on the railing, and he whispered into my shoulder: "Hold on tight, Brooklyn."

He kissed down the side of my neck to my collarbone and finally to my breasts. He took his time with them, drawing one nipple into his mouth and sucking gently, forcing my fingers tighter around the bars, before he moved to the other breast. He licked my nipples then tugged on them gently with his teeth eliciting protests from my mouth and hands.

"Put your hands back on the railing, Brooklyn," he said, running his nose gently over my right nipple.

I shook my head.

"Brooklyn," he said, and gathered my wrists above my head with one hand while his other snaked down my belly. "Do you want me to touch you?"

I squirmed.

"Well?"

I nodded, afraid to look at him. I don't know why. We'd made love nearly every day since we reunited. But it was something about him when he got in one of these moods. It aroused me, and I thought I shouldn't like it.

But I did like it—being told what to do—because his demands were gentle, and I knew he'd never abuse the power I entrusted to him.

"Look at me, Brooklyn," Ryan said.

I obeyed.

"Spread your legs."

I did.

"Wider."

I complied, spreading my legs until he grunted his satisfaction.

"I'm going to touch you, Brooklyn," Ryan said. "And then I'm going to taste you. Is that all right?"

"Yes." I sounded like I was in pain, but it was purely sexual frustration. I wanted him inside of me *now*, but when he was like this, he made me wait for it. He would touch me, lick me, taste me everywhere before intercourse, making it nearly impossible for me to hold out longer than two minutes once he slid inside of me.

I cried out when I felt a single fingertip on my clit, circling slowly and gently. Reflex or the intense sensation made me snap my legs together in one swift movement. I don't know why, but it embarrassed me.

"Let's try again," Ryan said, amused. There was a hint of laughter in his voice. "Brooklyn, spread your legs. And this time, keep them open."

"Just fuck me already!" I cried. "I can't take it!"

Ryan chuckled and kissed me softly on the lips. "I'm going to make up for those three years we were apart, Brooke," he said after a moment. "I've been telling you that for a year already. You should know. So I really need you to hold on to the headboard. And that's not a request."

I held on and spread my legs again, gasping at the feel of his finger circling my clit once more. He rubbed me endlessly, plunging his finger into me before taking it out to stimulate my clit again. I moaned and writhed, feeling my passion build quickly, afraid I would come too soon before we had intercourse. I tensed, fighting the sweeping pleasure.

"Brooke," Ryan said. "We have all the time in the world, you know."

I nodded, watching as his face dipped lower between my legs. I bucked involuntarily, twisting my fingers in his hair while his tongue lapped me, his fingers plunging inside of me, heightening my pleasure.

"Don't stop," I begged, pushing my hips into his face.

"I've no plans to," he replied, the words humming between my legs. He drew my clit into his mouth, sucking gently but firmly, fingering me relentlessly until I was begging for release.

I came hard, gripping his hair. I knew I was hurting him; he grunted but never took his mouth off of my delicate tissues until my body relaxed, languid and soft in the afterglow.

He hovered over me once more, staring at my face, into my eyes, and I thought I saw the guilt vanish from his own. Just like that. It disappeared to a faraway place.

"Marry me."

My mouth dropped open. He grinned.

"You're asking me now? While I'm naked in bed? After you just made me come?" I asked. "What kind of engagement story is that?!"

Ryan laughed. "Oh, don't worry. I've got a whole thing planned out. It's been planned out for two months, but I couldn't wait. I had to ask you now."

"What do you have planned out?" I asked.

"Yeah right," he replied, nudging my legs apart and sliding into me before I could protest.

"Marry me," he whispered, finding a slow, gentle rhythm. "Will you?"

"Oh my God, Ryan," I breathed, clutching his

shoulders. "Now you're asking me while you're inside of me?"

He nodded, thrusting hard and deep, and I arched my body, crying out at the pain and pleasure of it.

"Marry me," he said again.

I nodded.

"Say it, Brooklyn," Ryan demanded. "I need to hear you say it."

I moaned, grasping at his back, grazing his skin with my fingernails.

"Say it, Brooklyn," he whispered, stroking me softly.

I felt something strange stirring. I couldn't understand it fully, but it felt like another orgasm. I'd never had orgasms so close together, but I felt like I would have one now, and I also felt like I wouldn't survive it. It was building large and demanding in my legs and stomach, threatening to push out my tendons and bones, my organs and tissues. I struggled to escape it.

"No, Brooklyn," Ryan said. "Let me love you."

I whimpered.

"Tell me you'll marry me, Brooklyn," Ryan said. "Right now."

"Ryan . . ."

I screamed at the force of it. The pleasure, so great that it crashed up my body and down. Up and down, a tidal wave that swept up my fiancé, drowned him in the pleasure, too, until he was moaning along with me, gasping on the crest of the wave before we tumbled over. Down, down, down, shaking from the after effects, the tiny ripples of pleasure that were reluctant to recede altogether.

Ryan lay on top of me spent. I didn't mind the full weight of his body, though it made it slightly harder to breathe. I stroked his sweat-slicked back, feeling his lips on my neck, raining the lightest kisses that said, "Thank you."

"Ryan?"

"Hmm?"

"I'll marry you."

I felt his grin on my neck. "You're not just saying that because of the nuclear orgasm I gave you, are you?"

I giggled. "Well, the nuclear orgasm is a very good reason to get hitched. I admit."

His fingers snaked down my sides to tickle my ribs. I screamed and squirmed.

"Okay, I'm not just marrying you for the nuclear orgasm!" I squealed.

He stopped tickling me. "Then why are you marrying me, Brooke?" He wrapped his arms around me and rolled over, pulling me on top of him.

I looked down at his face and smiled. "Because I love you."

"Just like that?" he asked.

"Just like that."

END

Dear Reader,

I struggled for some time with whether I wanted to include a letter at the end of this book explaining the rape scene in Chapter Twenty. I understand that some readers will have strong (even angry) reactions to Brooke's orgasm, and felt like it was necessary to explain my research on involuntary orgasms during rape. Unfortunately there isn't a lot, and what's there is conflicting. Many speculate that this is because women are ashamed to admit it. As the nurse explains to Brooke, women feel like an orgasm questions the validity of their rapes or demonstrates their desire to be raped. That's why in the little bit of research I did find, statistics show anywhere from five to 21 percent of women experience orgasm during rape. That's a wide range.

I understand that this is a controversial topic. I've read arguments that involuntary orgasms are bogus, and that women must be emotionally invested in the sex in order to achieve orgasm. I've read psychiatrists' arguments that involuntary orgasm during rape occurs because of women's millions-of-years-old genetic dispositions to want to be dominated. I've read literature by MD's explaining that the part of the brain that triggers orgasms is the part that controls involuntary responses, so orgasms can actually occur apart from a woman's will. Drugs, hypersensitive G-spots, adrenaline, and fear have all been argued as aiding involuntary orgasms. Personally, I will always trust science over speculation, and science argues the validity of involuntary orgasms.

I encourage you to do your own research on the subject, but I decided to include orgasm during rape in my book because it's not talked about, and I think it needs to be. I hesitate to say that I included it to teach you something. I told my editor that I never set out to tell a story that teaches a lesson, because stories, by their inherent nature, will teach a lesson anyway. It's the lesson you, as the reader, decide to learn; not the one I'm shoving down your throat.

I really do not encourage any rape or sexual assault victims to read this book, but if you have and you need help, please talk to someone. The Rape Crisis Center hotline is open 24 hours a day: 210.349.7273. Do not be silent like the characters in my book. Talk. Seek help. Start to heal.

Love,
Summer

ABOUT THE AUTHOR

S. Walden used to teach English before making the best decision of her life by becoming a full-time writer. She lives in Georgia with her very supportive husband who prefers physics textbooks over fiction and has a difficult time understanding why her characters *must* have personality flaws. She is wary of small children, so she has a Westie instead. Her dreams include raising chickens and owning and operating a beachside inn on the Gulf Coast (chickens included). When she's not writing, she's thinking about it.

She loves her fans and loves to hear from them. Email her at swaldenauthor@hotmail.com and follow her blog at http://swaldenauthor.blogspot.com where you can get up-to-date information on her current projects.

Other Titles by S. Walden:

Honeysuckle Love
Hoodie

Printed in Great Britain
by Amazon.co.uk, Ltd.,
Marston Gate.